Ace Books by S. K. Dunstall

LINESMAN
ALLIANCE
CONFLUENCE

CONFLUENCE

S. K. DUNSTALL

ACE
New York

ACE
Published by Berkley
An imprint of Penguin Random House LLC
375 Hudson Street, New York, New York 10014

ISBN: 9780425279540

First Edition: December 2016

Printed in the United States of America
1 3 5 7 9 10 8 6 4 2

Cover art by Bruce Jensen
Cover design by Diana Kolsky
Book design by Kelly Lipovich

ACKNOWLEDGMENTS

Producing a book is not simply writing it. We would like to give a huge thank-you to and acknowledge, once again, the people who have been important to our getting this book out there.

Our agent, Caitlin Blasdell, and our editor, Anne Sowards. Without both of you, we wouldn't have this book.

Bruce Jensen, for another amazing cover.

All those people at Ace involved in making this book.

And, of course, copy editor Sara Schwager, who put our commas in the right places again.

Our beta readers, Alison, Arthur, and Jenny. Thank you for reading the book and for your feedback. It was invaluable.

Dawn, your encouragement and support were timely and appreciated.

Our family, who are there for us always.

Helen, you have taken care of our garden so wonderfully and have been such an ambassador for our little books. Thank you.

And, of course, you, our readers, who took the time to read our books, to send us encouraging messages, and to tell us you cared what happened to these characters we had created.

NEW ALLIANCE DEPARTMENT OF ALIEN AFFAIRS—
LIST OF LINES AND THEIR PURPOSES

LINE	REPRESENTS
1	Health of crew and lines
2	Small mechanics 1—air circulation, heating, cooling, power. Overall comfort and running of a ship.
3	Small mechanics 2—tools. Interact individually with other lines for repair, maintenance, management.
4	Gravity
5	Communications
6	Bose engines (engines with the capacity to take a ship through the void)
7	Allows ships linked by line eleven to move autonomously
8	Security
9	Takes ship into the void
10	Moves ship to a different location in space while in the void
11	Links ships together. Allows them to move/behave as a single unit.
12	Actual abilities unclear, but known to communicate across all lines and appears to have some control over other lines

ONE

✦

EAN LAMBERT

EAN LAMBERT'S QUARTERS on Confluence Station were in the same area as Jordan Rossi's, with a brand-new titanium-bialer-alloy door between them and the rest of the station. The first apartment inside the blocked-off section had been gutted, and the newly opened space filled with state-of-the-art surveillance equipment, some of it of human origin, some salvaged from the damaged alien ships in the *Confluence* fleet.

It had been secure when Rossi was the only linesman here. Now it was triply secure.

Ean gave it a cursory glance and turned to the more immediate problem.

His bodyguard, Radko, had inspected Ean's apartment with a thoroughness that bordered on paranoia. That was before she'd dropped the news that she wasn't staying.

"You're staying with the *Lancastrian Princess*."

Radko scowled at one of the screens. "It won't be for long."

Ean didn't know line one on Confluence Station as intimately as he did the line on the *Lancastrian Princess*, but he knew Radko, and he could hear a strong undertone of worry.

"But why?"

"Family business," Radko said.

Ean knew nothing about her family except that she was a distant relation of Crown Princess Michelle. "Will you be all right?"

"I'll be fine, Ean. So will you."

She shouldn't try to lie when the lines knew her so well. She was worried about something. And if Radko was worried, so was he.

The song of Confluence Station changed. Jordan Rossi,

Yaolin's level-ten linesman, had arrived. This was Rossi's home, and the lines welcomed him.

"Be careful, Ean. Don't do anything—"

"Stupid?"

"Don't do anything that would upset Vega. At least, not until I get back."

How long would she be away? "I'll be a model linesman."

Ru Li, who—like the rest of Bhaksir's security team—was pretending to work at the screens while Ean and Radko talked, snorted. "That will be the day."

Bhaksir frowned at him before turning to Radko. "The shuttle is ready to depart. And Captain Helmo only has a small jump window. We'll take care of him for you."

Radko nodded and glanced at her comms. "Remember, Ean. Be sensible."

She took off at a run.

Ean looked around. Everyone in Bhaksir's team pretended to be busy again. There was an underlying hum of worry from line one. It echoed the worry from line one on the *Lancastrian Princess*, for Crown Princess Michelle was going home on family business, too. Her father, Emperor Yu, had demanded her presence.

"Will Radko be all right?"

Bhaksir shrugged. Ean was glad she hadn't tried to lie. He was glad, too, that Rossi halted in the doorway then. It stopped him from asking what the problem was with Radko's family. If she'd wanted him to know, she would have told him.

"This is cozy," Rossi said. "I go away for two days, and look what moves in."

Ean ignored him. Through the lines, he saw Radko run onto the shuttle. The bay doors closed, and air was being pumped out before she'd even clipped herself in.

CAPTAIN Helmo called as soon as Radko was back on her home ship. "We're ready to jump, Ean."

On board the *Lancastrian Princess*, Michelle patted Radko's shoulder. Radko tried to smile; couldn't. Something was seriously wrong, and Ean had no idea what it was.

"Ready." Ean pushed the worry to the back of his mind.

Being distracted when you worked with the lines was a disaster waiting to happen. "Fergus?" Fergus was on the *Lancastrian Princess*.

"Ready." Fergus's line hummed with anticipation.

At least someone was happy.

The *Lancastrian Princess* was part of a fleet of six ships, joined together by the alien ship, *Eleven*. Until recently, they'd only been able to jump the fleet as a single entity. Then they had discovered that line seven could be used to allow a single ship to move on its own. They'd tried it before—of course they had—as often as they could get jumps. But every other time, Ean had been on the ship that had jumped.

Please let it work.

"*Of course it will work,*" the lines told him.

Fergus started to sing.

Ean could see it as clearly as if he were on the *Lancastrian Princess*. The ship lines connected. Line seven to every other seven in their mismatched fleet of six ships and one station. He heard them as song, saw them as lines of light, different colors for each ship. Every line had a knot at each end, tying the ships tightly to each other. Ean smelled fresh bread, tasted it, as the colors ran together and turned white.

"Ready, Captain," Fergus sang.

"Prepare to jump." Helmo's voice was calm although Ean could hear the nervousness underneath. Helmo always said it wasn't the jump that captains worried about; it was coming out the other end.

Line nine moved the *Lancastrian Princess* into the void, with Fergus's line seven linking the fleet ships.

Line ten came in, and the *Lancastrian Princess* jumped.

Then they were out of the void. Helmo's relief swamped the lines momentarily.

Ean checked the lines on each ship in the fleet. All were good. All were strong and straight. The song of the Galactic News ship had changed. They had a new engineer on that ship. He was surprisingly strong. Ean hadn't realized he was a linesman.

The navigator on duty on the *Lancastrian Princess* said, "Confirming position 33.76785.23.45." The first digits were the sector—33 was Lancia.

It was the first time Ean had been in a different sector from the *Lancastrian Princess* since he'd started working for Lancia.

Helmo opened the comms to Abram Galenos, and to everyone on ship as well. "This is Captain Helmo, from the *Lancastrian Princess*, calling Admiral Galenos on Haladea III."

"Receiving your call loud and clear, and in real time," Abram said.

A spontaneous cheer went up from the listeners. For this was history. The first time two humans had ever communicated officially in real time between sectors.

"Ean?" Helmo asked.

Ean could hear and see the *Lancastrian Princess* as clearly as if the ship were nearby rather than half a galaxy away. Michelle and Radko were entering shuttle bay eight. Vega and two teams entered with them. He normally knew everything that happened on ship, so why hadn't he known about Radko?

"Ean?"

He dragged his attention back to his job. "Everything looks normal. Are you sure you have moved?"

He didn't need to ask, for the leaving of the *Lancastrian Princess* was already causing a flurry on both media ships. The producer on the Blue Sky Media ship was saying, "Find out where they went," while Coral Zabi, the reporter from Galactic News, said, "We're supposed to be part of the entourage. They could have told us where they were going."

Captain Helmo laughed. "Look at the view from outside this ship, Ean." He pushed the view through the comms to Abram, but not to Ean. He knew Ean would see it, anyway.

A purple-tinged planet. Lancia.

The shuttle exited from the ship, and Ean couldn't see Radko or Michelle anymore.

BACK in the common outer area, Bhaksir's team were swapping gossip with Rossi's bodyguards. Bhaksir glanced at Ean and looked as if she was going to say something, then thought better of it.

Ean forced himself to break the awkward silence that had fallen. "We've still got full comms with the *Lancastrian Princess*. It's in real time."

Even if they got nothing more from the eleven-line ships, this one ability, that of being able to communicate instantaneously between galactic sectors, would revolutionize trade. Communication within sectors was instantaneous. But to relay a message to another sector, a ship had to jump into that sector first. Until now. The companies that made a fortune providing message ships would lose out, but everyone else would win.

"And full comms with Lancia," Ru Li said. "Look, all the latest shows."

"You already have the latest shows." Ean didn't watch them; he hadn't watched anything from Lancia in ten years, but the crew loved them. Helmo bought them in batches. They were no more than a week old.

"But these are happening on air, right now," Ru Li said. "Look, *Cry for the Stars*." He changed the channel on the largest screen to where a woman in a scarlet dress was kissing a green-tentacled alien—which looked nothing like the real aliens. "Happening right now."

"Turn it off," Hana said. "We haven't seen last week's episode yet."

Ean sang a different channel up for them. This one was a news channel, with a striking black-haired newswoman with a high-class Lancian accent, saying, "Her Royal Highness, Crown Princess Michelle, has arrived at Lancia and is believed to be making for Baoshan Palace to—"

Bhaksir turned it off.

No one looked at Ean. What didn't they want him to know? Never mind. He could look it up later, in his room. For now, he had work to do.

He forced himself to stop thinking about what was wrong with Radko—and maybe Michelle, too—and spent the rest of the afternoon communicating through the lines with Sale's team on the *Confluence*, with Abram on Haladea III, and Captains Helmo, Kari Wang, Wendell, and Gruen on their respective ships, testing what they could and couldn't do between sectors.

He was so busy trying not to think about Radko that initially he didn't notice the activity on the Galactic News ship.

"Wait," he said, midsentence, and pushed through images from the media ship, where people were gathered around the new engineer, who was gesturing at a screen. "Something's happening."

They were watching a newscast, where the black-haired Lancastrian reporter was saying, "His Imperial Majesty is hosting a party tonight to welcome home his daughter, Her Royal Highness, Crown Princess Michelle. There are rumors that an announcement will be made tonight."

"I tell you, this is real-time," the engineer said. The linesman. "The *Lancastrian Princess* only arrived there today." He waved his comms at the man Ean recognized as the producer. "Call someone you know in the newsroom at Lancia."

"What? I haven't got time, Christian."

"Do it, Coop. This is important."

The producer took out his comms. "You'd better have a point to all this."

"Trust me. You'll be sorry if you don't hear this. What's the lag?"

"To Lancia? Anything up to an hour."

Ships couldn't communicate between sectors in real time. Or they hadn't been able to before today. Other ships would record the message, then relay it after they jumped. A regular message ship jumped between the Lancian sector and the Haladean sector nowadays, but it only jumped every hour. In less-traveled sectors, the messages could take days, or even weeks.

The producer called up the Galactic News office on Lancia.

"This is Bob Cooper. Can I talk to Harper Fuji?"

The answer was immediate. "Coop. Haven't heard from you in months. So they let your ship tag along with the royal yacht, did they?"

"I told you." Christian slapped his comms triumphantly into the palm of his other hand. "We're in real time."

Cooper looked at his comms. "Where are you, Harper?"

"Where? Baoshan, of course. Covering the party tonight. If you're down on planet, let's meet for drinks."

Baoshan was the capital city of Lancia.

Cooper looked at his comms as if it were about to bite him.

"Ean." Bhaksir waved a hand close to his face, then stepped back quickly as he focused on her. "Admiral Galenos is talking to you."

"Sorry." He forced himself to concentrate on his comms. "Abram?"

"Can you turn instantaneous communication off for the media ships?"

The media ships were part of the *Eleven*'s fleet. "No."

Bhaksir leaned over and said into Ean's comms. "Begging your pardon, Admiral, but we're also receiving and broadcasting real time on Confluence Station. We've already discovered we can get broadcasts from Lancia here."

Abram blew out his breath. "Right. In that case, we might postpone these experiments for half an hour while I prepare a press release. I'll call you when we're done, Ean."

He signed off.

When Ean turned away, Jordan Rossi was leaning in the doorway, arms crossed, amusement leaking through his lines.

"Lambert strikes again." He waited expectantly, then looked around as he was ignored. "What? No defense? Where's Radko?"

"On leave," Ean said, and tried to make it neutral, but Bhaksir said, at the same time, "Mind your own business, Rossi," and Ean heard the interest quicken in Rossi's lines.

ABRAM'S press release was a brief, recorded vid pushed out to all media outlets.

"The New Alliance confirms that initial tests of the new intersector-communications device have been successful. You might experience small pockets of extended communication over the next few days as we continue these experiments. If you require further information, please contact Spacer Grieve at the Department of Alien Affairs."

As press releases went, it was almost a nonevent. Definitely not worth half an hour's delay in testing. Although . . . they had put Grieve onto answering any questions, and Grieve wasn't someone you wasted on simple inquiries. Ean would have liked to talk it over with Radko, but Radko wasn't here.

When Sale and her team arrived back from the *Confluence* that evening, they sat down to a shared meal. Rossi joined them, and Ean got the feeling he was glad of the company.

Group Leader Sale was Bhaksir's boss. Bhaksir's whole

team—Radko was part of Bhaksir's team—were assigned to mind Ean, while Sale, and Sale's other team, led by Team Leader Craik, spent most of its time working on the *Confluence*, the other eleven ship. They knew more about the ship now than Ean did.

"We found the hospital today," Sale said. "At least, it's similar to the area on the *Eleven* that Captain Kari Wang thinks is the hospital. Except that it's ten times the size."

The *Confluence* was four times the size of the *Eleven*. It had a fleet of 128 ships in tow and was the size of a small city.

Craik slid in beside Sale. "Not that we planned on going into that section at all. We were supposed to finish mapping sector three first. This is two floors down and a quarter of the ship across."

"So how did you find it, then?" Ean asked. These were trained soldiers. If they were supposed to map sector three, that's what they would do.

"We got a wild-card day."

"Wild-card day?" Bhaksir asked. Ean was glad she was as mystified as he was.

Sale said, "People get bored doing the same thing day after day. So we decided to do a random exploration."

"She decided," came unbidden into Ean's mind, the thought tinged with satisfaction. *"Showing, showing."* The *Confluence*.

"What made you choose that particular corridor, Sale? Out of all of them?"

She shrugged.

"We showed."

"Nice work," Ean said, but he didn't push Sale. She could deny it as much as she liked, but he'd ask again later, when there were fewer people around. Had the ship just shown a nonlinesman where to go? If so, how had the lines known she wanted the hospital?

Sale scowled. "We've already got what feels like a hundred scientists and medical experts wanting access to it." She scowled again. "I don't know how they find out so fast. This is supposed to be a top secret mission. Thank the lines Galenos insists we leave as much as we can on the *Confluence* untouched, that any experiments we do come from the *Eleven*. Kari Wang can deal with the requests."

Selma Kari Wang, the captain of the other eleven-line ship, didn't suffer fools. When Sale had a ship of her own—and Ean was sure that one day she would, for she would make a good ship captain—she would be a lot like Kari Wang.

"Do you want me to—" Not that he was sure what he could do, short of asking Abram to say something, and Sale would be horrified if he did that.

"Thanks, Ean, but no. I'm just sounding off. Admiral Galenos keeps them off our back." She scooped up grains and beans from her plate, paused. "Speaking of experiments, after the press release, we all took half an hour to call up family."

Bhaksir had let her team do the same.

"It was instantaneous. Like they were right next door. And clear as clear. If I didn't know, and you'd just told me we were in another sector, I wouldn't have believed you." Sale spooned the beans into her mouth and choked. "What is this stuff?"

The kitchen staff on the *Lancastrian Princess* cooked for royalty and her guests. Even Ean had to admit that Ru Li and Hana, who'd been on mess duty, were not in their class.

"Borrow one of the chefs from Lady Lyan's ship." Rossi glanced Ean's way. "After all, we do have a level-twelve linesman on board."

Ru Li filled Rossi's wineglass. "Another glass of this will make the food taste better."

They had Lancian wine. An entire pallet of it. Ean had seen it delivered. He'd wondered at the time how much wine Helmo thought he and Rossi would drink. Ean looked at his own glass, shook his head when Ru Li offered to refill it for him.

Sale leaned back. "So, how do we think this instantaneous communication works?"

"I would have thought it obvious," Rossi said. "Lines do communicate instantly within a sector, after all. If line seven links the lines through the void, then there is effectively no void for those ships."

"So what makes a sector, then?" Sale asked. "And how can linked ships communicate through them?"

Back when humans had first left Earth, they had divided space into radial sections, 360 of them, one degree each, radiating out from a nominated central position on Old Earth. But after they'd discovered the lines, the old measurements had been replaced by sectors, which was an area of space in which line ships had instant communication.

The sectors were constant, but different sizes. There was no known mathematical theorem that could calculate why each sector was the size it was. The smallest was the Grent Anomaly, less than a light-year in area. One of the largest was the Lancian sector, which was how—back when the New Alliance had been the Alliance—Lancia had gained so much power.

Rossi said, "Sweetheart, if we knew how linked ships communicated through sectors, human ships would have been doing it years ago." He paused. "One might surmise that the fleet model—multiple ships common to a line eleven, with the sevens keeping individual ships linked—was the default model for alien ship movement."

Say what you might about Jordan Rossi, he was a linesman at heart, and he was serious about line business.

Some of that respect must have leaked through the lines, for Rossi lost track of what he was saying momentarily and looked at Ean strangely, before continuing, "Especially given the way the *Eleven* is so ready to integrate any and every full set of lines it can. One might say that the only line that doesn't provide added value to standard ship travel is line twelve."

Ean ignored that.

Rossi looked around. "Where *is* Radko again?"

Ean ignored that, too. As did everyone else.

"Imagine," Sale said. "Instant communication everywhere in the galaxy. What a shake-up that would be."

"Especially for Gate Union," Rossi said. "If you had instant communication, you could automate the jump process."

Gate Union's main advantage in the war at present was that they controlled the jumps. Would that mean the end of war?

Except the New Alliance only had two elevens, and Ean, to link the ships together.

Sale's and Bhaksir's comms sounded then, along with that of the senior of Rossi's two bodyguards.

"Heart attack." Bhaksir looked at her comms as if she didn't believe it. She looked at Rossi, then Ean. "But there's been no—"

No strong line-eleven activity, she meant. Ean might not

have reacted, but Rossi would, for he was easily overcome when line eleven was strong.

"I'll check it out," Sale said. "Craik, Losan, with me. Ean, watch us in case it's a setup."

They left at a fast walk.

Ean sang to lines eight and five, and asked them to track Sale through the station. He put it onto the closest screen. "Where's she going?"

"Station manager's office," Bhaksir said. "Apparently, the station manager has had a heart attack."

The station manager was the equivalent of a ship captain. If he'd had a heart attack, wouldn't the lines have registered something? A little distress, maybe. If Captain Helmo had a heart attack, the lines on the *Lancastrian Princess* would go crazy. If someone had attacked the station manager—which was why Sale was checking it out—wouldn't the lines have reacted?

Ean sang up the station manager's office on another screen. The room was filled with paramedics, along with an older, tired-looking man who was speaking to one of them, and a distressed younger man.

"Station staff," Bhaksir said. "The older man works directly for Patten."

Patten was the station manager.

"The younger one is new. Also works for Patten. Nothing untoward." Bhaksir called up Sale. "Looks clear so far."

Rossi snickered. "Nothing untoward. You people take your job so seriously."

Maybe one day, a heart attack could simply be a heart attack instead of paranoia. Until then? Ean watched as Sale, Craik, and Losan entered the already overcrowded office.

Why hadn't the lines become distressed?

TWO

DOMINIQUE RADKO

THE RADKO ESTATE looked the same as Radko remembered it. Kilometers of vineyards, deepening now into purple as the leaves darkened for autumn. She hadn't told Ean that most of the wine he drank on the *Lancastrian Princess* came from her family winery.

Golden Lake, named for its color, sat like a massive gem in the heart of the estate. Hectares of trees and gardens set around smaller lakes made a gracious panorama as the car flew in. The morning sun caught the rose quartz and mica in the granite of the stone blocks of the house, making it sparkle and glow.

It had been afternoon when she'd left Confluence Station. Radko sighed. On top of everything else, it was going to be a long day.

She received three messages from her mother in the time it took to walk from the parking station to her apartment, and another one as she dropped her kit onto a shelf in the nearly empty wardrobe room. This time, Hua Radko leaned on the signal until her daughter answered.

"Mother."

"You're late."

She wasn't. She was seventeen minutes earlier than she'd told them she'd be, but there was no point saying that. "When you're traveling with Michelle, you travel on Michelle's time."

"I suppose you can't argue that. Although you'd think she'd try to be on time for her own father."

"Are we going to hold this whole conversation through the comms?" Radko asked. Her mother was perfectly capable of doing that though her apartment was just down the corridor from Radko's. "Why don't I come and talk face-to-face?"

She dropped her comms back into her pocket and moved swiftly down the corridor to her mother's claustrophobic quarters. Hua Radko had collected jeweled eggs all her life. The heavy black timber cupboards that were de rigueur for displaying them lined the walls. That, combined with the individual display lights to show off each egg, always made Radko think of a cave alight with phosphorescent growth.

Her mother hadn't changed. A tall, elderly woman who held herself as straight as a soldier on parade, Hua must have spent time in the military; for how else could she hold that posture so long? Radko had never asked, for her mother didn't encourage personal questions. They'd never been close.

The long entertaining room was crowded with people. That was normal. Hua entertained as much as her sister Jai—the Emperor's mother—did.

There were new faces. After years serving under Abram Galenos, checking out potential threats to the Crown Princess of Lancia, Radko recognized many of them.

Prominent among them was Tiana Chen, a minor functionary in the Emperor's outer circle. She didn't have much influence with the Emperor himself, but she had a knack of ferreting out secrets from those who did and using those secrets to control them. She had no reason to associate herself with an out-of-favor branch of the Yu family like the Radkos. Nor did Ethan Saylor, the slender youth sitting beside her, whose family were part of the Emperor's inner circle.

Saylor leaned his head close to Chen's, curled his lip, and said in an undertone meant to be heard. "Look what just walked in."

Chen rapped his fingers with her comms and said something too low to hear. Given Chen's lower standing in court, an action like that should have been social suicide. Instead, Saylor scowled at Radko, as if she were to blame for the reprimand.

Radko moved around to get close enough to hear them.

Both of them fell silent.

Her time in the fleet had made her suspicious of everyone. She had to remember that people behaved strangely without ulterior motives.

Hua saw her then. "Surely you could have changed out of

that dreadful outfit before you came to me." If her mother had
been given to histrionics, she would have put her hand to her
forehead in an overt display of the hopelessness of the task.

Out of the corner of her eye, Radko saw Saylor nod. Chen
rapped his fingers again.

Hua beckoned two of the guests toward her with an imperi-
ous snap. "Messire Zheng, Messire Tse. Do what you can."

Tse and Zheng circled Radko.

"At least she has the family looks," Tse murmured.

"But her hair," Zheng said. "What a disaster."

Hua beckoned again. "Messire Coles."

Pieter Coles had been doing the hair for the Radko family
ever since Radko could remember. He'd been the first and only
person to cut her hair until she'd left to join the fleet. He'd been
simply "Pieter" back then. Messire was an old term, once used
for a master of a craft but now mostly fallen out of favor.
Maybe it was coming back into fashion, for Ean's voice coach
insisted on the title "Messire" Gospetto, as well.

It wasn't hard to tell what the other two were, with their
striking outfits and their comms extended to full slate mode.
Clothes designers.

Radko stood patiently while the designers made their
sketches. She'd done this often enough as a child to know they
would have come in with their designs mostly complete. After
all, what designer threw something together in half an hour
when it would be worn to an audience with the Emperor of
Lancia? This part of the designing was for show.

"So excited to be a guest of honor at tonight's party," Hua
said. "And Michelle will be there. I haven't seen her in . . . oh,
I forget how long."

Radko could have told her mother that Hua had last seen
her grandniece 287 days prior, at a function held the day
before Michelle had left to supposedly investigate the confluence. She didn't. Instead, she stood silent and thought about
her own upcoming meeting.

Emperor Yu had a habit of springing nasty surprises when
he called a member of his family in for a royal audience, and
Radko's invitation had come separate from Michelle's, which
meant the Emperor had plans for both of them.

She didn't know which was worse. Worrying about what

the Emperor wanted or worrying about what might happen to Ean while she wasn't there to protect him.

"Dress her to show how important her family is," Hua said to the designers. "After all, she is the Emperor's cousin."

A cousin the Emperor didn't remember existed most of the time.

Radko's oldest niece, Claudette, drifted over to talk to Chen and Saylor. Claudette was two years older than Radko. Hua hadn't wanted a second child—after all, Henri was happily married and already producing grandchildren. But Hua's nephew, Yu, insisted the family bloodline be carried by more than a single child. And who would argue with Yu, then newly ascended to the Lancian throne?

Saylor couldn't hide his boredom although the occasional glare from Chen kept his acidic comments under control.

What had happened in the Radko family that made Chen desperate to stay on their side?

"Take off your jacket," Tse commanded. "I need to see your arms."

Radko did so.

Tse clapped her hand to her forehead. "Look at them. They're . . . hard."

"And she has no chest at all," Zheng said. "Or nothing to speak of."

Radko couldn't tell if they were acting for their audience or genuinely upset. "Muscle tone never hurt anyone." If they wanted curves, they wouldn't get them from a Lancastrian soldier, especially not someone who worked for Abram Galenos.

Commodore Vega now, for Galenos had been promoted to admiral.

Zheng walked around Radko. "I could make her arms a feature. It would be unusual."

"No," Hua said, and her horror wasn't faked. "It would be a show of strength. We don't want to challenge anyone. Cover them. Cover them now," and she picked up Radko's jacket and thrust it at her. "I don't ever want to see them again."

Radko pulled on her jacket. She recognized genuine fear when she saw it. Had her mother always been so scared of the Emperor?

"Messires Zheng and Tse will come up with two designs

each," her mother said. "You must choose one of them. While it's being made up, I'll send Messire Coles in to attend your hair. In the meantime, do us all a favor and go and wash and change."

"I wouldn't mind some sleep." Radko was a soldier. She could nap when she needed to. "It's evening where I've come from."

"You won't have time," her mother said.

Radko thought she might snatch a nap, anyway.

Claudette caught up with her outside the apartment. "Take the Tse outfit. Grandmama has promised that the designer you don't choose can design my dress, and I already know what I want."

Radko's childhood had been made up of bargains and counterbargains like these. "Make sure Tse designs me something I want to wear, then. I don't plan on looking stupid because you want the other designer."

"I'll find a way to send Tse along to your apartment," Claudette said.

Radko missed her uniform already, and she was still wearing it.

"I want a dress I can move in," Radko told Tse, when she was alone in her quarters with the designer. "And I want hidden strength." She was a soldier. She was dangerous. Emperor Yu would do well to remember that. Then she remembered her mother's obvious terror. "Maybe not the strength." She didn't want anything to reflect back negatively on her family.

"Clothes you can move in are not fashionable."

"I'll take a Zheng design then."

"Your niece wants the Zheng outfit." Tse took out her comms and extended it to a full drawing slate. "I can't design a new dress in half an hour." She paused, and looked at Radko. "You seem naïve—unusual for someone of your position—but your mother is a good customer of mine, so I'll give you some advice for free. Don't antagonize Emperor Yu. I've seen other people try it, like young Ethan Saylor back in your mother's rooms. It gets you nowhere except out, and if your family want to retain any position they have, they would then have to disown you."

"Is that what Saylor's family did?"

Tse cocked her head to one side and studied Radko, then the design on her slate. She didn't answer.

Radko looked at the design. A sheath dress, so tight she'd have to mince. "I can't wear that. I need to move when I want to."

"I'm thinking." Tse changed the image. The new design was much better. "This I designed for the Crown Princess herself. All designers do, you know. In case they are ever asked. Not that we're ever likely to, of course—Her Royal Highness has her own designers. But we all have half a design ready to build on. A classic, just in case."

Tse modified the design and held up the final image. Tightfitting leggings with a swirling, full-length tunic over the top. The tunic had side slits that went up to the waist. "You'll be able to run in this."

Not without pulling it up, but at least you *could* pull it up. If she was desperate, Radko could fling the cloth over her shoulders.

"The beauty in this is the cloth it's made from," Tse said. "It took me five years to come up with the design. But a soldier like you wouldn't appreciate the finer things in life."

"Even soldiers like to dress well."

Tse sniffed. "I'd believe that more if you'd stopped to change before you went to your mother's rooms." She held up the design.

Radko nodded approval.

Afterward, Tse lingered.

"Is there something else?"

Tse still hesitated. Finally, she said, "Your mother is one of my best clients. I hope whatever you're involved in doesn't endanger her."

"What I'm involved in?" How much did Tse know about Radko's job? How much did she know about Ean?

"Your mother has a lot of new friends. All acquired after we heard you were coming home."

Radko had only been summoned ten days ago.

"You don't need friends like Tiana Chen or Ethan Saylor.

They'll discard you as soon as you've finished being useful. As will their mentor, Sattur Dow."

"Thank you," Radko said. Her mother knew better than she did what a minefield Lancian politics could be. She would know this already.

The swirling design on the outfit Tse produced reminded Radko of the creation scene on the wall in the large crew room on the *Eleven*.

Pieter waited with his gels and brushes. "I hardly know what to do with it," he said. "The dress takes over."

"What about an electrostatic halo," Radko suggested. If she was to wear an outfit based on an alien design, she might as well wear her hair the way it often was when she was around lines.

"It's plain," Pieter said, doubtfully, when he was done. "But it's striking enough, I suppose."

It felt like home. "I'm used to its being like this."

Pieter looked appalled. "Isn't it dangerous to be close to so much static all the time?"

Radko smiled, thinking of Ean, who could throw a man across a shuttle bay with the help of the lines. "Of course it's dangerous." But perfectly safe, too.

HUA Radko kept up a constant, strained chatter in the aircar on the way to Baoshan. Radko thought the chatter covered nervousness and a bit of one-upmanship.

There were six of them in the car. Radko, her mother, Claudette, Tiana Chen, Ethan Saylor, and another close friend of her mother's, who'd been around seemingly forever.

"It will be nice to see Michelle again," Hua said. A subtle reminder to people like Chen and Saylor that Michelle was a relation. "*She* dresses so beautifully."

Her mother hadn't commented on Radko's dress. Claudette hadn't either, but Radko had seen the expression on her niece's face. Tse had gotten herself another client out of this and probably started a new fashion.

"You work with Her Royal Highness," Chen said to Radko. "You must see her every day."

"No." If Chen thought Radko had easy access to the Crown

Princess, it was time to disabuse her. "I'm part of a team. We have other duties as well." She could get to Michelle more easily than most of her team could, through Ean, but that was none of Chen's business.

"Like guarding the linesmen on the alien ships," Saylor said.

That wasn't general knowledge. "Occasionally," Radko said. "Her Royal Highness has a linesman on her staff." That was known.

It was night on Confluence Station. Ean would be in bed.

"And we'll have access to that linesman." Saylor rubbed his hands together. "Imagine. We'll own the universe."

Lancia was never going to get free access to Ean. Not without Michelle as intermediary. Nor without Radko at Ean's back to protect him. Yet most Lancastrians assumed that because Ean was Lancastrian, they had an advantage over the other worlds. Radko wouldn't have thought anything more about his comment except that Chen jabbed her fan into Saylor's leg as he opened his mouth to speak again.

It was supposed to be unobtrusive, but any trained observer would have picked it up.

Why did Chen want Saylor to shut up?

"Have you ever been on one of the alien ships?" Chen asked, in what Radko thought was a deliberate attempt to change the conversation.

"Captain Helmo arranged for the crew of the *Lancastrian Princess* to see the *Eleven*." She'd been plenty of times before that visit, of course, and afterward, but she knew how to deflect this conversation. "We wore suits and UV goggles. You couldn't see much."

"Suits?" Chen asked. "So the air isn't breathable?"

Radko shrugged, like a junior guard who didn't know much about the atmosphere on the spaceship and didn't much care. "Orders," she said.

The *Eleven* was fully oxygenated now, not a trace of alien atmosphere left. The *Confluence* only had oxygen to the small area between the regular shuttle bay they used and the bridge, plus a few other areas they had explored thoroughly.

"What was it like?" Chen asked. "The ship, I mean."

Everyone was interested in the ship. "Big," Radko said.

"You walk a long way to get anywhere. There wasn't much to see, really."

"And the equipment?"

Radko shrugged. "It was alien."

"But linesmen can read the boards?"

Chen seemed to know a lot about the alien ships. The question made Radko uneasy.

"That's the theory." It was common knowledge that linesmen were required for the alien ships.

Hua Radko said, "We've a Lancastrian in charge of the project, but what have we seen? No alien technology. Not using the ships to attack Gate Union. When does Lancia get some benefit from this?"

Civilians always expected things to happen immediately. And to happen solely for their own world's benefit. "One ship has been crewed." Or partly crewed, anyway. "These things take time."

"We've been at war months. We should have blasted Gate Union out of space by now. We've seen what the ships can do."

"Maybe the New Alliance is preventing Lancia from acting." Chen watched Radko carefully, as she added, "After all, Galenos has only recently been promoted to admiral. Maybe he finds himself outclassed."

No one had ever accused Abram Galenos of being outclassed before. He'd worked with the admirals on Lancia as an equal, even when he'd only been a commodore.

It was time Radko started shutting Chen down. She laughed. "I doubt it. I've seen some of the trials. The ship is dangerous. The New Alliance doesn't want civilian casualties. They'll bring the ship out when they need it."

They landed then, to her relief, for she didn't want to spend hours talking about the alien ships. Not with these people.

They waited in a private room off the public concourse of the palace. Radko saw four cameras. The people who were watching them would be part of her own unit. The Royal Guard.

The Royal Guard was split into three branches. The largest was the division that dealt with the security for the Emperor himself and was headed by Commodore Sergey Bach. As a child, Radko had been scared of him. Thinking about it now, she realized it was her mother's fear, for her mother had impressed on her early that Bach had the power to kill them if they so much as looked at Yu the wrong way.

Her mother must be terrified of Emperor Yu.

The Crown Princess's division was headed by the recently appointed Jiang Vega.

The third division, the group that looked after other members of the royal family, was run by Captain Ah Ning, who answered to Commodore Bach.

Finally, it was time.

EMPEROR Yu was a striking man, genetically tweaked to be handsome and powerful. He was approaching sixty years of age but looked half that. Two Royal Guards stood inside the door, on either side, another two on either side of the throne, and two more partway between, close to where the visitors would stand when they had their audience.

Aside from the throne, there was only one other seat in the room, a long chair placed at right angles to the throne. The seat was already occupied by Sattur Dow, a close friend of Emperor Yu's.

Sattur Dow's presence was worrying.

Radko bowed low and held the bow for as long as protocol demanded, and a bit longer. After all, she didn't plan on disgracing her family.

She kept her face expressionless. "Your Imperial Majesty."

He said nothing.

The Emperor was famous for keeping his visitors waiting. Sometimes, he'd make the visitor wait ten or fifteen minutes before he spoke.

Radko knew how to deal with that. She stood at ease, hands behind her back, and stared ahead as if she were at parade assembly. She could stand that way for hours. Although she would have preferred better shoes to do it in.

Maybe it worked, for the Emperor broke the silence in less than two minutes. "Cousin." Or maybe the short time was for Sattur Dow's benefit.

"Cousin." Radko bowed again.

Emperor Yu steepled his hands. She couldn't tell what he was thinking. "I trust you are well."

"Thank you, I am. And yourself, likewise?" Dow hadn't been introduced yet, so she didn't inquire after his health.

"Of course," the Emperor said, as if there was never any doubt. "I hear you are protecting my daughter."

"It is an honor to serve as one of Her Royal Highness's guards."

"Yet you are not guarding my daughter at all."

"I beg your pardon?"

"You are bodyguard to Linesman Lambert."

"Who is a member of Her Royal Highness's staff, and Her Royal Highness herself has requested that protection." Was this what he had called her home for? To reprimand her?

"You spend a lot of time on the alien ships."

He'd better not ask her to spy for him because this conversation was going straight back to Vega and Galenos. "I have spent some time on the alien ships, yes."

The Emperor smiled. "You see," he said to Sattur Dow. "I promise, and I deliver."

Saylor and Chen's belief that they would soon get access to a linesman suddenly made sense. Especially given Tse's earlier comment about their mentor being Sattur Dow.

That was going straight back to Vega and Galenos as well.

"But I have been remiss, cousin," Emperor Yu said. "I summoned you here for a reason. Please allow me to introduce your future husband, Sattur Dow."

It wasn't a surprise. The Emperor didn't invite relatives like her to the Imperial Palace for any other reason. Most of the family members Radko had grown up with had already received their summonses. Radko fully expected that when the time came, she would do her duty as well.

She went down on one knee and bowed deep—partly in acquiescence, partly to hide her dismay.

"My cousin accompanies the linesman to every function," Emperor Yu said, above her head to Sattur Dow. "You will have ample opportunity to speak with him."

How did Dow did think he was going to get access to the functions Ean attended?

"My cousin is a dutiful soldier. She is also a dutiful employee of the Crown." He directed the next words to Radko. "Cousin, you will take every opportunity to allow your new husband to speak to your charge."

Never. If she allowed Dow access to Ean, she was failing her job. She wasn't going to be Yu's pawn. But the Emperor had given her an order. If she refused, it was treason, and he had every right to kill her.

If she was going to die, she'd do it her way.

Radko looked up. "I wish you had spoken to me earlier, in private, Cousin." Not the Imperial form of address, for this had to sound personal, not professional.

It *was* personal.

It was also her job—her right—to protect Ean. Giving Sattur Dow access wasn't protecting him.

She stood, breathing deep to stop the tremble that threatened, and bowed to Sattur Dow. Lower than she might have otherwise. "No insult intended, Merchant Dow, but I have a career, a life. It doesn't include a partner." It might have included a partner, but not the one Yu was proposing.

Emperor Yu's expression didn't change, but his voice was cold when he said, "You insult me with your rudeness."

"You insult both of us by not discussing this with me privately first." She bowed to Sattur Dow again and hid her icy hands in the folds of material.

The stance of the guards changed subtly. None of them had moved, but Radko could see they were ready. She couldn't take on six guards on her own. Not Royal Guards. Right now, she would have liked Ean and line eight backing her up.

"You forget yourself, cousin," Emperor Yu said.

"No. You forget *yourself*, Cousin. There is nothing in the laws of Lancia that says another Lancastrian must marry a person of the Emperor's choosing." If she had to make such a futile stand, she might as well do it properly. "The only reason other members of the family have done so is because you are head of our family and have arranged the marriage."

And because they were scared of him.

He was about to kill her, and she couldn't do anything about that. Not that he'd kill her himself; he wouldn't soil his hands. One of those guards standing tense with their hands near their weapons would do the deed.

She hoped Ean's new bodyguard would look after him properly.

The Emperor looked at the guard to Radko's left.

Radko looked at him, too. He'd better look her in the eye while he shot her.

"Wait." Sattur Dow spoke with such urgency that the guard paused at his command. How much power did Dow have?

Emperor Yu's eyes narrowed. He shifted his cold gaze from Radko to Sattur Dow, and maybe, just for a moment, Dow remembered how easy it was to fall out of favor with the ruler of Lancia. At least, Radko hoped he did.

"I will not have my orders challenged."

"Your cousin is emotional and overwrought." Dow held Yu's gaze. "If we give her time to reconsider, I'm sure she'll come around."

The Emperor's face darkened into a scowl.

"I have already made *plans*," Sattur Dow said. "The wedding. Our future. I would hate to see them *ruined*."

The emphasis was so slight that if she hadn't been listening for it, Radko wouldn't have heard it.

"Plans. Of course." Emperor Yu waved dismissively at Radko. "Get out of my sight before I change my mind."

She bowed to Dow, ignored the Emperor altogether, and kept her back straight as she walked to the door.

"And cousin."

Radko looked back.

"Prepare for your wedding."

THREE

EAN LAMBERT

A WHUMP IN the walls and the sudden movement of the station jerked Ean out of a restless sleep. The wee-wah of a hull-breach alert brought him upright hurriedly, only to fly out of bed as something hit the station with enough force to turn it.

"What's happening?" he sang to the lines.

Line eight came in strong. *"A ship. Firing at us."*

"Which ship?" Ean made for the cupboard containing his space suit, the location of which Radko had ensured he knew before she left. As he pulled it on—it still took fifteen seconds—two suited guards burst in. Hana and Gossamer.

Hana checked his suit.

He only half noticed, sorting through the images from the exterior of the station, trying to match them to the sound of the ship the lines had sent him. That one. A freighter, the type that delivered the station supplies every three days. He listened to the lines, heard the damage to lines two and three, watched the bulwarks slam shut, heard the station chatter through line five.

". . . Exploded in the shuttle bay."

"We're under attack," Ean said. "Something in the shuttle bay exploded." The external air lock had bowed out, but inside was a gaping hole that went for half a corridor. The inner air lock must have been open.

The station rocked again. There was another soft whump along the walls. "That's a bomb," Gossamer said. He pushed Ean out into the central area.

In the central room, Sale was trying to pull up screens. Nothing. She pounded on a panel in frustration. "We put in state-of-the-art equipment, and it doesn't work."

"That's because the lines are down, sweetheart." Rossi was still pulling on his suit.

"What? All of them?"

They wouldn't have air in this part of the station if that were the case.

"No," Ean said. "Where the damage is." He was already singing to the damaged lines. Line six, first, because it was more damaged than the others. Why did everyone try to damage line six? Because they controlled the engines, he supposed, but there were other ways to disable a ship.

"What's happening?" Sale demanded of him.

What did she need to know? What would Abram or Michelle, or even Radko, want to know? "There's a freighter firing at us."

"Show me."

He sang up the station control center and the call going out right now. "Emergency. Emergency. Confluence Station is under attack." He routed lines farther, to the other ships in the *Eleven* fleet, and only realized he'd sent the signal to all of them—the media ships included—when he saw the flurry of activity it caused.

Another bomb hit jerked him off his feet. Ean stayed on the floor. More damaged lines. He sang them straight, aware of Rossi singing with him.

Sale opened the comms to the *Eleven*, the *Wendell*, the *Gruen*, the *Lancastrian Princess*. And to Abram—still pulling on his shirt—on Haladea III. "Are you getting this?"

"Affirmative," Wendell said. "The attacker is an unmarked merchant freighter but those weapons are military grade. Could have come from anywhere. We'll be an hour reaching you." The ships—except the *Lancastrian Princess*—were already moving. The *Wendell* had six bombs, the *Gruen* none. The *Eleven* was the only ship that could save them.

"The freighter will be ready for us," Kari Wang, captain of the *Eleven*, said. "As soon as we get close they'll jump. Meantime, they'll do as much damage as they can."

"Who let them get that close?" Captain Gruen demanded.

"No idea," Sale said. "How heavily armed is their ship?" She scowled at the screen, then turned to look behind her.

"Ean." She was beside him in an instant. "Do you need oxygen? What's wrong with you? Why didn't any of you notice?"

"Nothing's wrong." Ean got to his feet. "I'm fine, Sale."

"What are you doing down there, then?"

"I fell." The recoil as another bomb hit the station knocked him down again. "You wanted something."

"I want to see that ship. I want to see their specs."

He had no idea what she meant, and Radko wasn't here to translate. He guessed, and pulled a feed from one of the cameras on the bridge of the attacking freighter.

He'd prevented a nonfleet ship from using weapons once before, hadn't he? But that had been by stopping the order going out through line five rather than by stopping the actual firing of the weapon.

Sale tapped a board on the image he'd put up for her. "Give me a close-up of that."

He zoomed in. It looked like the weapons board on the *Lancastrian Princess*. The stats looked the same, too, with everything green and the bars high.

"Shit. There'll be nothing left of us in an hour."

Dead bodies lay everywhere on the station. People in the outer sections crowded into the inner sections, trampling the slow and the weak.

Another explosion, this one from a slightly different place. The freighter was moving down the side of the station, planting minibombs as it went. Ean pulled the feed tracking the freighter from an external camera on the *Wendell*.

Sale pounded the board. "We're a sitting target, and we can't do a thing."

"Isn't the station armed?" Ean asked.

"No." Sale looked away from the bodies. "Let's get you to a shuttle, Ean." Her voice was bleak, full of the horror of walking away from all this. "You, too," to Rossi.

They couldn't walk away and leave a station full of people to their fate.

"Can't we do something?" Ean asked.

"Our job is to protect you. Not them. Let's move, Ean. Before they clog the shuttle bays in their panic."

"Too late for that." Ru Li indicated the shuttle bays on the side of the station opposite the freighter. The passageways were jammed with people headed for the shuttles.

"Where's the station manager?" Sale demanded. "He should be stopping this."

"In hospital, sweetheart." Rossi had stayed calm and immovable throughout. Did he ever panic? "He had a heart attack last night. Remember."

How convenient was that heart attack now?

"What about his second then?"

"Fighting fires," Ean said, and he meant it literally, for the older man who'd been present in the stationmaster's office last night was using a fire extinguisher to put out an electrical fire. "What can we do, Sale?"

"Get you to safety."

That wasn't what Ean had meant.

"The shuttles are too dangerous," Bhaksir said.

Leaving by shuttle was only going to save those on the shuttle. There were two thousand people on Confluence Station. Ean looked around for inspiration. The station was part of the *Eleven* fleet. Could the lines do something?

"Are they shooting at shuttles, or just at the ship?" Sale asked.

"The ship, but they're not dodging the shuttles either."

Another explosion spun them in a crazy circle until line four—gravity—kicked in.

Sale looked at the screens. "They've another layer of station to destroy before they get here. Ready some lifepods for the linesmen." She turned to Ean and Rossi. "You two do what you can to disrupt them in the meantime."

"I hate to point out the obvious," Rossi said, "but mere tens need to be closer to the lines to do much."

"Ean then. I don't care what you do. Put static in the lines for all I care. Blast them with noise at full volume. Anything to distract them."

Noise might be a deterrent. Ean chose someone having hysterics and forwarded it through to the freighter. He pushed the volume up on the comms and continued to keep it up.

As a deterrent, it worked for about two minutes.

He had to hold them off for an hour, and according to Kari Wang, the freighter would jump before their own ships got close enough to attack, anyway.

He couldn't hold them off for that long.

How did he reduce the time for a ship to get there, to fight them? There was only one way that he could think of. Through the void.

The only fully armed ships were the *Lancastrian Princess* and the *Eleven*, and the *Lancastrian Princess* was not around.

Ean sang to the lines on the *Eleven*. *"We're being attacked."* He showed them the freighter and Confluence Station. *"You need to jump close enough to defend us."* He changed his tune to target specific lines. Line seven, to keep the ships together in the void, but to allow them to jump a single ship. Line nine, to enter the void, and line ten to make the jump.

Rossi lunged at Ean. "Stop him. He's crazy. He'll kill us all."

He was too late, for they were in the void.

In the infinity that was the void, Ean had time to straighten the damaged lines on station.

That wasn't right. The *Eleven* was supposed to jump, not the station.

They exited the void. Ean couldn't tell who was swearing the loudest. Sale, Kari Wang, or the freighter captain.

"Ean," Abram said, and Ean concentrated on that, for everyone else was yelling at him. "You've switched places with the *Eleven*, and Captain Kari Wang is heading at full speed for the freighter."

The station wasn't supposed to jump.

"Ean," Abram was insistent. "If you don't do something in the next three minutes, she'll hit it."

The *Eleven* rocked then anyway, under a shot intended for Confluence Station.

"Protect yourself," Ean said to the *Eleven*. *"That field."* For it was the only thing he could think of. Then added hurriedly, *"But don't kill us."* The field had a limit of two hundred kilometers. Abram insisted each fleet ship stayed at least twice that distance apart.

"We won't destroy you." The lines were a comforting sound in his head. *"You are of our line."* The resonance on line eight changed to include the special song that was the green protective field.

Inside the freighter, the captain was yelling, "Reverse thrusters. And for the lines' sake, get that jump ready."

The song extended in a thick, green stream. It reached the first of the fleeing shuttles, flicked them like motes of dust. Ean thought he heard the sonorous song of the void underneath it.

It reached the freighter.

"Jump," the freighter captain said.

The freighter lines disappeared.

Ean pushed Rossi away and dragged himself to his feet. There was a difference between a jump and a push, and that had been a push. But where had the *Eleven* pushed the freighter to? The void? He thought he'd heard the void come in at the end.

Rossi snarled. "You are insane."

"Nicely done, Ean," Abram said.

Ean looked around the room. Everyone was laughing. The insane after-battle-adrenaline laughter. Through the comms, he heard Wendell say to Kari Wang, "Nice control there." It was seconded by Helmo and Gruen.

"Thank you." Kari Wang was still swearing. "No thanks to Lambert. But when we've learned to use this thing properly, we'll be able to turn it on a pinhead."

Ean decided to keep out of Kari Wang's way for a while.

THE attack was midnight news. Here, and—if you believed Ru Li—throughout the Lancian sector as well. Ean hoped Radko's family was keeping her occupied enough to keep her away from the vids.

Abram gave a press conference in person this time. Ean watched it from his rooms on Confluence Station. He didn't go into the shared area, for Rossi still twitched when he came near. He seriously considered singing Rossi's lines calmer, but that wasn't going to end anywhere good.

He watched the Blue Sky Media feed. Sean Watanabe hadn't been so animated in months.

"Is the New Alliance ready to move against Gate Union at last? Yesterday, they unveiled new technology in the form of intersector communication. Today, they showed what power the alien ships have given them. An hour ago local time, a disguised freighter attacked Confluence Station and was repelled by one of the alien ships. Is this the next step in their war against Gate Union?"

Ean flicked over to Galactic News, where Coral Zabi was interviewing someone in a mottled purple uniform. "And what of the rumors that the New Alliance staged the attack themselves to demonstrate how powerful the alien ships are? We have with us Admiral Markan, from Roscracia."

Markan was the military commander of Gate Union, although—according to Abram and Michelle—he was struggling to keep that command right now. Especially given that his plan to win the war by denying the New Alliance access to jumps wasn't going as well as he'd planned. Not only that, the Redmond/Gate Union accord was shaky right now, and that had to be worrying Markan, for the line factories were all on Redmond worlds. If Redmond went its own way, Gate Union was as vulnerable as the New Alliance. It was all very well to control the jumps, but if Gate Union didn't have line ships to jump with, they weren't any better off than the New Alliance.

Zabi turned a professional smile on Markan. "Before we start, can you tell us where you are right now, Admiral?"

"Merchett," Markan said.

Merchett was the major Gate Union world in the Lancian sector. Ean smiled. It must have hurt Markan to say that. Especially since Markan's home world, Roscracia, was three sectors on from Lancia and half a galaxy away from the Haladean Cluster. He would have made the trip specially to find out if the rumors of instantaneous communication were true.

He was finding out they were.

"And I'm Coral Zabi, from Galactic News, currently situated close to the New Alliance capital, Haladea III. Galactic News is making history tonight, being the first to report live in real time between sectors." Zabi smiled her professional smile again.

From the scowl on Markan's face, he hadn't planned on being part of that history.

"Admiral, did Gate Union attack Confluence Station earlier?"

Ean sighed. Markan's answer would be as slippery as one of Abram's.

Sure enough. "We are at war. Why would we hide the fact that we are attacking our enemy by disguising the attacker as a freighter?"

Maybe because a Gate Union battle cruiser wouldn't have gotten anywhere near as close.

"So you believe this was a message from the New Alliance," Zabi suggested. "Showing what they could do. You think they would pretend to attack one of their own bases?"

"It's hard to know what to think," Markan said. "I don't know what the New Alliance planned. Fact. Gate Union is at war with the New Alliance." He paused long enough for Zabi to open her mouth to ask the next question. "I imagine the New Alliance was waiting for an opportunity to show off that particular piece of technology. A controlled experiment might be safer for them than taking their showpiece into a real war situation, and the New Alliance might well consider the station expendable.

Expendable. All those people who had died. Yet Zabi was nodding.

Ean switched back to Blue Sky Media. They were showing the jump and what had happened after.

From the outside, looking in, it didn't look much. You couldn't see the explosions. The station spun a little, but not as noticeably as it had when you were on it. If it hadn't been for the feed Ean had sent through—which was showing on half the screen—you might not have known it was under attack.

Suddenly, Confluence Station wasn't there and the *Eleven* was. Heading at speed toward the freighter.

They weren't getting the *Eleven* feed. Ean was glad about that.

The *Eleven*'s green field pulsed out. Both the *Eleven* and the freighter fired thrusters. The green field enveloped the freighter.

Ean switched off the vid.

As well as the freighter, they had destroyed every shuttle in a two-hundred-kilometer radius. Shuttles with people on them. Innocent people who'd been trying to escape. Innocent people who'd been going about their business ferrying goods, until Ean had unleashed the *Eleven*.

He would have liked to talk to Radko about it. She wouldn't

judge. She wouldn't say, "It's war, don't worry about it." She'd listen.

What was the problem with Radko's family, anyway? Radko had once said the crew on the *Lancastrian Princess* was her family. That Abram Galenos had given her a life.

Why wouldn't anyone talk about what was wrong?

The lines must have picked up some of his worry, for Jordan Rossi's own thoughts came through the lines. *"Hey, Bastard, sing your own lines straight rather than corrupting everything on the station."*

Ean sighed and lay back on his bed.

FOUR

DOMINIQUE RADKO

IRIS RECOGNITION GOT Radko into the barracks, where she hunted up an old squad mate she hadn't seen in years. Toll had been at headquarters forever.

"It's a little early for partying," Toll said. "Incidentally, your hair's sticking out like you've plugged your arm into an electricity supply."

She fixed that by pulling off the cleverly designed hairpiece Pieter had made for her. "Do me a favor, Toll. I'll owe you forever. My kit is in the Emerald waiting room at the palace. Can you send a guard to collect it?" Toll was a group leader. He'd have the authority to send someone.

"Emerald. We do live the high life. A little too grand for a simple spacer now. Or are you team leader?"

Another advantage was that Toll knew about her family.

"Please, Toll." She was begging, and he could see it.

"Owe me forever, right."

"Thank you. I'm going to wash this makeup off."

She recycled the fresher twice before Toll arrived back with her kit, but she couldn't wash the stupidity out. What was done was done. Should she warn her family?

"Your kit's here," Toll said. "And the guard I sent said there were a lot of minor dignitaries in that room. All twittering."

Twittering. What an apt word. Radko smiled as she came out to dress.

The bag vibrated. Her comms. She ignored it while she pulled on her uniform.

"And she said someone wants you really badly. They called you four times on the way across."

Radko could imagine what it was about. She ignored it.

Dressed, cleansed of all her makeup, she felt capable of thinking again.

She had to tell Vega and Galenos what had happened. Vega was here, on Lancia, but she'd be at the palace. Not the smartest place to talk when you wanted to inform on Emperor Yu. Should she go back to the ship and report to Captain Helmo instead?

At least Dow had given her enough of a reprieve to report to someone.

"That's much better. You look like you." Toll focused on the braid on her shoulders. "Royal Guard. We are moving up."

Radko slung her kit bag over her shoulder. "Thank you, Toll."

"Although seriously, Radko. Don't stay too long in the Royal Guard. It's a career killer."

"It's been fun, lately."

Her bag vibrated again.

She didn't want to talk to them. Unless . . . maybe it wasn't about her. Maybe it was about Ean. She snatched the comms out of her bag.

Vega.

She clicked it on.

"I hope you haven't done anything stupid," Vega said, by way of greeting.

It wasn't about Ean. It was about her. "I might have done, ma'am."

Vega sighed. "Where are you?"

"At the barracks, ma'am."

"*Which* barracks?"

"Baoshan Barracks." As if there was more than one.

"So you're still on Lancia?"

"Yes, ma'am."

"That's something to be grateful for. Report to me. Now. I'm at the palace."

"Yes, ma'am." That solved one problem. Vega must know something already. She'd want to hear the rest.

"It will take you twenty minutes. If you're a minute late, I want to know why."

"What a dictator," Toll said, as Radko slipped the comms into her pocket. "Who is she?"

"My boss. Gotta go. Thanks, Toll. I owe you." Radko took off at a run.

RADKO arrived at the palace barracks as paramedics wheeled a stretcher out. It was Sasha Martinsson, one of Michelle's bodyguards.

Vega took her job as head of Princess Michelle's security seriously. Anything that got in the way of her doing her job upset her. Sure enough, she was scowling at the empty space in the assembled team where Martinsson would have been.

"What are the chances of one of my crew collapsing two minutes before they're due to escort Her Royal Highness to the Emperor?" Vega demanded of Radko.

"Low," Radko said.

Commodore Bach, in charge of the Emperor's Royal Guard, stood beside Vega. "We can supply a guard for you."

"One I don't know? I'd rather go in understaffed."

She wouldn't, of course, and she couldn't go in herself. That would look bad. "You," to Radko. "Get in line."

Radko obediently got in line. Yu wouldn't recognize her. She hoped. He didn't recognize house staff or guards. They were like furniture, and just as dispensable. But Bach's soldiers would.

Or maybe not. She was in uniform now, without the makeup that had covered her face. They might recognize her as a relative of the Emperor, but he had lots of relatives—particularly illegitimate ones, for Emperor Yu's relationships had been prolific in his youth—and there were half a dozen in the fleet.

It was too late, anyway, for they were already marching out the door.

"Wait." Vega put a hand to Radko's arm to stop her. The whole team stopped as a synchronized unit. "This stupidity of yours. How urgently does it need fixing?"

Sattur Dow wanted something. He'd organized a reprieve.

Could it wait? Probably. Unless Emperor Yu recognized and killed her this time.

"It can wait," Radko said, and the team marched out.

Down the corridor, away from anyone who was likely to pry, Radko said quietly to Ashleigh, beside her. "In case I don't survive tonight, tell Vega I don't trust Sattur Dow. He has plans."

Ashleigh's shock was palpable. "You think Sattur Dow was behind the bombing of Confluence Station?"

Radko misstepped—she never misstepped—and concentrated on getting back the rhythm.

"No," but then they were outside the princess's apartments, and Michelle was walking out to join them. They surrounded her, like the well-trained protective machine they were, and marched her to the throne room.

Radko's training let her make the right moves, which was just as well, for she wasn't thinking about them any longer. What had happened on Confluence Station?

Was Ean all right?

What if Ean wasn't there to protect? What if he'd been killed in the attack? What would that do to the line ships? No wonder Vega had asked if she had done anything stupid.

They entered the throne room.

Radko took in the changes at a glance.

Sattur Dow had gone. The guards had changed.

Michelle moved to sit on the seat Sattur Dow had been sitting on before. She was smiling. "Father. It's good to see you looking so well."

Of all the Emperor's family, the Radko branch included, Michelle was possibly the only one who retained a genuine affection for the Emperor.

"One cannot say the same of you," Yu said. "You are looking tired. That last news conference you gave." He waved a hand. "Perhaps you are working too hard."

Radko stared straight ahead. She couldn't tell if the comment was genuine concern, delivered badly, or a veiled dig.

"It won't be forever," Michelle said. "It's for Lancia, and we both want the best for our home."

"For Lancia. Yes. Although, Daughter, I have some concerns regarding what you perceive as good for Lancia."

"I do not understand."

"It is for this reason I have called you home. Without your shadow."

"My shadow?" Radko couldn't read the look Michelle gave her father. "It is unusual for you to be so oblique, Father."

"Then let me be blunt. Lancia has half a garrison on Haladea III, plus a number of high-ranking executives and statesmen."

"Hand-chosen," Michelle agreed. "People who will bolster Lancia's standing in the New Alliance."

"Therein lies our problem, doesn't it? They have been chosen by you. You and Admiral Galenos. Yet you block me and my representatives."

Michelle stilled. "I assume we are talking about my refusal to allow Sattur Dow to set up offices on Haladea III."

Sattur Dow again. Had Michelle's refusal triggered Yu's plan to provide Dow access through Radko?

"Your refusal. Or Galenos's?"

"Mine." It was firm. "The worlds of the New Alliance associate Merchant Dow too closely with the palace here at Baoshan. They believe that anything Dow does is with your tacit approval, and with some advantage to you. We cannot afford to lose all our goodwill. Sattur Dow's reputation as a ruthless businessman who destroys everything that gets in his way is well deserved."

"So is that of Merchant Pact, from Yaolin, and Merchant Fanko—"

"As is your reputation for swooping in after Dow has destabilized commerce and taking concessions for Lancia."

"Only a foolish man would ignore something ripe for the picking. Ignore it, and other worlds get the fruit."

"Rightly or wrongly, the New Alliance sees Sattur Dow both as a threat to the economy of Haladea III and as the beginning of Lancia's attempting to take control of the New Alliance government. They see it as Lancia's attempt to take over the commerce of the Haladean worlds. And once we own the commerce, to control the government, for that is what happened on Pasko."

Michelle paused. "I see that, too." She sounded calm, but her back was damp. "We cannot afford to lose what support we have by bringing in people other worlds don't trust."

The Emperor stood to pace. Radko watched him, while the guards on either side of her kept their eyes on the Emperor's guards. "In the old Alliance, Lancia never had problems placing people."

"The old Alliance was losing a war," Michelle said. "This is not that Alliance. This is a new governing body with a different structure. Lancia cannot simply walk in and take over. They have equal power with sixty-nine other worlds."

"And we agreed to that?"

"We did. You know as well as I do that had we not, we would be a second-rate Gate Union world right now. Or at the top of a third-rate Alliance with maybe ten worlds left."

"I took my daughter's advice. Maybe I was misinformed."

Michelle sighed. "Maybe you are getting bad advice from elsewhere, Father. Or your wits have finally left you permanently."

Yu swung around. "My daughter certainly isn't giving me any advice. Other than to stay away."

The turn placed him face-on to Radko. If he recognized her, he didn't show it. Radko watched his movements without seeming to.

"Maybe I am not the one getting bad advice. Admiral Galenos also voted against my request."

He swung around to face Michelle again. "What advice is he giving *you*, Daughter?"

A flush flamed Michelle's skin, and fire sparked deep in her eyes. She lifted her chin, and her tone crackled ice as she said, "You should apologize for that. Abram Galenos works for Lancia."

An answering spark ignited in her father's eyes. He turned away. Radko thought his lips quirked in the beginnings of a smile, quickly tamed.

"So ready to defend him." Emperor Yu resumed pacing. Maybe it hadn't been a smile. Radko couldn't tell if he was genuinely angry or acting.

"I am the ruler of Lancia. Where is *my* seat on the council? Where is *my* vote on matters concerning my world? Where is *my* voice? Last week, the council voted that each world would crew its own alien ship. What power do we have?"

"Equal power with other worlds, and whatever our alliances can bring. We are trying to build alliances."

"Daughter, I have been building alliances for longer than you have been alive. Now you tell me I don't know my job." He started to pace again.

Michelle's pause seemed interminably long. "Yes. I am. We are doing what we can to keep Lancia powerful."

The only reason Lancia had any real power was because their representatives—Crown Princess Michelle and Admiral Abram Galenos—worked hard to prove they weren't a threat. Radko should have told Vega about her earlier meeting with Yu and Dow.

Emperor Yu stared at Michelle. "Sometimes it seems, Daughter, that you are happy to allow Lancia to decline to a second-rate world, to allow other worlds to bully you."

Michelle chided gently. "Bullying me in return, Father? That worked when I was five. It doesn't work now." She sat up straighter. "I want Lancia to be a power as much as you do. We have to remain in the New Alliance long enough for us to become that power. And I don't want us feared by everyone when we do. I want us to be a respected ally."

"Power brings respect," Yu said.

"That sort of power is not respect, it's fear, and the problem with fear is that people who are afraid are likely to destroy what they are scared of if they can."

"My own daughter lectures me on politics. Me, who has twice her experience and ten times her power."

"We are trying to make a future for Lancia."

"We?" Yu turned so fast every soldier in the room instinctively put their hands to their weapons. Radko was pleased to see that on average, Vega's team was a second faster than Bach's. "You and who?"

"All of us working with the New Alliance," Michelle said.

"You and Galenos."

"We are both in charge."

"Maybe that's the problem," Yu said. "Galenos forgets that he is *not* in charge, that he answers to you. Instead, he fills your head with foolish notions like respect supposedly earned by showing how harmless we are."

"They're not just his notions. They're mine as well."

"Are they, Daughter? Maybe I left you too long under the protection of a man who chooses not to put Lancia first."

Michelle opened her mouth to argue. Yu silenced her with a hand. "Do you know what I call someone who refuses to put Lancia first, when they are employed by the government of Lancia?" He waved her quiet again. "Traitors. That's what I call them."

"You can call it what you like, Father, but you know as well as I do that Galenos only works for the best of Lancia."

"Not according to my sources. As head of Alien Affairs, and with his seat on the council, he has more power than anyone in the New Alliance, you included. Has power gone to his head? I ask again. What has he done for Lancia? Where are our ships? Where are the secrets from those ships? Where are our benefits?"

"The alien ships are a shared New Alliance resource," Michelle said. "Lancia is already getting more access than anyone else."

"Then why do we not have instant communication with Haladea III? Why are we not jumping ships the way you jumped that alien ship earlier?"

Michelle could still smile. In her place, Radko wouldn't have been able to. "That was an emergency. One of our bases was under attack. We would prefer not to have jumped the ship the way we did today without a lot of testing beforehand."

Alien ships moving unplanned sounded like Ean. As soon as this meeting finished, Radko would find out what had happened.

"As for instant communication, is that not what we have done?" Her voice hardened. "Is this not the first time we have communicated between sectors? Between the *Lancastrian Princess* and a small number of designated ships back in the Haladean sector."

A lot more had happened than Radko realized.

"Would Galenos have mentioned this if it hadn't made the evening news? I think not."

"You would have known once tests were completed."

"Are you certain of that, Daughter? Of course not." Emperor Yu moved back to sit on his throne. "It is time to tip the balance of power our way."

Radko hadn't thought Michelle could get any stiller, but she did.

"How?"

Yu put his palms together in what might have been a bow, or an attitude of prayer, and rested his chin on his fingers as he smiled. "How many votes do we need for a majority in the New Alliance government?"

"Fourteen. Seven worlds if both the military and civilian councilors vote the same way. They will be difficult to get. We will alienate worlds if we push too hard."

"I can get you twenty votes."

"How?" Michelle asked again.

"I have ten worlds who would take full membership in the New Alliance and support Lancia in all things."

"Who?" If Michelle looked wary, who could blame her? Most worlds were rushing to join Gate Union, sure that line restrictions would soon mean the end of the New Alliance as any real power. That would have happened already if the New Alliance hadn't had the alien ships.

And Ean Lambert.

"The Worlds of the Lesser Gods," the Emperor said, and waited for her reaction.

He got a puzzled frown in return. "The Lesser Gods? If they affiliate with anyone, surely it would be Redmond."

Yu's smile was wide. "I, too, have been making alliances, my daughter. While you sit in parliament too scared to oppose those who oppose you, listening to the advice of a man who has let power go to his head."

Michelle's mouth became a straight line, but she remained silent.

"I have been building a power base for Lancia's future. The Worlds of the Lesser Gods recently fell out with Redmond over mineral rights on Satan's Gate. They came to us, for Lancia has the only other known supply of pelagatite."

"Which was mined out two centuries ago. Not to mention

that it's beneath Settlement City, and you gave that to Sattur Dow years ago."

Yu waved dismissively. "I have offered Sattur something in return."

Access to the line ships through his new wife.

"Maybe so," Michelle countered. "How will the Factor feel when he realizes you have duped him? One worked-out mine is not enough to create an alliance."

Yu smiled. "The mine was only the start of negotiations, Daughter, and the Factor has evinced a certain . . . interest in my bait."

"Which is?"

The New Alliance would certainly be interested in the Worlds of the Lesser Gods, for while they were small, politically, they shared space close to Redmond. Having access to ten worlds in the same sector would make it easier to strike at the enemy.

"Tell me, Daughter, would not a bloc of ten votes—twenty votes—be to our advantage?"

"Of course it would. If we could be sure the Worlds of the Lesser Gods would vote for us. They are known to be unfriendly to Lancia. What bait did you use to get them to agree?"

"A close binding of our worlds. You, Daughter, will marry the Factor of the Lesser Gods."

Michelle laughed. She was the only person who would have dared. "Maybe." She stood up. "I will investigate the Worlds of the Lesser Gods and take your news back to the New Alliance so they can prepare for their request for membership."

He walked with her to the door. "And Daughter, beware of who you take advice from. When I say something is to happen, I expect it to happen."

Michelle glanced back. "I hear you, Father. Loud and clear."

VEGA had a replacement guard ready when Michelle left the throne room.

The team followed Michelle while Radko waited with Vega.

"Turns out Martinsson's allergic to his own world," Vega said. "Or the pollution in it, anyway. He hasn't been back here since Sattur Dow extended his factory at Settlement City. Airborne particulates."

Like any world, Lancia had minimum clean-air requirements, but those requirements were specific, and easy to get around if you had the money or power to buy exemptions.

Vega scowled in the direction of Settlement City. "So let's hear how bad it is."

Radko was strongly aware of Commodore Bach at his desk. These rooms, used exclusively by the guards working for the Emperor's household, were as secure as the *Lancastrian Princess*, but after what she'd heard, Radko thought that anything she told Vega would go right back to the Emperor.

"I left my kit at the barracks, ma'am. I'll need to collect it if I'm to leave now."

Vega nodded and walked with Radko. One thing about Vega. She picked up messages very quickly.

They were both silent until they were in the aircar taking them over to the barracks.

"What happened at Confluence Station?" Radko asked, for that was safe talk. Anyone would want to know about it. "I hear it was attacked."

Vega's eyebrows rose. Radko didn't have to guess what she was thinking. If she hadn't known about Confluence Station, how could she have done anything stupid?

"It's all over the vids. Galactic News and Blue Sky Media filmed it for us."

"I haven't seen the vids."

"I'm surprised." Vega folded her hands in her lap. "Confluence Station was attacked by an armed ship disguised as a freighter. It did a lot of damage."

"And Ean?"

Vega's tone turned dry. "The linesmen are safe. Before the freighter could destroy it, the station switched places with the *Eleven*, leaving the two ships to battle it out."

No one listening would have understood what Vega had

told her in those short sentences. They hadn't known before today that two ships—or a ship and a station—could switch places. Ean was the only person who could have done it.

"There is some conjecture in the media as to whether the *Eleven* destroyed the freighter or whether it jumped," Vega said. "And the captain of the freighter hasn't come forward to say, one way or the other. I'm sure you will make up your own mind when you see the vids."

Judging from the grim way Vega smiled, the freighter had been destroyed.

The aircar landed.

"Thank you for taking the time to inform me, ma'am," Radko said, as they stepped out onto the tarmac.

The aircar lifted on auto and whisked itself away.

It was safe to talk now, but Radko kept her voice low. "Did you see Michelle's audience with her father?"

"I did."

"Did you see my audience, earlier?"

"No."

She wouldn't have had a reason to.

"Sattur Dow was there. I think he wants access to the alien ships." Radko reported the whole conversation as precisely as she could, including her own pending marriage. "Not only that, I traveled to Baoshan in an aircar with Tiana Chen and Ethan Saylor. They're connected with Sattur Dow. Saylor let slip that they believe they'll have access to Lambert soon."

"That's worrying. Especially in light of the later meeting."

They walked together in silence around the parade ground at the barracks. "Your kit is at the palace," Vega said, eventually. "Let's hope Bach doesn't realize."

There was no excuse for clumsiness like that. "Sorry, ma'am."

Vega waved that away. "Emperor Yu does not like people who defy him. He's just as likely to change his mind and call you in for an accounting, no matter what Dow says."

An accounting like that only ended one way. With the accountee being wheeled out dead.

"If you stay on the *Lancastrian Princess*, he can call you

in at any time. Even if he doesn't, you become Dow's access to the alien ships because they have plans, and you're important to them."

She'd expected it, but a slow hatred started to burn against the two men who would destroy her life.

"You could always transfer me." Her voice wasn't as steady as she wanted it to be.

"We could. But why break up a good team? We'll send you away temporarily, for your own safety, until we work out what the plan is and find a way to circumvent it." Vega smiled, albeit grimly. "Let's hope Dow has overreached himself this time, and we can take him down for it."

That was almost treasonous talk. Radko glanced around, instinctively taking in who might have been listening to them. No one.

"Lambert won't take it well. Especially if he knows you don't want to go." Vega looked at her. "Unless you do want to go, that is."

"No, ma'am." It came out more fervently than she'd planned.

Another grim smile. "Lambert will do fine without you." Then Vega amended that to, "Well enough, anyway. Personally, I'd prefer you there to handle him, but under the circumstances—"

"He doesn't need handling, he needs understanding."

"He's like an out-of-control weapon. You never know whether the recoil will kill you."

"But it's more likely to turn around and hit the enemy," Radko said.

"So far. But don't worry, I'll keep him safe until you get back. Inasmuch as I can because we all know Lambert."

The brusque words relieved Radko, for she had wondered if she would be allowed to return. "How long?"

"As long as it takes. We'd best get you off now. Make it look as if you were already assigned, rather than us bundling you off in a hurry."

Vega stopped and tapped something into her comms. "A temporary promotion, I think. I'm trying you out as a team leader. The lines know, you're long past ready for it."

Ean had once told Radko that he could sometimes hear when people like Abram or Helmo or Michelle made decisions.

"It's like a snap," he'd said. "A sharp color, and they're done. Instant decision, with a whole plan behind it. As if they'd spent hours thinking it out."

Radko would bet Vega had just made a decision like that.

"Hah," Vega said. "And I've the perfect job here, especially in light of your recent information. You'll like this one. You've done covert ops before."

It wasn't a question. Before she'd come aboard the *Lancastrian Princess*, Vega had studied everyone's dossier. Radko answered anyway. "Yes, ma'am."

Not many, but enough.

"And your Redmond-language skills are good?"

"Yes, ma'am." In fact, all of Radko's covert operations to date had been on Redmond, for her parents had planned a career for her as a diplomat long before she'd chosen to join the Lancian fleet. She was skilled in three languages outside Lancian and Standard. Redmond, Carina, and Aquacaelum—and had spent time on each world as a child.

Interestingly, they were all in what was now enemy territory.

"Get yourself some clothes," Vega said. "Formal business attire. I'll have someone collect your kit and send it home."

When Radko came out of the tailoring machine, Vega had gone, but her orders were on Radko's comms, coded and backdated.

A Redmond trader, Callista OneLane, has acquired what she hints are details of groundbreaking experiments on linesmen. Further, she hints that the records include the data from the last six months, when the parameters changed, and they started getting real success with the experiments.

Six months ago the then-Alliance had discovered the alien spaceships. And realized that current line theory was flawed. And made massive leaps in communicating with the lines, themselves. Radko's breath quickened. They had to be using what the New Alliance had learned from Ean and his work with the alien lines.

As you can imagine, we're keen to see those plans.

So was Radko.

They were offered to Sattur Dow, who has bought
contraband from OneLane before. Until your report, we
had no idea why. Now we do.

Sattur Dow was never getting close enough to Ean to use
what he might have learned from those experiments.

Dow is sending Tiana Chen to purchase the report.

Vega was right. Radko did like it.

We'll delay Chen for twenty-four hours.
    You are ideally situated to know what the report shows
and how important it is. Check it out, pay what you think
we should offer for them.
    Above all, don't get caught, and don't get yourself
killed.

That was Vega, blunt and to the point. Abram Galenos
would never have said that. He would assume she was smart
enough to stay alive. Radko rubbed her eyes. Change was
inevitable, and she liked Vega, but everyone on ship had been
comfortable with the old regime.
    They'd been happy, Ean had said.

You have been assigned a small team. Your "other" job—

Based on the quotes Radko assumed this was unofficially
as important to Vega as the first.

—is to assess them for line ability. Every one of them
went through line training and failed certification. I want a
full report on each of them, including their level and your
assessment of their capabilities.

Radko wasn't a linesman, but she was better equipped than
most to recognize the individual songs of each line. Vega must
have been planning this part of the operation for a while.

There's a ship leaving for Mykara at 1800 hours. Be on it. Leave the ship at Shaolin. Lancia has a cache there. You can arm yourself, and from there you can catch a ship to Redmond.

She had exactly fifteen minutes to make the shuttle Vega had booked for her. Radko shouldered her bag and ran.

FIVE

EAN LAMBERT

EAN AND ROSSI fixed as many of the damaged lines on Confluence Station as they could, and the twenty linesmen Ean had
been training came out the next day to finish off. Abram came
along as well.

Ean listened to the trainees' work.

"There isn't much more I can teach them," he told Abram.
"They know how to listen now, and how to sing the lines
straight."

"That's good," Abram said. "There's a push to train more.
We've every world in the New Alliance scouring for suitable
linesmen for you to train."

Singing to the lines wouldn't be a secret much longer.

They suited up so that Abram could inspect the damaged
areas.

"Some worlds have agreed to leave their trained linesmen
here to help you," Abram said. "Provided they can train others
from their own world."

"Hernandez?" Hernandez was a ten. She had spent so much
time around the eleven ships, she'd have problems if her home
world of Balian took her away.

"Of course," as if that was a given. It probably was. Admiral Katida of Balian would like her own personal ten knowing
everything that went on. "You lose Tai." Tai was the chief
engineer on the *Lancastrian Princess*. Ean had never expected
him to stay. "Chantsmith will stay on the *Gruen*."

Chantsmith had always defended the *Gruen*. "I'm glad."
The *Gruen* would be happy.

"At least this attack has galvanized those councilors and
admirals who were uncertain before. They're seriously looking for line crews."

Finally.

"We're also training paramedics from the various worlds to work with line-related problems. You'll work with a mix of experienced and inexperienced paramedics for a while."

"So when does the *Confluence* get its crew?"

He could tell from the way Abram paused that he wouldn't like the answer.

"It doesn't. Not initially. They're still arguing over who should crew it."

"It's not fair the other ships get crews—and captains—while the flagship doesn't. Besides—" He broke off.

"Besides?" Abram looked wary.

"I promised it was next."

"I can't get you a captain, Ean. Not the way we got Kari Wang. This one will take all the politicking—and more—that the first one didn't."

How was Ean going to tell the *Confluence* that? "The lines won't wait forever. Lines need people." The more permanent crew a ship had on board, the more aware a ship became. The *Eleven* was markedly different from the lonely ship they had found in the outer depths of space all those months ago. "How are they crewing the other ships if they're not crewing the *Confluence*?"

"We've promised every world a ship of its own, provided they agree to remain on permanent loan to the New Alliance fleet."

That would take some politicking of its own, for there was a range of ships. Fleet carriers, which were the largest outside the eleven ships and had smaller one- and two-man ships on board. There were twenty of them. Patrol ships, smaller than the carriers and not as heavily armed, but some of the weapons were massive. Then there were sixty smaller, faster combat ships with lighter weapons and bigger engines. Lastly were the scouts, which carried six people.

Every world would want the larger ships though many of them were damaged. One of the fleet carriers and two of the patrol ships would have to be rebuilt before they could take crew.

What did the aliens do when their ships were damaged so badly? What could cause that sort of damage, anyway?

It was good to know that the ships were getting crew, but the flagship needed crew as well. "Why don't you make each supply a crew member for the *Confluence* as a condition for getting its own ship?" The *Eleven* had a full linesman and a single-level linesman from each world; the *Confluence* should have the same. "Two crew. A single and a full."

Abram smiled. "I'll see what I can do. I may be able to get you a crew even if I can't get you a captain."

They arrived at the internal air lock that blocked off the more damaged areas of the station. Once through the air lock, the still-intact passages gave way to a structure of struts and clear plastic, separating the inside from the outside.

Ean's stomach flipped queasily. Sure, he knew that there was nothing except space outside a ship or station, but he'd rather not see it. Not an empty black expanse like this.

Abram looked around. "That freighter did some damage."

Yet Confluence Station wasn't majorly distressed about it. Even though the lines were damaged, and their station manager was still in the hospital, the station song was more of fixing things and of everything under control. The *Lancastrian Princess* would have been distressed if its "Ship"— Captain Helmo—was missing.

"Do you think only ships, and not stations, bond with their captains?" Ean asked.

"Do you?"

"No." Although both Piers Wendell and Jita Orsaya believed that going through the void increased the bond between ship and captain, and Ean knew his own link with the lines expanded every time he went through the void. "Maybe. I don't know." Ean would still have expected some recognition from Confluence Station that its "Ship" was damaged.

CAPTAIN Helmo called at midnight to say he was returning to Haladean space. Fergus and Commodore Vega were on the bridge with him.

Ean already knew one person was missing. "Is everyone—"

"There is a line-security issue I need to discuss with you, Linesman," Vega said over the top of him. "Make yourself available on the *Lancastrian Princess* at the earliest opportunity."

"A security issue?"

"At the earliest."

He could get subtle—and not so subtle—hints.

Ean let Fergus sing them in, while he checked the surrounding lines to ensure there were no ships nearby. This was a sanctioned jump, ordered in the name of a freighter half the galaxy away, but Gate Union knew by now that the New Alliance was buying jumps on the black market. How could they not?

Ean trusted the *Eleven* fleet ships to stop any intruders, but Captain Helmo wasn't as trusting as he was. It was Ean's way of reassuring Helmo that everything was all right. Maybe one day, Helmo would believe it enough to jump cold.

The galaxy would turn into a black hole first.

He went out to the shared common room, where Ru Li and Gossamer were on duty. "I need to go to the *Lancastrian Princess*."

"Now?" Gossamer asked.

"There's a problem." Vega might have wanted him to wait until morning, but she had said at the earliest.

Ru Li sighed and went to wake Bhaksir.

"If it's line-related, couldn't you fix it from here?" Gossamer asked.

If it was line-related, he could have. "Vega said a line-security issue. And to make myself available, at the earliest." Besides, he wanted to know what had happened to Radko.

Bhaksir came out with Hana. Hana rubbed sleep out of her eyes. Sale came out from her room.

Guilt swamped Ean. He looked at the growing crowd of people. "It can probably wait until morning."

"Ean," Sale said. "Once you've asked for something, don't weaken your position by saying it's not important."

"Besides, it'll be good to have Radko back," Bhaksir said.

Except Radko wasn't back, and her own team leader didn't know that yet.

Jumps weren't permitted close to other ships. They waited in the shuttle for the *Lancastrian Princess* to come in closer before they went to meet it. If human ship lines developed to the level of the alien ship lines, there would be no need to jump so far out. If they could jump as accurately as the *Eleven* had earlier, they'd simply jump directly into position.

Ean listened to the chatter of the ships as they waited. Abram was going out to the *Lancastrian Princess* as well.

Bhaksir and Hana listened to the Lancastrian news feeds— no longer in real time although still more current than they had been—switching between channels when something bored them. Ean hadn't kept up with Lancian news. He didn't plan on keeping up with it, either.

Some of the news was about the war. Gate Union had attacked the mining colonies at Aratoga.

"At least it's a change from the usual complaints about how restrictions on jumps are harming the New Alliance world economies," Bhaksir said. "Wait," as Hana poised to flick the channel again.

The reporter was the striking woman Ean had seen on the news vids earlier, Maxine Oroton. On-screen behind her was a picture of Michelle, wearing a formal blue jacket encrusted with jewels. Her dark hair was swept up in an elegant chignon, and she wore a tiara glittering with more jewels.

"News in from the palace," Oroton said. "His Imperial Majesty, Emperor Yu, has announced the betrothal of his oldest daughter, Her Royal Highness, Crown Princess Michelle, to the Factor of the Lesser Gods."

The image changed to display a man—equally formally dressed—with cropped black hair and a wide, sensuous mouth.

He looked—to Ean's prejudiced gaze—like a man who thought a lot of himself.

"We go now to Professor Ghyslain, to tell us about the Worlds of the Lesser Gods."

The image crossed to a man standing in an open area, long coat streaming in the wind. A massive castle filled the screen behind him. "I'm standing here in the capital of Aeolus, the largest and most populous of the Worlds of the Lesser Gods."

He had a booming voice that didn't so much compete with the wind as quell it. "The building behind me is the Factor's primary home. This is where Her Royal Highness Princess Michelle will reside after her marriage to the Factor."

Michelle had four and a half years left on Haladea III before she went anywhere. New Alliance council members were elected for a term of five years.

"Professor Ghyslain, can you tell us more about the people and the worlds Her Royal Highness is marrying into?"

"Of course. There are ten Worlds of the Lesser Gods. They're in the Redmond sector." A galactic map filled the screen. Six worlds were highlighted in the center. "These are the Redmond worlds, which we all know." The image moved to the top right corner and zoomed in to an edge of the sector. "These are the Worlds of the Lesser Gods. They are named after ten of the gods in Greek mythology. That's an Old Earth mythology," he added. "Aeolus, Asclepius, Amphitrite, Dionysus, Hebe, Hellas, Maia, Nemesis, Pan, and Persephone. Named, I might add, because the first three worlds discovered personified these gods."

Ean had never heard of them.

"Aeolus is the god of winds, and as you can see, this place is most definitely windy. Asclepius is the god of healing. It was on Asclepius that we discovered the restorative compounds so vital in regeneration. Amphitrite is the goddess of the sea, and that world is totally covered in water."

The overlay disappeared, and the image returned to Ghyslain.

"The worlds are relatively new and unknown. They are 150 years old, and most of their trade to date has been with Redmond, so this political marriage is a major step up in galactic power for them.

"They have a lot in common with Lancia, in fact, and a lot to offer us. Like our own world, a single family has ruled since humans settled there. The leader of that family—of the whole ten worlds—is known as the Factor. His full title is the Factor of the Lesser Gods."

"And when her Royal Highness marries the Factor? What is her title?"

"She doesn't take a title," Ghyslain said. "She becomes the Factor's partner. She will retain her own titles at home, of course, and on other worlds she will still be known as Lady Lyan, but on the Worlds of the Lesser Gods she is a commoner, at the command of the Factor in all things."

The Factor sounded like someone Michelle should avoid.

Even Maxine Oroton looked a little nauseated. "Her Royal Highness is a working royal. I cannot see her accepting that."

Ean liked Maxine Oroton a lot better, suddenly.

"I am sure our princess is willing to do what needs to be done for the good of the New Alliance."

Ean couldn't imagine Michelle giving up on her duties or ceding power to a husband.

Oroton seemed as unconvinced as Ean. "The Worlds of the Lesser Gods have been closely associated with Redmond until now. Why do you think they seek an alliance with Lancia?"

The wind was so strong, Ghyslain's smile was almost pasted on. "Emperor Yu is famous for initiating political alliances that benefit Lancia, and a pact with the Worlds of the Lesser Gods certainly will be that. Particularly as Lancia requires only fourteen votes on the New Alliance council to gain a majority. I am sure His Majesty must be considering that."

So would the rest of the council, many of whom were worried about Lancia already. Ean could name three worlds immediately that would look askance at this. Probably more.

"It's perfect timing," Ghyslain said. "Some months ago, Redmond and the Worlds of the Lesser Gods had a falling-out. Redmond stopped supplying pelagatite, which is essential to manufacturing on the Lesser Gods worlds. The Factor had been sounding out Gate Union—"

"Aren't Redmond and Gate Union allies?" Oroton asked.

Ghyslain laughed. "Of course, but there's no love between those two, and both of them will use any political clout they can get. Anyway, it's too late, for His Imperial Majesty stepped in. For, you see, the only other known pelagatite mine is on Lancia."

If you asked Ean, a world—or worlds—so dependent on one mineral was not a stable world or a rich world.

"The mine under Settlement City? Wasn't that closed down years ago?"

"It was, yes, but it may be viable to reopen it, especially if Lancia is prepared to mine it at a loss in order to bring the Worlds of the Lesser Gods into the New Alliance. And it's already being rumored that the marriage agreement is dependent on the Factor's bringing his worlds across. This could be counted as a coup for Emperor Yu, who single-handedly brings ten worlds into the alliance, while strengthening Lancia's position and power."

The unemotional words went on.

Ean watched Bhaksir and Hana, both of whose faces lost all expression as they listened. Radko sometimes went blank-faced. Usually when she didn't want people to know what she was thinking.

It was a pity they were in the shuttle. On ship, Ean could have worked out how they really felt about it.

AFTER seemingly forever, the *Lancastrian Princess* came into range, and their shuttle moved toward it. They docked just after Abram did.

Abram waited for Ean. Since Vega was pacing in Michelle and Abram's workroom, Ean went with him. Ship mood was anxious. Ean sang to the lines as he walked, but it was nothing he could fix. Should he ask about Radko? Maybe not right now. It didn't feel like a good time.

Helmo joined them outside the workroom.

So far as Ean knew, Vega had never been in Michelle's workroom since her introductory tour, and while Helmo talked to Michelle a lot, he often did it from the bridge. Yet Michelle wanted them here. She felt safe here. That came through on line one.

Michelle should feel safe anywhere on the *Lancastrian Princess*. Was this about her impending marriage?

Michelle settled onto her couch with a sigh. "Where do I start?"

There were no preliminary explanations, and she didn't treat Ean as if he shouldn't be there. Ean sat down quietly in his regular seat, as if he had every right to. Abram had a regular seat as well, but he didn't sit there today. Instead, he sat beside Michelle, leaving Helmo and Vega to sit on his couch.

"One month ago, my father sent a delegation from Lancia to help on the council. He does that all the time," she said to Ean. He was the only one who didn't know that, for everyone else nodded. She looked around at the others, so the next bit was for everyone. "He wanted Sattur Dow to head the delegation."

"Not exactly a smart move, politically," Vega said.

"No," Michelle agreed.

When Ean was a boy, Emperor Yu had gifted Sattur Dow

with Settlement City. Dow had given the residents two days to get out. On the third day, he'd sent in demolition crews. By nightfall, the city was razed. Those people who hadn't got out in time were dead. The rest had flooded in as refugees to the slums at Oldcity, where Ean lived, causing turf wars that lasted years.

It would be a kind of justice for all those people Ean had known if Yu kicked Sattur Dow off that land now so they could reopen the old mine under it. Especially since he'd spent billions of credits in the intervening years building a factory on it.

"Naturally, we told him he couldn't come," Michelle said.

She rubbed her hands together as if they were cold. It was an uncharacteristic movement from Michelle, who could normally keep her feelings hidden when she needed to. Ean could hear through the lines that this next bit was important. "Then my father called me home."

"To talk about Dow?" Ean asked. Or to talk about her forthcoming marriage?

Vega said, "I recorded the feed if you'd prefer me to show it."

"Thank you. I would."

They watched in silence as Emperor Yu accused Abram of treason, then attempted to trump that by telling Michelle she was to marry the Factor of the Lesser Gods. They sat silent a moment longer after it finished.

Abram blew out his breath. "I knew there were rumors about a blowup regarding pelagatite, but I cannot see the Worlds of the Lesser Gods allying with Lancia and the New Alliance over it. Not unless there's something in it for them. Something big."

Maybe they thought the New Alliance would win the war and wanted to be on the winning side.

"The Factor has a smooth tongue," Michelle said. "Even so, my father isn't normally taken in by clever words."

"Not unless he has plans of his own," Abram said.

Like gaining an extra twenty votes in council for Lancia. "We heard about the engagement," Ean said. "It made the news."

Michelle made a face. "I would have preferred more time to sort that out privately. However, that's not my concern. My father is paranoid. I have seen how he acts when he believes someone is undermining his power. He starts to worry aloud whether that person truly supports him. He starts to believe his own questions. I have seen other people, good people, destroyed for that."

And Yu was questioning Abram now.

"He's getting really bad advice," Vega said.

"And Settlement City," Helmo said. "Why give that away when he's already promised Michelle? He has to compensate Sattur Dow then."

"As to that," Vega said, and her look at Ean was veiled, "I expect it's an excuse. I imagine he's promised Dow one of the alien ships. Or access to it, anyway. If you won't let Dow come here as part of a business delegation, he has every right to come here to see his wife. Her Royal Highness isn't the only one who was betrothed yesterday."

She glared around at them all.

"He's also remarkably well informed, for he knew exactly whom to target." Her glare stopped at Ean.

What had he done?

"Radko," Michelle said.

At first, Ean didn't understand. Then he did. "Are you saying Radko is to marry Sattur Dow?" The ship lines sang with his incredulity.

Helmo winced.

"Worryingly well informed," Abram said.

Yu had no right to tell Radko or Michelle whom they were to marry, and Sattur Dow was not getting anywhere near Radko. Not if Ean could prevent it.

"Where is Radko?" Ean asked.

Vega glared at him again. "Spacer Radko is on special assignment. Organized *two weeks* ago. I'm trying her out for a team-leader position."

Two weeks. "She didn't tell me she was on special duties."

"She didn't know about it until last night, Ean," Michelle said. "You should pretend you both knew about it."

"When will she be back?"

"When this business is over," Vega said. "Not before."

If Ean had anything to do with it, it would be over soon.

"So what do we have?" Abram counted them off. "A plan

involving Sattur Dow and access to the linesman. A plan to bring votes into the New Alliance by allying Lancia with the Worlds of the Lesser Gods. Are they related, do you think?"

"My father always has many plans on the go."

"Probably not, then. And we have Emperor Yu starting to question my abilities as admiral."

"Because you're not doing what he wants you to," Vega said.

Abram worked for Lancia, and anyone who had listened to the lines would know that. Except Yu, it seemed.

Abram blew out his breath. "Misha, unfortunately, you'll have deal with the fallout from the Lesser Gods. I'll help where I can, but you'll get the brunt of it."

"It might even be a good thing," Michelle said. "A base that close to Redmond might give us a chance to strike at them."

Close was only relative when you were talking distances in space.

"Or it might simply make the Lesser Gods an immediate target," Abram said, and Vega and Helmo nodded. "Take them out before they have the New Alliance behind them." He blew out his breath again. "If I were the Factor of the Lesser Gods, I'd be asking Lancia for protection, just in case."

"Have they?" Vega asked.

Abram shook his head. "Which is worrying in itself."

Redmond was building ships based on alien technology. They were building weapons based around the same. Kari Wang had been testing them, back before her world, Nova Tahiti, had defected from Gate Union to join the fledgling New Alliance.

The Worlds of the Lesser Gods were pastoral worlds. If Redmond chose to attack them, they wouldn't stand a chance. Even if there were only six Redmond worlds to the Lesser Gods' ten.

If Gate Union chose to help—not that Redmond and Gate Union were working much together at present, but they were still formally allied—the fight would be over even faster.

"What about Dow? If he wants access to Ean, he'll find a way to get out here."

Vega looked as sour as Ean had ever seen her. "You have

already denied him access to Haladea III. There is only one place he can come."

The *Lancastrian Princess.*

"I must host him when he comes," Michelle said. "He is a close friend of my father's."

"I can deal with Dow," Vega said. "If Radko's not here, he has no access to Lambert. But it would be better if Lambert wasn't on ship at the same time at all. They can't help running into each other. Lambert will have to remain on Confluence Station." Vega had always wanted Ean off the *Lancastrian Princess*, but right now, she looked as happy about it as Ean was.

"I'll put Orsaya in charge of the confluence linesmen's security," Abram said. "She's got Rossi there as well, so she has a reason to own it."

"Let's hope we get Ean back," Michelle said. "She'll love to have Ean under her charge."

Everyone laughed, and the sudden relaxation of tension emphasized just how much there had been in the room beforehand.

The worry soon flooded back as little eddies of song—different tunes for different people. Vega's worry was about the ship and how she would make it secure. And about Ean, which was unexpected. Then, she didn't know Orsaya, who didn't ally herself with Lancia—she was part of the other main power group in New Alliance politics—but was line obsessed. Orsaya would look after Ean. She wouldn't give away line knowledge if she could prevent it.

Helmo's worry was centered around Michelle, and line eight was strong.

Abram's worry likewise had a lot of Michelle in it, but it was normal Abram, only stronger. Ean took that to mean these were the things Abram normally worried about. Like keeping Lancia strong, keeping Michelle safe.

Michelle's worry was a swirling crescendo full of the sound of Abram, so loud it almost drowned out the others.

"Bhaksir's team will stay with Lambert, of course," Vega said.

Abram nodded.

"Everyone in Sale's teams will need to stay on station as well because if he can't get Ean, that's who he'll try next."

Abram nodded again.

At least Ean wouldn't be totally alone although he wasn't sure how Bhaksir and Sale would take the news that their temporary relocation wasn't as temporary as it had been.

Michelle blew her breath out in a manner reminiscent of Abram. "Any suggestions for what we do about the Worlds of the Lesser Gods? The New Alliance will see this as a power grab by Lancia, which it is. We are not going to make friends with this."

They didn't mention the other issue. Emperor Yu and Abram. Ean knew they weren't going to.

Everyone went silent for a moment. Even the ship went quiet.

"Emperor Yu has already made news of the engagement public," Vega said.

Through the lines, Ean heard the green snap of Abram making a decision. "Give them something else to think about. Something they've been asking for a while. Let's send the *Eleven* on a mission."

"Is she ready?" Helmo asked.

"When is ready? We won't send her into a full battle situation. Not yet anyway. A skirmish somewhere, a small battle to show the power of the *Eleven*."

The song of the *Lancastrian Princess* lifted. There was hope in the tune now.

"Gate Union attacked the mining colonies at Aratoga two hours ago. The Aratogans are defending," Abram said. "As you can imagine, they're severely limited with the jumps they can get."

Fighting a war when the enemy controlled the jumps was no way to win. The Gate Controllers would deny any New Alliance jumps direct from Aratoga to the war zone. The *Eleven* didn't need a controlled jump—at least, Ean was sure it didn't—but no one was prepared to test it. Maybe this time Abram and Kari Wang would let him do it.

"And how do we get a jump for the *Eleven*?" Vega asked.

"We don't," Ean said. "We trust that the *Eleven* won't jump into space occupied by another ship."

Silence greeted his words.

"We switched the *Eleven* and Confluence Station yesterday. That's a tiny jump window, compared to what we usually have."

"We also knew where both ships were," Helmo said. "I won't risk a cold jump. Kari Wang won't either."

Marcus Helmo was not a man who scared easily, yet he had a deep-seated fear of jumping cold. That fear was starting to freeze the *Lancastrian Princess* lines right now.

"They've done it before. If you listen to your ship, you'll be safe," Ean said to Helmo.

"Can you guarantee 100 percent—absolutely 100 percent—that we won't jump into another ship?"

Could he? If he was wrong, he condemned everyone on the *Eleven* to death. He didn't want that. "We need a jump, then."

Abram bought jumps on the black market. It was an expensive business, and fraught with danger, for eventually the Union of Gate Worlds would realize what the marketeer was doing. There was always the worry that this time, the jump would be a setup, and they'd be sent into another ship, or into an asteroid.

Abram checked his comms. "The only one I have in the next two hours is close to Roscracia."

Two hours. Abram planned for them to go right now.

Michelle managed to laugh. "That would go down well. Why, hello Admiral Markan," for Roscracia was a populous Gate Union world, and home to Markan, who headed the Gate Union war effort. "We're just dropping by to get a jump."

"Actually"—Abram's eyes gleamed—"it might work. Are we likely to be refused a jump from Roscracia? Especially if Ean taps into one of the military ships there and uses that to request it."

It was even safe, for they knew Ean could control the lines on other ships.

"You are certifiably crazy, you know that." But Helmo was grinning. "It's insane enough to work."

Abram reached for his comms.

"Might I remind you," Vega said. "You are taking our only level-twelve linesman into the heart of enemy territory. A member of Her Royal Highness's personal staff. Someone from whom that same enemy recently tried to get information."

"They'll only be there long enough to get another jump," Abram said. "The jump window we have is for a civilian ship. It won't be anywhere near the warships."

The captain of the *Eleven* came up on the comms.

"Captain Kari Wang, we are deploying the *Eleven* to the incident at Aratoga. Linesman Lambert will accompany you. We'll send you a situation report and plan of action. Execute it as soon as the linesman is on board."

"Not that I like losing our twelve," Helmo said. "I would prefer Lambert stayed here."

At least Helmo thought Ean was part of the *Lancastrian Princess* crew.

Vega had taken out her comms as well. "Bhaksir, you and your team are assigned to active duty on the *Eleven*. Protecting Linesman Lambert. Prepare to move out in five."

"Yes, ma'am."

Through the lines, Ean heard Bhaksir call up the rest of her team on Confluence Station and relay those orders.

Ean stood up. When they made decisions around here, they moved fast.

"Ean," Abram said. "You know what you have to do?"

"Use another ship's comms to book a jump." It would be so much easier to jump to Aratogan space. He forced himself not to rub his palms down his sides. He wished Radko were here. It wasn't a hard job. He'd listened in to other ships' comms before. He'd stopped them firing on the *Lancastrian Princess*.

"Choose a military ship, if you can. They'll get jumps fast."

Ean nodded.

"And don't, whatever you do, sing the enemy ship into the fleet."

"I'll try not to." He couldn't promise something like that.

Sale, Bhaksir, and Craik had discussed at length how lucky they'd been with Wendell and Gruen. Wendell had been in the wrong place at the wrong time, and his home world of Wallacia had branded him and his crew traitors. Wendell had no love for either side, but the New Alliance let him keep his ship, and that was the most important thing to him. As for Gruen—she had left the Roscracian military after Admiral Markan had refused to get back her captured ship. They wouldn't be lucky a third time. If Ean sang a Gate Union military ship into the *Eleven*'s fleet and they kept the captain on, he'd be singing a spy into their midst.

"Thank you."

Michelle stopped him. "Take care."

"You too, Michelle." And Ean smiled at her. "Everything will work out." He didn't mean just the upcoming battle, which he deliberately wasn't thinking about.

"What happens if Lambert mucks up?" Vega asked.

The smile in Abram's tone was reflected by a red-mint-cinnamon spurt of amusement from Michelle. "Ean can be unconventional, but he usually manages."

At least it had stopped that awful worry that had been circulating through the ship earlier.

Abram opened his comms again. "Galenos here. Get me Admirals Orsaya, Katida, and MacClennan."

They were the other admirals in the Alien Affairs Department of the New Alliance, which was the department in charge of the alien ships. Abram would have to get their agreement to run this trial. Or did Abram, being in charge, decide, and just tell them?

"Battle." The song of the *Eleven* was pleased. *"Fight."*

Sometimes the ships seemed a little bloodthirsty to Ean. He forgot they had been warships.

And behind all that, the thread of a sad whisper from the *Confluence*. *"If we had a crew, we could fight, too."*

SIX

DOMINIQUE RADKO

ON THE SHUTTLE, Radko received another package of data from Vega.

Radko was tapping out a careful set of instructions for Bhaksir:

> Just because he wears the uniform, don't expect Ean to
> know everything. He hasn't had the training. Explain
> things. He doesn't think like a soldier; he thinks like a
> line. Lines don't think the way we do.

She paused over the SEND button, and deleted it instead. The team would cope perfectly well without her. Ean would, too. Then took a moment to compose herself before she opened Vega's message.

> OneLane's shop is in the FourDogs district of Bane, the
> largest city on Satan's Gate.

Satan's Gate was the main Redmond world. Radko had spent time in Bane, even knew of the FourDogs district although she'd never been there. It was a well-to-do area full of high-class boutiques and antiques shops. She pulled up images to view the address Vega had supplied.

The shop had a narrow entry, with artfully displayed artifacts in the window. The window was crisscrossed with a grating that glowed a soft blue around the edges. A security field. Whatever OneLane had in there, she liked it well protected. Radko saw four cameras at the front of the shop, and although she couldn't see the back, they would be there, somewhere.

A discreet plaque on the wall advertised LoneField Security—one of the best in the business.

Radko turned back to Vega's comms.

> You have a team of three. They'll join you on the freighter to Shaolin.
>   Theodora van Heel works in surveillance. She has worked in intelligence for twenty years, the last six behind a desk. She is a class hacker and can break into most systems. A reliable person when you need to break into a system or to cover your tracks, but every year she is called in for remedial target practice. That, and her level of fitness, are the main reasons she is behind a desk rather than in the field.

Bless Vega for telling her the important things she needed to know about the people she was working with.

> She is the only one of your team who has worked off world before.
>   Yves Han is military police. He works in the main barracks at Baoshan.

Han was a high-caste Lancastrian family name. Combined with a French first name like Yves, his family would move in the same circle as hers. In which case, Radko knew him. Renaud Han's son.

She brought up the image. The resemblance to Renaud was strong. Yves Han was three years older than Radko. She'd last seen him when she was nine, and he'd been twelve. Her family had been visiting the Hans and she'd found Yves Han standing over his tutor—seventy years old if he was a day—forcing the old man's hand onto the red-hot heat supply of the furnace.

The tutor screamed as Yves forced his hand down.

"Stop that now," Radko commanded.

Yves had laughed at her. "Go away, little girl. Keep out of things that don't concern you." He'd pushed the tutor's arm down again.

So she'd beaten him up.

She was the one who'd gotten into trouble. Yves had needed regen, and the tutor claimed he'd burned his own hand. She hadn't seen Yves since. He'd tested high on the Havortian tests and taken up the offer of an apprenticeship from one of the big cartel houses.

Yet she'd always liked Yves's parents. Even though Renaud and Amina Han were part of the Emperor's inner circle, they always had time for the Emperor's aunt, and for the almost-forgotten young cousin.

Radko frowned at the image. The boy she'd known had bordered on sadistic or worse. She hoped fleet training had knocked some of his nastiness out of him. He definitely wasn't someone she'd ever introduce Ean to, linesman or not.

I have worked with Han before, back when I spent two years as a captain on Baoshan. I found him reliable and easy to work with. A good man to have at your back.

He didn't sound like the Yves Han she remembered. Radko turned to the last name.

Arun Chaudry is six months out of training. His psychiatrist says he has a death wish. Joined the fleet to get himself killed.

The preliminary psych tests should have picked that up.

They put him in Stores—on base—where he'll never see combat. His group leader is surprisingly protective of him, says he's lost and needs to find something he can do.

Radko flipped the name to see who the group leader was and wasn't surprised to find it was Lee Toll.

Van Heel was the only person with any experience in this kind of work. As for the other two—a man who might or might not like power over others and a man with a death wish. Did Vega believe they were dispensable? Or was there something more?

The something more came on the next line.

Yves Han trained ten years at House of Sandhurst.
Theodora van Heel, seven years, House of Xun. Arun
Chaudry, six years, House of Isador. Van Heel and
Chaudry failed certification.

According to Ean, six years was the absolute minimum for
a line apprenticeship. The apprentices started in their teens—
although a cartel master would take them earlier if they
showed real promise—and couldn't be tested until they were
seventeen. The ones the cartel masters thought would fail
were tested early. Van Heel and Chaudry probably hadn't
shown much ability.

Vega hadn't said how old they were, but Radko could guess
from their images that van Heel had trained a generation earlier than Chaudry.

I need to know what lines they are and if they are suitable
for line training.
    Han certified as an exceptionally strong seven but
received head injuries in an accident not long after
certification. The doctors say there is nothing physically
wrong with him, but after the trauma, he lost any line
ability. I want you to assess whether Lambert may be able
to fix his line problem.

THE only ships getting jumps to and from Lancia nowadays
were unaffiliated merchants. Mostly small, second-class
freighters, and right now they were making a fortune. The ship
was crowded. Every ship leaving Lancia was.

Radko didn't have a cabin. There was a netted-off area in
the bar to stow her kit, for she and her team would leave the
ship in four hours.

Them and a hundred others.

She recognized Yves Han immediately. He stood like a
member of one of the Great Families, as if he expected people
to move around him, rather than him to move around them.
Sometimes, Radko knew, she did that herself.

She pushed forward to stand beside him. "Han."

If he remembered the last time they'd met, it didn't show. "Team leader." Or maybe he'd had time to decide to ignore the memory. Vega must have sent their names through to the whole team—without the other identifying information Radko had received—or otherwise he wouldn't have recognized Radko. That was unusual for by-the-book Vega. Radko had a code she could use to identify herself to the other three. That was what she would normally use on an operation like this.

The title felt strange, and not something she planned on getting used to. She liked the job she had.

"This is crazy crowded," Han said. "I hope we arrive safely."

She tapped in the identifying code and touched her comms to Han's. Identity established. "Yes," she said, and looked around. "Somewhere in this crowd, we've two other people."

Her comms chimed. Van Heel.

"Never mind," van Heel said, when she answered. "I can see you. I'm nearby." She pushed through the crowd. "This overcrowding. It's dangerous."

It would get worse before it got better. Unless Ean could convince the New Alliance to jump cold.

As Radko touched her comms to van Heel's to establish identity, the bell chimed to signify the ship was about to enter the void. She paused and looked around to be sure her charge was safe this time. Weird things happened around jumps.

But, of course, Ean wasn't there.

She waited until they jumped, then went back to her comms. No one else had noticed; no one else cared. She'd forgotten how normal jumps were on other ships.

The public address blared over the top of her attempt to contact Chaudry. "All passengers leaving at Shaolin please assemble at the shuttle bays. Be sure to collect all luggage prior to disembarking."

"That's us," Radko said, and thumbed the comms open to the other member of her team. "Chaudry. This is team leader Radko. We'll meet you at the shuttle bays."

"That's early," Han muttered. "Can't wait to get rid of us, obviously."

Personally, Radko couldn't wait to get off the ship.

They found Chaudry standing, arms crossed, in the middle of the shuttle queue. He wasn't much taller than anyone else, but he was wider. His arms were bare, and the muscles bulged. Despite the crowd, people moved a long way around him.

"He's enough to scare anyone's grandmother," Han said.

Radko frowned at him.

"Arun Chaudry," Han said.

Chaudry narrowed his eyes. "Who's asking?"

"I wasn't asking, I was identifying." Han gave a half bow. "Your teammate, Yves Han, and with me I have Theodora van Heel and Team Leader Radko."

"I need a code," Chaudry said.

Radko tapped in the code and touched her comms to his.

Han had names and images to identify the team. So had van Heel. Chaudry hadn't. "I'm surprised you know us all," Radko said to Han. "I only got them on my comms as I was coming out here."

Van Heel was a hacker. If she was as good as Vega said, then she could find out who she was working with. But Han? He was a policeman on base.

"I have contacts."

"I see." Radko made a mental note to let Vega know. Military police shouldn't have been able to get that detail.

Han watched her face. "I like to know what I'm getting into. And we do have orders on our comms."

"Those orders shouldn't be something you can get from your contacts." Radko looked around at the crowd waiting to exit the shuttle. "We'll discuss it when it's more private."

RADKO'S team was directed to a small, eight-man shuttle. They were the only passengers for Barth, the fourth-largest spaceport on Shaolin.

"We get people like you every four, five trips," the pilot said. "They think because it's busy and on the southern end of the continent, it's a good place to come if you need to go south. But there's nothing but cargo sheds. Passengers don't usually get off here. Most people go on to San See and take an aircar across the continent."

Which was why their equipment was stored at Barth. "It's close to where we need to go," Radko said. "And provided we can hire an aircar, does it matter if there's nothing there?"

"Lady, your aircar will have to come from San See. If you were thinking of saving money, this is not it." The pilot turned abruptly and waved frantically at Chaudry, who'd been about to strap himself in beside a small, refrigerated crate. "Not on that side. Can't taint the special orders, can we."

Chaudry squeezed in between van Heel and Han instead.

Radko looked at the crate. She recognized the logo. "Gippian shellfish. Here?"

"You'd be surprised where we take these babies," the pilot said. "Here. The center of the galaxy. The outer rim. We go from Lancia to Redmond, Roscracia to Yaolin, and everywhere between. Anyplace someone is prepared to pay for them."

Including Haladea III, where the Lancastrian ambassador served them to his guests.

It was a pity this particular delivery wasn't going straight to Redmond.

"Gippian shellfish," Han said, salivating.

"Spacers can't afford shellfish on our wage," van Heel said. "You'll never get to taste it, Han."

Chaudry shuddered. "I had one once. It was awful."

"Gunter Wong is a friend of my father's," Han said. "He brings it over sometimes when he comes for dinner. Fresh as."

Van Heel and Chaudry might not have understood the reference, but Radko did. Gunter Wong owned the Gippian shellfish company. His beds were on the coast in the province of Han, across the river from the main Han estate, in fact.

"Wish I had friends like that," the shuttle pilot said. "I've never even tasted the things. That little box is a week of my wages."

"Some people say they're an acquired taste." Radko smiled as she thought of Ean, politely swallowing shellfish, then washing it down with a mouthful of wine.

"It's a taste I wouldn't mind acquiring."

The discussion as to the merits of whether it was worth acquiring lasted until touchdown.

The pilot let them off with a cheery wave. "Order your aircar now," he said. "It's got to come half a continent. You'll be here awhile."

Radko didn't tell him the aircar was already on its way, courtesy of Vega's well-laid plans.

He off-loaded his precious cargo into the drone that waited for it, and he and the drone took off at the same time.

Han looked around. "We must be the only humans for hundreds of kilometers. What a dismal place."

"We've an aircar coming," Radko said. "Let's collect our gear." Their gear was stowed in a cargo container on the edge of the field.

"They couldn't have gotten it out any farther away without taking it all the way back to San See." Han clapped Chaudry on the back, making him jump. Chaudry had been looking around nervously. "You don't have to worry about other people. There's no one here."

Radko suspected that was the problem. "Have you been out of the city before, Chaudry?"

He shrugged. "Maybe." It was a mumble.

There was a cure for that. Take his mind off the wide-open spaces. "Van Heel, you're in charge of our equipment. Tell us what you want. Chaudry, you pack it. Han, you're on guard."

She watched what van Heel chose. She definitely skewed to the surveillance and electronic side.

"Add two sheets of explosives," Radko said. If all else failed, they could blow themselves out of trouble. "Some hand weapons. A blaster each. And spares."

She checked the stats of the ship they were to travel to Redmond on. It was a commercial liner. "Van Heel, what can you hide from the ship security?"

"You don't hide something like this from a ship," van Heel said. "You bribe the staff. I've got that in hand."

Radko hoped she was right. "More weapons then." Something that didn't look like a weapon. Something they could put in their baggage. "A tranq gun. And that Pandora field diffuser, there."

"That's not a weapon," van Heel said. "I don't even know why it's in the container. It's practically an antique."

Radko hid a smile. Commodore Vega, who collected ancient weapons, had an early-model Pandora field diffuser on her wall. "You never know. It might come in useful." It wouldn't be the first time one had been used as a weapon.

"If we come across a meteor shower," Han said, picking it

up and handing it across to Chaudry. "We'll let the captain know we've got one in our luggage."

"Any other crazy suggestions?" van Heel asked.

"No," Radko said. "I'm sure you think one is enough."

ONCE in the aircar, the extended day caught up with Radko. All she wanted to do was sleep. Instead, she spent the trip to the spaceport going over the job and getting a feel for her new team.

"You all know this is a covert mission," she said. "Secrecy is vital and will likely save your life. Don't discuss the mission where we can be overheard."

"Are you sure it's covert ops?" Chaudry said uneasily. "I don't think I'd be good at that."

It wasn't a comment Radko would have expected from a man whose psychiatrist said he had a death wish. Radko thought Toll's assessment might be more accurate.

Van Heel pulled out her comms and held it up to him. "What do you think that code means?"

Radko craned her neck to look. Van Heel had brought up her mobilization orders.

Chaudry looked at the orders as if he'd never seen them before although he had.

Van Heel put her comms back into her pocket. "You can't say you didn't look at it, for you're in casual clothes, like the rest of us."

"I was on leave. My kit's in my bag."

"And I was pulled out of a training course I'd waited two years for," Han said.

One soldier on leave, another on a training course. Vega must have scrambled to get this together so fast. Even if Vega's main reason for choosing them had been their line ability, surely there were more than three available linesmen in the Lancian fleet.

Perhaps Vega didn't trust the Lancian fleet right now. Sattur Dow was getting his information from somewhere, and it was more likely to be inside the fleet than out of it. Radko could understand that Vega might go outside the usual channels to put her covert-ops team together.

Which meant Chaudry and Han wouldn't have had the usual pre-op training. Vega would deal with it when they got back. In the meantime, a quick overview of the basics would be a good start.

"I hope you all understand what a covert op entails. No uniforms. No comms out until we've completed our task. In fact, you should all have received new comms before you left."

They nodded.

"You should have left your own comms behind."

This time van Heel was the only one who nodded.

Should she make them wipe their comms? She could, because they'd compromised the job by bringing them. If Redmond got hold of either comms, they would know who they had. But then, they hadn't known any better.

She coded a security override into her own comms. "Give me your personal comms."

Chaudry handed his over first. She pushed the override through and handed it back. "Iris and fingerprint recognition." Radko waited until Chaudry had held the comms up to his eyes, then pressed his thumb on the screen. "You, and only you, can use it. If anyone else tries, the whole thing will be wiped clean."

Han handed his over but didn't let go of it. "Mine's already set for that." She could see it was true. "My family is paranoid about security."

Radko remembered Renaud Han as an easygoing man. Still, it had been years. Maybe he'd changed.

"Give me permission to check the settings."

He did. It was way more secure than she'd made Chaudry's.

"Right. Don't use your personal comms for anything. Turn it off and pack it away in your bag. Use the issued comms from now on."

Han scowled down at his hands.

"Han?" If he refused to do this, she was going to take his comms away. Or maybe try to use it so that it wiped itself.

"Understood." Han depressed the back panel to turn his comms fully off. He looked at it, then held it out to her.

She almost took it, shook her head at the last moment. "You're responsible for your own shit, Han. Look after it."

He slipped it into his pocket.

"Same for you, Chaudry. Don't use your personal comms for anything."

Preliminaries over, it was time to get back to the job in hand. "We're going to Redmond, where Tiana Chen—that's me—will attempt to buy a stolen report. You are my bodyguards."

Han stretched himself out in one of the seats, arms crossed behind his head. "Tiana Chen. You don't mean that loathsome woman who hangs around court and blackmails everyone?"

"I do."

Chaudry cleared his throat. "Redmond is enemy territory."

"Of course it is," van Heel said. "Covert ops. Remember. You do them in enemy territory."

You didn't always, but Radko didn't correct her.

Chaudry pulled at the knuckles on his right hand. "I don't speak Redmond; I work in Stores." He didn't state his question aloud, but Radko understood, anyway.

"They haven't made a mistake. You were specifically chosen. All of you were."

"Why?" van Heel asked. "So when we do get this report they can catalog them properly in Stores?"

"That's better than the other option," Han said. "That we're disposable."

"No one is disposable," Radko said. "I intend to bring us all back." Herself included. "We do this carefully, and we do it safely. I'll take Chaudry and Han with me. Van Heel, I want you on surveillance, and as a backup if anything goes wrong."

Van Heel nodded.

"As for not understanding the native Redmond language, Chaudry, you don't have to. The person we are meeting knows where we are from. She'll expect us to speak Standard."

SEVEN

EAN LAMBERT

KARI WANG WAS in the middle of a ship check when Ean arrived with Bhaksir and Hana. Even so, she took time out to meet them at the shuttle bay.

"Touch my ship without my agreeing to what you are doing—without my knowing what you plan—and I will personally boot you off the ship."

"Understood," Ean said because there was nothing else she wanted to hear.

"Good." Kari Wang turned to Bhaksir. "Keep him out of my way until I need him."

Bhaksir looked dubiously at Ean. "Isn't he supposed to work with you? I mean—"

She should have done what Radko would have done, which was say, "Yes, Captain," then let Ean work anyway.

"I've an undercrewed ship; no one is battle trained. I don't have the foggiest how many weapons I've got or how to use them. I don't need Lambert in my way. I'll call you when I'm ready."

Kari Wang headed back to the bridge, opening her comms as she went. "Mael, is level three secured?"

"All good," Mael said.

Ean started after the captain.

Bhaksir hesitated. "Shouldn't we wait till she calls us?"

"No." Because no matter what she said, Kari Wang would expect them on the bridge soon. "Listen to the lines," Ean said. Ship lines were a song of anticipation and calculation. "She says she's worried." Worry seemed to come with captaincy. "But she's looking forward to it."

The human lines were mostly calm—some nervous. Kari Wang had done a lot of training with these people in a very short time.

Ean sang softly to the lines as he followed the captain through the ship.

"Ready to fight," the lines sang back, and Ean could taste the anticipation.

The alien ships were all warships. They would be used to fighting. Had that eagerness come from their prior crew or their current captain?

They reached the bridge. Kari Wang continued her checklist. She was nearly at the end, for Ean could hear the nerves and excitement.

Finally, "Dubicki?"

"Line eight is good."

"Abascal?"

"Line seven is ready."

"Lambert?"

"Here," Ean said.

"Good." She opened the comms—to Abram and to the other *Eleven* fleet ships. "This is the *Eleven*. Preparing to jump. Lambert."

Ean started singing direct to the sevens, linking all the line sevens in the fleet, so that when they jumped through the void, they wouldn't lose contact.

"Lambert. You have the coordinates."

Yes, but how did he translate them to something the lines could understand? The captain usually keyed the coordinates on human machines. They didn't have any way to set the jump on the *Eleven*.

He stopped singing. "We have a problem."

The alien ships didn't understand human references. In their practice runs, one of the human ships had always set the jump. He would have to bring one of the other fleet ships with them to set the coordinates.

He sang the comms open to the *Wendell*'s bridge. "Captain Wendell. I need you to come with us. I need you to set the jump."

Captain Wendell never slept. Well, he must, but Ean seldom saw him away from his bridge. He was on the bridge now. Ean wondered if he used the lines to tell him when things were happening.

"Unarmed, into enemy territory."

He shouldn't have known where they were going.

"You're not unarmed. You've six bombs. And we won't be there long."

"If we do this, I want a full complement of weapons on this ship afterward."

It didn't have the snap of the quick decisions Abram and Helmo made. Then, Wendell must have been planning how to get his weapons back. No doubt he'd worked out long ago all the possible ways he could do it, and this was one of them.

"I can't promise that," Ean said.

Kari Wang's impatience was a wave battering at him. The *Eleven* joined in the chorus. *"Battle."*

"Of course you can," Wendell said. "You're a level-twelve linesman."

"We'll lose our jump window soon," Kari Wang said.

"I can't promise weapons," Ean said, again. "I'll talk to Abram about it, but that's all I can do."

How could he explain to the *Eleven* where it had to jump? There would be a way to translate human coordinates into something the ship could understand. He just didn't know what it was yet. It would be like line seven, explaining what it did, but it had taken them months to work out what it meant. He didn't have months. He had minutes.

"A pity," Wendell said. "What are the coordinates?"

"I haven't promised any weapons."

"I understand that."

"We have two minutes left in the jump window," Kari Wang said. She pushed the coordinates through to Wendell herself.

Ean started singing again. *"Only the* Eleven *and the* Wendell. *The rest of you remain where you are."*

Underneath the song, he heard Wendell's crisp directions. "Ship, prepare to enter the void."

He had the usual forever in the void to check the lines. There were only two sets—the *Eleven*'s and the *Wendell*'s. That bit worked, at least. Both sets of lines were clean. Both sets anticipating what was to come.

He realized he'd forgotten to clear Wendell's coming with Abram. He sent a hurried song back. *"Wendell*'s coming with us."

Then they were back in normal space, with the chatter of the lines from the various ships in this sector, and Wendell and Kari Wang's now-familiar relief at the safe passage through the void momentarily swamping the lines.

Kari Wang didn't give Ean time to relax. "Find me a military ship close by."

How was he supposed to pick a military ship from a non-military one?

He sang to line five on the *Eleven*. He'd heard military ships before. They were nearly always busy, with information being passed through. They also contained plenty of weapons.

Kari Wang didn't wait for an answer. She turned to her own crew. "What have we got?"

Her crew was singing, too, bringing up line-five traffic on each of the nearby ships, singing them down again when Kari Wang shook her head. Kari Wang herself was going through ships on the small human screens set around the captain's chair.

Through the lines, Ean could hear Wendell's crew doing the same. He sang the lines open from the *Wendell* to the *Eleven*, and vice versa. It was easier to do that than have to explain everything later.

For a while, there was no sound except the two ships' checking off and discounting possible ships.

There had to be an easier way. Like asking. Ean raised his own voice and directed it out through line five. *"Which of you have been in battle?"*

He got the instant attention of fifty ships, probably more. He chose the strongest. "That one," and pointed to it on the screen. He had no idea how far away it was.

Abascal sang the comms open.

The multiple messages going in and out made a jumble of sound. Ean concentrated on new messages, pushing them through.

"This is the GU *Packard* calling Weapons Supplies."

"Go ahead, GU *Packard*."

"We ordered fifty fusion warheads. You sent us heat-seeking missiles."

"Get us a jump," Kari Wang demanded, close to Ean's ear. He hadn't realized she'd moved.

He nodded. "Be ready to order a jump. Like you normally

do," and sang to the lines on the GU *Packard*, *"We're going to borrow your lines for a moment."* It was disorienting that he didn't get an answer—he was used to the alien ships, which answered back—but the lines waited for him. He opened the lines to the gate station in this sector—all linesmen knew how to do that though he'd never had to request a jump before.

The clerk on duty sounded bored. "This is the Roscracia Sector Gate, what can we do for you?"

"This is the GU *Packard*." Kari Wang made it crisp and military. "We require a jump to Aratoga sector 123.2143.23, effective immediately."

"As you are aware, we are in a war situation here, and there might be a slight delay in obtaining codes. I'll need to confirm your—"

"Just get me the jump and stop mucking around."

Ean looked at Kari Wang. She looked back. The clerk put the line on hold—which didn't stop Ean's hearing it—and said, "Military. All the same. Must have it now. There's a war on." He took the line off hold. "Sending an identity check through now. Please reply with the correct response, or I will be unable to provide the jump."

Ean sang the check on through the *Eleven* and back to the GU *Packard*. *"Confirm it. It is correct. Send back the right code."*

For a moment, he didn't think it would work. He changed his tune to include line eight. *"Send the confirmation through."*

Something went back, and Ean held his breath until the clerk said, "Codes confirmed. Please wait while I set a jump for you." His tone changed, to a monotonous cadence. "Please be aware that requesting an immediate jump incurs a surcharge of 200 percent. You must confirm this and accept the surcharge as part of the jump contract." He said it like it was something he'd recited hundreds of times before.

"Accepted," Kari Wang said.

"This acceptance must be confirmed by the officer in charge of your ship, the ship second, or the ship third."

"I confirm as officer in charge." Kari Wang wound her finger in front of Ean, as if wanting him to do something.

What did she want?

A signal came through then. "Please use a thumbprint and retina scan and return this as the authorizing officer."

She held her comms up to scan her eyes, then pressed her thumb against the screen. "Sending confirmation through now."

She sounded as if she'd done it a thousand times.

Kari Wang circled her finger at Ean again. This time he understood what she wanted. He sang the confirmation through. He didn't route it via the other ship. All they wanted was confirmation that she was captain and that she was authorized to request this.

"Thank you, Captain. Setting your jump now."

The clerk whistled tunelessly as he set the codes. Kari Wang twitched as they waited. Wendell paced.

Ean tuned them out. He had lines to thank. *"We appreciate you letting us borrow your lines."*

The human ship lines didn't respond in words, but he thought they were pleased to be talking to other lines.

They were so weak compared to the lines on the *Eleven* and the *Wendell*. He could hear Wendell's boots as the pacing got faster.

Grayson, Wendell's second-in-command, was at the comms. He moved. Ean wouldn't have interpreted it as anything, but Wendell did and stopped.

"Enemy ships have noticed us," he said.

"Coordinates coming through," the clerk said, seconds later, but it felt like hours. He pushed them down line five. "Thank you, Captain Kari Wang. Have a great trip."

"Thank you," Kari Wang said, and clicked off.

Ean kept the line open and sang the clerk's comms open, so he could hear what came next. Sure enough, "Wasn't that the GU *Packard*?" the clerk said. "Shouldn't that have been Captain Packard?"

He punched in a code to the ship Ean had used. "Captain Packard, confirming the jump you recently requested."

Kari Wang pushed the codes through to Wendell. "Lambert."

Ean began singing to the sevens.

"Ship, prepare to jump," Wendell said.

They entered the void.

IN Aratogan space, all was quiet.

Somewhere, close to one of the weapons bays, Spacer

Tinatin was talking to Spacer Qatar. "They didn't want him on the *Lancastrian Princess* anymore, so they sent him to Confluence Station. But Confluence Station didn't want him either, so now he's here on the *Eleven*, until they can work out what to do with him."

"You are full of it, Tinatin," Qatar said.

On the *Lancastrian Princess*, Abram was back at his old desk in his and Michelle's workroom, talking to Admiral Dirks, from Aratoga. Dirks must have been on Haladea III, for Ean couldn't get any information other than what he could hear through line five.

"Now in Aratogan space. No ships close by." Kari Wang used her human screens to tell her that. "Moving toward the battleground."

"Thank you, Captain." Abram looked toward Dirks's screen. "We now have real-time communication with the Aratogan sector, Admiral. The comms is yours."

"I could get used to this." Dirks's grin was a toothy baring of teeth. There was something about admirals. They showed more teeth than other soldiers. Maybe it was a seniority thing. He clicked on his comms, through to another admiral. A woman this time. "Brant. Dirks here."

Ean sang the feed going to Abram's screens onto one of Kari Wang's screens. She nodded her thanks.

"This had better be important, Dirks. We've a situation at this end."

"I know. We're sending you reinforcements."

"That's going to be a lot of use. This battle will be over in six hours."

Six hours. How did she know with such precision how long it would be?

Brant looked at the comms. "You're in real time. You're in the Aratogan sector?" She was animated suddenly. "What are you sending us? And how long will they be?" Ean heard her say quietly to someone, "Get Commodore Summers on the comms."

"We're two hours away," Kari Wang said.

"Who in the lines are you?"

"Captain Kari Wang, ma'am. New Alliance governance fleet."

Governance fleet? Ean had never heard of it. Neither, by her frown, had Brant.

"We are in the Aratogan sector and making at speed toward—"

"Kari Wang. The *Eleven*? You're sending me one of the alien ships?"

"Affirmative," Dirks said.

"Admiral Brant, Admiral Galenos here. Understand that this is a trial run. We are still testing the *Eleven*. Results might be unexpected." A strong sound of Ean came through with that. "We ask that you give the ship space to do what it needs to do, and if Captain Kari Wang asks your people to do something, then they should do it. It will be for their safety. Sometimes our control is . . . erratic."

"Give us access to that green field," Brant said, "and I don't care how erratic you are. Even the sight of the ship should scare them. Hell, it scares me and it's on our side."

"Command of the *Eleven* is yours, Admiral Brant."

"Commodore Summers is the man in charge at the scene." Brant switched in another line. "Are you there, Commodore?"

"Admiral."

"Situation report."

"We've ten enemy ships surrounding Asteroids 527 and 629," Summers said. "Ships range from a two-hundred-crew Class Three warship to one-hundred-crew Class Five." He put the data and maps on-screen as well. Ean pushed that through to the *Eleven* and to the *Wendell*. "These asteroids contain the offices and supply stores for the whole belt. If we lose them, we lose control of the asteroids. We've five Aratogan ships. With the exception of the ship I am on, all are smaller warships with less than a hundred crew. We have five battle cruisers two light-years away, but we can't get jumps for them."

"Sounds bad," Brant said. "But you're about to get re-inforcements."

"We'll be glad of them." Summers stumbled, then righted himself.

It took Kari Wang's saying, "He's under attack," before Ean realized what had happened.

"They hit him?"

Kari Wang nodded.

Summers glanced over to where someone was giving orders, then looked back. "How many? What class? When will they be here?"

"One ship," Brant said.

Ean didn't need the image on Abram's screen to see Summers wince.

But they didn't have one ship, they had two. And one of them was effectively unarmed.

"Class—" Brant looked at Abram. "Does it have a class?"

"Eleven," Abram said.

"Never heard of it," Summers said. Then he did a double take, much like Brant had before. He looked from Abram to Dirks to Brant. "One of the alien ships?"

"Affirmative."

"How long to get here?"

"One hundred and fifteen minutes," Kari Wang said.

Ean tuned them out. He'd brought the *Wendell* along; he had to make sure Wendell and his crew were safe.

The conversation between the admirals, commodore, and captain was done. The Aratogans clicked off, leaving only the *Eleven* fleet ships online.

"Wendell," Kari Wang said, "you should stay here. We'll collect you on the way back."

"No," Ean said. "He should come inside the protective field."

"I've been meaning to ask," Abram said. "Was Wendell's coming along an accident? Or deliberate?"

He hadn't gotten Ean's message. Another thing they knew now. You couldn't send messages while you were in the void.

"We couldn't set the jump on the *Eleven*," Kari Wang said.

"I can see that might be a problem. I wonder how the aliens did it." Abram gave a wry smile. "Maybe you should have used one of the media ships, Ean." Ean wasn't sure if he was joking. "This could be an impressive show."

"Wendell," Ean said, for Wendell wasn't making any attempt to move.

"Sure, I'll come along," Wendell said. "But I'm not going

in close. Not even to ensure my protection. Not at the speeds we're traveling."

"It was safe when the *Lancastrian Princess* did it."

"The *Lancastrian Princess* wasn't traveling at full speed toward a battle. No thank you, Ean. I'd prefer to take my chances following behind."

"Not to mention he'll slow us down," Kari Wang said. Which was true, for the alien ships could travel twice as fast as the Bose engines could drive human ships.

Admiral Brant called back. Commodore Summers not long after. Kari Wang and Mael were soon deep in tactical discussions.

"War is mostly waiting," Bhaksir told Ean. "With occasional exciting moments. Hanging around you, it's more exciting than normal."

Ean liked life quiet. The lines, his crewmates on the *Lancastrian Princess*—especially Radko, wherever she was—and the alien ships. His preferred adventures were discovering new things about the lines.

He listened to the lines and kept out of Kari Wang's way.

Ten minutes later, a ship jumped into space close enough for the *Eleven* to register the lines. Then another. Then a third. The three of them started to move toward the *Wendell*.

"Damn." Kari Wang didn't sound surprised. She called up Wendell. "You've three ships closing in on you."

"We can see two of them. Where's the third?"

Ships broadcast their location, but because communication within a sector was instantaneous, most ships ignored anything outside a known radius of their own ship unless they were specifically contacting another ship. Otherwise, they'd drown in the information overload.

Kari Wang gave coordinates.

Ean looked at the positions. Sure, the ships were thousands of kilometers apart—but that was normal for jumps. These three ships had arrived in close succession, and had arrived close to where the *Eleven* had jumped.

Now they were making for the nearest ship.

Ean had brought the *Wendell* into this battle and left him there. "We have to go back and rescue him."

"We have a battle plan. Other ships are working to our timetable, have already started moving. What do you want me to do? Call them up, and say, 'Sorry, we'll be delayed'?"

Yes, he did. "We can't leave one of our own fleet."

"This is war, Lambert."

Another ship arrived. Then another. Gate Union intended to make sure of their kill.

War or not, Ean couldn't leave Wendell there to face five ships. He opened his mouth to sing.

Kari Wang took out her blaster. "You jump us back to that ship, and you're a dead man."

Bhaksir jumped up hurriedly. "I can't let you do that, Captain."

Ean didn't think Kari Wang would kill him, but she would knock him out, and he wouldn't be any use to anyone then. He closed his mouth.

Maybe he should try singing Wendell home. Or . . . "Why don't I swap? Like we did with Confluence Station? That won't cause too much delay, and we know it works."

"Last time we did that, we weren't traveling at this speed," but he could see she was considering it.

"The *Eleven* knows what to do. And it's not like we're doing anything dangerous." He hoped. "We're switching places."

"Can you guarantee that?"

He wanted to lie. "No."

She put her blaster away. "If you'd said yes, Lambert, we wouldn't be thinking of this."

If he couldn't guarantee it, why was she thinking of it? "I will do my best to make it as safe as we can."

"I'm not sure that's the right approach with you." Kari Wang turned to the screen. "So, Wendell, you've five ships headed toward you. I'm sure you'd like to fight your way out of it, but Lambert has a suggestion."

"They're not good odds this end," Wendell admitted. "We only have six warheads. I'll listen to any suggestions."

His crew were already making plans. Ean could see them, calculating distances and trajectories.

"We're thinking a swap, much like Lambert did with

Confluence Station. We don't want to swap too often, or I'll lose too much trajectory."

"Minimum number of swaps." Wendell scratched his chin.

"Minimum number any *sane* person would do. I don't want to die of fright doing it."

Was she talking about him or about Wendell?

"Give me some calculations, Piers, and a safety margin."

Wendell came up with three jumps to get all five ships. "We could do it in two, but you'll be getting close to one of the ships."

It meant a change in course, and Wendell had planned that so it looked as if he were trying to avoid one of the ships, which in fact took him into the path of another two.

"With luck, they'll see what you do to the first two, and the rest will retreat to regroup," Wendell said. "That's what I would do."

Provided everything worked as planned.

They watched the ships move closer to Wendell. Too close. What if the *Wendell* was destroyed before the *Eleven* swapped? Atmosphere on the *Wendell* was calm, ready for battle. Wendell paced around the bridge, slow and careful, as if he wanted to cover every centimeter of surface.

On the *Eleven*, there was a lot of nervous excitement. Kari Wang continued to drill her crew, treating it like a training exercise. Ean wasn't sure if she believed it was, if it was to keep them calm, or if she thought they needed more training.

Two hours ago, Ean had been listening to Michelle tell them Emperor Yu had called Abram a traitor.

The *Eleven* drew closer to the battle. The *Wendell* grew closer to the warships.

"Shields up," Wendell said, as the first ship fired. "Take evasive action as needed but keep heading toward those ships."

Eventually, the two ships were as close as planned. The *Wendell* took some damage, but Wendell's crew were good and the Gate Union ships wary, so damage was minimal.

Wendell stopped pacing. "We're in range."

Commodore Summers came online. "You are within range of our sensors, *Eleven*."

"Good," Kari Wang said. "Ean. Switch."

Ean sang the request. *"Switch places, with the Wendell, please. Like you did the other night with Confluence Station."*

"Preparing to enter the void," Kari Wang said, but by the time she'd said it, they were out the other side.

"Captain Kari Wang?" Summers said.

"One moment," Kari Wang said. "Status report?"

"We're about to get shot," Mael said.

"Thank you, Mael, that's truly helpful!"

But Mael was already adding, "One ship at 234.23.33, one at 235.24.186."

"No one in range here," Wendell said. "But I see a lot of ships within ten to twenty minutes."

"Ean. Turn on the field."

Ean sang the protective field on.

"Mael, set a course between the two ships. I want the *Eleven* to pass within nine kilometers of the first, then be ready to swing around and do the same for the other."

The enemy ship frantically fired side rockets to turn. It was too slow. The protective field triggered at just under ten kilometers and spread outward from the *Eleven*. This time, Ean was listening for the quick, deep dirge of line nine. The enemy ship disappeared, its lines with it.

The *Eleven* and its crew sang with triumph.

A whole ship, gone in seconds.

Ean didn't join the singing.

The green field spread out inexorably farther. Two hundred kilometers farther, then it stopped, held for thirty counts, then began to recede. All the while, the *Eleven* moved closer to the second ship.

Through line five on the second ship, Ean heard the captain requesting a jump. He held his breath. Abram always had a jump ready. Please let these people have a jump ready.

Mael counted off the distance on one of the human screens. "Two hundred eighty kilometers. Two hundred seventy kilometers. Two hundred sixty kilometers."

The clerk assigning jumps sounded the same as the one in the Roscracian sector. "Please be aware requesting an immediate jump incurs a surcharge of 200 percent. You must—"

"Confirmed and accepted as officer in charge," the captain said. "Now send me the jump, or you'll kill us all."

"Please use a thumbprint and retina scan to confirm that you are the authorizing officer."

"One hundred thirty," Mael said. "One hundred twenty."
The ship disappeared.

"One hundred ten. Ship has jumped."

"Captain, please use a thumbprint and retina scan to confirm you are the authorizing officer," the clerk at the other end of the now-empty line five repeated.

Ean blew on his hands, which were icy.

"They jumped cold." Kari Wang shivered. "Ean, swap us back."

Ean dutifully switched the two ships and breathed deep as he listened to the celebration around him. He should have insisted they trust the lines to jump them safely into Aratogan space. Then the first ship wouldn't have been sent into the void, and the second wouldn't have taken that desperate jump.

Now they were stuck in the void forever. Ean had been in it long enough to know how horrible that was, and based on the condition of the original crew of the *Eleven*—stuck in stasis like the crew of the *Balao*—the aliens must hate it as much as he did.

"Why did you send them into the void?" He used the sound for line nine because he didn't know how to differentiate between the line that took them into the void and the void itself.

"Void?" line one on the *Eleven* replied. *"Not the void. We sent them."* What came through was the heavy strength of line six.

"You used the void to flick them into line six?"

"Not line six. This."

The second time around, Ean heard subtle changes in the sound. It was fainter, deeper, heavier. Stationary. He'd heard the sound on the *Eleven* back near Haladea III. He'd never been sure what it was.

"Quick. Kind."

Bose Engines were mostly energy. Was the *Eleven* telling him it had flicked the first enemy ship into a massive energy source? Like a sun?

Summers was relieved to see the *Eleven* back. "I wasn't sure what happened there," he said.

"Some Gate Union ships tailing us." Kari Wang glanced over to Ean, looked as if she would say something, then didn't. "There are another three ships. We might need to jump again to eliminate them."

Summers nodded. "You will be back in time though?"

"Yes. Currently on track to arrive in ten minutes," Kari Wang said. "Any changes to our plan?"

He looked bemused at that, as if wondering why she asked. "Negative."

That plan had been agreed to and valid five minutes ago. In that five minutes, they'd destroyed a ship full of people and lines, and forced another to jump cold.

And no one but them had noticed. Ean shivered. He'd never get warm again.

Kari Wang let her crew celebrate for another five minutes, then called them back to their tasks. She glanced at Ean occasionally but said nothing, although she did look at Bhaksir once, and incline her head toward Ean.

Bhaksir came over and sat beside Ean. "Is there a problem?"

"No," Ean said. "Missing Radko, actually."

He didn't know why he'd said it, but Radko's absence was an ache that wouldn't go away. He'd have given anything to have her nearby, even if she was making him do laps on the *Lancastrian Princess* when his throat was burning, and he couldn't breathe. His throat was burning now, too, and he hoped Bhaksir wouldn't ask him any more questions. He wasn't sure he could answer.

"Me too, Ean. Me too," Bhaksir said.

Wendell watched the boards carefully. "The third ship's definitely slowing. So are the ones chasing us."

Two minutes later, all three jumped out, one after the other, at intervals of half a minute.

"That's one problem out of the way," Kari Wang said. "I wish the ships around here would do that." She looked at Ean. "Do I need to state the obvious? No shield here, or we'll annihilate ships on our own side."

She hadn't needed to state it, but Ean said, "Understood."

Kari Wang opened her comms to the whole ship. "Positions."

Line one echoed with the wave of anticipation and nerves. "Abascal, Dhalmans. Ready on the weapons?"

"Ready, Captain," from two different parts of the ship.

Ean moved over to Mael. "Which ones are friends; which ones are foe?"

Mael sang the IDs for the enemy first. "Here, here, here, and here. Enemy."

Ean sang them back to the ship. "*Enemy*. And the Aratogans?"

Mael sang their IDs.

Ean sang them back to the *Eleven* as well. "*Friends.*"

He hoped the lines could distinguish between the terms.

After which, they waited some more. War seemed to be one long wait, with tiny bits of action between.

On the *Lancastrian Princess*, Abram was making tea for himself and Michelle. Captain Helmo wandered the decks, stopping occasionally to talk to crew. The lines were melancholy. They were melancholy on the *Wendell* as well. Captain Wendell was sitting—a rare still moment for him—staring at the screens as if he expected the enemy ships to jump out of the void again. Ean didn't think he thought that at all.

The only ship that had any real life was the Galactic News ship, where the engineer who'd been so animated two nights previously was animated again.

"I tell you, Coop. We're getting live news again. This time from the Aratogan sector."

And, of course, from Spacer Tinatin on the *Eleven*. ". . . Lady Lyan, and no one is happy about it because it means she's trying to make Lancia back into the power it used to be back in the Alliance."

That news was only two hours old. Where was she getting it from?

"Combat ship coming into range," Kari Wang said, crisp and clear, making Ean jump.

The whole ship seemed to brighten.

"Abascal, Dhalmans. Are you ready?"

"Ready, Captain."

"We're ready too," Tinatin said to Qatar.

"We're on the wrong side of the ship for fighting."

"But we're still ready."

"Ready," the ship echoed.

"Fire on my command. Three, two, one, fire."

Line eight sang. Two twangs, and seconds later—it felt like hours—Abascal said, "Missile gone." Dhalmans said the same, almost on top of her.

Did the other ship realize they had fired? Ean sang gently to the lines on the other ship to find out.

Yes, and they were firing rockets now, moving away. But the *Eleven* had fired first.

"They're taking evasive action," he said. "And they fired at us."

"Calliope. Fire jets eighty-seven and eighty-eight. Five seconds on half thrust."

Calliope sang instructions to the ship, and the ship responded instantly.

The *Eleven*'s missiles hit the enemy ship then. It bucked against the force.

"Fire again, on my command. Three, two, one, fire." Two more missiles headed toward the ship. The enemy ship's own sudden, evasive acceleration turned it into their path. The ship lines jangled and stayed jangling.

Ean clasped his fingers together, saw Kari Wang glance at them, and crossed his arms instead.

"Weapons ready," Abascal said, and Dhalmans, almost on top of her again. "Ready."

"Ready," line eight echoed.

Ready to pound other lines into oblivion. Then, that was what battles were for, and this was a warship.

"Missile will pass fifty meters from port side," Mael said. "And two vessels have broken away from the main fight, making toward us. Staying within two hundred kilometers of Aratogan ships."

"Acknowledged," Kari Wang said.

"Ready," line eight sang again. A persistent tune under everything that was happening on the bridge.

"Line eight is ready," Ean said. *"Ready to do what?"*

The answer that came back was quiet and blue and smelled like hot blood.

"Not your green field." They'd kill everyone within a two-hundred-kilometer radius, friend and foe.

"Not the automatic defense system. The . . ." Quiet, blue, hot blood.

"Ready to what?" Kari Wang asked.

Use? Do? "The thing."

"That's really helpful, Lambert. I need more information." She opened the comms. "Those of you not at active stations, see if you can work out what Lambert's talking about."

"It's line eight," Ean said.

What questions would Radko ask?

Is it a weapon? How do you use it?

"How does it work?"

In line eight's song, the tune twisted and turned into a hot, blue ball.

"I think it's a weapon," Ean said. *"Can you fire at a specific ship?"*

"Of course."

"The GU *Salvan* has fired," Mael said. "Two missiles, coming this way."

Kari Wang checked her boards. "Calliope. Fire jets eighty-seven and eighty-eight. Five seconds on full thrust."

"Can you fire at that one?" Ean made the sound for the GU *Salvan*.

For a moment, they were in the void. Line eight released something, then they were out again.

"Lambert. Do that again without my permission, and I will kill you personally."

A bright blue ball of flame engulfed the GU *Salvan*. The metallic smell of hot blood swamped Ean momentarily. The lines on the GU *Salvan* went dead.

Ean put a hand to his mouth. Lives and lines, so easily wiped out.

"And what did you do, anyway?" Kari Wang asked.

The three single eights started cheering.

"GU *Salvan* has been neutralized," one of them—Boleslav—said.

"How do you know this?" Kari Wang demanded.

"Didn't you see it, ma'am?"

"No, I didn't."

"There are no lines left alive on that ship," Ean said.

"Another missile leaving the GU *Salvan*," Mael said. "And another. No, scratch that. Lifepods exiting."

At least something had come out of it alive.

Ean watched the exiting pods while Kari Wang turned her attention to the next ship Summers had assigned her. "Can we do it again?"

She had to stand right in front of him before he realized she was talking to him.

"Can you?" Ean asked line eight.

"Time. Wait."

"Not yet, I think."

"Let me know when it can."

Ean nodded and went back to watching escaping pods.

The sounds of war went on around him. The *Eleven* destroyed another ship, and damaged two more. It was hit twice, neither time badly.

"Ready," line eight said finally.

Ean took a deep breath.

One of the Gate Union ships disappeared. It had jumped. Then another, and another. In five minutes they were all gone, scattered no doubt over the galaxy to whatever jumps they'd been assigned.

Ean blew out his breath.

Summers was all smiles over the comms. "Thank you, Captain. Your presence here routed the enemy. It was good to see you in action. Most impressive."

"We're still learning the ins and outs of the ship," Kari Wang said. "Once we know it, then you'll see impressive."

The lines sang with pleasure. *"You will."*

Kari Wang patted the console, then called up the *Wendell*. "If we're to jump together, I'd prefer to be closer. We know how much space we have to clear."

A lot, because Abram didn't like the ships too close together. But at least Kari Wang was prepared to jump home cold. Although, really, when you had instantaneous communication between two sectors, and feeds from ships in the other sector, how dangerous was it? The jump took a milli-second, and you knew what was there.

Even so, Ean was going to make good and sure the jump was a safe one.

Afterward, while the *Eleven* made for its rendezvous with the *Wendell*, Kari Wang walked around the ship.

"Walk with me," she said to Ean.

He wanted to sit and think, but he could tell from the lines that she'd insist if he didn't. He trailed her out, and Bhaksir trailed him.

Kari Wang stopped and talked to some of her crew close by. "Well done," she said. They talked some moments, then moved on. As they moved off Ean noticed she listed slightly to the left. So the fight hadn't been as easy as it looked. He was glad about that.

"You should sit down," he said.

"I need to check my crew," she said. "Was this your first fight?"

"No." He'd been in a battle before, back when he'd been with Orsaya on the shuttle, escaping from Markan. Kari Wang wouldn't be satisfied with a no. She'd keep on at him until she got to the root of what she thought was the problem. All Ean wanted was to forget what had happened. "Today was . . . it was so easy to destroy a ship full of people. Normal people like you and me. And they didn't have a chance. We just—"

Either ship—the one they had destroyed with the green protective field or the one they had destroyed with the hot blue ball that no one but the eights had been able to see—and the *Eleven* was as bloodthirsty as its crew. But then, ship sentience came in part from its crew, so a warship would think that was right.

"It makes you wonder what damage the aliens did to each other," Kari Wang said.

They knew what damage they did. Some ships looked as if they'd been bitten in two; on other ships, the lines were so bad Ean still hadn't fixed them properly.

"That weapon I couldn't see. Does every ship have that?"

"I don't know. I'll ask later." When he could work out a way to formulate the question. Maybe he should approach each ship and ask it if it had one. "There is so much we don't know."

Kari Wang stopped to talk to more crew. Ean waited, quiet beside her.

After they resumed their walk, she said, "You did well today."

"Thank you."

"And it's comforting to know that our leading linesman isn't going to opt for the kill every time if he can help it."

EIGHT

DOMINIQUE RADKO

THEY HAD A two-room suite on the liner to Redmond. An outer room for Tiana Chen's staff, and an inner room with a huge double bed that was bigger than Radko's cabin on the *Lancastrian Princess*.

The screen on the wall, tuned to a news channel, was as tall as she was.

"I could get used to this." Van Heel looked around the outer room with satisfaction. She settled onto a comfortable couch. "Toss me some fruit, Chaudry," for Chaudry was inspecting the contents of the bowl on the table.

"I don't even know what most of it is," Chaudry said.

"I don't care. Send some over."

"I need sleep," Radko said. This was the third time zone, and third set of daylight hours she'd been awake for. "Stay in quarters. Do any prep you think you might need, but if I don't get some rest, I'll be useless."

She jerked awake when they turned up the sound. The first word she heard was "*Eleven*," followed soon after by "alien ships." She recognized the voice of the man being interviewed. Admiral Markan of Roscracia.

Radko rolled out of bed and went to see what was happening.

Markan looked calm, but Radko had seen enough of him to know that underneath he was ready to blow.

"It is only one ship," Markan said. "It can't be everywhere at once."

"But there are another 130 ships in orbit around Haladea III. And one of those is larger than the *Eleven*."

"Half those ships are damaged too badly to use. The rest have no crew. Including the *Confluence*. It will be months before they can use them. The war will be over by then."

"Even one ship can do massive damage, as we've seen."

The reporter had a Roscracian accent. It was the first time Radko had seen Markan put on the spot by his own people.

"Of course it can," Markan said. "But as I mentioned, it is only one ship. If it arrives at a battle, we know how to counteract it. We can simply jump away until the ship leaves, then come back. The New Alliance cannot get the jumps. *Everything* is under control."

"There is a rumor the alien ships don't need jumps. That they can jump cold. What do you say to that?"

Markan stared straight at the camera. "I say that is an absolute lie. Furthermore, if the New Alliance is jumping cold, they risk the lives of billions of people every time they do so. These are the monsters we are fighting."

"Sometimes I admire that man," Radko said.

Han gave her a strange look.

She ignored it. "What happened?" but the screen had already changed.

Filming a battle was difficult, for the distances were huge and ships relatively small. News crews deployed drones to a battle and used them to create composites, with the distances compressed. Hundreds of drones, tiny little mechanized cameras that clogged up the spaceways and could be more dangerous than incoming fire.

"They deployed one of the alien ships," Han said.

She could see that. The *Eleven* loomed closer and closer, then suddenly it wasn't the *Eleven* anymore.

"They swapped with the *Wendell*." That was the kind of thing Ean would do. Kari Wang would never switch ships like that, and Radko bet it had been a cold jump.

"They swapped with the enemy," Chaudry said. He looked as pleased as if he'd arranged it himself. "They planned that ship would be destroyed in place of them."

"I bet the captain's having kittens," Han said.

Not Piers Wendell. He got calmer the stronger the action. There was nothing around the *Wendell* that posed a danger to the ship. That meant the fighting was elsewhere. "Can we see what the *Eleven* is doing?"

"It's hiding, waiting for someone to destroy the Wallacian ship," Chaudry said.

"You need to learn which ships are on our side."

"It's the *Wendell*," Chaudry said. "He is a spy."

Radko looked at her team of three. Even van Heel was nodding. "The *Wendell* and its crew are part of the New Alliance fleet. They have no love for Gate Union, or for Wallacia. No one calls them spies. Understand."

She didn't miss the look that passed between them. She didn't comment either.

On-screen, the *Eleven* switched places with the *Wendell* again.

Radko watched the rest of the battle. The alarm on her comms sounded as the first of the Gate Union ships disappeared, making them all jump.

"I need to get ready," she said. "The rest of you, do what you can to disguise yourselves, but not obviously. Makeup or clothes, nothing more. I want you to look different." If they got into trouble, they could quickly change clothes and remove their makeup. It might be enough to get past any blocks set up to stop them.

She made for the fresher.

Ean had been on board the *Eleven*. They couldn't have done a ship flip like that without him. He'd probably made for his own fresher afterward. He wouldn't have liked the battle.

The sooner this job was over, the happier Radko would be.

Except they still had the problem of Sattur Dow. Until that was sorted, she couldn't go home.

She dressed carefully in the classic-cut business clothes fashionable across the galaxy right now and added a black wig with a heavy, coiled braid. She'd thought about dyeing her own hair black, but Chen had long hair, and it would be difficult to explain a sudden haircut. Not only that, if they needed to escape, she could get rid of the wig, and no one would recognize her.

She hoped.

As she applied careful makeup to broaden her chin and flatten her cheeks, she thought about what she knew of Tiana Chen. Most of it came from Galenos's intelligence gathering, but she had seen her around the palace occasionally. And at her mother's house. Yesterday now.

She'd once heard Chen put a highly placed palace official

in his place. At the time, Radko had wondered how she dared, for the man outranked her. It was only after she started working on the *Lancastrian Princess* that she discovered Chen was blackmailing half the people in the palace. Not badly enough for them to do away with her but enough for her to enjoy some role reversal when she could get it.

And now she had an in with Sattur Dow. Had Chen blackmailed Dow, and if so, with what? Or maybe Dow had simply offered her patronage in return for her knowledge.

THE shuttle down to Redmond was a classy, six-passenger vehicle. The sort a wealthy woman would hire. What was Tiana Chen doing right now? How long had Vega been able to delay her?

It was a silent trip. Radko used the time to check her comms, which was what Chen would do. Had done, in fact, on that earlier trip with Radko and her mother. She'd talked then as well, but that was to equals. She wouldn't talk to her bodyguards.

Chaudry—almost unrecognizable with a cleverly applied makeup that looked as if he'd recently come out of regen—pulled at the knuckles of his right hand. It was his only sign of nervousness, but she suspected if she could hear lines, there'd be a note of distress in there somewhere. It was a pity it was out of character to try to calm him.

Once on the ground, she hired an aircar. A luxury model. Again, what Chen would hire.

"I could get used to this," van Heel said again. "None of my jobs to date have been like this. Usually, we're mechanics or service people."

"Not much fun being the servant," Han said. "I never realized how boring being a servant would be."

"It has to be better than a military policeman."

"Clearly, you've never been a military policeman."

Radko routed the aircar halfway across the city from where they planned to go. Call her paranoid, but she didn't want to go straight to her destination.

"I've been meaning to say, Chaudry, your disguise is brilliant." If anyone came looking for them, they would look for someone with regenerated skin.

It calmed him, which it was meant to, but it was honest, too. "As children, we played doctors and symptoms."

It wasn't a game Radko had ever heard of. "And you were the doctor?"

"I preferred to be the symptoms."

"Strange games where you came from," Han said.

"It was fun. You had to do the symptoms right."

Radko thought it might have been. A combination of art and medicine. She'd like to hear more, but right now they had other things to worry about. "Pick the smaller blasters. Use a back holster. Make sure it can't be seen under your jacket." It would take vital seconds to get at them, but OneLane would ask two armed bodyguards to remove their weapons.

She felt naked without a weapon at her own side. Chaudry looked as if he'd never worn one in his life. He probably hadn't, outside of drills.

Radko breathed out, long and slow. This was an easy job. Remember that. A quick in, look at the plans, see if they were worth buying, then out.

And then what? Would Sattur Dow be gone by then? Unlikely.

Vega would send her on another job—possibly already had it planned, in fact.

THEIR roundabout trip gave van Heel time to set up some of the surveillance equipment. She passed each of them a tiny disc. "The shop is a communications black hole. I can't trace you while you're in there, but I'll know the second you come out."

Radko looked at the screen. One had to assume OneLane was selling pricey stolen goods to warrant such security. "Do a flyover, then circle around to land."

"Nearest park is two buildings away," van Heel said. "Whoever heard of a shop that doesn't have roof landing?"

Ean had said there were whole blocks where he'd grown up that didn't have parking for aircars. Although, the area they were flying over wasn't that sort of place.

"What do you think?" Radko asked.

"It looks normal. Like a high-end shopping center. Right

number of people, right amount of traffic." Van Heel dropped neatly into a carspace.

"Let's go," Radko said to Han and Chaudry.

Radko had been in shops like Callista OneLane's before. As a youngster, trailing after her mother for another jeweled egg, or for a high-end gift for a member of the Great Families her parents needed to impress. Or later, on her own, when she found something to interest her. It had been a shock the first time she'd entered one wearing a spacer's uniform, to find the proprietor thought she'd come to sell stolen military property.

Radko smiled ruefully. She'd been young then.

The shop was quiet.

Radko recognized Callista OneLane immediately. She was ushering a client out the back, into the private offices. A man around her own age, in casual clothes, with the pale skin of a spacer who seldom came on world. The quick glance he gave them as they came in made her think he was selling rather than buying.

There were two shop assistants and one other customer—a well-dressed businessman examining a long, pointed obsidian stick that looked as if it might sit well on Commodore Vega's wall. He looked familiar.

An assistant handed something small and black to the businessman. He clicked it onto the middle of the stick, holding himself stiff while he did so. Radko bet he was wearing a corset under his clothes, something that pulled in his waist and forced him to stand straight. She smiled at the small vanity that gave the otherwise colorless businessman a measure of personality.

The other assistant came over to Radko. "May I help you?"

"Callista OneLane is expecting me. Tiana Chen."

"Of course." They'd been primed, for he recognized the name. "Madam OneLane is with a customer at the moment. She won't be long." He indicated a luxurious sitting area off to one side of the store. "While you wait, can I offer you some refreshments?"

"No." Radko made it sharp and dismissive, like Tiana Chen would. "I'll browse." She felt safer on her feet. More in control.

He hovered, offering information about various items, until she said, "If I require information, I'll call you."

He bowed. "Of course," and blessedly left her alone with Han and Chaudry.

Han kept an easy pace behind her, whistling softly to himself. It wasn't recognizably a line tune; it was a popular song. Had she ever heard a linesman sing popular songs? Ean, for sure, wouldn't know any. The lines were his life.

Chaudry wasn't as comfortable. He stared around the shop although his gaze kept returning to the other customer.

"Don't stare obviously, Chaudry," Radko said, quietly, so that only the three of them could hear. "Do it unobtrusively, with sideways glances when you're looking at something else."

"He's staring at us," Chaudry said. "And there's something—"

Radko glanced over at the man. He was watching them, frowning as if they weren't supposed to be there. She glared at him discouragingly through narrowed eyes.

He winked at her, hefted the obsidian spear in his hands, and looked down over it, as if looking down a barrel. He seemed to be pointing it directly at her.

Radko remembered the movement, recognized the man. Last time he'd lifted his arm like that, he'd had a blaster in his hand and had been about to kill her.

Stellan Vilhjalmsson. Assassin, and close friend and confidante of Admiral Markan, head of the Gate Union fleet.

"I've got it," Chaudry said triumphantly, making Radko jump. "He's wearing a surgical brace. That man has injured his spine."

Vilhjalmsson turned back to his weapon. Though his attention seemed to be off them, Radko knew he watched them as carefully as she was now watching him.

"Be wary of him. He's an assassin. He could kill us from where he stands if he wanted to."

Why hadn't he?

"He's injured," Chaudry said.

She didn't think that would stop him.

AN older woman burst into the shop. Radko wasn't the only one who swung around. Vilhjalmsson did as well. Chaudry was right. He did move carefully.

"Where's Callista?" She reminded Radko of Governor Jade in build and in imperiousness. Her voice was familiar. Distinctive, and parodied on many comedy shows across Lancia and Haladea III. The wife of the head of government of the Redmond worlds.

An assistant hurried forward. "Madam OneLane will be with you in a moment, Partner Nataliya. Meantime, can I offer you refreshments?" He tried to lead her over to the elegant couches, but she paced the shop as if a demon were after her.

"I *am* in a hurry."

"She won't be long, ma'am," the sales assistant said smoothly, while the other assistant slipped quietly out the back.

Moments later, OneLane came out with the seller she'd exited with earlier. They shook hands. The seller looked satisfied. No doubt he'd gotten a better deal than he'd expected, given OneLane hadn't had time to bargain.

The shop assistant moved up discreetly to stand beside Radko. "We apologize for keeping you waiting, Madam Chen, but Partner Nataliya is a regular at the store, and it *is* an emergency for her."

Partner Nataliya looked like a person who had emergencies all the time.

"Can I get you some refreshments?" and he once again tried to usher Radko across to the couches.

Another time she might have sat because she could tell it would be a long wait. But not now, not when it put her in a corner with a master assassin roaming around.

"I am enjoying browsing," Radko said. "I have everything I need." She moved closer to OneLane and Partner Nataliya, partly to get rid of the shop assistant—for he wouldn't persist close to other customers—and partly to put a barrier between herself and Vilhjalmsson. She made sure Chaudry and Han followed. It was her job to keep them alive. The move brought her close enough to hear the conversation between storekeeper and customer.

"I am in dire straits, Callista," Partner Nataliya said. "I'm catching a ship tonight to Aeolus, and I need to take a gift to the Factor of the Lesser Gods to celebrate his upcoming wedding."

Why would the wife of the ruler of Redmond buy a betrothal

gift for a man whose world was supposed to be enemies with hers? Why would she be going to said enemy's planet?

Vilhjalmsson hadn't moved.

OneLane picked up a striking latticework in a greenish-brown metal. "What about this? It's made from pelagatite."

Nataliya made a face. "Pelagatite's not rare anymore. Not on the Worlds of the Lesser Gods. They've a big mine coming up to production on Hellas, and another one on Pan."

Hadn't Emperor Yu offered Michelle's hand in marriage and a pelagatite mine in exchange for the Factor's support?

They eventually settled on a small etching by the preline artist Tamas Abbat. Radko conservatively priced it at five hundred thousand credits.

Partner Nataliya left happy.

One of the shop assistants had a quiet word with OneLane. She nodded and came over to Radko.

"Madam Chen. I am so glad you came promptly. Offers like this don't come on the market every day. I already have other interested parties."

Did she half glance back at Vilhjalmsson when she said that, or was it a trick of the light when her eyes moved? Vilhjalmsson definitely smiled.

"May I see the merchandise?" Radko asked. And the back door, if they had one. Or would Vilhjalmsson expect that?

OneLane raised her hand to her staff in a discreet signal. "This way," and started toward the back. Radko, Han, and Chaudry followed. Radko kept her hand close to the knife in her boot.

Vilhjalmsson raised the spear. It was, indeed, a weapon. They were close enough that Radko could see the buttons on the top, and the miniscreen that lifted. Unfortunately, too far away for her to use her knife for anything except throwing.

"I wouldn't mind sitting in on this," Vilhjalmsson said.

"Touch my people, and you're dead," Radko told him.

"Believe me"—and he sounded fervent—"I have no intention of harming any of your people right now. Not until I know where I stand."

"I am glad we understand each other."

Behind them, something heavy thudded to the floor. He was good. She hadn't seen him move. A second thud.

She knew what it was without looking. OneLane's assistants.

OneLane glanced back but didn't move toward them.

Chaudry started toward the fallen salespersons. "Chaudry," Radko said, "leave them. They're either dead already, or they'll be fine."

"It's a general anesthetic," Vilhjalmsson said. "They'll come out of it in around four hours." He moved the spear OneLane's way when she surreptitiously tried to take out her comms. "Drop it on the floor."

"That weapon is a ceremonial Traaken spear," OneLane said. "Deadly when it's loaded, but in my shop it isn't. You might be able to stab us with it, but you can't do much else."

"Now there's where you're wrong," Vilhjalmsson said. "I was in here yesterday." OneLane nodded at that. "Today, I came prepared. It is fully armed now, even the tip, as you can see by what happened to your staff." He tapped the small black piece he'd clipped on earlier. "Anesthetic and poison darts," then tapped the length of the spear farther down. "Voltage here. Drop your comms."

OneLane complied.

Chaudry moved to do the same.

"Not you, Chaudry. You keep your hands clear and away from your body. All of you. I know how fast you people can get a weapon out."

She shouldn't have mentioned Chaudry's name. It was too late now. Radko kept her arms away from her body and ensured that Han and Chaudry did likewise.

Vilhjalmsson indicated the office door. He waited for them to walk into the office, and Radko thought there might be a hint of sweat on his brow. Maybe he was weaker than he looked. Could she use that?

Chaudry moved alongside Radko. "It's a rigid lumbar brace," he said quietly. "He's recently out of regen. He's had spinal fusion. He can't move fast."

He'd kept his voice low, but the assassin heard him. "It makes me slow, Chaudry, but I don't need speed for accuracy."

The Alien Affairs Department had calculated Vilhjalmsson would be out of action for six months after Ean's inadvertent use of line eight. "You're walking well for someone who should still be in hospital," Radko said.

"I am. A new surgery technique. It came from the military hospital at Goed Lutchen. Pioneering work done by Dr. Arnoud and his team. I'm sure you appreciate the irony."

Appreciate wasn't the word Radko would have used.

Chaudry lifted his head, almost scenting the air. "Dr. Arnoud's team specializes in nerve and bone regeneration."

It wasn't knowledge Radko would expect a young recruit in Stores to pick up. Or maybe she should have, given Chaudry's childhood game of doctors and symptoms.

They entered OneLane's office.

The far wall was covered with screens. Each screen—except the central one—showed a view from the security cameras. The shop; outside the front door; the alley at the back. There was a door in the wall on the left, cleverly hidden in the paneling. Radko had to look twice to be sure it was a door.

The office was dominated by a huge wooden desk—made of the same black timber that Radko's mother used for displaying her jeweled eggs—so polished they could see their reflections. The desk was bare.

Radko stepped forward, and the spear crackled hot against her cheek.

"No sudden moves," Vilhjalmsson said.

It was more, she thought, to ensure they all respected the spear than from any worry about her moving. She touched her finger to her face. He'd gone close, but he hadn't burned her. Even she couldn't shoot that accurately. Especially not with a weapon that had been on a store shelf fifteen minutes ago.

"You're very jumpy," Han said.

"One needs to be with a soldier like her. Especially since, as Chaudry here has noted, I am a little sore at present. Right now, I intend to shoot first, before anyone gets near enough to harm me."

It was a warning. And a threat. Radko moved back.

Vilhjalmsson glanced over to where Callista OneLane waited. "Let's see this famous report."

OneLane was calm. Either she'd been held at weapon point often enough to realize she was in no danger for the moment, or she had a secondary protective system, and backup was already on its way. Radko hoped it was the latter.

"I don't give things away for free," she said. "If you want it, you'll have to pay for it. In fact, I would have preferred you steal it after my client left. Not here. This is bad for business."

"I did plan on stealing it afterward," Vilhjalmsson admitted. "Until I recognized Spacer 'Chen,' here." He waved the spear at OneLane, but he spoke to Radko, "You're not minding people anymore?"

Radko didn't answer.

OneLane said, "I am taking a comms out of the drawer." She'd definitely had a weapon trained on her before. "Incidentally, your own comms won't work in this room. You can't record. This is the only copy you will get."

Han moved his hand to scratch his back. He was going for his weapon. Radko caught his eye and shook her head. Not yet. As Stellan Vilhjalmsson had just illustrated, Han wouldn't stand a chance.

OneLane held up the comms, then turned it on and pushed the data through onto the larger screen in the center of the wall behind her. "The report."

There were two logos on the title page. Redmond Fleet Military Service and TwoPaths Engineering.

So, a combined military-commercial exercise.

Radko had come across TwoPaths Engineering before. They built spaceships based around the original line ship, the *Havortian*. They'd had the plans for over ten years now. Line ships. Linesmen. How coincidental was that?

She crossed her arms and watched as OneLane moved the report on to the next page, which contained a list of names associated with the report. She recognized one. "Hold it."

OneLane stopped scrolling.

The second name down. Latoya Jemsin, currently sequestered in a New Alliance prison on Haladea III, after an early incident where she'd tried to question Jordan Rossi, and failed.

"You said this was new data. Dr. Jemsin has been in prison for months. If she wrote the report, it's old."

"This report has been ten years in the writing. Dr. Jemsin was part of the team." OneLane pointed to a line farther down. "You will see as we scroll through that none of the later reports are hers. Dr. Adam EightFields has taken over her work."

If she knew this much about every illegal item she sold,

then no wonder she asked so much money. Radko nodded and let her continue to scroll through the pages.

OneLane scrolled through the first ten pages of the report slowly, then flicked through others, faster, and again slowed at the end. "It's a massive report. Ten years of data here, and their conclusions."

"How much?" Radko asked. And how did she buy it and keep it out of Vilhjalmsson's hands.

Movement caught her eye, and she looked up to the screens. On the screen depicting outside, soldiers jogged into view. Five in at the front. Four at the back. A full team, dressed in military uniform. Redmond soldiers.

Callista OneLane smiled.

There had to be an emergency button here in this room. OneLane must have pushed it when she'd entered. Although it had only taken five minutes to respond. With such a quick response, one could almost think the whole thing was a setup.

For Chen? Or for Vilhjalmsson?

It didn't matter who it was for. Radko couldn't let herself or her team be caught or questioned by Redmond soldiers.

The soldiers in the back alley had to break the lock. Good. They'd arrive a minute after the ones who came in the front.

"Chaudry, Han. Get down behind the desk. Use it to cover yourselves while you cover me." And Radko watched carefully—one eye on the screens—to see what Vilhjalmsson would do.

He inclined his head toward the office door. Maybe, today, they were on the same side. She'd soon find out.

She nodded and pulled her blaster from the holster at her back. It was good to be armed. She took a position to the left of the door. Vilhjalmsson took the right.

The door blasted open.

OneLane's reinforcements had arrived.

"These people are—" OneLane said, as the lead soldier glanced around quickly.

The soldier turned his weapon toward OneLane and blew her away.

Radko's answering blast went straight to his heart. Beside him, his companion went down. She and Vilhjalmsson seemed to share the same enemies. For the moment.

They downed two more before the Redmond soldiers realized they were a threat. A blaster fired over her left shoulder took down the final soldier in the first group. Han, as accurate and reliable as Vega claimed him to be.

The soldiers hadn't been expecting trouble, so why a full team? To prevent a back-door escape? Or to remove all witnesses?

The soldiers from the alley arrived then. They expected victory, and the battle to be over before they got there. They were seconds too slow. Radko and Vilhjalmsson stepped out and took down two each before they even knew they'd lost.

NINE

DOMINIQUE RADKO

RADKO CALCULATED THEY had less than five minutes before Redmond sent reinforcements. There was no one in sight yet.

She waved to Han and Chaudry. "Go, go. Before the next
lot get here."

They scrambled out in an awkward run.

Radko snatched OneLane's comms a second before Vilhjalmsson did, and the two of them ran out together.

Her comms started beeping as soon as they were outside.
Van Heel. Radko flicked it on as they ran.

"I've been trying to call for five minutes," van Heel said.
"A team of Redmond soldiers went in there."

"We found them."

"There's a backup team waiting one street south."

They were headed south. Radko beckoned to the others and
veered east. "How close can you get the aircar?"

"I'll need at least two blocks if you think they'll come after us."

"Meet us two blocks east then."

"Wait," Vilhjalmsson said. "Maybe we could work together
a bit longer. You have transport out. I have codes that should
get us past Redmond military."

His face was gray, covered in a film of perspiration. He
couldn't run far, or fast. He'd get caught quickly. Given the
number of Redmond soldiers in the area—more when they
saw the carnage inside the shop—they would find it hard
enough to escape themselves.

He was Gate Union, Markan's man, so he was likely to
have codes he mentioned. Redmond and Gate Union weren't
working together at present, but they were still, officially,
allies. They'd honor their ally's codes.

"Give me the spear and we'll drop you off on the other side of the city." Radko hoped she'd made the correct decision.

He hesitated, then stumbled, winced, and tossed the spear to her. "It's all yours."

She covered him while he ran. From the way his back twitched, he didn't like it any more than she did. Good.

They reached the aircar as the first soldiers came running around the corner.

"Go, go," Radko said, and van Heel took off in a straight lift that pushed them all to the floor.

Vilhjalmsson grunted, the sound quickly cut off.

Radko pulled herself up, blaster trained on him. "Han, Chaudry. Cover him. If he moves—even a twitch—shoot him." She didn't look away as she backed across to van Heel. "How soon can we dump him?"

"It's hard not to twitch," Vilhjalmsson said to Han and Chaudry. "Not when I know she's ready to shoot me."

The two blasters were close together. Chaudry's left arm against Han's right. All Vilhjalmsson had to do was reach out, and he could grab them both.

Why did a left-handed linesman hold his blaster in his right hand?

"Move away from him," Radko said. "Make him work if he's going to take the weapon off you. A blaster set to burn is as deadly at two meters as it is at one."

"Who is he?" Han asked. "Why so leery of him?"

"He's a professional assassin. Reports personally to Admiral Markan."

"So why help him?"

"He helped us," Chaudry said.

If Chaudry thought like that about one of Gate Union's best assassins, Vilhjalmsson would walk all over him. "He has codes he can use to get us past Redmond security," Radko said. "We have an aircar. Mutual benefit, Chaudry."

"We're being pursued," van Heel said. "I can drop him, or I can run, but I can't do both."

These were Redmond soldiers on their home territory. They couldn't outrun them. How long would it take for Redmond to identify the aircar?

Radko looked at Vilhjalmsson. "Those codes you promised." If he was working with Redmond, surely he would have
let the soldiers capture them back at OneLane's shop.

Vilhjalmsson stood up carefully.

"You should get your back seen to," Chaudry said. "You
shouldn't be doing strenuous physical movement yet."

Chaudry was never going to make a decent soldier. He
didn't have the personality for it.

The speaker crackled. "Aircar D-J-12351. This is Redmond
Fleet. Please land in the nearest available landing space."

"I need to call base over the aircar's comms," Vilhjalmsson
said.

Radko nodded and held her blaster close to his back while
he used the comms system on the aircar to call base. She
didn't relax even when an irate Redmond voice came through,
demanding to know what was going on.

Vilhjalmsson explained—in Redmond as good as hers—
that the attack on OneLane's premises had interrupted a sting,
and the team following them should remove themselves before
they totally ruined it. He provided further codes, good enough
that the Redmond carrier climbed high with a burst of speed
and disappeared over the city.

"It won't hold them long," Vilhjalmsson said. "Redmond
doesn't share information about lines or line experiments."

It was long enough for Radko. "We'll find somewhere public to drop you off. The parking lot at SevenWays Plaza," to
van Heel. It was the largest shopping center in the city.

Van Heel set the controls.

Radko motioned Vilhjalmsson's hands away from the controls with her blaster. He put them on the table, facing up.
Empty. "I'll buy the report off you."

She laughed at him.

"Shopping center coming up." Van Heel landed the aircar
neatly.

"No?" Vilhjalmsson turned for the door. "I appreciate your
not killing me this time."

He winced and almost fell. Radko let him right himself.
"Young Chaudry is right. I would have liked more leave." He
climbed out of the car like an old man.

"Vilhjalmsson. Catch." She tossed him the spear. "You'll need a weapon." She didn't trust Vilhjalmsson not to have put a tracer on it somewhere, and she didn't have time to investigate, which was a pity because Vega would have liked that weapon. She turned to van Heel. "Go, before he shoots us all."

Van Heel took off in a vertical lift.

They were five minutes in the air when Radko realized the comms she thought she'd rescued from OneLane's dead hands was a military-style comms. The brand favored by Roscracian military.

BACK in their rooms, Radko tossed the comms across to van Heel. "See if you can hack into that."

Vilhjalmsson's comms would be like their own. Provided especially for the mission and nothing personal on it.

"He seemed so nice," Chaudry said. "And he was injured."

Radko couldn't work out if the niceness was supposed to prevent an assassin from stealing things, or if his injury was. She didn't care. She wanted to shoot him.

"He must have swapped as we picked it up." OneLane's comms hadn't been out of Radko's pocket since. Or the comms she thought was OneLane's.

She had to admire the cleverness of it. If she'd known he had picked up the comms first, she would have demanded it from him at blaster point. Instead, he'd offered to swap his comms for this one. She should have taken him up on his offer and seen him wriggle out of it.

"We didn't see him swap it," van Heel said. "Are you sure this isn't the report?"

"Hack it and see, van Heel."

Half an hour later, van Heel admitted, "There isn't much on here. A code I can't read. A ship booking from Roscracia to here. A restaurant payment for last night. He ate at a place called Sahini's. He's staying at the Grande Hotel."

Radko would bet he wasn't staying there anymore.

Like her own comms, there'd be deeper information if van Heel hacked further, but nothing to incriminate Vilhjalmsson, and it would wipe itself if they tried to discover more. One thing was certain. The comms with the report on in wouldn't have last night's dinner bill on it.

She dug into the tools on her belt. A tiny screwdriver. A metal knife. Some wire. She unscrewed that back of the comms, pressed the knife into the wiring, and wound the wire around the knife. She wound the other end of the wire around the screwdriver.

She was about to jam the screwdriver into the other end when she stopped. This would short the comms. There was a tiny piece of line five in each comms. She was about to destroy a line. Or a piece of one.

Could she do it?

She looked up to see all three of them looking at her.

"Are you okay?" Han asked. "You look green."

Comms lines weren't intelligent like a ten-line ship, but all the same. Was it murder?

"I'm fine," Radko said, and jabbed the screwdriver down.

Ean would have told her the line had disappeared. All she got was the smell of burned plastic and hot metal. And a tiny wisp of black smoke.

When did lines become sentient, anyway. Surely all the small pieces of equipment weren't. They didn't seem to think until there were ten of them together and they were much larger than a single sliver. Maybe she should think of the tiny piece of line in a comms as like regenerated skin, being grown to match a human DNA. Not alive in a sentient way.

She tossed the comms away. Vilhjalmsson wouldn't be able to track it anymore. Although it would be like him to bug something else.

"What if you were wrong about which comms it was?" Han asked.

"Then I've destroyed plans we were prepared to pay a lot of credits for."

The trick to a successful operation, covert or otherwise, was not to think about what-ifs like that until after the operation, when you worked out what you could do better next time.

There were other what-ifs she had to think about now. Like, what if Vilhjalmsson had bugged them?

"We should all change," she said. "Everything. Even our shoes if we have others. We may be bugged."

Han followed her into the room she shared with van Heel. She didn't see any signals, but van Heel lingered outside. "It's not such a big deal," he said. "Losing the comms, I mean. They can't expect newbies like us to be a hundred percent successful first time around."

What was he trying to tell her? "Han, with that kind of attitude you'll never make it in covert ops."

"I never planned for covert ops."

Neither had she.

"I like my job. I like that I can go home every break."

"I like my job, too," Radko said. She missed her job. She missed Ean. And she didn't have time for the small talk. "Tell me what you're trying to say. I like honesty."

Han looked at her.

"We don't have time for you to muck around."

He hesitated. She waited.

"Maybe you shouldn't take it so hard. Losing the report. It's okay to destroy his comms, but don't you think this bugged business might be going too far."

No wonder Vega liked him, but the Yves Han who'd burned his tutor's arm wouldn't ever offer advice like that.

"Humor my paranoia this once, Han. I know this man." A lot better than she had two months ago. "Let's all get changed and see if he has planted any bugs. I hear what you're saying, but I am your team leader in this. I'm not doing it because I'm upset he stole the comms from me. I'm doing it because I think he's bugged us."

"And that business with the comms before?"

"That is a totally different thing. I don't like destroying lines. Not even comms lines." She pushed him out. "Go and get changed."

Afterward, she checked their clothes. On the back collar of the business jacket she had worn as Tiana Chen was a tiny receiver.

Van Heel took it from her fingers. "Finest grade," she said approvingly. "Do you know how much a device like this costs?"

Radko was sure Vilhjalmsson hadn't worried about the price.

She tossed her jacket into the recycler, and got the others to dump their jackets as well. She sent the bug down with it.

"I can't believe I let him do that." She should have known better.

"He did save our lives," Chaudry said.

"Chaudry, he's a professional assassin." Who'd probably kept them alive because he wanted to hear more about the line ships and their plans.

To be safe, Radko had them pack up and move elsewhere. They hired a new aircar halfway across the city, swapped their equipment over, then took both aircars across the continent, where van Heel dumped the first one. After that, they went back to Bane and booked themselves into an apartment to make plans.

"What happens now?" Han asked. "We go home, tail between our legs?"

"No," Radko said. What kind of a team were they if they let a setback like that stop them? "We get our report from the source. What names can you remember from the list of contributors at the front of the report?" She remembered five. Jemsin, EightFields, Quinn, RiverSide, and Jakob.

"EightFields," Chaudry said. "And that one you mentioned. Jemsin."

"Jemsin, EightFields, and Quinn," Han said. "There was a Dr. Quinn who tested—" He paused, and visibly didn't finish what he'd been going to say. "I wonder if it's the same one."

Radko didn't push. Han had probably met Quinn as a linesman. She watched Han rub his eyes—with his right hand, again—and wondered. How likely was trauma to change one's handedness?

"Find out all you can about those five people. I want someone I can get the reports from. Or at the very least, I want to know where they're doing their experiments."

There were no records for Jakob, and it wasn't a Redmond name. They had the whole galaxy to search, and they didn't have the time or support to do it.

"There's plenty on Jemsin," van Heel said. "She wrote a lot of papers."

"Forget about her," Radko said. "She's in jail." If she'd

spilled any information, the Yaolins would already know about it. "What about Quinn?"

"He's still doing line experiments, apparently," Han said. "But there's nothing here about where he's doing them. Or where he's living now."

Radko noted the "still." Would he have a problem if they came up against Quinn?

"Concentrate on RiverSide and EightFields then." They were both Redmond-founding-family names, likely to be well-known in society. That was good in one way, because there was a lot of information about the founding families. They just had to find those particular names among all the noise.

"EightFields," van Heel said. "I can't believe the names these Redmond people come up with."

Radko's early studies of Redmond had taught her the importance of the names. "When the first settlers arrived on Redmond, they renamed themselves according to their surroundings. Thus, the EightFields family had a farm with eight fields. TwoPaths had two paths nearby." She tried to remember other founding names. "OneLane. FiveWays."

"They're still weird," van Heel said.

Radko got van Heel to hack into OneLane's records, while Chaudry and Han searched for other people listed on the report, and she tried to find out what she could about One-Lane's contacts. The woman had run a legitimate business over the top of her fencing activities. Radko could even have bought a jeweled egg her mother had been after for years.

A man named Daniel EightFields was a regular customer. It might only be coincidence, but once they were done with Adam, she'd get them to search on Daniel.

"Adam EightFields fancies himself." Van Heel pushed an interview onto the main screen. EightFields was being introduced by a young reporter.

"Dr. Adam EightFields is one of our foremost line experts here on Redmond, and—"

"Not only on Redmond," EightFields interrupted him. "One of the universe's leading experts on linesmen and line theory."

Apart from the fact that humans had only settled the one galaxy, there was a whole race of aliens out there whose children probably knew more about the lines than any single human expert. Radko would have bet Ean's expertise over a whole roomful of people like EightFields, anyway.

"So how does the news of a new line eleven affect line theory?" the reporter asked.

"If it is a new line," EightFields said. "The New Alliance claims it is, but is it really so?"

Radko checked the date on the interview. Not long after Michelle had been kidnapped, back when people were still arguing whether there really was a line eleven.

"Sounds like he took any opportunity he could to get on the media," van Heel said. "Or he used to. Haven't heard anything from him for months."

"Can you find out where he works? Where he lives?"

"Last known employer, TwoPaths Engineering. But they have fifty sites. His address is here in the city, but then that's the address of twenty other EightFields as well. Place must be a mansion."

Han was checking the social pages. "He's got a sister, Christina, who manages the EightFields estate. A brother, Daniel, who's a spacer in the Redmond Fleet."

"Only a spacer?" A founding family would have paid for a promotion for their son. Why hadn't they? "Find out more about Daniel, Han. Tell me if he gets on with his family." A disaffected family member might not be so loyal to said family. Or he might be broke. Maybe even sell a stolen report to a woman he shopped from regularly.

She went back to the shop records. "Callista OneLane sold a jeweled brooch to Daniel EightFields sixteen days ago. I want to know if that Daniel is Adam EightFields's brother."

Van Heel hacked into the city security system to view the records for the street near OneLane's premises that day, while Chaudry and Han went painstakingly through each face she brought up and compared it to the image Han got from the social pages.

Meanwhile, Radko worked on five different escape plans. They not only had to find which engineering complex Eight-Fields worked at, but they had to get off Redmond afterward, and the longer they stayed here, the harder it would be to get off.

Maybe they should go back to the original spaceport and convince the pilot who transported the shellfish to take them off.

But how long before he'd be back?

"Got it," Han said. "It looks like the brother."

Radko compared the images and had to agree. "So let's go after Daniel. Find out where he is and when we can get to him."

There was plenty in the vids about Daniel EightFields. He was a member of a well-off family, he was a lavish spender, and he was often in trouble. Much like the progeny of some of the Great Families on Lancia.

"Looks like his family sent him to the fleet to sort him out," Han said. "We get them on Lancia. The parents get tired of bailing them out of trouble and send them off to the fleet to learn some discipline."

Had that happened to Han?

"They're useless as soldiers, and we can't send them anywhere dangerous, or their family sues. So they stick around headquarters, getting into trouble, and we have to bail them out. Or we send them off to worlds where, if they do get into trouble, it doesn't hurt them or us."

Van Heel hacked the public comms codes, found Daniel EightFields's comms, and they tracked it until he left the base. Vega was right. She was a class hacker.

EightFields finally stopped at a nightclub.

"Let's go chat with EightFields the Younger," Radko suggested.

THEIR images from OneLane's shop were circulating on the news vids. According to the news, they were dangerous murderers, and anyone who saw them should call the fleet, not tackle them. Chaudry was unrecognizable as the regen victim, but his short, bulky shape was unmistakable. He looked nothing like the man on the vid, but anyone seeing him would report him because of his size. If the police investigated, they'd pass him over. Provided they didn't talk to him. If they did, they'd soon work out he wasn't a native, so they'd probe more.

Not the police, Radko corrected herself. The military. Redmond wasn't treating this like a civilian murder gone wrong. They were treating it like a military problem. Even at One-Lane's premises, there'd been no local police. It had been a wholly military exercise.

The report had been co-branded with Redmond military. How far were they prepared to keep the information secret?

Han was more recognizable. It might be smart to keep them out of sight if she could. Radko looked nothing like Chen. Best if she did it alone.

"Van Heel, can you get the feed from inside the club? Han and Chaudry, stay in the aircar with van Heel. If I need you, I'll call. Keep an eye on me." With luck, she could be in and out quickly, without any need for backup.

She waited while van Heel hacked into the club feed. Even the screen inside the club showed their faces, with the words DANGEROUS KILLERS in large letters underneath.

"Have you ever had to kill anyone?" Chaudry asked.

She wondered, for a moment, if he was serious, for she and Vilhjalmsson had decimated a team of soldiers.

"Before today, I mean."

"I'm not an assassin." Not yet anyway. If she came across Vilhjalmsson again, it might be a different matter. Murdered in cold blood. "I have killed people."

"Don't you mind?"

"I don't think about it." She didn't. It was her job. She was good at her job.

"I've killed people," van Heel said. "Three of them. If you think about it, Chaudry, it gets to you. Don't persist."

Radko was glad Chaudry hadn't harmed anyone earlier. Around about now, he'd be starting to feel bad.

"Thank you," Radko said to van Heel, and glanced at Han, who'd probably killed his first enemy today, too.

He knew what the look was for. "I felt nothing."

That just meant it hadn't hit him yet.

"Got it," van Heel said, and switched the camera view to pan on the patrons. They found EightFields with a group of people who laughed at every joke he made. Radko had had friends like that when she was a girl. The Yves Han that Radko had known as a child would have friends like that.

But she didn't know this adult Han at all.

Which reminded her. "Han." She took out her comms and tossed it across.

He caught it with his right hand.

"What do I do with it?"

"Nothing." She took her comms back. "Testing your reflexes." And his handedness. This spacer she had in her team showed a strong tendency to right-handedness.

Yet linesmen were always left-handed, and Yves Han had spent ten years with House of Sandhurst.

Ten years. Was he the real Han or wasn't he? If he was the real Han, but wasn't a linesman, then why had Iwo Hurst kept him on? Because he could be useful? Or because the man in front of her wasn't the same man Hurst had trained?

She was starting to suspect he wasn't the same man.

She pushed that question away. Tonight, they were here to get information from Daniel EightFields. She tucked her blaster into the back of her trousers and pulled on her jacket. Loose enough and thick enough to hide the bulge. "Don't come after me unless I really need help."

She swung out of the aircar.

THE nightclub was fashionable and expensive, full of shiny, glittering surfaces, and a lot of flashing lights. Radko bought herself a drink and turned to look around the room.

EightFields's friends were drunk. Their laughter overloud, their interactions with other patrons bordering on nuisance. In contrast, their host looked stone-cold sober, and he twitched every time someone entered the bar.

He twitched when Radko entered but relaxed when she ordered her drink. He twitched even more when a group of uniformed fleet officers entered and didn't relax until they'd passed through into a private room.

A man with something to worry about? And from the way he looked broodingly at the screen every time Radko and the others appeared there, it might have something to do with Callista OneLane. Even if it wasn't his brother's report, Daniel EightFields had bought or sold something to OneLane, and he was worried he'd get caught.

The woman closest to EightFields called for another round of drinks. EightFields paid with an absentminded flick of his comms. Radko couldn't tell if he always paid, or if he was just inattentive tonight.

Radko finished her drink and wandered over. "You're Adam EightFields's brother. Am I right?"

He looked at her, and there was no welcome in his eyes. "Who's asking?"

"A friend of Adam's. I haven't seen him in months. Where is he nowadays? I'd like to catch up with him sometime."

Daniel EightFields shrugged. "Don't know. Don't care."

She pushed her way in between the drunk woman and EightFields. "Of course you do."

"Hey," the woman said.

"What's more," Radko said, quietly, under the other woman's protestations, "you'll tell me, or I'll mention your visits to OneLane."

She felt the hardness of a blaster shoved into her side. "Say anything, and I'll kill you," EightFields said.

Good. He had something to hide. She didn't move. If Eight-Fields was desperate enough to pull a weapon on her, he'd use it, despite the consequences. "Why don't we go outside. They'll have security watching the patrons. If someone sees your"—she indicated with her chin, but didn't look down—"they'll call the police."

He looked around.

"Your friends are too drunk to be any help."

He stood up. "They're not real friends, anyway. The first sign of trouble, and they'll be squalling for a team leader." He stood close to her as they exited. "Do anything to draw attention to us, and I'll kill you as soon as we get outside."

"Trust me, I want to draw attention to myself as little as you do."

EightFields led the way out through the back. The staff seemed to know him, for they let him go through.

"You're well-known here."

"Comes from being one of their best customers." The back door led directly onto a street. "Keep walking. Straight ahead, then turn left at the black hole."

Black hole was an apt description. Radko hesitated before she stepped in.

Van Heel couldn't follow her here with the cameras. She'd have to assume she had no backup. She turned as she entered and chopped down and snatched the blaster out of Eight-Fields's suddenly inert hands.

He cried out. There was a squawk from the end of the lane. Or alcove, really, for it only went in two meters. A light flicked on. Two indignant faces peered at them from the end of the space.

"Find your own place."

"Get out," Radko ordered, pushing EightFields up against the wall so he couldn't escape with them. He struggled. She wondered if she could hold him.

"We were here first."

Radko waved the blaster at them.

Another squawk, but they scrambled out, grabbing their clothes as they ran.

EightFields stopped struggling. "You're stronger than you look."

"You're not so weak yourself. I'm going to step back, let you go. Do anything stupid, and I'll shoot."

EightFields stepped back into the alcove. "What will you do with me?"

"Where is Adam?"

"Why Adam, of all people?"

Instead of answering, she said, "Did you sell the report to OneLane?"

"What report?"

They heard running footsteps, pounding toward them. Radko stepped into the alcove beside EightFields. "Give us away, and I'll kill you."

The footsteps stopped.

"Radko?" Han's voice.

A bright light was shined into the alcove.

"Turn the light out," Radko said. She nearly added "no names," but that would draw attention to the fact that he'd used hers. "I said I'd call if I needed help."

"Van Heel couldn't see you out here," Chaudry said. "This section's not covered. And H—"

"No names," Radko said, sharply. Between them, they'd give the whole team away.

Chaudry looked first at Han, then to EightFields. "He said Eightfields pulled a blaster on you. We thought." He didn't say what he thought.

If Han had recognized the movement, there was a good chance security had seen it.

"Let's question him elsewhere." Radko gestured with the blaster. There was only one safe place, and that was the aircar. She called up van Heel. "We're bringing him in. Be ready for us." He'd recognized them and would be able to describe them, but she didn't feel safe in this alley right now. "Give me your comms," she ordered EightFields, and waved the blaster impatiently in his face when he didn't hand it over immediately.

He handed it over. She tossed it into the alcove, hard enough to shatter it, then jumped on it as it bounced back, and kicked it back in.

"She really likes to be sure," Han said to Chaudry.

"Comms are harder to destroy than you realize," Radko said. "Come on."

The back door of the club opened as they reached the corner. Her heart sped up. Two bulky security men made their way down to the alcove.

Van Heel dropped the aircar into the street. "Hurry, this is illegal."

Radko waited until Han and Chaudry were in the aircar, then shoved EightFields in and followed so close, she stepped on his heels.

Van Heel took off straight upward. Han, Chaudry, and EightFields fell; Radko, more used to speedy maneuvers, kept her feet. She patted EightFields down, checking for weapons.

EightFields hardly noticed. He was staring at Chaudry. "I know you. You're the people at Callista's shop."

"You do not," Chaudry said. "I don't even look the same."

Radko moved the blaster threateningly up to EightFields's throat. "Tell us about the report."

"Go ahead, shoot me."

"I wouldn't shoot you dead. Just enough to cause you so much pain you'll want to tell me."

"Go ahead. I'm used to pain."

It sounded like the truth.

Chaudry made a sound that might have been shock. "Do you like pain?"

"Of course not. But I've been beaten before. Starved. Burned. Shot." He looked at Radko as he said that.

"I'm happy to shoot you, too," Radko said.

"Of course you are."

"If someone treated you so badly, why didn't you report them?" Chaudry asked.

"Why would you care?" and there was bitter truth in the words.

"If you allow yourself to be a victim," Han said. "You will always *be* a victim." He seemed to have forgotten he was part of this mission and reverted back to the policeman he would have been on Lancia. Radko thought he might have been good at his job.

What had Vega given her as a team?

Linesmen. Who didn't always make the best soldiers, but they were damned good at what they could do.

"I don't care how much you were bullied," Radko said. "And you don't either," to Han and Chaudry. "We're here to do a job. Let's do it. Now," to EightFields. "Tell me about this report before I shoot someone in frustration."

EightFields laughed. "I wish I'd never seen that report." He sobered quickly, then looked at them speculatively. "But you were buying it, weren't you?"

There wasn't any point denying it, and if he'd been jumping at Redmond soldiers earlier, it was probably even beneficial. "Yes. Did you keep a copy?"

"I didn't even know what it was. It was just a comms Adam was fussing about." He took a deep breath. "I have to explain some history; otherwise, you'll think I'm crazy."

Radko looked at van Heel. "Are we okay with pursuit?"

"So far."

She was after Adam. She didn't really care about the report Daniel had sold to OneLane, but if they could relax him by letting him talk, maybe he'd let slip where his brother was. Provided they didn't run out of time.

"Go on," Radko said.

"Thank you." He settled into his seat, lance straight, like a soldier. "I hate Adam. I always have." She heard the truth of it in his voice and suspected that Adam might be the source of the pain EightFields had been speaking about earlier. "He made my life a misery when I was a boy. That's why I joined the fleet. To learn how to fight."

If he was trying for sympathy, he was certainly getting it from Chaudry. Radko couldn't read Han's face. Van Heel looked skeptical.

"I'm doing okay, actually. I was up for team leader." He stopped and took three quick, shallow breaths. "I hated Adam so much that when I was about fifteen, I spent three months following him around, trying to find something I could use against him."

Radko hoped this story was going somewhere.

"Back then, Adam was spending more than his allowance. Than both our allowances combined. He stole one of Mother's necklaces—Radiance of the Night, it was called—and took it down to Callista's shop. I followed him there."

Named necklaces were priceless.

EightFields's voice turned reverential. "Have you seen Callista? Isn't she something? She was my first crush. I kept going back though I had no money to buy anything. I must have spent my whole youth in that shop. I propositioned her once."

Radko raised an eyebrow.

"She turned me down. You remind me of her, actually. Ice queen."

"Thank you."

"I think she liked that I liked her. Adam visited occasionally. I was there often enough. I saw him go out the back. I used to ask her what he wanted, but she told me to mind my own business."

"So you tried to impress her by selling stolen goods?"

EightFields shook his head. "Adam came home to attend a function. Two hours before we were due to leave, a captain arrives with a full team as an honor guard. He wants Adam to finish something because they were about to get a twelve, and they—" He stopped, and stepped back. "What?"

Radko hadn't moved. At least, she hadn't thought she had.

"A twelve?" The chase had suddenly become personal. Her pulse pounded from the instant adrenaline rush.

"I don't know what it is, either. But Adam and the captain were excited about it. There was this massive fuss as they signed over the comms, like it was the most precious thing ever."

"Did Adam talk about it?"

"To me? Of course not. But he boasted about how important the work was, and it took a whole team to deliver it. Adam invited the captain to stay for a drink." EightFields paused, took a deep breath.

"I was up for promotion. Team leader. The captain mentioned it. Adam—" EightFields swallowed. "I turn up at work next day to start team-leader training and find I'm out of the program. That I'm unfit to be in charge of people. It's signed by the captain from the night before."

"So you decided to get your own back?"

"Not then. They placed me on special leave because no one knew what to do with me. My old position had already been filled. So I go home, and what should I see when I walk inside, but Adam's precious comms on the table. And no one around." He scrubbed at his eyes with the heels of his palms. "That's when I took it. I went straight around to Callista's shop."

"Didn't you think you'd get caught?" Radko asked.

"I had proof he'd stolen the necklace. If they traced the comms, I'd show them the proof about the necklace and say Adam had a history of selling things off." His mouth twisted down. "I didn't think it through. I was angry. There was this massive fuss about the missing comms, but they assumed I'd been at work all day. I was ignored."

"And you've been jumping at Redmond soldiers ever since?"

He nodded.

And no wonder. "What else did they say when they delivered the comms?" Radko asked.

"They didn't say anything. Except about how important and confidential it was. And how time was so short."

She thought he was telling the truth. "And Adam. Where is he?"

He shook his head and raised his hands when she instinctively raised her blaster. "I truly don't know. It's supposed to be secret."

Han stepped forward to stand beside Radko. "We've spent all this time hearing your story, and you haven't got anything for us. Not even a report."

"I don't know for sure, but I can guess where Adam is. If you'll listen before you shoot me."

"Talk faster, then," Han said.

"Adam was late." EightFields rushed the words out. "This function we both had to attend. It was a major event. Everyone in the Founding Families had to attend. You disgrace your family if you don't. We never miss it. But Adam nearly did this year. Because his lab was under lockdown."

If a lab was under lockdown, it was usually for security reasons or because something viral had gotten out of hand. Either way, the company wasn't going to publicize it. "We need more than that," Radko said.

"But Adam is also a name-dropper." EightFields watched Radko's blaster warily. "When he dines with someone important, you know about it. And he dined with the Factor of the Lesser Gods three times in the two weeks before he came home." He paused expectantly.

"Connect it for us," Radko said. "The Factor of the Lesser Gods isn't from Redmond." In fact, he was supposed to be turning against Redmond by marrying Michelle.

"The lockdown," EightFields said. "They had a lockdown at the Factor's palace on Aeolus. It made the news. The Factor had some important visitor. So important they locked down the whole palace and the streets surrounding it. No one could get in or out for two days. Timewise, it matches perfectly."

Van Heel ran checks. "TwoPaths does have a lab there. Although it's listed more as a store nowadays. It is close to the palace. Right against the walls, actually."

"Yes, but why put a comilitary operation on a world that's not your own? And why leave it there if the two worlds are close to being enemies right now?"

"Maybe that's what the twelve is about?" Han suggested. "Their plans to move."

Radko shook her head. "That's something different." She

watched EightFields carefully. She thought he was telling the truth. Otherwise, he was an accomplished liar. "Anything else you want to tell us?"

"No."

She looked at the others. Han shook his head. Chaudry didn't respond. Van Heel shrugged.

"Take us down somewhere safe," Radko ordered van Heel. "We'll drop him off."

TEN

EAN LAMBERT

ADMIRAL ORSAYA WAS delighted to be officially placed in charge of security for linesmen. She came out personally to reassure Ean he was in safe hands.

"I know that." Ean was on Confluence Station. The lines would look after him.

A pleased hum echoed through the station lines. *"We'll look after you well."*

"Thank you. I know you will."

Sale was less happy. "We're perfectly capable of looking after you. This business with Radko had better not take long."

Vega had called Sale as Ean had arrived back on Confluence Station, told her about Orsaya, then asked her to come in to the *Lancastrian Princess* after she finished work that day. Ean eavesdropped unashamedly on the call. Sale had just clicked off when Ean and Bhaksir rejoined them. Bhaksir had shrugged, and Sale had looked at her comms but hadn't asked anything else.

"You're coming out to the *Confluence* with us today, Ean." Sale looked at Orsaya, who'd smiled, and said nothing.

It had been a long night. Ean tried to doze while Sale and Bhaksir talked quietly off to one side, and everyone else pretended things were fine.

"No idea," Bhaksir said. "But everyone on board the *Lancastrian Princess* is on edge. Vega nearly bit my head off when I asked. It doesn't help that it's happened at the same time as this business with the Worlds of the Lesser Gods. That's all anyone's talking about on ship."

"I imagine not." Sale glanced over at Ean. He thought she was going to come and talk to him after that, so he looked away.

* * *

THE *Confluence* welcomed them. It was the only thing that seemed happy today.

"We'll have crew for you soon," Ean said.

"Crew is good. Lonely."

Ean knew that as well as the ships did. *"I know. We're doing what we can."* He was trying hard not to promise something he couldn't deliver, but if the New Alliance didn't make up its mind soon, he was going to assign linesmen himself.

"We choose, too."

He hoped he hadn't committed to choosing linesmen without the council's agreement. "I'm going for a walk," he told Sale. He needed to distract himself and the ship.

Bhaksir looked at Ru Li and Hana.

"On it," Ru Li said, and the two of them trailed after Ean.

"You realize," Ru Li said to Hana, "Bhaksir never made Radko take anyone with her. That means she thinks we're half the person Radko is."

"You are half the person Radko is," Ean said.

"Oh, that's mean, Ean. Especially when I know you really mean it."

He had meant it. Ean bit his lip. "Sorry. I didn't mean it that way." Don't compound your mistakes, Radko would say. Or would that be Sale? He took a deep breath. "You know what I mean."

Luckily for him, they did.

He stopped at one of the large crew rooms. On board the *Confluence*, there were always things to do. Except he couldn't think straight today.

Protection. That would be a good start. Ean and the ships had to be able to protect their people. Like he had before, with Radko, throwing the enemy across the room but a controlled throwing.

"I'm going to practice with line eight," he told the ship.

"Practice?"

What had the aliens done when they wanted to practice? Or were the lines so natural to them they didn't need to? He searched for another word to explain. *"Work with,"* he said finally. "Ru Li, Hana, you need to stay behind me."

"What are you doing?"

"Working with line eight."

"I'm not sure this is a good idea," Hana said, as they both moved in behind him. "Isn't line eight the one that throws people around?"

"That's why I have to learn to use it."

How did you work with something you couldn't see, you could only hear? You listened to them. And you tried to explain what you were doing because though you heard music, the general consensus seemed to be that it wasn't just music, it was your thoughts that conveyed the message.

"I want to build a field to protect us."

It built a field all right. Ean recognized the tune. The protective green field that surrounded the ship and when anything came within 9.7 kilometers of it, spread out, annihilating anything within two hundred kilometers.

"No. Not that one."

On the bridge, Sale grabbed her comms. "Ean. Whatever you did, don't. Turn it off."

Sale wasn't a linesman, but she was a good ship person. Especially on the *Confluence*, which she and her team knew better than anyone else alive, except Ean.

The green field died. Cut off instantly.

"It's off." Ean waited for his heart to stop racing. Thank goodness Abram insisted no vehicle ever went within two hundred kilometers of any of the alien ships without permission.

"What did he do?" Hana asked Ru Li.

Ru Li gave an elaborate, exaggerated shrug.

How did Ean explain to the ship what he wanted? Then, last time he had used eight that way, it had been on the *Gruen*, which was a different ship in a different fleet. Maybe only human ships did it. Maybe it was their equivalent of the green shield. Maybe it was the only thing they could do, for they didn't have the equipment to produce the other.

No. That couldn't be it. Both times, the ship had been protecting individual people.

"I was on the Gruen, *and someone fired at Radko. And we— I—knew he was going to kill her. So line eight made a protective field on the ship and stopped the other man's weapon."*

He still hadn't made himself understood to line eight by the time they left to go home.

ABRAM waited for him on Confluence Station.

"Wouldn't it be smarter for us to go to the *Lancastrian Princess*?" Ean asked, as they settled in with tea in Ean's quarters. Michelle liked it when Abram came back to her ship, and so did the crew. "Sattur Dow isn't there yet, and we'd know long before he arrived that he was coming."

Abram made a face that could have been a grimace. "Both Michelle and Vega feel it is better for me to spend less time on the *Lancastrian Princess* for the moment."

That was like kicking Michelle herself off the ship. It was Abram's home as much as it was hers. Or it had been. "Sometimes, I don't like change much."

"Change is inevitable," Abram said. "You go with the changes as they come, try to control them."

Abram and Michelle were both masters at controlling change and making it suit them.

"Do you ever regret becoming an admiral? Do you ever think that if you had to do it again you'd say no, and stay in your old job?"

He didn't have to hear Abram's reply to know the answer—the lines told him the truth.

Abram sidestepped the question anyway. "Have you met the other Lancastrian admirals, Ean? I can't think of one I'd like to see in Alien Affairs. Lancia's reputation is not undeserved. We have been too long in power. When we want something, we go out and get it, without thought to the consequences."

"But you think of the consequences."

"I think of the future, Ean. That is all." There was a strong sound of Michelle in the lines now. "I want Lancia to have a future."

He wanted it for Michelle.

"Emperor Yu is right to accuse me of controlling access to Haladea III. I do. Because I believe that is best for Lancia's future. I might be wrong. There are plenty of people who believe what they are doing is right, when it isn't."

"You are not wrong. And keeping you off the *Lancastrian Princess* is crazy."

"Michelle has her reasons. And I trust Michelle implicitly. If she thinks there's a problem, there's a problem."

What sort of problem would Michelle be worried about? It was Yu who had accused Abram of working against him, not Sattur Dow. Was Michelle expecting Dow to act as proxy for Yu? Or was there something more?

"What does Lancia do to traitors, Abram?"

Abram grimaced. "Treason has to be proven first."

That didn't answer the question. Ean waited.

"But that's not what I came here to talk about."

Of course it wasn't. Did Abram ever pay social visits?

Abram blew out his breath. "We're going to sing another ship into the *Eleven* fleet."

"Into?" Ean asked, just to be sure. They asked him to sing the ships out, which he couldn't. Not in.

"We are looking for the aliens."

Abram believed that if they didn't find the aliens, the aliens would find them one day. It was better, in Abram's opinion, that humans were the ones who did the finding. It gave them more control. Furthermore, Abram believed that Kari Wang's jump into alien space would have triggered an alert, somewhere. Ean had told the ship to go somewhere safe. Safe for an eleven ship was likely to be close to its alien home, in a sector with other alien line ships.

The aliens would have picked up the line signal. Especially if they were looking for it, for no one, not even aliens, would lose an Eleven-class ship and not be searching for it. Aliens would arrive one day, following the *Eleven*'s trail.

Humans didn't know how old the war was that the alien ships had fled from, or how close. All they knew was that the *Confluence* fleet had accumulated a lot of damage, and anything that could do damage like that would annihilate human ships. Abram's job in the Department of Alien Affairs wasn't just to learn how to use the fleet ships to their advantage, it was also to determine what threat—if any—the aliens were to humans.

Ean had heard other plans, too, at those interminable dinner parties the councilors loved so much. Plans for trading, plans for expansion. Plans for war.

"We want to start with the place you sent the *Eleven* to."

Where, according to Abram's theory, they would almost certainly meet aliens.

The *Eleven* had been under attack. A new weapon invented by Redmond, where four cloaked ships surrounded another ship they were attacking and sent a wave through that sliced the ship they were attacking into pieces. They had surrounded the *Eleven*, and Ean had told the *Eleven* to go "somewhere safe" until the field dispersed.

"Suppose I can't get back to the same place?" Ean didn't know where the *Eleven* had gone.

"We'll work that out when we get to it. We've astronomers and astrophysicists working on the images the *Eleven* brought back, to see if they can identify it." Abram smiled, a rare expression nowadays. "So far they haven't, but we'll get there."

He blew out his breath again. "I want to send Wendell."

Wendell would be perfect for a trip like that.

"I hear a but?" Ean wasn't sure if it was in the lines or the way Abram said the words.

"Many of the New Alliance worlds don't trust Wendell. Or his crew."

Wendell and his ship were prisoners of war. Normally, in cases like this, they retained the ship but ransomed the crew back to their world, but Ean had already sung the *Wendell* into the *Eleven*'s fleet, and the bond between ship and captain meant they couldn't send Wendell home.

They couldn't send the crew home either. They knew too much.

They were now dual citizens of Lancia and Yaolin, but really they were loyal only to their ship and their captain. As for Wendell himself, Ean had heard him say once that given the circumstances, he was loyal to whoever paid his crew and kept his ship supplied and powered.

"He's part of the *Eleven* fleet. We'd know everything they did."

"That doesn't matter to some people. Whether they believe it or not, they see this as an opportunity to get one of their own ships into the fleet, as a way to open up space for their world."

Or the mistake that brought an alien war to human space.

Abram blew out his breath again. "They'd be right, too, because whoever gets there first will have an advantage."

"So who?"

"It hasn't been decided yet. But it will be a functioning fleet ship. If this war is over before we've got someone, it might even be a Gate Union ship."

"Will the war be over?" No one else talked as if they thought it would be.

Abram shook his head. "And that's worrying enough in itself. We've two groups of aliens fighting each other, maybe more. I'd rather humans were all allied before we come up against them. Instead, if the Redmond–Gate Union split happens—as everyone expects it to—we'll be three fragmented groups. Not a good position to be in."

"Redmond is only six worlds. How dangerous are they?"

"Line factories," Abram reminded him.

Other worlds had factories that grew individual lines, like mass-producing line five for comms use, but now that the factories on Shaolin and Chamberley were gone, only Redmond could produce the full set of lines required to power a ship or a station. They couldn't afford to destroy Redmond.

Not even if the Worlds of the Lesser Gods gave them a military base close by.

Ean turned his attention back to the thing he could control the most. Another ship for the *Eleven* fleet.

"What about a Balian ship?" Admiral Katida supported Lancia—although she claimed she didn't always. Ean suspected it was less Lancia she supported than Michelle and Abram. He was fine with that. It was his definition of supporting Lancia as well.

"Unlikely. We're more likely to get someone who opposes Lancia. It won't be Nova Tahiti, for they have a captain on the *Eleven*. Maybe Yaolin, if they can talk hard enough."

Admiral Orsaya's passion was lines and linesmen. At least she'd want to know more about the ships and their lines than she would about finding new planets to explore. Or maybe not. Even Abram would be thinking about exploration for Lancia.

"Whoever we get," Abram said, "I want them to join in line training although most of them won't be linesmen."

Ean nodded.

"Speaking of line training. The events of the last two days have had most worlds scrambling to get people for us. They don't want to be left without trained linesmen."

When he said "events," Ean thought he meant the battle, and the *Eleven*, but there was a strong sound of Michelle underneath Abram's words.

The *Confluence* would be happy. "Good. We need crews for the ships. All of them. And captains."

"This batch of trainees will be bigger than the first group," Abram said. "We'll house them on the *Gruen* initially. Once it gets too many, we'll put them on Confluence Station, but that will take some organizing."

How many could they train at one time? A group session, Ean supposed, plus smaller groups. At least he had Hernandez and Fergus, and maybe Rossi, to help. And some of the earlier trainees.

Abram said, "We are also training paramedics from the different worlds to deal with line-related problems. That's going to be fun. We'll send them with the line trainees, but you won't have to train them. The paramedics who are already trained will do that."

"Do we have the room?"

"Captain Gruen has already complained about her cargo holds being kept empty for line training, rather than being put to use for storage now she has a full ship. We've promised her supplies every three days."

Ean grinned. Gruen would milk that for everything she had.

"As for the rest. We'll take it as it comes."

ELEVEN

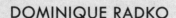

DOMINIQUE RADKO

BACK AT THEIR temporary home, Radko considered what they knew.

Callista OneLane's premises had been protected by Lone-Field Security. When OneLane had pressed the emergency button, the people who responded should have been LoneField employees, not Redmond Fleet soldiers. Not only that, if you were paid to protect someone's premises, surely you would know who they were, and not shoot them in the head the moment you entered a room.

OneLane had been Redmond's first target. Protecting the report, Radko thought. In case OneLane had read it? What was in that report?

Stellan Vilhjalmsson had the report now, but Redmond Fleet headquarters wouldn't know that because OneLane didn't have a camera in her office. Unfortunately, the cameras Redmond would see showed Radko introducing herself as Tiana Chen and saying she had come to buy something.

EightFields might or might not go to the authorities. If the story he'd told was true, he wouldn't, but that didn't stop the military putting the same names together that Radko and her team had. They'd get to him in the end. Radko wanted to be off world by the time they did. But Aeolus wasn't even a Redmond world. Why have a military operation off world?

"Do you think EightFields is sending us into a trap?"

"Why would he?" Chaudry asked.

"Don't trust anyone, Chaudry." But if EightFields had been telling the truth, they could verify it easily enough. "Van Heel, find out about the lockdown. It was supposed to be on the news. Han, see if you can find the Factor's guest list." On Lancia, it was easy to find out with whom Emperor Yu had dined. Most rulers had lists, and Han being who he was would know where to look. "Let me know if EightFields dined with him around the time or before the lockdown."

"What do I do?" Chaudry asked.

"Make us look as different as we can without drawing attention to us." They'd already changed once, but if Eight-Fields did go to the authorities, he would describe them and what they were wearing. And he had names.

Chaudry seemed to have a talent for disguise. Anything would help, no matter what, even if Chaudry himself stood out. EightFields had known him, even without a layer of fake regenerated skin.

"We need to look different," Radko said. "Shower, change. Let Chaudry make you up."

She dressed in the pants Chaudry had picked out for her, and a shirt she thought might have been Han's, then mulled over escape plans as she let him slick her hair back and use something from the cupboard to add a few dark streaks.

"Here's the lockdown," van Heel said. "Two weeks ago, for four days. Lots of speculation about who the Factor's mysterious visitor was, and the reason for the lockdown. All non-urgent staff were sent home. Staff who stayed said the visitor was masked."

"And I've got EightFields," Han said, not long after.

Radko looked up once to see Han across from her, almost a stranger with his hair flattened on top and his eyebrows clumping out. The droop to one side of his face made him look as if he'd had a stroke. She looked closer at the scab on the side of his mouth. It looked real and made her want to look away.

"I don't want to know," Han said. "Van Heel stared at me before, too." He looked back to his screen. "EightFields is a regular guest at the palace. He dined there a month prior to that, and three times in ten days before the lockdown."

Van Heel was not so much unrecognizable as noticeably older. Chaudry had done something to her face to make her look ten years older than she was. Her skin was a shade darker, and her nose and cheeks were red and blotchy with the broken veins of an alcoholic.

"Nicely done, Chaudry," Radko said. She didn't want to know what she herself looked like.

For his own disguise, Chaudry had paired his uniform pants with a loose shirt and casual shoes, and spiked his hair with gel, arranged so that it looked as if he'd lost a few clumps of hair. If he hadn't been such an obvious size, even Radko would have found it hard to recognize him.

"You're very good at this, Chaudry."

Chaudry frowned down at his trousers. "It feels wrong. Wearing part uniform."

"It can get you court-martialed," Han said.

"Han," Radko chided.

"Seriously, I pulled someone in for that the other day." Then Han grinned. "I won't tell. Your indiscretion is safe with me."

Chaudry tugged nervously at his trousers. "Maybe I should—"

"Wear them," Radko said. "It's the best disguise we've got. If you're worried about repercussions, then I order you to wear them. Van Heel, Han, witness that please."

"Duly witnessed." Van Heel glared at Han. "Leave him be."

They were starting to bond as a team, at least.

"Suggestions as to how we can get off this world," Radko said.

"Come in like we did to Bane," Han suggested. "Find ourselves a cargo port, and a shuttle that will collect us from there."

That had been organized by Vega, who had a whole fleet of resources behind her.

It wasn't only getting off world. They had to get on to a ship afterward. "We need that guy who delivers the shellfish," Radko said.

Maybe they could.

Radko looked at Han. He had implied that Gunter Wong was a family friend. Using contacts and calling in favors was a very Lancian way to work. "How well do you know Gunter Wong, Han?"

"Gunter?"

"Gippian shellfish."

"I know what he does, it's just unexpected you asking." Han considered it. "He's more a friend of my father's than he is mine. They're neighbors. They see each other often."

"What would he do if you asked him for a favor?"

"What sort of favor?"

"Send two orders of shellfish posthaste. One here to Redmond, the second to the Worlds of the Lesser Gods. We'd pay him, of course," as Han opened his mouth. They had a budget. "He just needs to prioritize it. And provide a ship that can carry four passengers."

"It's something my father would ask, not me."

"We'll try Wong first. If unsuccessful, we'll ask Renaud to do it."

"Keep my father out of this." Han's eyes narrowed. "How do you know his name anyway?"

"She's your team leader," van Heel said. "She knows more about you than your family does."

Did Radko imagine the whiteness around Han's mouth? She was sure there were things she guessed about Han that his parents didn't know. Like the fact that he wasn't Yves Han at all.

"My family knows yours," Radko said. "If we have to, I'll talk to Renaud, but it's best if we do it together." She'd prefer he did it alone, for Renaud was close to the Emperor. He wouldn't normally talk about Radko, but Michelle's wedding would be the main topic of conversation around Baoshan Palace. Someone might mention other weddings, and Renaud might casually drop into the conversation that he'd spoken to Sattur Dow's betrothed recently.

And if she was talking to Renaud, there was the other matter he might mention, so it was best to prepare Han for that. "You and I go way back, Han. One summer I smashed your face in. Did a lot of damage. I appreciate your not mentioning it, but Renaud might find it surprising we get along."

Han went still.

"You were twelve." She'd been nine. If this had been the Han she'd taken on, she wouldn't have beaten him.

"I'll get those numbers for you." Han stood up and went into the other room.

Van Heel laughed. "He doesn't like your remembering that, I take it."

"No. It was humiliating. I'm sure he didn't need to be reminded of it." Radko stood up. "I'd best make amends." She went inside, using the laughter of van Heel to hide the fact that she was stepping quietly now.

She came up silently behind Han, who was tapping something into his comms.

The comms in his hand wasn't the brand-new, generic model they'd all been issued, either. It was the high-end deluxe model she'd told him to put away at the start of the mission.

"Turn it off, Han. Before you compromise our location by sending an unnecessary comms while we're on a covert op, think about what you are doing."

He yelped.

"What were you planning? A message to your parents to find out information you should already know?"

"I don't know what you mean."

"I told you because it's an infamous incident in both our childhoods. Yves would have remembered it. I was nine, he was twelve. I thrashed him."

"You know, somehow I believe that."

Radko smiled. "You'd better believe it. Yves was a really unpleasant boy."

"And I'm an unpleasant man?"

"Yves might have been, but you're not Yves, are you." She watched his eyes but kept part of her gaze on his hands, to see if he'd go for his blaster. She nodded at the comms. "Doesn't your family think it strange, your calling them up to ask about yourself?"

His gaze was watchful. "I was in an accident. I lost a lot of memory of my past life. My memory's still not good."

"How long ago?" Although she already knew.

She thought he wasn't going to answer.

"Twelve and a half years."

Just after he'd completed training at House of Sandhurst.

If he'd been going to shoot her, the danger was past. Radko sat down across from him. "Your accent slips sometimes when you're stressed." Like now. His vowels broadened the way Ean's did, when Ean was tired. He'd be tired right now—if he was awake—for it was 02:00 hours Haladean sector time. "If I had to guess, I'd say you're from the slums."

"I didn't kill Yves if that's what you're thinking."

"I wouldn't blame you if you had. He was a bastard when he was a child. I imagine he grew into something worse."

Han made a wry moue. "How did you know?"

"You're right-handed." Not that Radko remembered Yves as left-handed, but he had been a linesman. "What happened to Yves?"

"I used to be Yves's stand-in." Han stared down at his comms, which was vibrating with an incoming message. He made another face, and held it up so Radko could see the name of the caller. Renaud Han.

Renaud could wait.

"Back when Yves was six or seven, someone threatened to kill him, so they found a double for public appearances. Me."

She nodded.

"We could have been twins. His family taught me how to speak and behave like him. I loved his parents better than my own. They would meet me whenever they came to Baoshan, and they invited me to dinner a lot. All *my* parents thought about was the credits I could make them."

"So what happened?"

"Yves liked to hurt people." It looked as if it took an effort to say.

Radko nodded.

"He got worse as he got older. The whole family was scared of him. My parents, my sister." Han rubbed his eyes. "Sorry, Yves's parents, his sister. Yet when he wasn't being a monster, he was charming."

A lot of monsters were. "How did he die?" Han wouldn't be running around pretending to be Yves if Yves were still alive.

"He hurt a young girl. Her mother tried to get him committed, but he was a Han."

She didn't need to interpret that. As a member of one of the Great Families, he'd have gotten off.

"She couldn't get it to trial, so she tried to kill him. She tried a couple of times. She nearly succeeded, so Yves asked me to stand in for him at a function he had to attend. I needed the money. Except . . . the girl's mother was as insane as Yves was. She booby-trapped the hotel where we were to change places. Killed herself and Yves and fifty other people as well."

"So you pretended to be him?" She hadn't known Han long, but he didn't seem the sort.

"The hospital got the records mixed. They thought I was Yves. I spent six months in hospital having my body rebuilt."

DNA was linked to one's identity at birth. There was no way the hospital could have mixed the records.

Han finally looked at her. "It sounds like an excuse, I know, but I lost my memory for a while. Or not so much lost it, but I got really confused because everyone was treating me like Yves, and I *knew* these people. I remembered them. I remembered having dinner with them. When I finally realized what had happened, I tried to tell them. A number of times, but something always came up, and we never got to the important part. Then I . . . stopped telling them."

His comms vibrated again. Han cut the call off.

"Sometimes I get a guilty conscience, but . . . I don't know. They get distressed when I talk about it."

Twelve years, he'd said. It was a long time to get away with pretending to be someone else. A long time to do it without being caught. The notes on Radko's comms said Han had joined the Lancian fleet eleven and a half years prior.

"So you joined the fleet."

"I thought that would solve things. It made it worse. And every time I go home—"

"But you do go home?"

Han shrugged.

"How often?"

"I'm at the barracks. We do three tendays, then ten days off."

Every break, in other words.

"I know. But I couldn't up and leave, and Annie is going through a stage right now, and Mother gets worried if I don't." Han shrugged again. "It's hard to cut off."

Even if the hospital had mistaken his identity, the fleet had rigorous security checks. The Great Families protected their progeny carefully. The DNA check for entry to the fleet should have exposed Han as an imposter. Yet it hadn't.

"Radko, court-martial me, do whatever you need to, but don't tell my parents. Please. They don't deserve it."

What if his parents already knew? Someone like Renaud Han had the contacts to change DNA records.

She didn't promise. She couldn't, for after this, she planned on visiting Amina and Renaud to see what they did know.

If she was allowed back on Lancia.

"I have to tell my boss," she said. "I'm here to test out a particular ability Yves had that you don't."

"That he could torture people better than me?"

Who knew what Han might do now that she knew his secret? Maybe it was time to share some secrets of her own. "He spent ten years at House of Sandhurst training to be a linesman."

"The doctors in the hospital explained that, before I regained my memory. It was the shock, they said. I might never regain my line abilities."

Radko laughed. "That won't gel with my boss. She'll observe you for five minutes, then she'll turn around and shoot you, for she'll know you never were a linesman, and therefore, aren't Yves Han. I'd rather tell her first. The Han family have influence." She stood up and stretched. "She's not a bad boss. A bit crusty, but okay for all that." Better than anyone had expected, but they should have trusted Abram Galenos to pick the right person. Even if, like everyone else, Radko would have preferred that Abram had stayed.

"That good, huh?"

"She's good, but everyone on ship will know. If—" She remembered in time not to mention Vega's name. Han had worked for Vega for two years. He'd have noted her promotion, would know for whom she worked now. "If my boss doesn't kill you, the rest of my team certainly will." In their job, someone pretending to be a linesman would be trying to get onto one of the alien ships.

"All in five minutes?"

"All in five minutes," Radko confirmed.

"What? They walk around with portable Havortian test kits?"

"Nothing so overt as that." She tapped the comms he was turning over in his hands. "They will see that you are naturally right-handed. They will ask what you see and hear." If he was near an alien ship. "And they will hear you sing."

"I'm doing the singing in five minutes?"

"Most definitely."

"So I walk on ship. You said it was a ship?"

She nodded.

"Singing, and holding something."

"Han, you holster your blaster right-handed."

"Oh." Han was quiet a moment. "And the singing?"

"Maybe ten minutes." More like an hour, given Vega would want to talk to him first.

"Seriously?"

"Seriously." She hoped her trust wasn't misplaced. "Han. It's a simple test, but it's classified. If you mention it to anyone, I'll bring up the secrecy act. And maybe I'll shoot you."

He'd been smiling. He stopped. "And you tell me this secret just after I tell you I'm not the person I'm pretending to be. Very funny. Even I got taken in."

He'd come around. Radko made her voice hard. "Don't mention what we talked about to anyone but me, Spacer Han. That's an order."

VAN Heel found an old, out-of-the way shuttle field halfway across the continent. It was busier than the one on Barth, but busy meant twenty ships a week, and it was cargo only. Radko used van Heel's comms—for her own was the contact for Tiana Chen in Callista OneLane's files—to order a box of fresh shellfish to be delivered there. The shuttle pilot was to collect a package from the same shuttleport. This parcel was then to be delivered, along with another box of shellfish, to the Factor of the Lesser Gods as congratulations on his forthcoming nuptials. The pickup from Redmond was to ensure that the same ship carried both orders.

Both orders were coded for urgent delivery.

"I hope that's not coming out of my credit," van Heel said, as Radko handed the comms back.

"It's coming out of our operations budget."

"You can always put in a chit for it if it does," Chaudry said. "We get that all the time in Stores. People charging things to the wrong account. It's form 55735."

"Wait," Han said. "You're telling me we have more than fifty-five thousand forms?"

"I've filled out about fifty thousand of them," van Heel said. "Intelligence likes to track where their money goes."

Radko had filled out the occasional order, but not many. "You should go onto a battleship. Not as many forms there."

"Are you kidding? That's worst of all."

Chaudry nodded glum agreement. "All the time. And we have to audit 5 percent of them."

"Audit?"

"What ship do you come from?"

Definitely not a ship where you filled out forms for everything. But then, no doubt Captain Helmo had that in hand. Radko would have to find out. "If anyone has to fill out a form for it, I'll do it."

She turned to van Heel. "Can you disable the tracker in the aircar?"

She nodded.

"Good. Not in the city," for in a populous area an aircar without a tracker was guaranteed to draw the attention of the police. "We'll stop somewhere along the way and take it out."

It was crazy to realize that it would take almost a full day for them to get to the cargo field. Around the same amount of time it would take a spaceship to get to Lancia, load some shellfish, jump, and send a shuttle to land on Redmond.

"Han, you can call Gunter Wong on the way. Let's go, people."

THE call to Lancia had a lag time of fifteen minutes.

That was unexpected. The lag between Redmond and Lancia had always been at least two hours. In wartime, it should be longer still. Radko checked to be sure the call really was going to Lancia. It was.

"Han." Gunter Wong's smile was wide and relieved. "Your father has been trying to contact you." The smile changed to concern. "What's wrong with you? Are you in hospital? Who is your doctor?"

Han looked startled.

"You're in disguise, dummy," van Heel hissed.

"Oh. No, Gunter, I'm fine. This is just a disguise. I'm supposed to look like this. I'm working undercover, and have been out of contact."

Cross-sector messages were always a little schizophrenic. Because of the lag, you fitted as much into the conversation as you could before the other person received it.

"We sent through an order." Han glanced at van Heel's screen. "WhiteRiver Company has ordered some Gippian shellfish for their base here at Redmond, and another order to go to the Factor of the Lesser Gods on Aeolus. We're hoping we can travel with the shellfish. That is, four passengers."

Fifteen minutes later, Wong's reply came back. Warm and reassuring, "Of course, Yves. But where are you? Your family is frantic. Your father called the barracks, and they told him you were on indefinite leave owing to personal issues. Are you sure you're well?"

"I'm fine. I'm working." That answer wouldn't get back to Wong for another fifteen minutes.

"If you have problems, you know you can go home to them."

Han rubbed his eyes. "I'm fine, Gunter. I just need passage off Redmond for myself and my friends. We're hoping to catch the shuttle your pilot brings the shellfish down in. It will need to carry at least four people. And we'll need to be able to book passage on the ship."

"I like your family," Chaudry said, as they waited for the signal to return to Lancia and for Wong to reply.

"Me too, Chaudry. Me too." Han glanced at Radko, looked away.

If Renaud and Amina Han knew he wasn't their true son, and were complicit in whatever had happened, Radko wasn't going to give him away.

By the time the next message arrived, Gunter Wong had someone with him.

"Papa," Han said, but that wouldn't get back for another fifteen minutes either.

How close were Gunter and Renaud, for Gunter to be able to call, and get, his neighbor over in less than half an hour?

Renaud Han looked haggard. "Yves. If there's a ransom, we will pay it."

"A ransom?"

Why would Han's father assume such a thing?

"No one said anything about a ransom, Papa. I'm working."

On a job that was getting more farcical by the minute. The longer this call went on, the more likely Redmond was to track it. Radko made winding motions with her finger.

Han nodded. "We need." His voice caught and he paused to breathe deeply before he could continue. "We need to get off this world. We sent an order through to Gunter. We want to travel with that order. We called hoping to fast-track the order, and to ensure we could get passage with it. Please, Papa."

Did he realize he'd added that last "please"?

This time, while they waited for the reply, Han muted the microphone on his comms. "I don't know what to say."

"Whatever we do," van Heel said, "let's not tell anyone we called your dad and asked him to get us out of trouble."

Even Radko managed a chuckle.

Van Heel added, "Provided he stops panicking enough to help us out, that is."

"I like him," Chaudry said. "He's worried."

"Yes, but why, Chaudry? It's a simple request. Please can you use your contacts to push this order through. Oh, and can you also make sure that whatever ship you send to do it picks up four passengers as well." Van Heel held out her hands, palms up. "Yet this man is running around in circles. Both of them are. Haven't you ever been away from home before, Han?"

"Of course I have. I work in Baoshan. My family lives in Han Province."

"Never off world then?"

"I've only been off world once," Chaudry said. "When I went to . . ." He trailed away. Radko strained to hear and thought the mumble ended in "Isador."

Chaudry had spent six years as a trainee linesman at House of Isador.

"We travel," Han said.

As van Heel had said, Han's request was simple enough. So why had Renaud and Gunter reacted the way they had? What was Radko missing?

Han blew on his fingers as if they were cold. He said to Radko, "My father's not normally—"

She nodded and cut off the rest of the apology with a motion of her hand. "If you can find out why he's concerned, do so, but I want you to wrap it up next time through. We can't talk much longer without Redmond picking up the signal." She looked at van Heel. "Let me know when they do pick us up. And disable the tracker as of now."

Han and van Heel both nodded.

It was closer to major population areas than she would have liked, but it might delay anyone associating this particular aircar with the call to Lancia. Redmond couldn't track the signal through their ops comms, for autolocation had been turned off, but they could triangulate the call, then slowly check the aircars one by one.

They waited in silence for the return message. It wasn't any less puzzling than the earlier communications.

Renaud struggled to speak. "I don't know what lies they used to get you to Redmond, Yves, but they're lying to you."

Gunter Wong cut in. "Don't do what they're asking, Yves. It's a trap. Cancel this order. They're setting you up. The Factor is allergic to shellfish. Sending a gift like this. It's as if you're threatening his life. If you accompany that delivery, they're sending you to your death."

Maybe that was all they were worried about. If Wong was correct about the allergies, then delivering the shellfish to the Factor would be perceived as a threat. But why all the talk about ransom payments at the start of the conversation? Worse, not only had Renaud confirmed that they were on Redmond; Wong had told the enemy where they planned to go next.

"Yves," Renaud said urgently, "I've contacted someone at Fleet Headquarters. They'll know what to do. They'll get you out of it."

Radko nearly groaned aloud.

Van Heel caught her eye, pointed to the screen. "Aircraft."

Closing in fast. That kind of speed meant military.

It was too soon for the military to have triangulated them. Too soon, even for Renaud Han's well-meaning—if misguided—request for help from Fleet Headquarters to have been intercepted by a Redmond spy.

"Wrap this up, Han," Radko said.

Han swallowed hard. "Papa, Gunter, I have to go. But please don't cancel that shipment." He clicked off.

"What weapons have we got?" Radko asked although she already knew. One tranq gun, six blasters, and a Pandora field diffuser.

She switched to one of the downward-facing cameras, to see what type of country they were flying over. Rocky outcrops.

"Can you set us down anywhere, van Heel?" On the ground they'd be stationary targets, but if the aircraft shot them out of the air, it would be worse. "Better yet, how far away are we from a town or city?"

Maybe they wouldn't have to fight it out at all if they could hide.

"Fifty kilometers from a twenty-person settlement, three hundred from one with twenty thousand."

You couldn't hide among twenty people.

"They might not be after us," Chaudry said.

It wouldn't matter. As soon as they got close enough to see the aircar, they'd stop it because no one went anywhere without a tracker.

"Maybe we should ask Han's family to pay Redmond off," van Heel said. "Since they're so ready to butt in."

"That was uncalled for," Radko said. "Especially since I was the one who asked for it."

"My family would help," Chaudry said. "If they could."

"We don't need amateurs," van Heel said. "Not from anyone's family, and I'm pleased to say that mine wouldn't. I haven't spoken to my mother in years, anyway."

"Clearly you don't move in the circles I do," Han said. "We ask each other for favors all the time."

He was right. Life was one massive game of requests and counterrequests.

Radko ignored the conversation going on behind her as she decided the odds.

The only weapon that might be of any use against another aircar was the Pandora field diffuser. They were designed for use in space, placed on the outside of ships to destroy tiny dust particles and meteor clouds before they got close enough to damage the ship. Radko needed a stable surface to concentrate the beam and to have something large to aim at. A diffuser at its normal setting could destroy micron-sized particles but nothing larger.

"Keep going for the moment," Radko said. "Head toward the larger town."

Van Heel changed course.

The aircraft behind them changed course, too.

Radko blew her breath out in a hiss. That wasn't triangulation. "They're tracking us."

Van Heel checked. "The tracker is disabled."

"Something is emitting a signal. Change course to the smaller town. Then see if you can find what it's using to track us."

Van Heel reset the course. The aircars followed. She rummaged through her bag of technology. "I'm sure I brought—" She pulled a small meter out triumphantly. "I did."

She set it up rapidly.

"Han, Chaudry," Radko said. "Check your weapons. I want them ready to use."

Han's would be fine, but Chaudry wasn't used to going armed, and she didn't want to single him out. Not at the moment.

"Got it," van Heel said triumphantly.

Her mobile tracker pointed directly at Han.

"Han," Radko said. "Empty your pockets."

"I really didn't think this day could get worse." Han pulled everything out of his pockets and dropped the contents onto the seat he'd been sitting in earlier. Among them was his personal comms, which he'd pulled out to check on Radko, back while they'd still been in the apartment.

"You left your personal comms on. I should toss you out of this car." In a way, she was as much to blame as Han because Han had shown her Renaud trying to call earlier. She should have insisted he turn it off. Of course, Redmond would intercept calls to or from Lancia. They were the enemy. The comms must have been transmitting ever since.

"Yup. It just got a lot, lot worse." Han picked it up to turn it off.

"Wait," Radko said. "Anyone else's comms on? No? Good.

Don't switch it off yet. We might be able to use it. Continue toward the settlement, van Heel."

She made her take the aircar low, near ground that looked less rocky. "As close as you can," she told van Heel, "and override the door for me."

Van Heel did.

Radko opened the door, leaned out, dropped the comms, then leaned back and wrestled the door closed again.

TWELVE

DOMINIQUE RADKO

"THAT MIGHT FOOL them for a few minutes," Radko said. And it seemed it did, for their pursuers didn't change course again.

"I apologize for getting us into this mess," Han said stiffly.

"Don't take all the credit, Han. Mistakes happen. We deal with it. Let's concentrate on staying alive now. Make for the town, van Heel."

If they were lucky, they'd get all the way there. It was simpler to hide in a town of twenty thousand people than it was to hide in the rocky terrain they were flying over.

"I'm glad it was you and not me," van Heel said to Han. "Being the first to muck up on a job stinks."

"I'm glad it was you, too," Chaudry said. "I'd have been devastated."

They could have made it worse by berating him, or by not saying anything at all. Instead, they tried to help although Chaudry's help could have done with some finesse.

They were fifty kilometers away from the town when van Heel said, "They've resumed following. A classic sector-search pattern."

"All of you, keep a watch for some cover where we might conceal the aircar."

"Have you looked at the terrain down there?" van Heel said. "We'll be lucky not to crash."

Rocky terrain made it harder to hide. Unless they could find overhanging rocks. "Put us behind something that will block our heat signature and get us down fast."

"Right." Seemingly seconds later, van Heel said, "Strap in. I'm going down fast."

Han would pull through, but it would be good to give him

something else to think about. Except she didn't need to, for Han was watching Chaudry's white-knuckled grip on the seat.

"You've never crashed before, Chaudry?"

Chaudry's grip became tighter.

Van Heel pulled up in a hard reverse thrust only meters from the ground. "I'm not that bad." They hit the ground with enough force to bounce. "She said go down fast."

"You know they have antigrav stabilizers," Han said. "You won't die, Chaudry."

"The force of the antigrav kicking in can cause more damage than outright impact. Because it kicks in so fast, it can cause trauma, cardiac contusions and atrial ruptures, asthma, traumatic iritis, and even orbital fractures."

"You know I only understood the first part."

Van Heel had brought them down in the center of a rocky outcrop. If they'd had something to cover the roof of the aircar, it would have been perfect.

"Nicely done, van Heel," Radko said.

"It was, wasn't it." If van Heel sounded smug, who could blame her? "Let's see what we've got out here."

They had to pop the emergency top for Chaudry to exit because the door didn't open far enough for him to squeeze out. Even then, it was a tight fit.

It took the three of them to boost him up, with Han doing the bulk of the work, grunting as he did so. "Lucky you're not fat, Chaudry."

"Fat is less dense than muscle."

Outside, Radko took time to appreciate just how cleverly van Heel had landed. They had cover from the rocks around them. The only thing that could get to them was a direct, overhead shot. She turned her attention to the Pandora field diffuser and started assembling the components.

"You know," Han said, "they set those things up on the outside of ships to destroy small particles. If you're thinking to use it to protect humans, it needs a stable surface. Holding it won't work."

Radko tapped the top of the aircar. "Define stable. Meantime, you and Chaudry take a quick look around to find enough shelter for all of us. If we bring an aircar down, it will fall right on top of us."

"Shelter. Right."

"Keep together and keep in constant comms."

"What's she doing?" Chaudry asked, as they moved off.

"I don't know, Chaudry. But that's a Pandora diffuser. She probably plans to use it after they've blown us to bits, to destroy any evidence we've been here."

Han would see.

Radko calibrated the diffuser until the beam was only atoms thick. She didn't test it. A deep gouge in one of the rocks would betray their location as fast as Han's comms had.

If they were lucky, the aircars would bypass them altogether. But they weren't going to be lucky. Redmond would have the technology to pick out individual heat signals. They'd find them. It was just a matter of how long.

Han and Chaudry returned from their circuit. "Not much to hide behind," Han reported. "A few overhangs, but more for one person than all of us. If they use lasers to cut into whichever rock each of us is sheltering under, we'll be crushed."

It would be safer if they moved away from the aircar. "Show me, Han. Chaudry, keep watch here with van Heel. Van Heel, can you slave the aircar screens to our comms?"

"These comms? These screens? You'd better all start thinking positive thoughts."

Chaudry looked as if he was doing exactly that. If he'd been on a ship, it might have worked. He was, after all, a linesman.

They set off together, Radko keeping an ear open for the sounds of aircraft and a careful note of the quickest, safest way back to the aircar. The ground was covered in loose rocks. It would be hard to run without turning your ankle.

The first part of their walk was silent. Radko nodded approvingly at one outcrop that might shelter them from the first pass of a strafing aircar.

"My father's going to the fleet?" Han asked eventually. "How bad is that for us?"

"It depends who he goes to. You know him better than I do. Whom would he approach?"

Han wrinkled his brow. "I can't imagine. Papa didn't have much to do with the fleet. I think he was scared of them. Especially Commodore Bach. He was always nervous around him."

Maybe Renaud had been worried Bach would find out he had changed Han's DNA, for the more Radko thought about it, the more convinced she was that it had been done with Renaud's knowledge.

"Back when I first joined the fleet, I was sure Bach was blackmailing him. I went to my father and asked."

"And was he?"

"He was . . . shocked, I think. Said of course not. That Bach would only do what was best for Lancia." Han shaded his eyes and squinted against the harsh sunlight, looking into the air for military craft. Radko could believe he'd welcome them, rather than this uncomfortable conversation.

Yet Han must have had a reason to suspect Bach. "So who was blackmailing him?"

"He never said. He changed the subject."

So Renaud was being blackmailed. Given it was around the time he'd "adopted" his new son, it was likely someone had found out about it. And was using it to what?

Blackmail didn't stop, not unless you stopped the blackmailer. Was that why Renaud tracked his son so carefully? Why he assumed that Han's going to Redmond meant a ransom payment first, or at best a trap, when others would assume a job for a soldier?

Her comms sounded. Van Heel.

"Two aircraft coming."

Two. Surely they could have come one at a time. Radko left Han behind in her run back to the aircar.

"Tell me where. Tell me when," she ordered van Heel.

Han arrived behind, breathing fast. "I never thought of myself as a slow runner before."

"Han, Chaudry. Weapons ready. Head for the cover you found earlier. Be prepared to avoid falling debris, and shoot everyone who exits." If anyone survived the crash, they would come out shooting. "Van Heel. Did you manage to slave the comms?"

"Yes."

"Good. As soon as I say, go with Han and Chaudry. If this thing comes down, it will come down hard.

Abram Galenos had always liked Pandora field diffusers. "They might not be enough to destroy a ship," he'd said, "but energy dispersed in a fine beam will still damage a ship enough to give you an advantage." They were old technology, replaced on many ships by stronger, newer field diffusers that you couldn't tighten the beam on.

Jiang Vega liked them, too, but that was because she considered them antiques, and she collected antique weapons.

Everyone on the *Lancastrian Princess* knew how to use them. And their strengths and weaknesses. It was also a test of skill, for matching a narrow beam to a high, fast-moving aircraft was well-nigh impossible. "Give me the coordinates of the first aircar, van Heel. Keep reading them out. One every two seconds."

Van Heel started to count off figures.

Radko counted with her, calibrating the diffuser as she went.

"Sixty eight five. Sixty eight four. Sixty eight three."

It was coming in a fast, straight line. "Go now. Quick."

She continued the countdown as van Heel ran. "Sixty seven nine. Sixty seven eight."

She pressed the button.

She couldn't see the beam, which was like a microns-thick, hot, molten wire. Didn't know she'd intersected the aircar until Han's, "Holy Jackson and Philtre."

"Take cover." And she raced for the nearest rocky overhang.

Pieces of aircar fell around her. One spinning propeller bounced and missed her by centimeters.

"Watch for survivors."

There were none.

The other aircar came down fast. Four soldiers exited.

"Stay under cover as much as you can," Radko said. "I'll take whoever is on the right. Han, take the left. Chaudry, center left. Van Heel, center right. Don't fire until we have to, for they'll know our range then." The Redmond soldiers would have longer-range weapons and could pick them off individually.

She moved fast around the rocks, rolling on one and sliding down. She waited, hardly daring to breathe, until she was sure the enemy hadn't heard her.

It gave her an idea. She reached down and picked up one of

the rocks. She hefted it in her hand, guessing the weight and balance.

She threw it as far as she could, off to the right of their attackers. Two soldiers headed that way.

Chaudry gave a small huff of understanding. Next moment another stone whizzed past. A good strong throw, it landed way past hers.

Radko waved her team on and out.

Then it was blaster to blaster. Hiding behind what little cover the rocks afforded. Firing when she could. She lost part of her sleeve taking the first soldier down.

Han fired past her, blaster melting the stone on the ground in front of them.

Radko ran forward. Again, and again.

A bitten-off scream behind her. Van Heel.

Radko took aim and fired.

A rain of stones from Chaudry, behind her, kept the Redmond soldiers occupied trying to defend their heads. She and Han picked the last two soldiers off.

VAN HEEL was down. They'd deal with her when the site was secure.

"Han, Chaudry, with me."

She entered the cabin of the Redmond aircar, fast, weapon ready to fire.

It was empty.

"Good. We'll take this aircar." It would be faster than their own, and right now, speed was the most important consideration. "Cover us," Radko told Han. "Chaudry, come back with me to collect van Heel. Then get back in here before any more aircars arrive."

Chaudry proved as strong as he looked. He picked van Heel up and ran.

"She's alive?" Han asked. He had the engines idling.

"I'm still conscious, idiot," van Heel said.

The weapon had caught her across her chest, burning part of one breast and the skin and flesh off the top of her arm.

"Let me see," Chaudry said.

"Take it up." Radko looked at van Heel. "Is there any chance that you know how to disable the tracking on a military vehicle?"

"Of course I can. But it will take hours and equipment we haven't got."

They didn't have the time, either. "When's Gunter's shuttle due?"

"Six hours," said van Heel.

This aircar was fast. They'd be at the spaceport in two hours. They'd have to hide for four. Even now, someone at Redmond headquarters—someone like van Heel—would be tracing their route. They'd work out where they were headed. Then they'd go through the expected deliveries at the spaceport. It wouldn't take much to associate Han's Lancian comms with an order coming from Lancia. They'd hack into Gunter Wong's call, then his sales records. They'd know where the shellfish were being delivered. They'd know exactly what Radko and her team planned.

What came after that would be far worse than anything they had encountered so far. If they continued with this plan, they'd be dead in four hours.

It was time to revise their plan. "Let's go steal a shuttle," Radko said.

THE closest spaceport with shuttles currently on the ground was a thousand kilometers away. Radko turned the throttle on full and set the autopilot. They'd be there in twenty minutes.

"Han, watch the boards, see if we're being followed. While you're doing that, see what shuttles will be in port, and identify them and where they're going."

Chaudry had already found the first-aid kit. He handled van Heel with a competence surprising for one who, according to his records, had been stuck in supplies for the six months since he'd graduated from fleet academy.

Radko watched him while she picked the lock on the first weapons cupboard. "You've seen action?"

"No, ma'am." Chaudry ducked his head and turned away, as if ashamed that he hadn't.

"But you've treated injured people before."

He didn't answer.

"Chaudry. It's not my business to know every personal detail of your life." Although a good team leader did. She was sure Bhaksir knew every detail of hers. "But if I have a skilled medical practitioner on my staff, I need to know it."

The cupboard door sprang open.

"My parents were doctors." She had to strain to hear Chaudry's mumble. "I was going to be a doctor."

Until he'd taken the Havortian tests. Did anyone ever refuse to go into line training?

Radko checked the contents of the cupboard. More blasters. Didn't they have better weapons? She moved on to the next cupboard.

"Speaking of knowing people," Han said. "You're very handy with a picklock."

"Thank you." Personally, she'd prefer a level-twelve linesman to open it for her. And what was Ean doing now, anyway?

Thinking about that—she apologized to the next cupboard as she broke the connection. "I am sorry, but we need the weapons." She didn't know if the Redmond aircar cupboards were line three or simply mechanical. Probably mechanical, and a linesman wouldn't have been able to open them.

She looked up to see all of them staring at her. "It's polite."

"Maybe I'm not the one you should be looking at," van Heel told Chaudry. She breathed in sharply as he sprayed painkiller on her wound, then out on a long hiss as the gel hardened. "That feels so good."

Radko went back to the weapons cupboard. This one, at least, had a long-distance armor-piercing gun. Not a big one, but large enough to put a dent into anything that might come after them. She handed it to Han.

The third cupboard held riot grenades. The smaller ones had a range of three meters, the larger ones could clear a large cargo space. Radko tucked all of them into her belt.

"We've three possible shuttles," Han said. "A small two-seater that will arrive around the same time we do. It's delivering machinery parts. A ten-seater delivering a shipment of iced Karamba mangosteen. It will arrive five minutes after we do. And a six-seater delivering passengers and cargo from a regular run between the Redmond worlds. It's been down half an hour already."

"We'll take the six-seater if we can." It had two advantages. They'd all fit, and it would be ready to leave—shuttles didn't stay long because of port charges.

They just had to get there in time.

Five minutes to go. Radko checked the location of the shuttle as the aircar slowed to descend and set them to land as close to the shuttle they wanted as she could.

She switched to manual at four minutes, for the automatic traffic controller would grab them if she didn't, and it would move them to a safer location. Five seconds later, the automated message came on.

"Attention, you are entering restricted airspace. This is an automated control area. Please hand control over to the automated controller."

She turned the volume down. "How's van Heel?" she asked Chaudry. "Can she run?"

"I can run," van Heel said.

Chaudry shook his head.

"Okay, you're responsible for her then. We'll try to stay with you. Get something to cover your mouth and your eyes." She tapped the gas grenades on her belt. "I might have to use these."

He nodded.

They were thirty seconds from landing when a human controller took over. "Back off, moron. You're in a spaceport, and you're too close to the shuttles."

She checked one last time to see if the shuttle was still on the ground. It was.

"The shuttle's there." She pointed in the direction the shuttle would be when they landed. Head for it." If they were lucky, the door would be open, and they could storm it. "Chaudry, get van Heel settled and strapped in. Han and I will take the shuttle."

Han looked at the weapon in his hands. "That's our plan?"

"The best plans, Han, are the ones you make up as you go along. They have an element of randomness. If you don't know what's coming, other people don't either."

They landed fifty meters from the shuttle. Better, it was partway through being loaded, so the doors were open. "Let's go." Radko set her blaster on stun and led the way down.

"I can walk," van Heel insisted, but was soon leaning heavily on Chaudry.

As they made their way across the tarmac, a ground car sped up from the other end of the field.

Radko waited until they'd slowed, then stunned the four occupants with her blaster. The ground car rolled to a halt.

"A bit extreme," Han said.

"Any closer, and they'd be in the shuttle blast when we take off. This way it's safer."

Radko quickened her pace. At the door to the shuttle, they were greeted by a blaster—not on stun. "I've called the authorities," the pilot said. "They'll be here soon."

Radko shot him. He toppled backward.

Chaudry made an inarticulate sound.

Radko hauled the pilot back into the shuttle. "Han, can you disengage the robots loading?"

"I—"

"I'll do it." Chaudry passed van Heel over to Han and moved over to the boards. Radko watched his swift hands as she prepared for takeoff. This was one thing he was used to doing.

"They do this in Stores?"

"All the time," Chaudry said. "It's Stores, after all."

She locked each door as the robots disengaged. "Han, disarm the pilot and strap him in." They could have ditched him, but it would take too much time to drag the body a safe distance.

Radko checked the fuel. Half-full. Enough for what they needed. She hoped.

"Pilot secure," Han said, at the same time as Chaudry said, "Robots clear."

Radko snapped the last door shut and fired the engines. Five seconds later, they started to rise.

How long before anyone came after them? It depended how long it took Redmond to link their missing aircraft with the stolen shuttle. Radko guessed they had an hour's lead, at best. She hoped it was enough.

In that time, they had to find the ship Gunter had arranged to transport the shellfish, intercept the shuttle pilot—who would already have started the delivery to Redmond—and convince him to collect them and return to his ship without making the delivery.

She counted on three things. First, that Renaud Han was genuinely fond of his son-who-wasn't; second, that Renaud and Gunter Wong were close friends; and lastly, that because it had been arranged at such short notice, the ship Gunter had called in to do the job was one that spent a lot of time ferrying shellfish for him. Which meant, she hoped, that Gunter had influence with the ship captain. Enough to convince him to pick up four strangers out of space, and order another jump, hours earlier than the one he already had.

She identified the ship. The *Mikasa*. The ship they'd caught off Lancia to Barth. How much was this diversion costing Gunter, for that had been a full passenger ship?

Half an hour. The timing was close.

"Han, I want you to call Gunter." Maybe it would have been smarter to call Renaud Han, but Renaud was probably still with Gunter anyway. "Tell him you have escaped from Redmond and that we're in space. We want to rendezvous with the shuttle that's delivering the shellfish to Redmond. We want the pilot to pick us up and return to his ship. We want the captain of that ship to organize his jump for as soon as we get on board."

They only had one chance at this. Further, they could only do it because the lag time between the two sectors was so short. Surely, someone had reported that by now. Radko couldn't see any reason for such rapid communication, yet someone had paid hefty premiums for that type of lag.

If this worked, Radko owed Gunter Wong and Renaud Han. A debt she'd be happy to repay.

Han opened his comms. "I hope no one at the barracks ever gets to hear about this."

So did Radko, but not for the same reason Han was hoping. She had to remember that Renaud had contacted someone at those barracks. Whoever he'd contacted would be looking out for Han.

If Renaud had convinced them it was serious.

"I mean it." Han looked at Chaudry and van Heel. "One word passes either of your lips, and you're totally dead. Or arrested on a trumped-up charge, at least."

Chaudry mimed zipping his lip. "Not from me."

"Van Heel?"

Van Heel struggled to reply, and when she did speak, it was through gritted teeth. Her wound must be bothering her more than she admitted. "I'll keep silent if you introduce me to your father. After all, I have to thank him for saving our lives."

Han looked at Radko.

"If you think this reflects badly on you," she asked, "how do you think it reflects on your team leader?"

"Badly," everyone agreed.

Radko laughed and checked the emergency suits as Han called Gunter.

There were six suits. Four of them were simple emergency suits with twelve hours of air and an emergency beacon. The other two were full suits, with controls. That was standard in a shuttle like this. The shuttle pilot always had a full suit—in case he had to do emergency repairs outside—and a standby suit in case that first one failed.

It was better this way. Han and Chaudry had probably never used suits outside of training. Ean had said his first time in space was terrifying.

"Yves." Gunter seemed to have aged in the time between calls. "We thought something went wrong."

"We were on Redmond. Have to avoid the enemy. Hello, Papa," as Renaud moved into sight as well. "I apologize for worrying you."

"We called Fleet Headquarters," Renaud said. "They will get you out."

Han kept talking, for they couldn't wait for the lag to catch up. "We got ourselves off Redmond. No need to stress, Papa. But I do need another favor from Gunter. I know it's a big ask, but people are chasing us. We need to get away.

"We booked passage on the ship that is taking the Gippian shellfish." He grimaced as he said it, but they all knew he had to mention it. "We're about to meet up with the shuttle. We want it to pick us up and take us back to the ship. We need you to tell the captain what's happening and that it's okay. We've less than half an hour before we intercept the shuttle. We need to do it fast. And you'll need to ask the captain to organize another jump. Before they realize what we've asked and stop him."

The delay for a reply took forever. Radko had time to think of five thousand ways that all this could go wrong. Renaud had a contact in the Lancian fleet. They might be listening to this call—but that could be advantageous. They might convince Gunter and Renaud to act fast.

Even if Lancia wasn't listening in, Redmond would certainly be. The only reason this plan might work was because even the military had to work with bureaucracy of the jump gates, and a captain who used the gates all the time might get precedence over someone who was trying to prevent that.

Chaudry moved over to check van Heel's wound again.

After the wait, it was Renaud who answered rather than Gunter. "Yves. We've organized a rescue. You'll be rescued soon."

Thankfully, in the background, they could hear Gunter talking. "Collect them and take them where they need to go."

"We don't need rescuing, Papa. It's a job. We ran into a little difficulty."

"Understatement of the century," van Heel murmured quietly to Chaudry.

"They might even compromise the mission if they try to help."

Radko nodded approvingly.

"We are nearly at the shuttle. We need to intercept it now."

Whoever Gunter was talking to was arguing back.

Gunter cut him off. "If you still want my business, you'll do this."

They were in range of the other shuttle and were out of time.

Gunter said in the background. "I'll give them the codes, Captain Engen." He repeated them aloud, much to Radko's relief. "The numbers are 436-243-043-341-094-334-234."

"Thank you," Han said, though the message wouldn't get back to Gunter for fifteen minutes. "We appreciate this, Gunter. And we'll repay any expenses as soon as we get home. Look after Papa and Mama for me, please." He clicked off, then sagged into his seat.

They had to keep moving. "Suit up." Radko chose the full suit for herself and gave van Heel the second full suit.

"I like your family," Chaudry told Han.

So did Radko, but this still had to be the strangest operation she'd ever been on. She punched in the code.

"Captain Engen. Gunter Wong called you a moment ago, asking you to change some plans."

Engen had a broad, flat face and a yellow net covering her brown hair. At least, Radko thought it was a net until it moved a tendril.

"You're not who I'm expecting."

Thank the lines for instantaneous communication within a sector. Han leaned into the call with her. "That would be me. I won't introduce myself, as I suspect people are listening."

"We're nearly at your shuttle now," Radko said. "As soon as your shuttle acknowledges it's ready to collect us, we'll suit across."

Captain Engen nodded and opened another comms line. "Come in, Leonard. Change of plan."

"These babies have a restricted shelf life. We can't change too much."

It was the same shuttle pilot who'd brought them on planet initially.

"This one pays more," Captain Engen said. "You're about to receive some visitors. Let them in, then return to ship."

"I'm in space."

"So are they." The captain clicked off, clicked back on again. "If the port authorities call, ignore them." She turned back to Han and Radko. "Here's the code for the shuttle." She pushed it through. "Tell Leonard to let me know when you're on board."

"Thank you." Radko clicked off and turned to check each suit before she clipped them into a line. Chaudry behind her, then Han, and lastly van Heel. Van Heel might be injured, but at least she'd done some ship work. "I'll do all the work. You stay put. If it gets too bad, close your eyes."

"What about him?" Han asked, looking at the still-unconscious pilot.

"We put the ship on auto and set a beacon. He'll come around in two hours." The biggest danger for the pilot was that Redmond would reach the shuttle before he returned to consciousness and blast him out of the sky. Unfortunately, she wasn't going to stay around to ensure he was okay. And she definitely wasn't going to mention that possibility to the others.

She zipped him into one of the remaining emergency suits. At least that way, he'd have a chance.

"You said he was staying here," Chaudry said.

"Just in case," Radko said. "Are we ready?"

The air lock was too small to fit all four of them. She broke the link between Chaudry and Han. "We'll go first."

Outside, through her helmet, she heard Chaudry swallow.

"Keep still, Chaudry," and made her voice commanding, and hoped he'd instinctively follow the order. "Close your eyes."

She linked herself magnetically to the side of the ship as she waited for the air lock to recycle, and listened to Chaudry gag in his suit. She'd once told Ean how important it was not to be sick in your suit, but if she even mentioned the word, then Chaudry's stomach would rebel properly.

"Are your eyes closed?" She snagged Han as he exited and clipped his line to Chaudry's belt. "If any of you have problems, close your eyes."

"But you still know." It was little more than a whisper from Chaudry. "You can't hide from it."

Radko fired her jets. The sooner they were in the other shuttle, the better.

The trip took seven minutes. Behind her she heard nothing but heavy breathing and choked-off gasps. One of them was hyperventilating, probably Chaudry. "All of you, keep your eyes closed." Didn't they take the trainees out into space anymore during training?

It felt like the longest suit journey Radko had ever undertaken.

She called Leonard when they were close enough for Leonard to track them from the shuttle. "Leonard, Captain Engen told you to expect us."

"Don't know that I'd like to be doing what you're doing."

Radko didn't mind. She liked space. She shifted, and changed direction to aim for the air-lock door she could see. "We're close to your hull. Can you let us in, please?" She turned her magnets on and clicked onto the hull.

The air lock opened. "Two of you at a time," Leonard said.

She unclipped Han from Chaudry again and pushed Han and van Heel into the air lock. "Be gentle. One of them is injured."

Outside, while they waited for the air lock to recycle, she said, "Chaudry, are you listening to me," and kept saying it until he was. "We're up against the side of a shuttle now, and I'm attached to it magnetically. You're safe."

As safe as he could be in a suit without any controls. It was for emergencies, after all.

"Ready?" Leonard asked, and opened the outer air lock.

Radko made her way in and dragged Chaudry in with her. "You're safe now," she said again. "You're in the shuttle."

Chaudry didn't relax until they were in the shuttle cabin proper.

"It's not how I'd choose to travel," Leonard told them, as Radko stripped off her suit, and helped Chaudry, then Han, out of theirs. Van Heel was struggling out of her own. "Hello, I remember you lot. I told you San See was a better port." He called up the ship. "Captain, I have our passengers. Heading back to the ship now."

"You realize," he told them, "that we spoiled an order of shellfish for you."

"They were our orders," Radko said. "I don't see why we can't eat them at dinner. We owe you."

"As if," Leonard said.

THIRTEEN

EAN LAMBERT

WORLDS THAT HAD stalled on providing line trainees suddenly managed to find extra linesmen in their fleet. There were so many trainees that eventually the Department of Alien Affairs put a hold on arrivals while new modules were ordered for Confluence Station because the *Gruen* was full.

"One can only imagine," Ean heard Helmo say wryly to his second-in-command, Vanje Solberg, "how they've all scrambled to get this far."

Fergus was a lifesaver. He organized the groups, organized which trainers were training who, and kept Ean sane.

He'd been Jordan Rossi's assistant before he'd come to work with Ean. "Rossi must be really sorry you're not still working with him," Ean said.

"Jordan's life isn't the same as it used to be. He hasn't got the same need for an assistant."

Ean couldn't see that Rossi was doing much different than what he'd always done. Fixing the lines. True, he was behind a protective curtain of military security now, but he was working harder than ever. Although, from what Ean could gather, a lot of Rossi's old life involved politicking, for it was no secret Jordan Rossi had wanted to be Grand Master of the line cartels.

Leo Rickenback—Rossi's old cartel master—was Grand Master now.

"Does Rossi still want to be Grand Master?" Ean asked.

"Even if he could, Orsaya wouldn't allow it," Fergus said, which wasn't an answer at all. "Not unless it benefits Yaolin."

Rossi as Grand Master of the line cartels wasn't as useful to a world going to war as a level-ten linesman who could communicate with the lines.

"Does he mind?"

"More important is do we think he's ready to train linesmen on his own?"

Ean could take a hint.

THE trainees were personally escorted and introduced by admirals of the fleet. Ean hadn't expected that.

"Let them come," Orsaya said, when Sale protested. "Don't hide him away like some relative you're ashamed of."

"The whole point of putting Ean on Confluence Station is to keep him away from people."

"Specific people. Let these people have their say. He's proxy for the one person they can't say it to."

The first to arrive was Admiral Trask of Xanto.

"Governor Shimson sends his regards," Trask said, as he looked around the area Sale had made public. It was bleak at the moment, with temporary chairs and tables bolted onto the floor, the only furniture in the room.

"And please pass my regards back to him," Ean said warmly. He liked Governor Shimson. Most people did, which was rare this high in politics. "Tell him he's welcome out here anytime he wishes to come," for Shimson was a single-level linesman himself.

He could feel Sale's disapproval right through his bones but ignored it.

"Allow me to introduce you to the Xanto linesmen." Trask moved over to where four soldiers stood at attention. "Spacer Thomas Peacock, Engineer, currently stationed on the *Foundation*." Peacock had six bars under his name. "Group leader Lina Vang, currently part of our own training team at Xanto barracks." Vang also had six bars under her name. "Spacer Alex Joy, also of the training department." Joy had no bars under his name. "And team leader Nadia Kentish, from the *Elysium*." Likewise, no bars.

"I'm delighted to meet you," Ean said. "I look forward to seeing you all at line training."

Kentish's stare back at him was more of a glare. Ean and Fergus had planned on splitting the linesmen into smaller groups for future training. They'd already worked out the groups, and they'd put Kentish under Hernandez. Maybe they should rethink that. Two strong personalities might clash.

Who would have thought, twelve months ago, that juggling people based on how well they got on with other people would be part of Ean's job description?

He said, half to Trask, half to the trainees, "We're putting the initial batch of trainees on the *Gruen*." It had worked last time, and it would get them used to being on line ships while he, Ean, still had control of the ship.

"So I hear." Trask looked at the soldiers. "Dismissed."

They marched out. Ean was glad to see Sale, and Captain Auburn—from Orsaya's staff—intercept them at the door and lead them down to a smaller room, where they could wait for their admiral in comfort.

"Can I offer you a drink? Tea?" Ean asked.

"A whiskey would be nice."

What did he do about that? He looked at Bhaksir, standing on guard with Hana, Gossamer, and Ru Li. Bhaksir tapped something into her comms.

"Please, won't you sit down," Ean said, before the wait got too long.

Trask sat. "So what level do you think the two singles are?"

The admiral hadn't given them a chance to speak. "I won't know until I hear them sing."

Trask nodded. "They have a choir on the *Elysium*. They put on two concerts a year for the crew. Team Leader Kentish was in that choir and most upset that we pulled her off two weeks before the show. Her captain wasn't happy either. Tried to get us to wait two weeks."

"It must be a good concert."

"Their captain thinks so. Thinks it is good for the ship. Morale is high for weeks afterward."

"Interesting."

"I thought so, too," Trask said. "Thank you," to Bhaksir, as she came across with the whiskey.

Bhaksir brought one for Ean as well. He didn't know what to do with it.

"Kentish was the lead female voice in that choir. Her opposite, the male, is left-handed as well, although he didn't do any line training. He should have been invalided out of the fleet years ago. A nerve in the left hand was severed, and the regen didn't take. Not a problem if he were right-handed, but a big issue when it's his primary hand. The captain downplayed the damage because apparently the ship is calmer when he's there."

What role did a captain have in retaining linesmen on his ship? If a ship liked a soldier because he or she was a linesman, was the captain more likely to keep them on? If so, maybe they should look at the more stable ships.

Trask gave a grim smile. "We'd never have known if we hadn't been looking for linesmen. Handedness is faster to search for than who did line training. It's in the crew medical records."

If Trask asked what level Ean thought the other man was, Ean would evade the question by saying he'd need to test the linesman, but he already knew he'd be a one. The ones monitored line and crew health. Combine that with a man who had a natural affinity for working with people, and no wonder the captain wanted to keep him there.

"You should have brought him in with the other line trainees."

Trask scowled into his whiskey. "I should discipline the captain."

How did you discipline a good captain without their ship taking umbrage? "How do his crew feel about him?"

"It's my most stable ship." He tossed the whiskey back in one swallow. "I wouldn't mind a little more stability in the New Alliance council right now."

Neither would Ean.

"Bringing in the Worlds of the Lesser Gods is a clever idea. With Redmond trapped between us and them like that, we might get rid of Redmond once and for all. But it was poorly done."

Orsaya must have known this was coming. She could have warned him. He might have known what to say. Ean swirled the drink he didn't want, then cupped it in his hands.

"Personally, I hadn't realized the split between them and Redmond was quite that bad, but sometimes the luck runs our way. Even so, we—as a council—could have offered the Factor enough if he had shown any interest in joining the New

Alliance." Trask put his glass down carefully and stood up. "Unfortunately, the way it was done makes it look like a power grab by Lancia."

Ean stood up, too. What did Trask want him to say? "I'll mention your concerns to Abram and Michelle."

"I'd appreciate it if you did. Maybe not mention any names. Only that some people are concerned."

Ean nodded.

"I'd best get these linesmen across to the *Gruen*." And Trask and the new trainees were escorted down to the shuttle by two members of Craik's team and two of Orsaya's.

Ean looked at the whiskey in his hand, looked at Bhaksir.

"Don't give it to me," she said. "I'm on duty."

Ean went to find Orsaya.

"Did you know he was going to say that?"

"People are concerned. *I'm* concerned. It was badly done, and exceedingly poor timing, with Lancia just managing the numbers."

"It wasn't Mi—" He stopped. Orsaya wasn't his friend, and he had to remember that.

The lines around Orsaya's mouth tightened. "That's what we're afraid of."

TRASK wasn't the last. A steady stream of admirals brought their linesmen along to meet him, and, "By the way, while I'm here, I'm a little concerned with Lancia's handling of the Worlds of the Lesser Gods. We're happy the Worlds of the Lesser Gods are considering joining the New Alliance, but the way it was done, allying Lancia with the Worlds . . . You might mention that it looks like a grab for power on Lancia's part."

Not mentioning any names, of course.

Sale took her concerns to Vega. Ean heard it through the lines.

"I don't know why we bothered taking Ean off the *Lancastrian Princess* if Orsaya lets in all and sundry."

"Believe me, I don't like it any better than you."

"Then I can stop it?"

"Admiral Galenos thinks it is beneficial."

"Damage control," the lines sang underneath Vega's words.

Sale might have talked to Abram as well, for she disappeared for hours one day, and when she came back, she stopped complaining about the visits.

Damage control.

The one person he could talk it over with was on a special mission. And Vega still hadn't told him where she'd gone.

Radko could look after herself. But still . . . *"If Radko calls Vega—or anyone on the ship—I want to know about it. If anyone mentions Radko, I want to know about it."*

The fleet ships hummed in assent.

So far, all his snooping had done was pick up Hana saying to Ru Li, "If Radko were here, you wouldn't dare say that."

Ean had no idea what Ru Li had said.

EAN was pleased when Admiral Katida joined them for dinner.

"It's like a flipping public house," Ean heard Sale mutter to Craik, out in the main watch room. "He'd be safer on the *Lancastrian Princess*. We should open a bar and charge for the drinks." She came over to the arch between the mess hall and the watch room proper. "Everyone who comes here hands over *all* weapons, Admiral Katida. Even you."

"Sale. Katida's a friend."

"Sale is doing her job." Katida handed over her blaster. Her lines were stronger today, more in tune with Confluence Station.

"You're listening to the lines," Ean said. She hadn't come to him for training, but her lines skill had improved. Hernandez? "Why didn't you come to me?" Ean had offered. Plenty of times.

"Lancia cannot be seen to favor Balian, Ean. Balian cannot be seen to be too close to Lancia." It was what she had always said. "But I am exceptionally happy I chose Hernandez for that first group of line training. She was my strongest linesman although at the time I wondered if I should have chosen someone with more stability."

Hernandez had certified as a level-seven linesman. She was, in fact, a ten.

"How long has she been training you?" Ean couldn't imagine Hernandez with the patience to teach anyone. Especially not an admiral of the fleet.

"Since you started training her. With time out when she was on the *Gruen*."

Ean spent dinner quizzing Katida about her training and how she was doing. He made her sing to the lines and listened critically, gently nudging her lines straight when they needed it.

"Not bad," he conceded eventually.

If Hernandez could teach Katida, she was certainly ready to train others. And if she could, then so could Rossi. Their plan of combined initial training until the linesmen could hear the lines, then splitting them into groups, should work well.

"High praise indeed. But how have you been, Ean? Without Radko when you need the support?"

Was she getting that from the lines?

"I'll be glad when she's back," he admitted. He could speak honestly to Katida. "Sometimes I want to—" He stopped. Admitting the urge to do harm to another person wasn't something one should say aloud. "The other part of it doesn't help."

"Other part?" Katida's voice was sharp suddenly.

Sale came to stand in the archway again.

"The Worlds of the Lesser Gods and Yu."

Katida's eyebrows rose at that.

"It's not really part of it, it just happened at the same time." It would be forever ingrained in Ean's mind as one thing, not two. "And while no one knows for certain, everyone thinks Yu told Radko she was to marry Sattur Dow in exchange for the mine Yu is going to give the Worlds of the Lesser Gods. Sattur Dow's mine, I mean."

Sale sighed.

Let her sigh. Katida would already know this. Abram and Radko both said she ran the best covert ops of any world.

"And everyone is telling me how foolish the whole thing is and how it could have been handled better. Abram and Michelle already know this."

"They come to you because they see the three of you as representing Lancia here at the New Alliance. If, as they fear, Lancia is moving to strengthen its power base and become de facto leader of the New Alliance, then saying it to Galenos or Lady Lyan will weaken their own position in the future."

"It wasn't Michelle's idea."

The song that was Katida's lines drooped and slowed. "Ean, that's the last thing anyone needs to hear."

"Why?"

"Because that means Emperor Yu is behind it, and Lady Lyan can't stop him."

"She *is* trying," Ean said.

"Perhaps if *someone* shared her problem, she'd get more support."

He didn't need Sale's, "Ean," to know not to say any more. He shook his head.

Katida sighed. "I'll be around if you need to talk, Ean," and moved on to discuss the line training that was to commence the following day.

AS they arrived on the *Gruen*, the antagonism of the first batch of trainees hit Ean like a wall of sound. It was a rancid taste at the back of his throat, a dizzying buzz that kept trying to pull the lines out of tune.

"Phwagh," Hernandez said. Ean had Hernandez and Sale with him but was without the support of Fergus, who was running experiments on the *Wendell*, and Rossi, performing emergency line repairs on a badly damaged warship. Right now, Ean would have preferred to be doing the repairs, leaving Rossi here with the mob.

Captain Hilda Gruen accosted Ean as soon as he stepped out of the shuttle. "I don't want these people on my ship."

Bhaksir and her team moved in to surround him. He was grateful for the protection.

"They're linesmen," Ean said. "This is the training ship."

"They're breaking my ship lines."

They certainly were. There were strong linesmen in the group, and some of them really didn't want to be here. What had they been told? "I'll do what I can." He sang line one as straight as he could. *"As soon as these people know who you are, they'll be better."*

Sale set the pace to the large cargo hold that was the de facto training area. "I'll talk to them first."

Ean nodded. Sale would give the usual pretraining spiel.

"These are the oxygen tanks, here's what to do if someone is overcome by the lines. Oh, and by the way, if the person next to you isn't looking at me, nudge them," for some multilevel linesmen got caught up in the ecstasy of line eleven and stopped thinking about anything else.

The first time he'd run line training, a Gate Union ship had tried to destroy the fleet. Today, at least, should be quieter.

He moved in to stand quietly behind the group while Sale gave her talk. He nudged one of the linesmen caught up in the ecstasy of line eleven and found it was Lina Vang. All four of the Xanto linesmen were together, Nadia Kentish looking as if she wished she weren't, the others looking just as aggressive.

He couldn't have familiar trainers at his back all the time, but today he wished for Fergus Burns and Jordan Rossi. And Radko, of course.

Sale followed the regular spiel with an extra talk. "I remind you that this program is top secret. The penalty for giving away these secrets is death. You have all signed agreements to this effect." She looked toward Ean. "Linesman Lambert. All yours."

He moved up to stand on the podium after Sale stepped down. Sale shouldn't be here either. Normally, she'd be out at the *Confluence*, and he could hear that the *Confluence* wasn't happy about her and her team not being there.

Nobody was happy today, it seemed.

"I'm going to sing a greeting to the lines," Ean said. "I want you to sing back, exactly the same tune. Don't be surprised if the lines answer back."

"Why is Lambert training us?" one of the linesmen demanded.

Ean hadn't been introduced to him via admiralty, but he knew him anyway. Arnold Peters had trained at House of Rigel. He'd made the first five years of Ean's stay there miserable. Or tried to, but Ean had been too happy just to be training.

"Lambert's not a linesman," Peters said. "He does everything wrong."

Sale moved back to stand on the podium beside Ean. "What's your name? Peters? Lambert is the leading linesman for the New Alliance. He is your senior. Treat him as such.

Continue with the attitude you have now, and you will be kicked off the program."

Not a good start at all.

Not for him, and definitely not for Peters, for the lines could feel the animosity, and the music was starting to change.

"Gently," Ean sang. *"They're new. They're not sure what they're doing."* Then he said to the trainees, "Introducing you to the ships, one line at a time. I'll name the line and the ship first, then I'll sing hello to them, then you sing back. Match my tune exactly."

He was used to the sea of faces looking up at him, wondering what was going on.

"Line one, the *Gruen*." He sang hello to the line. "You sing now. Remember, exactly the same tune."

"I'd rather be at my own choir practice," Nadia Kentish whispered to Alex Joy.

"Everyone sing," Ean said, for some of them hadn't. "Don't insult the lines by being rude to them."

"He is seriously as crazy as he used to be," Peters muttered to the linesman next to him.

Ean tuned him out. "Line one, Confluence Station."

FOURTEEN

EAN LAMBERT

AS EXPECTED, WHEN Ean introduced the trainees to line eleven, the surge sent most of the multiple linesmen to the floor. Even Hernandez.

Especially Hernandez.

Unfortunately, there were more linesmen than they'd ever had before, and half the paramedics were trainees as well. They'd trained in the techniques, but experiencing it firsthand was something else again. They struggled, because there was little you could do to help a linesman whose heart was trying to change its rhythm—except give them oxygen and wait until things settled back to normal.

Ean grabbed an oxygen tank and moved over to the closest linesman having trouble. It was Lina Vang. He pushed the mask over her face. Mind over matter, where the linesman's mind was trying to control the body. Luckily, human bodies were resilient.

"It's important to ensure they get oxygen," Ean told the two Xanto singles. He nodded at the other Xanto multilevel. "See how he's having trouble breathing. If you're not sure, oxygen never hurts."

Kentish grabbed another canister.

There were still a lot of unattended multilevel linesmen with breathing difficulties.

Ean raised his voice, amplified it through the *Gruen* speaker system. "Those of you who are still standing. You all know the theory about what to do for line-related incidents like this. If you're still standing and not administering oxygen, why aren't you?"

For a while, attending trainees was all he had time to do.

Afterward, he sat on the dais, elbows on his knees, and watched the paramedics attend the final few who still needed attention. Four paramedics attended one linesman. Ean could hear the distress in her lines. She was a four.

"Fix," the *Eleven* offered, and the other ships in fleet agreed. *"Fix."* Ean could feel the ship lines tapping at the edges of the line four.

"No, no. You're too strong." He could taste the strength and the alienness in the lines, even those of the human ship, who were learning fast from their fleet parent. Ean could almost see the linesman turning gray. He jumped up, but even as he stood, the four lines disappeared.

No.

He hurried across.

Sale stepped in front of him. "You can't do anything, Ean."

He knew he couldn't. The lines were gone. "But—"

"They sign a waiver. They know the danger."

No one expected to die from a line-induced heart attack, even if it sometimes felt as if you were going to.

"I hear you're killing off linesmen now," Rossi said at dinner.

They were all there tonight. Orsaya, Rossi, and Orsaya's people; Sale, and Craik and Bhaksir with their teams.

"Only the ones he doesn't like, Rossi," Ru Li said.

"I'll be careful, then," Rossi said.

Ru Li looked at Hana. "Did he just—?"

Orsaya took a sip of Yaolin whiskey and visibly savored it. Everyone had alcohol tonight. Nearly everyone, anyway. Hana and Ru Li weren't drinking, and nor was one of Rossi's minders. Ean wasn't sure if everyone else was drinking because Orsaya was there, because they were off duty, or because it had been a truly bad day.

"We've had preliminary results from the autopsy," Orsaya said. "Linesman Park showed evidence of narrowed arteries. Her medical records show no indication of it."

"Those medical requirements aren't there just so we have the healthiest crew in the fleet," Sale said.

Orsaya knew that already, and Ean could hear through the lines that Sale was only saying it to vent some of her own frustration.

"The medic on her last ship but one—six months ago

now—recommended surgery. She was booked to go in after her current tour."

Until the alien ships had come along, and everyone wanted linesmen. Or maybe they had planned all along she would arrive after her surgery, only there'd been this mad scramble to supply linesmen since Emperor Yu had announced Michelle's engagement.

Ean hated Yu more than he hated anything in his life.

Except, perhaps, Sattur Dow.

Rossi gripped the table. "A little strong, Linesman. We don't all need to share." He gritted his teeth, and Ean could hear the effort it took to loosen his hold.

"Sorry." But Ean couldn't stop it all, for little eddies of anxiety about Yu—and yes, some hatred, too—whirled around him and the ship.

Orsaya watched them.

Sale leaned across. "Are you okay, Ean?"

"Fine." It was a lie. Ship was agitated, and he with it.

Except, he wasn't on the ship. He was on Confluence Station, and the agitation was coming from the *Lancastrian Princess*. Coming from Ship himself.

Ean had never heard Captain Helmo express such strong negative emotion.

"If you—"

He held up a hand to silence Sale.

Whatever had caused Captain Helmo to momentarily lose his customary calmness was gone.

"Nothing," Sale said, putting away the comms Ean hadn't seen her take out.

"Nothing on my end either." Orsaya had her comms out as well.

The *Lancastrian Princess* was a flurry of activity. Ean could hear it, but couldn't tell what was happening. He asked the lines, and got literal answers.

"VIP module brought online."

He could tell that for himself.

"Welcome. Unwelcome welcome." The kitchens were busier than normal. Preparing for something.

Visitors. Unwelcome ones. Sattur Dow was the most unwelcome person Ean could think of.

"Sattur Dow is coming." Surely he didn't warrant that much activity. And not only from the *Lancastrian Princess*. The linesman on the Galactic News ship was getting excited.

"Coop, you have got to see this."

"I've a news show to deliver."

"No, no. You have to see this. A ship's arrived." He put it on Cooper's screen.

It was a massive fleet carrier, bearing the colors of Lancia. Apart from the mother ships—which were too expensive and big to move around much—this was the largest ship in the Lancian fleet.

"So," Cooper said. "Another warship. We're surrounded by the line-blamed things, Christian, and I have a show to get out."

Ean sang the image onto the main screen. If the other linesman were interested, so was he.

Everyone around the table stopped and watched, seemingly transfixed.

"But look, Coop." Christian zoomed in to a close-up of the ship, where there was an enormous pattern of light displayed on the hull.

A familiar pattern. Ean saw it every day on the shoulders of his crewmates.

"That is the Lancian flagship. That's—"

"Emperor Yu," Orsaya said.

JUDGING from the grim look on Orsaya's face as she rose and went into her apartment, closing the door behind her, Yu's arrival wouldn't be well received.

Ean left, too, into the semiprivacy of his own room, where he could still see—and hear—the others, silent at the table.

Michelle was sitting on Abram's couch in her workroom, staring at nothing. He heard a song of resoluteness, and a whiff of steely gray determination. Michelle had known her father would come. That was why she had insisted Abram stay away from the *Lancastrian Princess*, as well as Ean.

He sang gently to the comms lines. Yu would be hours yet. He got that from the ship chatter.

Michelle looked up. "Ean."

He could smell the fizzy citrus smell the lines associated with her. "Are you okay?"

She gave a smile that came out more like a grimace. "I'll be happier when it's over."

"One way or another," the lines whispered underneath her. Whose thoughts were they picking up? Ean shivered.

Michelle had never been one to let depression get in the way of practicality. She said now, "Sometime soon, I will invite you to a function to welcome my father and to introduce the Factor. I know you will be too busy to attend."

He didn't need the stress on "too busy" to understand what she meant, but right now he was more concerned about other things. "The Factor is here, too?"

"Of course. That is why my father has come. To introduce me to my betrothed." And by the sound of it, to make himself wildly unpopular. "No doubt, while he's here, he will petition to address the council."

Which, from the way she said it, was the real reason she thought the Factor and her father had arrived.

"But, Ean—"

"I understand. I'm a busy, busy linesman."

It got a smile out of her even if it didn't have a dimple. "Take care of yourself."

"I will. The lines will take care of you, too, Michelle."

THE *Lancastrian Emperor* departed as soon as Emperor Yu had settled into quarters on the *Lancastrian Princess*. How long did he plan on staying?

Sattur Dow arrived with the royal party. A day earlier, that would have been the worst of Ean's problems. Now it was the least of them. Radko was safely away. Ean hoped it was safely, anyway.

Dow brought his own entourage. Two servants and two assistants. With Emperor Yu's own Royal Guard, and the Factor's guards and support staff, the ship was nearly as full as it had been when Michelle and Abram had first gone chasing the *Eleven*.

How many support staff did one need?

Commodore Bach, in charge of the Emperor's security,

didn't need the sophisticated surveillance equipment he set up in the VIP area Helmo set aside for him.

"I am sure we'll be aware of any security issues that crop up long before Bach is," Helmo had said, aloud on the bridge, the day after that had been set up.

"Naturally," Ean sang, through line one.

Vanje Solberg, Helmo's second-in-command, looked at him in query.

Helmo smiled. "Message received, Vanje."

Solberg didn't ask. He and Helmo weren't as close as Wendell was with his second, Grayson. One day, Solberg would take a promotion and captain his own ship. The lines would notice his going, but they wouldn't miss him the way they missed Abram's not being there.

What made specific humans important to the lines on a ship?

Ship itself—the captain—was always important. But the ship singled out specific members of the crew as well. Esfir Chantsmith, for example, was a *Gruen* favorite. And no doubt Trask's singer with the damaged arm was a favorite on his own ship.

Sometimes, the lines didn't have anyone else. The *Confluence* looked favorably on Sale and the team she took across with her, but they were the ones who spent most of the time on ship. Who else did the *Confluence* have? Would the ship give up Sale when it got a new captain? Ean didn't think so. That was something else he would have to talk to Abram about.

But not right now, not while Yu and the Factor were here. Nor while Sattur Dow was, either.

Sattur Dow's staff's whole job seemed to be to find Radko. One—a youth named Ethan Saylor—kept calling Vega and demanding to see Radko.

"Spacer Radko is on special duties," Vega said, every time. "As soon as she arrives back on ship, I will notify Merchant Dow."

Saylor said the same thing every time after he clicked off. "Stupid bitch. You won't last long. I'll be sure Merchant Dow personally requests your dismissal."

Ean never heard him ask it of Dow, so he didn't know if

Saylor meant it, but he wasn't above a little petty meanness of his own in return.

"Too cool," he sang to line two, directing heating into Saylor's room; and when Saylor complained about that, *"Too hot."*

Which lasted until Captain Helmo twigged to what was going on, and said sternly to both Ean and the ship, "Not on my ship, you don't."

FIFTEEN

EAN LAMBERT

EAN HAD JUST strapped himself into the shuttle on his way to training the next day when a request came through from Abram.

Linesman Lambert, as the senior New Alliance Linesman, you are required to attend the *Confluence* today.

Ean wasn't sure if it was a real summons or another of those he was supposed to be too busy to attend.

"Do I say I can't go?" he asked Bhaksir.

"You can't ignore a summons from Admiral Galenos."

"But suppose he doesn't want me to go?"

"He wouldn't have asked you if he didn't, would he?"

Ean checked the whereabouts of Michelle. She could tell him if he was supposed to attend or not.

Michelle was breakfasting with her father. Talking reasonably, but the *Lancastrian Princess*'s lines had a faint brown taint that told Ean she was choosing her words carefully.

"Everyone who visits the alien ships must request to, and be cleared by the committee. I cannot send Merchant Dow with the Factor."

"And who controls this committee, Daughter?"

Not a good time to interrupt her.

"Shuttle's waiting for you, Ean," Sale said, through the comms. "We need to get there before the main party."

He still didn't know if Abram meant him to go or to refuse. He called Fergus and Hernandez. "Can you run line training today, please? I need to go out to the *Confluence*."

"The grand tour," Fergus said. "We heard about it. We'll treat your trainees gently."

Ean jogged down to the shuttle bays, Bhaksir's whole team behind him.

THE *Confluence* was happy to greet them.

It had been a patient ship, waiting for its crew, and there were some people Ean didn't want on it. Like Arnold Peters. Maybe he could convince Abram to let the *Confluence* choose its own crew. It wouldn't choose Peters.

The song of the *Confluence* changed to a pleased purr.

"Ean. What did you do?" Sale asked.

Ean was glad Sale's comms beeped then. "*Lancastrian Princess* Shuttle Four requesting permission to dock."

A team of Yaolin guards stepped out, followed by Admiral Orsaya.

They'd left Orsaya on Confluence Station. Shuttle Four must have collected her on the way. Why hadn't she come with Sale and Ean? How close behind them had Shuttle Four been all this time?

Governor Jade of Aratoga stepped out next, then the Factor of the Lesser Gods. It was hard to pick who wore the most gold jewelry. The Factor was followed by his bodyguards—six of them—and after him, Abram.

The Lancastrian soldiers on board the *Confluence* saluted. Ean didn't.

One of the bodyguards was smiling.

The Factor moved up to where Governor Jade halted.

"Linesman," Governor Jade said to Ean, and the chill that had come in with the visitors rolled away with the warmth of her words. "Allow me to present the Factor of the Lesser Gods. Factor, this is Linesman Ean Lambert, leading linesman for the New Alliance."

"Welcome to the *Confluence*," Ean said.

Abram nodded at Ean, as if he was supposed to be there. Ean was relieved.

"A ten." The Factor glanced at the bars on Ean's shirt. "I thought all the higher-level linesmen worked with Gate Union."

Ean didn't need the lines to know he was lying. It was common knowledge that both Ean's contract and Jordan Rossi's belonged to the New Alliance.

"We have two level-ten linesmen working with the New Alliance." You couldn't hear the smile in Abram's voice, but it came through clearly on *Confluence* line one.

Abram wasn't lying, for if you took Ean to be a level twelve they still had two other tens. Jordan Rossi and Ami Hernandez. Not that Grand Master Rickenback had certified Hernandez yet. For the moment, Admiral Katida preferred that no one knew the Balians had a ten as well.

Abram indicated the cart that waited for them.

Sale didn't like the cart. She made her crew march to the bridge most days. "If you exercise while you're here," she'd said once, "you don't need to go back to ship and spend hours in the gym."

Ean thought it was because the *Confluence* didn't like the cart, but he'd never told Sale that. The *Confluence* didn't see the point of the cart. *"Not need. Faster,"* and showed an image of something that looked like a pipe. He'd drawn a picture of the image and shown it to Sale, who'd shaken her head. She'd not seen anything like it. Maybe Ean had misinterpreted the image. Whatever it was, one day he'd find it. Or Sale would.

The cart was a long box with an electronic motor at the front, a seat for a driver—Craik—and a long, flat tray at the back others could stand or sit on. A raised bar along the center allowed you to hold on.

"I hate these things," Governor Jade said, stepping on and gripping tight. Two of Craik's team stepped up either side of her. The others stepped on as well, all except the bodyguard who'd been smiling.

His face was alight with wonder.

A linesman, though he didn't have bars on his shirt.

Confluence line eleven surged—not Ean's doing.

The linesman gasped and tried to breathe. Sale reached for the nearest oxygen with a scowl, while Craik and Losan stretched the linesman out on the floor. Craik placed the oxygen mask over the man's face.

Abram's voice was hard. "There is a reason we asked you not to include linesmen in your party."

"A linesman." The Factor looked bemused. "Surely you are mistaken." The overriding emotion emanating from him was irritation rather than surprise. He glanced at the bodyguard beside him.

The bodyguard's nod was so slight, Ean wondered if he had imagined it, but he'd had a lot of practice lately interpreting the secret deals people in power made. He recognized an agreement when he almost didn't see it.

"Our linesmen undergo rigorous training before we allow them on board the alien line ships," Orsaya said. "The lines are too strong for them. We need to acclimate them first. Without that training, the strength of the alien lines can be incapacitating on occasion."

Training Ean should have been conducting right now. Hernandez was berating the linesmen for their sloppy responses. Or she had been, until the surge of line eleven. Now she was waiting for the paramedics to declare everyone all right. It was another new batch of paramedics. Ean would be glad when they were all trained. He hadn't realized how much they had come to rely on the paramedics Abram had supplied, or how skilled those paramedics had become.

"Given that this gentleman is here without bars on his shirt"—Orsaya indicated the linesman on the floor—"one can only assume he is here dishonestly." She looked directly at the Factor as she said it.

"So it would seem." The Factor frowned down at the gasping linesman.

"I take full responsibility for this." The bodyguard looked at the Factor. "My apologies for the deception, sir. I was aware of what this man was. I'd heard about the ban. I thought it was a security measure. I didn't realize it was for their own safety."

He couldn't say anything else, could he. Not if the Factor still wanted to see the ship.

"I am disappointed in you, Captain Jakob," the Factor said. "We had strict instructions to bring no linesmen."

Jakob bowed in apology.

If it had been Michelle in the Factor's place, she would have admitted she'd been part of it and not made Abram—for Ean was sure from the way he moved and spoke that Jakob was more than a simple bodyguard—take the blame.

The linesman improved enough for Sale to help him sit up. "The confluence. I thought it had gone. It's . . . amazing."

Ean knelt beside the other man. "Linesman?" He made it a question.

"Glenn. Linesman Glenn. House of Sandhurst. Level seven." It was an automatic reply, one linesman to another.

Ean hid the disquiet the information gave him. Linesmen level seven and above remained with the cartel houses. They also wore house colors. The fact that Glenn hadn't meant what?

"How do you feel?"

"I'm fine, I think." Glenn smiled again. "I was at the confluence, but it was nothing like this."

Sometimes, it seemed to Ean that he was the only linesman who'd never visited the *Confluence* back when no one had known it was a ship trapped in the void. "Good." He stood up. Based on his experience with linesmen, Glenn would be fine.

"The linesman stays with the shuttle," Orsaya said. "The stronger lines on the bridge could kill him. We had an incident yesterday where the lines accidentally killed a linesman."

The Factor nodded, as did Governor Jade. News traveled fast.

"So how dangerous are these ships?"

"You saw the news the other night, Factor," Governor Jade said. "Deadly, I'd say."

"To their own side, I mean."

"Dangerous," Ean said, because he wanted them to realize that.

"Dangerous and deadly." *Confluence*'s lines sounded smug.

There might have been a bit of miscommunication there. Not to its own side, surely. *"Surely that's not how you want to be thought of?"* But he'd forgotten, this was a warship.

He'd also forgotten he hadn't planned on singing in front of the Factor.

"The singing, Linesman?" the Factor asked. "What does that signify?"

He'd jumped on a single tune very fast. Almost as if he'd been waiting for a song so he could ask the question. How much did he know?

"Are you kidding?" Linesman Glenn said. "That's Crazy Ean Lambert. He always sings."

"Sings?" the Factor asked. Did Ean imagine it, or was it taking an effort to keep up the friendly facade?

"And he's famous right now," Glenn said. "Because the New Alliance is so desperate for tens, Lady Lyan paid millions of credits for him. Even though he sings. The linesmen are still talking about it." He looked at Ean. "Sorry, I didn't mean that the way it came out."

But he had, and everyone on ship knew it, including the *Confluence*, and the ship didn't like it. Or was reflecting someone else's dislike of it, rather. Ean guessed it was Sale, and was warmed by her unspoken defense.

"I'm used to it," Ean told Sale though Glenn had been the one to speak.

"We're not. And we don't appreciate the insult to our linesman."

"Not here. Wrong place. Wrong time."

Something must have got through, for Sale straightened and looked at Abram. "Sorry, sir."

Yes. The *Confluence* was listening too much to Sale, and she was listening back.

"We should move on," Abram said with a slight smile. "We've a trip ahead of us."

And Abram would have shut down the conversation long ago if he hadn't wanted to hear it.

Sale looked at Bhaksir. "Leave someone to guard Linesman Glenn."

"Yes, ma'am."

Bhaksir chose Ru Li and Gossamer, and she stayed as well.

Ean listened to Glenn talk to them as the tour made the long trek up to the bridge.

"It's hard, not wearing the uniform when you're from a cartel house. You feel as if you've suddenly become invisible."

Ru Li danced around the shuttle bay, seemingly unable to keep still. "I hope they paid you a lot of money to do it, then. *I* wouldn't become invisible for anyone."

The dance took him around the whole bay. It was a Ru Li-style sentry march.

"They're not paying money." Glenn rubbed his hands together. "I get to take part in an experimental program House of Sandhurst is supplying linesmen for."

Captain Jakob let go of the center rail momentarily, grabbed it again as Craik turned into another corridor. Ean leaned over. "Are you all right?"

Jakob didn't pay any attention to Ean.

"I get to work with people like Dr. Quinn, who's done so much to open line theory recently," Glenn said.

"How do you open line theory?" Ru Li asked. "Make it available to the public?"

Jakob twitched.

He couldn't be listening to Glenn. Could he? How?

"Of course not." Glenn looked at Ru Li as if wondering if he was a little simple. Which was exactly what Ru Li would have been aiming for, knowing Ru Li. "Information like this is so classified even the linesmen don't know about it."

Ru Li and Gossamer would find out what they could from Glenn. Ean's job was to stop the snooping. He sang under his breath, searching for unknown line fives on the ship. Yes. There.

And there. And there.

Someone was leaving listening devices along the way. He was tempted to send a high-pitched noise through line five, to see what Jakob would do. No, it was better if he didn't know they had been discovered. Not yet, anyway.

They stopped and stepped off the cart to look at the immense image on the wall of the crew room. Another listening device joined the others.

"Impressive, isn't it," Governor Jade said. "I predict a new art movement will sweep the galaxy over the next few years."

One of the Factor's bodyguards stepped close. The ship seemed to consider him while he considered the image.

"No, not that one," line one said, and the other lines agreed.

That was strange. The whole ship was a little strange today. Ean would be glad when the Factor and his people were off the ship.

"Or that one," as they moved on and another of the party stopped to inspect a door.

"Not that one, either," the other lines agreed.

If Ean had been alone, he would have asked what the ship was doing. But he wasn't alone, and he didn't trust the Factor or his so-called bodyguard.

Back at the shuttle bay, Ru Li was saying, "According to Jordan Rossi, the only good line scientist is a dead one."

"You've met Jordan Rossi." The lines were full of Glenn's awe.

"A couple of times. Haven't you?"

"Not Jordan Rossi. Or Rebekah Grimes, either. What's she like?" He asked the question as if he thought she was still alive, working for the New Alliance.

Ru Li looked at Bhaksir and Hana.

"I don't think we met her," Bhaksir said.

Beside Ean, Jakob relaxed.

The group moved on, Sale, Abram, and Orsaya answering questions.

Another five joined the chorus of strange line fives. Should Ean do something about it? Like ask Jakob to empty his pockets? Not yet. Wait until their visitors were gone. Otherwise, they'd plant something else, something harder to detect.

They reached the bridge. Sale and Abram started explaining the setup to the visitors. Only one person really saw anything. The woman who'd stepped out of the shuttle in front of Glenn. Ean was certain she could hear the panels.

The Worlds of the Lesser Gods had come well prepared. A multilevel and a single-level linsman.

Should Ean say anything? Or pretend he hadn't noticed?

Orsaya came over to stand beside him. "Is everything all right?"

Ean looked at the single-level linsman.

"I hear you." Then, as the Factor came over to join them, "How are you finding it so far, Factor? Somewhat of a letdown when you cannot even read the boards."

"It's impressive just in the size," the Factor said. "I have warships whose whole crew would fit onto this bridge. And everyone on board would be deaf and blind to it. As am I. Tell me, Linsman," to Ean. "What do you see?"

The correct question was, "What do you hear?" but Ean chose to interpret it literally. He knew what Sale couldn't see. "Flickering lights. A starfield."

"And only linsmen can see this?"

Most people didn't yet know about single-level linsmen. "Certified linsmen, and those who failed certification," and

Ean looked deliberately at the single level the Factor had brought with him.

The Factor followed his gaze. "I see."

"We all see," Orsaya said. "Let's ensure it doesn't happen again. You won't get off so lightly another time." She smiled, all teeth. "You have used up some goodwill already."

Governor Jade was talking to Sale. "I'm not sure," Sale said. "Ean?"

He moved across to them.

Behind him, the Factor turned to Orsaya. "I believe you made a study of linesmen, Admiral."

"I have, yes."

"Particularly the higher-level linesmen. Did you study Lambert at all?"

"Of course."

"He came out of nowhere to become the leading linesman for the New Alliance."

If the Factor had been a linesman—which he wasn't—he would have felt the chill sweep the ship though Orsaya's voice retained its normal crusty tone. "Out of nowhere, Factor? He was the only linesman working with high-level lines for six months."

Had the Factor timed his question so that only Orsaya and some of the guards were close?

Abram moved to join Orsaya and the Factor. Jakob intercepted him, asking about something on the wall. Abram stopped to answer him.

Deliberate? Or coincidental.

If it was deliberate, then the Factor hadn't heard Ean could listen through the lines, for otherwise he'd know that no matter how he kept his voice down, or how many people Jakob kept away, Ean would hear him.

"So Lambert was lucky. In the right place, at the right time. The rumors of his abilities . . ." The Factor let the words trail off.

Yes, he had been in the right place, and no one could deny that. Ean couldn't help his smile.

"It depends what you mean by rumors, Factor. Maybe if you asked straight out what you want to know, I could answer your question."

The Factor looked at her as if no one had spoken to him bluntly before. Maybe they hadn't.

Orsaya waited for his response.

"Admiral Orsaya, you have a level ten of your own under contract. Surely it irks you that Lambert was elevated above him merely by a combination of circumstance and birth. Jordan Rossi is a strong ten. Possibly the strongest now that Rebekah Grimes has gone."

He knew Grimes was dead even if Glenn didn't.

"Yes, Rossi is strong." Orsaya bared her teeth in another smile. "But Factor, don't make the mistake of assuming Lambert is weak simply because of his reputation. It takes resilience and determination to get where he is."

Was it a warning? Or a threat?

Abram joined them. The Factor nodded and turned to where Sale was explaining how they had integrated the human equipment alongside the alien boards. The guards were asking plenty of questions. Intelligent questions. Expert questions. Ean was pleased when Sale gave one of them a flat stare.

"That's classified."

Eventually, Abram glanced at his comms. "I'm afraid that's all we have time for on this visit."

"Surely a few more moments," the Factor said, although Ean had the feeling he was as impatient as Ean was for this trip to be over.

Abram sounded regretful. "Apologies, but our time is heavily scheduled. I am sure your time is, as well. Governor Jade is to address the council this afternoon, and Admiral Orsaya and I have a meeting with Admirals MacClennan and Katida."

"Of course." The Factor smiled although his smile didn't reach his eyes.

Jakob secreted one final device, and they all stepped back onto the cart.

Governor Jade gripped tight. "Surely the aliens had a better transport system than this. Or did they run all the way to the bridge?"

"We don't know, Governor," Abram said. "We certainly haven't found anything we identify as transport yet."

The ship was considering the single-level linesman again.

"*Yes?*"

"*No*," Ean said. "*She's banned.*"

"*But she is promising,*" the ship said.

"*No.*" He was singing in front of people he didn't want to sing in front of, but he couldn't stop there. "*She works for bad people.*"

"*We like her.*"

Ean sighed. "What's your name?" he asked the single-level linesman. If Michelle did marry the Factor, then theoretically she could be one of the crew. And why was the ship suddenly considering who was suitable and who wasn't?

"*You said we could,*" the ship reminded him.

He had?

The linesman didn't give her name. Ean didn't care. He'd get it later. Abram would know.

"I realize this is a miracle ship," Governor Jade confessed to Sale, as the cart made its way back the way it had come. "But it still scares me. I'm happy to get back to something human."

She didn't have to say it aloud.

"*We don't mind,*" the ship lines said comfortingly in Ean's mind. "*We don't want her anyway.*"

Ean didn't answer that. There was nothing he could say.

The *Confluence* responded more to nonlinesman than the *Eleven* did. Was that because most of the people who came to it were nonlinesmen? Or was it because—being a larger ship—it had housed nonlinesmen in the past?

AFTER the shuttle had left, Ean said, "Jakob is not coming back on this ship."

"Give us a reason. We can't ban someone just because you don't like them." Sale paused to think about that. "Or can we?"

"What about leaving bugs around?"

Ean sang them through the ship, finding the tiny line fives. As he found each one, he channeled the signal back to the other devices that had been placed. When he was done, the only things these little lines were communicating with were each other. Sale picked them off the wall as he located each one.

"Normally we'd leave them." She tossed the last of them into a container. "Doctor them to send back misinformation. Are you sure that's all, Ean?"

"I think so."

"We'll take these back as evidence. That woman. She was a linesman?"

"Did you know?"

"A blind man could have seen the way she reacted to the boards."

Smugness washed through the lines. It came from the ship, not from Sale. You couldn't fool its people.

Its people? *"These are not your people. They're Helmo's."*

Did he imagine that the ship deliberately ignored that? Could lines indicate deliberate ignoring anyway?

"This ship," Ean told Sale, "is acting strangely."

"You have to expect that, Ean. It's just had unpleasant visitors."

Sale was as bad as the ship.

WHEN he got back to Confluence Station, Ean called Vega. He made the line secure.

"No," Vega said. "I haven't heard anything. On jobs like this, Lambert, you don't, and you don't want to, either."

He hadn't been calling about that, but it was good to have the report.

"What if she's in trouble?"

"We expect her to get out of it herself. The only time she'll send a message is if she's in so much trouble she can't get out of it. It's called a dead man's message, for obvious reasons, so you'd better hope we don't hear from her."

Ean fervently hoped they wouldn't, and equally fervently hoped she'd be back soon. "I need to talk to Linesman Glenn." Glenn had mentioned an experimental line project, and Ean wanted to know more. He might not tell Ean, but he would tell Jordan Rossi. If Rossi chose to cooperate, and given it was line business, he would.

"You're too late."

He hoped she meant they'd sent Glenn home, and not the way she'd made it sound.

"Glenn had a line-induced heart attack on the way back in the shuttle. They couldn't do anything for him."

Ean stared at her image. "Line eleven's been quiet all afternoon."

Lemon-sour Vega washed over him. "So say the linesmen on board this ship. Someone didn't like his being outed as a linesman."

A heart attack. Someone had come well prepared.

"We're going over ship records now," Vega said. "If you can think of anything he said or did that might have triggered an outcome like that, let me know."

"Glenn was about to start working on a top secret line project. House of Sandhurst was involved. And someone called Dr. Quinn. It's probably not important, but Jakob didn't like his talking about it."

"I'll see what I can find out," Vega said.

The first thing Ean did after he clicked off was send a request to all the fleet lines. If Radko called, he wanted to know the instant it happened.

Vega called back half an hour later. "You have good instincts. We'll never make a decent soldier of you, but you can be useful on occasion."

That was just Vega's manner. Ean could hear through the lines that she was pleased with what she had discovered. "Your friend Dr. Quinn works for TwoPaths Engineering."

TwoPaths Engineering was a Redmond company. They made spaceships based on the plans of the *Havortian*, the alien spaceship that had been discovered five hundred years earlier. They didn't realize the New Alliance knew that. Or the fact that TwoPaths' sister company—FiveTrees Consolidated— was building weapons based on those same plans.

"Aren't the Worlds of the Lesser Gods enemies with Redmond now?"

"Supposedly," Vega said. "Which makes you wonder why the Factor is running around with a Redmond-based linesman on his staff."

Ean sighed, and Confluence Station sighed with him. And speaking of which, Confluence Station was still too chirpy for a station whose equivalent of its captain was in intensive care.

"Are you still there?" Vega asked. "Because I've nothing else to say. I'll keep you informed." She clicked off.

Ean stared thoughtfully at the comms. The ships were quiet. The *Lancastrian Princess* was the most uneasy. Helmo—and Michelle's—worry about what would happen now permeated the whole ship. On the *Wendell*, Wendell was dyeing his hair, and everyone on the ship exuded satisfaction about that. What was the story there?

The *Gruen* was content. Hilda Gruen was pacing her ship, pulling the occasional trainee into line. "I don't care if you're a level twenty. On my ship, you do as I command."

Ean had always thought linesmen were treated as special. It didn't seem to be the case on fleet ships. Or maybe it was because Gruen didn't have any crew but the trainees.

"We've got crew," the *Gruen* lines told Ean, and showed him. The two original Aratogan teams who'd been assigned to the ship. Along with Esfir Chantsmith.

The Blue Sky Media ship's captain was drunk again. He always drank.

The Galactic News ship buzzed with enthusiasm. Christian, the engineer, was talking to Cooper, the producer, about something.

And Confluence Station was going along as if everything was normal.

Maybe, for the station, it was.

"Where is Ship?" Ean asked, and used the tune that denoted the station. Had he upset the station by asking the obvious, when the station commander was still unconscious in hospital?

Confluence Station obligingly showed him a dimly lit passage where the tired, older man Ean recognized from Patten's heart attack was talking to a mechanic.

That was Ship?

Ean could sense, roughly, where on the station it was. *"I need to talk to him."*

Line five obediently opened a line.

"It's okay," Ean sang. *"I'll do it face-to-face."*

"Face-to-face?"

"Human to human," and Ean tried to convey the idea of two physical beings talking together. He wasn't sure he succeeded.

"Why, when you have the lines?"

"Because." Why? *"Because Ship doesn't have lines like we do. Not the same."*

He got brown confusion and the scent of eucalyptus.

He looked around for Radko, remembered she wasn't there. "I'm going for a walk," he told Bhaksir.

"Do you need to?"

Did he? He was doing his job, finding out more about the lines. "Yes."

"Where, and for how long?"

"I need to talk to the man who was in Patten's office when he had the heart attack."

"Can't you use the comms?"

"You sound like the station."

Bhaksir gave him a look that showed she didn't understand what he said. "It would be safer."

"I've a station of lines to protect me."

"That doesn't stop you getting into trouble," Ru Li said. He snapped to attention as Bhaksir glared at him. "Sorry, ma'am."

"For that, you're on bodyguard duty," Bhaksir said. "You and Gossamer. Keep your comms open, and I want to hear from you every five minutes."

"Five minutes is a little excessive, ma'am."

"Why don't I show you my route, so you can see us all the time." Ean sang it up on screen for her. "And hear us."

"Did you just volunteer for bodyguard duty?" Gossamer asked Ru Li, as the three of them left. "You knew she would pick you because of what you said."

"It's more fun than being stuck in a boring control room," Ru Li said.

Should Ean remind them that Bhaksir could hear everything they said?

CONFLUENCE Station Ship had moved on to the engine room by the time Ean caught up to him.

Bose engines were reputedly quiet, but they still made a lot of noise up close.

A station didn't need a Bose engine for everyday running, but it needed one for the initial jump through the void to position the station, and since the biggest cost was the engine itself, the Bose also powered the station.

Ean looked at the line chassis. Where did it end if they didn't have a bridge?

Up close, the man the station had identified as Ship looked more tired than he had the other night, if that was possible. The name on his shirt was Ryley.

"Nonstation personnel aren't allowed in this area," Ryley said.

"We're part of the fleet," Ean said. Did Ryley know that he meant *Eleven*'s fleet?

"Even fleet personnel need clearance." Ryley turned and led the way back. "I don't know how you even got through the doors."

"I do," Ru Li murmured, as they turned to follow.

Ean hurried to walk abreast of Ryley. "How long have you been on this station?"

"Is that any of your business?"

"Twenty years," the Station sang in his mind, and Ean smelled eucalyptus again, only this time it was younger eucalyptus.

Ean blinked. Twenty years. These were human-built lines, cloned from the *Havortian* and from the *Havortian*'s descendants. They'd had five hundred years of human conditioning. Unlike alien lines, they understood the concept of years.

"I didn't know you were that old."

Ryley looked at him.

"Older," the lines said.

Ean got a black sense of a long period of time. Alien, yet familiar, intermixed with human years. That, and something he'd experienced not all that long ago, a time when he'd been talking to Katida. He frowned, trying to place it. And got it. The fresh, new-cloned feeling of the station Governor Jade had co-opted for Aratogan use before the fleet had moved to Haladea III.

"You can remember what you were before? The Havortian*?"* All human line ships had been cloned from the *Havortian*.

"Havortian*?"*

Ean sang the tune that had recognizably been the freshly cloned station he remembered from months earlier. He was unsuccessful, for all he got was lime-green uncertainty in return.

"How old is the station?" Ean asked Ryley.

Ryley looked at him again. "Thirty-six years."

"And you've been on it for twenty?"

A strong, purple unease flooded the lines. This man was Ship all right.

So Ship didn't have to be the captain. Which meant Sale might still be able to be Ship on the *Confluence*, if she wanted to be.

"If you knew that already, why did you ask me earlier?"

"I didn't know before. The station told me."

The purple unease grew.

Ryley stopped at a door. "Here's the no-go zone." He tapped the yellow warning sign. AUTHORIZED PERSONNEL ONLY BEYOND THIS POINT. "See that. It means you."

"I don't think that's going to stop him," Ru Li murmured.

He got a sharp glance from Ryley. "Or your friends."

"I am a linesman. My responsibility is the welfare of the lines on this station."

"Jordan Rossi looks after the lines on station."

He did. And he was doing a good job. Say what you might about Rossi, where lines were concerned, he delivered. Especially now he'd started singing to them.

"And as for being a linesman," Ryley said. "I spent six months on this station with linesmen like you." He glanced contemptuously at the ten bars above Ean's pocket. "Not one of you lifted a finger to do any work on the lines in all that time."

Ean bit his tongue, so he didn't say that Rossi had been one of the linesman here then, and he hadn't.

"This is *our* linesman," Ru Li said. "He's not like the others."

"I don't want to see you down here again," Ryley said. "If I do, you can be sure I'll have a word with your team leader." He looked at the bars on Ean's shirt. "Or your cartel master."

"Thank you for your time." Ean led the way back, aware of Ryley, staring after them, a little cloud of purple unease.

"That seemed pointless," Ru Li said. "Bhaksir's right. Couldn't you have done that through the comms?"

"No." Because what would he have learned through the comms? Nothing. Instead, he now had a strong sense of the man who controlled the station.

BACK in his temporary new home, Ean called Abram. He made the line secure from habit although today he could feel something tapping at the edges, asking to be let in. It was a familiar sound—the *Lancastrian Princess*—and for a moment Ean almost let it hook in.

Except . . . why was the *Lancastrian Princess* listening in?

"How are you, Ean?" Abram asked.

Ean held up a hand to silence him and sent a quick query down to *Lancastrian Princess*'s line eight. Was the ship asking to listen in?

"No."

He followed the tentative whisper of sound back. It was on the *Lancastrian Princess*. There. And there.

By now Helmo had heard what was happening, and the sudden surge of fury—they were doing this on his ship, his beautifully protected ship—galvanized line eight.

Eight surged. The lines trying to listen in disappeared.

Ean's comms chimed. Helmo. He sang Helmo into the connection with Abram.

"What's going on?"

"I'm checking to see if the lines are secure now," Ean said.

He sang every single line on the *Lancastrian Princess* and got answers from them all. There was no untoward activity. He sang to the other lines in the fleet. Nothing on the *Wendell*, nothing on the *Kari Wang*, nothing from Confluence Station. There were two illegal comms on the *Gruen*. Both of them with trainees. Ean got the *Gruen* to short them out. The media ships were sending to their usual spies, but nothing that the New Alliance wasn't aware of.

"All clean," he said, eventually. "The *Lancastrian Princess* was the only affected ship."

Helmo, his arms crossed, looked and sounded the unhappiest Ean had ever seen him. "Our security is usually good."

"Yes," Abram said. "I almost wish you hadn't destroyed them. I suspect if we'd been able to investigate the codes, we'd find they came out of Palace Security. No one else would have been able to slip anything in."

Palace Security. Vega was Palace Security. But then, Ean realized after one horrified moment, so was Commodore Bach.

"Bach is spying on you?"

"He won't be doing it without a specific request." Abram's tone was grim.

"Yu?"

"Yes. Spying on his daughter."

"I'll ask Vega to investigate," Helmo said, and Abram nodded.

Ean said, "I'll ask the ship to let you know if it happens again, Helmo."

"Thank you."

After he clicked off, Ean realized he hadn't talked to Abram about Confluence Station. Or about Sale.

SIXTEEN

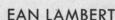

EAN LAMBERT

AFTER THE DISCOVERY of the *Confluence* fleet, the Alliance—as it had been then—had taken control of Confluence Station, and the New Alliance had used it for a temporary headquarters until they'd moved to Haladea III. Most people believed it had been handed back to its former owners afterward, and that its owners had continued to lease it out. After all, it wasn't needed at the confluence anymore. There was nothing there now.

They were wrong. The station was an official spoil of war, and though Patten and his staff retained corporate dress, they were employed by the combined governments of the New Alliance. The governance fleet, Kari Wang had called it. It was an appropriate name.

Access to the station was restricted.

The Factor requested permission for Captain Jakob to meet with Linesman Rossi. Orsaya couldn't see it, but Jakob was with the Factor, sitting out of sight of the screen.

Ean heard the request, for he was listening carefully to all comms to and from the *Lancastrian Princess*. And Orsaya's frosty reply.

"Our linesmen are busy, Factor. It might have escaped your notice, but we have a lot of ships to repair and limited access to cartel linesmen. I cannot approve of anything that takes them away from their work. Especially not Linesman Rossi, who is one of only two tens we have available."

"Admiral Orsaya, why not let Jakob tag along when Linesman Rossi is repairing lines, then. That way, he could work while they talked." The Factor's smile was meant to charm, Ean could tell.

"I have just explained, Factor. He is *busy*. I don't need him distracted by foolish questions."

"I am sure they wouldn't be foolish questions, Admiral."

"To a linesman, talking to a nonlinesman, every question about lines is foolish. Or haven't you noticed."

"We would not annoy him."

Orsaya snorted. "Everything annoys him."

"Surely one visit."

"Factor. There is a war on, and every single member of the New Alliance wants access to my linesman. I am pleased he is popular, but tell me why I should put you ahead of them?"

She clicked off.

She didn't see the expression the Factor made afterward. Ean did.

"I doubt you'll charm that one," Jakob said.

"If she didn't have a linesman, I wouldn't care."

Ean should let Orsaya know about this conversation. Or maybe Vega would, for she was listening as well.

"She won't be a problem," the Factor said. "We can get at Rossi anytime, no matter what she says. I am sure you can get to Confluence Station. We only need to find out when he's there."

Jakob nodded. "What about line training? He assists there, doesn't he? Why don't we go along to that? It should be easier."

Not if Ean had anything to do with it.

It wasn't the only conversation Vega was listening to. She was listening in on Michelle, entertaining Sattur Dow in one of the VIP lounges. Vega looked to be giving that conversation more attention.

"I had thought to see my betrothed here."

"My cousin Dominique?"

"Yes."

"Sattur." It was strange to hear him called by his first name. Ean had never heard him referred to as anything but his surname or his full name. Even the media used his full name. "Dominique is a soldier. You need to talk to her commanding officer, Commodore Vega."

"Commodore Vega is being particularly obstructive. I was

hoping you might do a friend of your father's a favor and perhaps intercede for me."

Ean was sure the "friend of your father" was a pointed reminder that Sattur Dow was, in fact, a close friend, and that Michelle would do well to remember that.

"I could do that. Although I must warn you, I have little to do with the soldiers who run this ship." Which was an out-and-out lie, but Ean would bet she'd pass any lie-detector test they cared to use on her.

Michelle nodded to Lin, who tapped something into his comms and brought it over to her.

In her office, Vega switched both channels off and sat up straighter—if she could sit straighter than she normally did—before answering Lin's call. "Vega."

"Her Royal Highness, the Crown Princess Michelle," Lin said, and handed the comms to Michelle.

If they had to go through that process every time Michelle answered her comms, she'd never get much work done. Lin wouldn't either.

"Your Royal Highness." Vega's voice became respectful. She inclined her head in a half bow. "What can I do for you?"

They hadn't talked to each other like that since the first day Vega had come on board.

"My guest, Sattur Dow, would like to meet his betrothed, my cousin Dominique. I believe she is part of your staff. He is upset you have denied access to her."

Vega didn't pretend not to know who she meant. "Your Highness. I have already explained to Merchant Dow that Spacer Radko is away on a covert operation."

Her tone wasn't exasperated, which it should have been. Or would have been if she'd been talking to anyone else. Who was the act for? Sattur Dow? Emperor Yu? Or both?

"Surely you can send her a message to contact us. Or bring her back and put someone else in her place."

Surely, Sattur Dow wasn't fooled by this farce.

But they kept on going.

"Unfortunately, no," Vega said. "On a covert operation, you do not contact the operatives. It endangers the mission."

"My Lady Dominque is in a unique position. Surely, once

you knew she was betrothed—by the decree of the Emperor himself, no less—you would have reconsidered."

"Had I known about it, yes." Some of Vega's natural bite was back. "But this mission was planned two weeks beforehand. Spacer Radko always meant to leave after seeing her family. Maybe if she had mentioned her changed circumstances, I might have reconsidered. Unfortunately for you, she omitted to do that." She quivered with apparent righteous indignation that didn't come through the lines. Line one reflected wariness more than anything else.

"My Lady Dominique is a low-ranking spacer," Sattur Dow said, and Ean had to hold his own lines in at the insult. "Surely it is unusual to send a spacer on a covert mission?"

"Not that unusual. On operations like these, you take the one with the strongest abilities in the area. Not to mention I also wanted to see how she would perform as the leader of a team."

"Abilities." Sattur Dow's eyes gleamed. "So it was to do with line ships?"

"Why ever would you assume that? Especially on a covert op. No, sir." Vega's tone was flat. "Radko has more specialized skills than that. She speaks perfect, unaccented Redmond."

"Redmond." Sattur Dow started.

His reaction triggered a response in Vega—and maybe in Michelle, too—for line one jangled. Strong enough and loud enough for Helmo, eating a late meal in the mess, to pull up a screen of the bridge and watch what was happening there while he ate. He was looking in the wrong place. He should have been looking in Vega's office.

"Apparently her parents planned for her to be a diplomat. Instead, she joined the fleet."

THE first thing Vega did after she clicked off was call Ean. "Lambert, were you listening?"

"Why would you think that?"

"Names were mentioned. I'll assume that's a yes. I want to know everyone that man calls, and I don't want him to know we're checking him."

How did you explain that to the lines? "I'm not sure I—"

Vega might have been reading his mind. "You won't be the only one looking. I want the stuff others are unlikely to catch."

"I'll do what I can." Ean clicked off. So he was a spy now. And Vega was getting very used to the tools at her disposal. Which weren't even her tools, they were Michelle's.

Still, Vega had given him something.

Michelle and her people lied by telling the truth, most of the time, and Vega had told Sattur Dow that Radko was somewhere her language skills were required. Therefore, she was on one of the six Redmond worlds.

How could he use that to find out more?

TODAY, Jordan Rossi accompanied Ean to training. Fergus was there, too, along with Hernandez.

"This ship smells like it's been through a sewer," Rossi said.

Captain Gruen bristled. "Are you insulting my ship, Linesman?"

"The people on it are polluting your lines."

"Exactly. I have tried telling Linesman Lambert that. He doesn't listen."

"You're not a line, sweetheart. He doesn't hear you."

"She *is* a captain," Ean said. He heard her all right, and Rossi knew that, so it was just another pointless point-scoring exercise.

"They'll come around," Fergus said.

Maybe. The antagonism crackling through the lines wasn't helping, for the lines considered Ean as one of their own. His biggest worry right now was that the trainees would make enemies of the fleet lines before they did come around.

Even now, the lines were promising, *"We'll protect you."*

"Thank you." For you couldn't turn their protection away.

At least Rossi's brooding presence kept most of the trainees awed and cowed today.

Everyone except Arnold Peters.

"Why is Lambert training us, when Linesman Rossi is here?" Peters demanded.

Rossi, who was close to the Xanto quartet at the time, listening to Nadia Kentish, narrowed his eyes. "Are you talking to me, or about me?"

"I'm just saying—"

"You think, I, Jordan Rossi, should waste my time on a level-six linesman like you."

A chorus of something defensive washed through the lines. No linesman liked the implication he or she was inferior.

"If you think you're so good," Nadia Kentish said, "why are you here?"

Rossi turned his narrowed gaze on her. "I am here because some bastard sold my line contract, and my new contract owner demands I come."

Ean seized the silence that followed. "You are *all* here because you've been ordered to come. It's part of your job." He watched them think about that, heard the song of the lines change. "If you'd rather be elsewhere, let me know, and I will arrange to have you returned to your fleet."

"That is a joke," Peters said.

"What, that I can't have you returned to your fleet?"

"You know, and we know, that you can't back out of a top secret project like this unless you're kicked out."

"So put up with it, then, or you will be kicked out." Maybe even for their own safety, for the lines were starting to pick up on Ean's exasperation. "Now. We have training."

It wasn't the best training session. The only thing of interest that came out of it was that Jordan Rossi spent a lot of time listening to Nadia Kentish.

"She's not Jordan's type," Fergus said, later. "He likes his women curvy."

Nadia Kentish had no curves at all.

Ean laughed and felt in control for the first time since the start of the session. "Fergus, there's only one thing a linesman really cares about." Especially at line training. "It's not her body he's interested in. I will bet you she's a high-level line."

SALE had been out on the *Confluence* all day. "How was training?" she asked at dinner.

"Okay."

"Only okay?" Sale made a face at what was on her plate. "Who is cooking, these days?"

"Ru Li and Hana," Bhaksir said. "I think they do it badly deliberately, hoping we'll get someone in."

"We can suffer bad food for a while," Sale said. "It's just until we get rid of the tourists. Only okay, Ean?"

Maybe she'd already heard how bad it had been.

"They're still antagonistic. A couple of them, especially."

"Your old cartel mate being one of them?"

Peters wouldn't like being called a cartel mate. Why single him out, particularly?

"If he gets to be a real problem, let me know. You can get him kicked off the project."

What he'd really like is for Peters to accept the new way of communicating with the lines and to come on board. Ean would just have to work out some strategies for doing it.

And as for strategies. "If you wanted to find out who on your ship called anyone in Redmond, Sale, how would you do it?"

"Redmond." Sale pushed her bowl away and stretched her legs out. Radko used to do that, too. Ean missed her suddenly, so much it hurt. "Am I doing it, or you?" Sale asked.

"Both of us."

"Me, I'd go to Vega. She'll be looking for anything like that. She's got access to all the messages that go out and come in, and she'll be checking their origin and what they say."

"And me?" It would be interesting to have Sale's view, given she'd worked so closely with lines over the last six months.

"I'd ask the lines, of course."

"How do you recognize something from Redmond? I mean, how do you know it's not from Lancia, say? Or Aratoga?"

"Identifying Redmond. Are they talking or not?"

"Maybe."

"Well, there's the language. Redmond uptrill at the end of their sentences." She tried to put an uptrill at the end of her own, failed miserably. "You get the gist."

He nodded.

"Otherwise, you can't pick them. Not like Lancastrians,

who are racially distinct." Then Sale looked Ean over. "Mostly, anyway."

Ean nodded again, not really hearing her. Suppose he asked the ship to listen for words. Or sounds. Would it work?

Back in his room, he settled down with a primer on the language of Redmond and memorized a hundred basic words. He turned it into a song, to make it easier to remember. When he had it down well enough, he turned to the lines. All ships, on both eleven fleets.

"Tell me when you hear sounds like these." He concentrated on getting them right, for with the lines, the sound had to be exact. *"Greetings, yes, no, today . . ."*

EAN was in the fresher, seriously considering whether he could convince one of the ships to jump to Redmond and back to see if he could identify it as a place, when the *Lancastrian Princess* said in his mind, *"Words,"* and suddenly he was looking at a place on ship he'd never been but recognized as part of the VIP area that was set aside for visitors. Of whom Vega had said, fervently, she hoped there were no more.

Jakob's room, and Jakob was there, speaking into a comms. Ean stopped the fresher midcycle.

Every sentence had an uptrill at the end of it.

Afterward, he watched Jakob slip the comms into a side pocket of his bag, pick up the bag, and walk down to the shuttle bay. Vega waited there, two guards beside her, along with the woman they had identified as a single-level linesman.

Jakob indicated to the linesman that she enter the shuttle.

"I'm sorry to hear about your mother," Vega told Jakob. "I hope she improves soon."

"Thank you, Commodore." Jakob disappeared into the shuttle as well.

Neither of them mentioned the linesman. Moments later, the shuttle was gone. Vega watched it go.

Ean called Vega. "Where did Jakob go?"

"He's going home. His mother is ill."

That was as likely as Sattur Dow's being a suitable partner for Radko.

"And the linesman?"

"He offered to take her. Said he hadn't known she had failed line certification."

"And you believed that?"

"I believe they didn't expect us to pick up on it so easily. She's a virtual prisoner here. What else could he do but send her home?"

Where she would tell everyone what she'd seen. Single-level linesmen wouldn't be a secret much longer. If they were now, for why had the Worlds of the Lesser Gods brought a single-level linesman if they didn't think there was good reason to?

"Are you listening to Jakob's cabin?"

"Naturally."

"You should listen to the last fifteen minutes then."

"I'll do that."

Ean was in the fresher again when Vega called back. He sighed and stopped the fresher. At least this time, it was nearly at the end of the cycle.

"You might tell me what happened in Jakob's cabin," Vega said. "For I can't see a problem."

She couldn't? Maybe he was wrong about the language. He didn't know it really. But he had recognized the sound of some words.

"Not even what he said?"

"He didn't say anything."

"But what about—?" Vega must have heard him talking into his comms. "I want to see the security tape."

He thought for a moment she was going to refuse. Instead, she said, "This had better be a secure line."

He sang it as secure as he could, then watched, disbelievingly, as Jakob settled onto his bunk with a tired sigh, closed his eyes, then lay there for fifteen minutes before getting up—with another tired sigh—and leaving the room.

"That wasn't what I saw."

"So I gathered. Security on this ship is badly compromised." He could feel the rage coming through on line one. It wasn't directed at him. Vega liked to be in control.

The ship—and thus Helmo, too—didn't like it either. And the emotion was building.

"How do I tell the ship what to watch for?"

"First we work out how he did it. Then we can work out how to prevent it. Now, I'd like to hear what Jakob said."

Maybe Jakob's people were listening in. But, *"No,"* from line eight, *"Secure."* Ean tried to stop worrying and concentrated on remembering what he could. "He was talking into a comms. Words like . . . " He gave what he could remember, which wasn't much. "Then he put his comms in his bag and went down to the shuttle bay. Can you check if his mother really is sick and that he is going home to see her?"

"No. The Worlds of the Lesser Gods don't like strangers, and to date, they've never been considered a threat."

"So you don't think it's important?"

"I'm saying Lancia doesn't have anyone on the ground there, and even with this alleged marriage coming up, they're still blocking us sending anyone in. Subtly, of course, but we know we're being put off."

So they couldn't check. Ean clicked off and spent the rest of the night wondering how he could protect the ships from people like Jakob.

SEVENTEEN

EAN LAMBERT

"I THINK YOU should run the training today," Ean told Hernandez and Fergus. He thought about including Rossi, who was there as well, but that was something to keep in reserve. Right now, having Rossi listening from the sidelines was just as good.

"Can't take the pressure?" Rossi asked.

"No."

Sometimes, with a short answer like that, Rossi would go for the jugular. Today, he just sniffed. "Radko's a long time coming back, isn't she."

And sometimes he simply attacked from a different angle. Then, so could Ean.

"I'm glad you're missing her, too, Rossi."

Rossi's eyes narrowed.

"You must be. You keep talking about her."

"It's nice to see you get in a hit occasionally," Bhaksir said, approvingly, as Rossi turned away.

Rossi probably did miss Radko. She was strong enough to stand up to him, and Rossi had to respect that. Maybe he should work with Rossi to get rid of Sattur Dow.

As if.

Although if Rossi could be persuaded, it was to his advantage.

"If you're making plans"—from Rossi—*"you shouldn't do it in a room full of raw linesmen in the middle of line training."*

Ean turned his attention back to the lesson, where Peters was complaining that now they had a seven running the training.

Hernandez, who was a ten, but still wore the seven bars she'd been certified with, bared her teeth. "If you think you can do better, why not come up and do it?"

Ean made his way to the front.

"And not just a seven," Peters said. "Aided by a linesman's assistant."

One of his companions nudged him. Ean heard through the lines the quiet warning Peters's friend gave him. "Fergus Burns is Jordan Rossi's assistant."

Hernandez seized on the silence that followed. "Line one," and started greeting the lines.

Ean moved to stand with one foot raised back against the wall. He couldn't do it for long. Radko did it for hours. What was Radko doing now? Who was she working with and did she like them as a team?

Did she ever think about him?

Peters started arguing again.

This was something Ean had to control. Even though Sale had hinted, the previous night, that they would take care of it for him if he needed them to.

"Linesman Peters." He used Gospetto's training to increase the sound, and pushed it out through the lines as well. "If you have issues, bring it up with me and your commanding officer outside of the scheduled training sessions. There's a war on, and the sooner you learn these new techniques, the sooner you will become useful to the New Alliance. Don't hold everyone else back because *you* don't like what you're doing."

The lines on all ships on both fleets joined in, for Ean hadn't stopped to target the *Gruen* lines only. It was so strong that all the trainees stepped back. And, of course, all the captains checked to see what was happening.

"I'm holding us back?" Peters said. "What about what we were promised? We were promised alien ships, but we're stuck here on a piece of Gate Union junk."

The captain of that piece of "junk" was listening in right now. Peters had just made himself an enemy.

"You're not going anywhere until you learn correct line technique."

"Correct line technique. That's a joke."

Nadia Kentish said, "So we come all this way off our own ships—at great inconvenience to us—and we won't even get to see the alien ships."

"I didn't say that." Of course they would introduce them to

the ships, and most of them would end up as crew. "But no one, especially not me, will take unwilling linesmen onto a ship that uses lines like the alien ships do." For their own benefit, rather than the ships'. "I'm not taking you anywhere until you show some appreciation of the lines."

"*You're* not taking us." That was Peters again. "Who made you the arbiter of what we can do and can't do?"

"The New Alliance council," Rossi said, before Ean could say anything. "They made Lambert senior linesman. All line matters go through him, particularly anything to do with the Department of Alien Affairs." He glanced at his comms. "And most of us have better things to do than sit around making power grabs."

It quietened them, although Ean wasn't sure it helped. Wasn't sure it was meant to. It definitely gave them more to complain about though at least they did it quietly. Except, of course, Ean heard muttered comments through the lines.

"The Department of Alien Affairs is controlled by Lancia."

"Jordan Rossi should be the senior linesman."

"They're using a junior to train us."

He made a point of moving over and standing close to each mutterer, to listen to their singing.

Hernandez continued with the greetings.

In the middle of the trainees' chorused reply, one of the *Confluence* fleet ships joined in. A song of welcome.

They usually restricted training to the *Eleven* fleet.

First, the *Confluence* itself tried to choose its own crew, now this ship was doing its own thing. Ean checked which one it was. That one, the little scout right on the edge of the fleet. Scout Ship Three.

Ean changed his song to target that specific ship. The lines answered, happy at the attention. Happy to be getting visitors.

"*Visitors?*" Ean heard air being cycled out of the shuttle bay on the scout, then being cycled back in.

A shuttle had landed.

"*Who?*"

"*Lines.*" And there were lines. Ean could hear them as they made their way onto the ship. The single-level linesman from the Factor's trip to the *Eleven*. Another single. Plus a third with the characteristic sound of a trained, multilevel linesman.

Ean sang the lines open to the fleet ships. The *Eleven*, the *Lancastrian Princess*, the *Wendell*, the *Gruen*, and the *Confluence*. "Someone has boarded a scout ship." He pushed the image up onto the main screens of each bridge.

"Do we know who?" Captain Helmo asked.

On the scout ship the boarders were using in-suit comms to talk to each other. That was line five. Ean pushed the comms through as well.

"Never mind. Anyone know Redmond?" for there was a distinctive uptrill at the end of each sentence.

The *Lancastrian Princess* and the *Gruen* both nudged Ean. *"That sound you were looking for."*

"Thanks." Wasn't it obvious he was already listening?

"That is too advanced for these trainees," Hernandez said. Ean blinked at her.

"How long?" Helmo asked the other captains.

"Four hours for me," Kari Wang said.

"Five." "Five point six," from Wendell and Gruen. Wendell's navigator was already calculating the fastest way.

"And six for me," Helmo said. "Can they jump the ship, Ean?"

"I don't think so." And Ean said to the ship, *"Don't let them take you away from the fleet."* He changed the tune to talk specifically to line eight on the scout and on the *Confluence*. *"You'll keep the ship safe."*

A ragged echo followed his song. *"Keep the ship safe."* The trainees.

Hernandez threw up her hands.

"Safe," promised the eights, while the scout showed Ean its new lines.

Without a level-seven linesman—and one who knew what he was doing—they couldn't jump the scout ship without jumping all the ships. The question was, did they know how to jump the ships at all? And if they didn't, what was the point of boarding it? Did they think they could camp there while their linesmen worked out what to do?

"Boarded safely," said one of the suited figures, this time in Standard, and Ean recognized the speaker. Jakob. "Come in *Iolo*."

"Receiving you loud and clear."

Ean was getting used to juggling multiple ships and lines. While he concentrated on the scout and its immediate lines, he heard Vega call Helmo. "The *Iolo* is the ship Jakob caught to go home. It jumped at 23:11 hours last night."

The communication was real-time. How long had the *Iolo* been in this sector?

He knew one person who would know, for she was paranoid about strange ships.

"Captain Kari Wang. When did the *Iolo* arrive?"

"Five days, twenty-three hours, and six minutes ago." Kari Wang knew the exact date and time of arrival and departure for every ship in the Haladean cluster. "It arrived with the *Lancastrian Emperor.*"

Vega said, "Yet to all intents and purposes, it jumped at 23:11 hours yesterday."

"No it didn't." Kari Wang was positive.

"Redmond has a cloaking device," Wendell said. "And some of these people were speaking Redmond. They would have cloaked, then moved away."

But the *Iolo* wasn't a Redmond ship. It was registered to the Worlds of the Lesser Gods; for otherwise, it would never have been allowed anywhere near the New Alliance headquarters. Although, given that Jakob had sent Redmond a message, it was likely Jakob was working with them.

"Ten minutes to jump," the captain on the *Iolo* said.

On the scout ship, there was a flurry of activity. Two of the linesmen held a U-shaped bar—as big as they were and twice the length—against the wall. Their knees were bent, their faces red with the effort.

The third linesman gave a thumbs-up.

"Electromagnetic loops in place," Jakob said. "Decloak when ready."

"Acknowledged," from the other ship. "Decloaking. Engaging magnets from this end." Whatever the linesmen were holding thumped against the wall, dragging them with it, nearly knocking them off their feet.

The linesmen stepped away.

"Enemy ship has decloaked," Helmo said. "We can all see it now."

"Run test," the captain of the *Iolo* said. "Reverse thrusters at 0.01 speed."

Ean didn't notice anything, but a minute later Captain Helmo said, "Scout ship moving at same speed and direction as enemy ship. Electromagnetic field detected. Strength, forty Tesla."

It must have been a strong magnet, for no one commented on how close the ships were.

"Eight minutes to jump," the *Iolo* captain said.

Last time Ean had prevented a ship jumping, it had been with the cooperation of all the line eights in the *Eleven* fleet. Could he do the same thing with the *Confluence* fleet?

"Can you hold the ship?" he asked the eights.

"Hold?"

How did he explain it? *"Stop the* Iolo *jumping through the void."*

"But they're not jumping."

The lines didn't understand the concept of future. They understood now.

On another ship—seemingly forever away right now—the engineer for Galactic News was calling his producer.

"We're recording," the producer said in an angry whisper.

"Coop. Something's happening. Something big. You've got to check it out."

"We're on air."

"Coop, you have to listen to this."

"Take over," the producer told his assistant, and stalked out of the studio.

Ean had to meet that linesman one day. He should be here, training. "The media's about to get involved."

Someone, he wasn't sure who, pushed that through to Abram.

Six minutes.

Ean didn't know what he had done last time to hold the ship in their space, and he didn't know how to convince the lines to do it. If he couldn't prevent the ship from jumping, what could he do?

What did he know?

The *Iolo* had one jump. If they couldn't get a jump, they

wouldn't move their ship. Therefore, Ean only had to hold it until the jump window was gone. Or until their own people could capture the ship. Which was four hours for the *Kari Wang*, more for the other ships.

Unless he moved the ship closer. Which would prove, once and for all, that ships *could* jump cold.

"Move that ship cold, bastard, and I'll kill you myself."

Jordan Rossi had never trusted the ships the way Ean had.

"If I don't, Redmond will get the scout." And possibly, the whole fleet.

"You'll kill us all," Rossi said.

Rossi was wrong. Ean wouldn't kill them. The lines would ensure ships didn't jump into each other. He changed his song to target the enemy ship.

"I need you to come." He tried to visualize the place in space that the ship needed to come to. He could hear the ships in his mind. A symphony of sound, where each sound placed the ship in a certain position, and he could tell where they were in relation to each other. *"When they tell you to jump—"* But he couldn't tell them where yet because they'd jump there now, and that meant the jump would be wasted. He had to make the captain of the *Iolo* think his jump was gone.

Rossi grabbed Bhaksir's blaster. "If you won't stop him, I will."

"Jump in four minutes," the *Iolo* captain said.

Bhaksir grappled for her blaster. But Rossi was determined. Ru Li and Hana came running to assist.

"You have no idea how dangerous he is." Rossi managed to get his finger through the trigger of the blaster. He fired as Bhaksir chopped her hand down on his.

Hot pain lanced Ean's thigh. The bulk of the burn went onto the deck, left a sizzling hole in the floor.

Gruen would kill them.

Bhaksir chopped down again. Something cracked, and Ean shared the pain of Rossi's broken wrist as it washed through the ship. It didn't stop him. Not until Ru Li and Hana wrestled Rossi's arms behind his back and put them into a restraining band.

"He's got a broken wrist," Ean said.

"I don't care what he's got," Bhaksir panted. "He's insane. And I am more than happy to kill him right now."

Two minutes. Ean's leg was agony, and he could feel waves of pain from Rossi as well.

"I'm not the insane one," Rossi said. "He has no right to play with our lives like that."

Nadia Kentish snatched Bhaksir's blaster off the floor and pointed it at Bhaksir's throat. "You have no right to treat a level-ten linesman like that."

The trainee linesmen surrounded Bhaksir and her crew. Many of them had their own blasters out now. The only ones who stood apart were the three Lancastrian linesmen. But they didn't help their fellow Lancastrians either.

"One minute to jump," the *Iolo* captain said.

Peters turned his blaster onto Ean. "I don't know what he was doing, but if Linesman Rossi didn't like it, then I don't like it either."

Line eight couldn't protect them all. Or could it?

The paramedics, waiting around the walls, drew their own weapons.

The paramedics. Here for line eleven. Yes, Ean could use that.

"All blasters on stun," Bhaksir said, to her own team and the paramedics. "No unnecessary injuries."

Ean called up the two elevens. *"Talk to me. Strong, please. Stronger than you've ever been."*

The two lines came in loud and clear, felling half the trainees. Even Ean, who was expecting it, fell to his knees.

It stretched the skin on his leg tight, pulling the skin where his leg was burned.

He couldn't breathe. Except he had to, for the *Iolo* captain said, *"Jumping now."*

"Here. Jump to here," and Ean sang a position to the ship. He had no idea where it was, he just knew it was close.

"Jump complete," the navigator on the *Iolo* said.

"Confirm position," the captain said. "Jakob, we have—"

"Sir." Something in the navigator's voice stopped the captain.

Behind it all, Ean could hear the *Eleven* fleet captains

swearing. "I'll kill Ean personally one day," Kari Wang said. "I wish he'd tell us what he's doing before he does it. Mael, change course for the *Iolo*."

Gruen burst in with a team of soldiers. She was already firing. Blasters on stun. Trainees went down under the combined onslaught of the *Eleven*, Bhaksir's team, and Gruen's team.

"Get me the local gate station," the captain of the *Iolo* said.

Ean redirected the request—and the signal from the bridge on that ship—to the only place he could at the moment. The other fleet ships.

Kari Wang answered the call. "Captain, your message isn't getting through. You are in New Alliance space, attempting to steal New Alliance property. Prepare to be boarded."

The captain ignored her. "How long till they get here?" he asked one of his crew.

"Thirteen minutes."

"Damn." He called Jakob.

Ean thought about rerouting that one as well, but what was the point.

"Jakob. The jump didn't work, and they're jamming our comms. The nearest ship will be here in thirteen minutes. The *Eleven*. I'll give you five minutes to get your shuttle here."

"Thirteen minutes should be enough to get another jump," Jakob said.

"They're jamming our comms." Did Ean imagine the gritted teeth that went with it? "You've four minutes, forty-five seconds to get your shuttle here, or I'll abandon you."

Because Jakob was on the scout ship, Ean knew how seriously he considered staying. The decision to leave was a bitter chocolate on Ean's tongue.

"Get to the shuttle," Jakob told the linesmen.

"No," wailed the scout ship.

It wouldn't take much for Ean to hold them there, but that would mean he was giving the ship to these linesmen, effectively giving the enemy a ship.

"Let them go. They're not yours. They're trying to take you from your rightful crew."

"Who is our crew?"

"You have to wait your turn. But it's coming."

The *Confluence* came in loud and strong. *"You promise and promise, but we never get anything. Make good on your promise. Lines for my ship,"* where "my ship" was the distinctive sound of the scout ship.

If he didn't give them something, they'd take the enemy linesmen. They couldn't afford to do that. Ean looked around. Two of the Xanto linesmen, Alex Joy and Thomas Peacock, helped Lina Vang to her feet, while Nadia Kentish, bound with the same restraining tags as Rossi, scowled at them.

"These. What about these ones?" The ships were to go to individual worlds, weren't they? Well, Xanto had got itself a ship.

"Shuttle leaving Scout Three," Kari Wang said.

Ean sagged with relief.

"Ours." Scout and parent ship inspected the four. The *Confluence* didn't complain about the scout getting assigned linesmen before it did, which was worrying. But then Ean already knew the *Confluence* was choosing its own crew.

Rossi started laughing.

"What's wrong with him now?" Bhaksir asked.

"You're out of control, Lambert. You're as crazy as the *Balao*, and you're in charge of all this."

Ean ignored him, listening instead to the talk between the ships as they discussed battle tactics. "Too close to fire," Kari Wang said. "And I don't know these weapons well enough yet. We're as likely to hit one of our own ships."

"They'll cloak as soon as the shuttle is on board," Wendell said. "Make us think they jumped."

Which was exactly what they did.

"Ship has disappeared," Captain Wendell said.

"No it hasn't," Kari Wang said, and a surge of ferocious joy swept the *Eleven*. "You can't hide a line ship from us."

"What do you need me to do?" Ean asked. He didn't want to think about the mess here on the *Gruen*. Not yet.

"Keep us linked to the cameras and sound on the bridge of the *Iolo*," Captain Helmo said promptly. "Prevent them calling the gate station. We'll do the rest. Nicely done, Ean."

Ean looked around the cargo bay, at the stunned bodies lying on the floor, at Gruen and her crew with weapons poised to shoot anyone who made a wrong move. It wasn't nicely done at all.

At least Rossi had stopped laughing.

Out in the corridor, Bhaksir was supervising the return of the trainees to their cabins, talking quietly through the comms to Sale, on the *Confluence*. "It blew up out of nowhere."

"Is everyone okay?"

A paramedic came over to Ean, checked his leg, sprayed painkiller onto it. The cessation of pain was so good it hurt. The dull throb of Rossi's wrist became the dominant pain. "You need to look at Rossi's wrist," he told the paramedic.

"I don't need help from you," Rossi said.

The paramedic finished dressing Ean's leg, then moved over to Rossi. "I have to cut the restraints," he told Captain Gruen.

She nodded, then glared at the final person still under restraint. Nadia Kentish. "If we let you go, will you behave like a rational human being?" And to the other Xanto linesmen who were hovering close. "You three as well."

"Yes, Captain," Lina Vang said although the words came hard.

Kentish looked at Rossi, whose wrist had swelled up around the restraint. "He's a level-ten linesman. You're treating him like a—" She stopped, as if she couldn't think of anything bad enough.

Gruen pointed to the damaged floor. "Nobody damages my ship and gets away with it." She moved on to help with the cleanup, and to ensure all the linesmen were taken back to their rooms. "You're all under lockdown until this is sorted."

Rossi laughed again. "She's as crazy as he is," he told Kentish.

Gruen was a little unbalanced where her ship was concerned, but who could blame her since it had been taken away from her once before.

"If this is what the New Alliance line program is about, then no wonder we're losing the war," Kentish said.

"You're part of that program, Kentish," Ean said. "If you stay in it, you'll have a say in how it goes." He sounded like Sale. "You can change it from the inside once you're in, but if you get kicked out, you lose your chance."

"It's self-destructing from the inside. It has been ever since they put a nobody in charge instead of a respected linesman like Jordan Rossi."

Fergus, who'd been nearby checking the last of the downed linesmen, stood up and came over to join them. "Yet without that 'nobody,' people like you and me wouldn't be linesmen, Nadia."

The other Xanto linesmen moved in front of Kentish, as if she was under attack.

"So they say. I haven't seen any evidence of line ability yet."

"Maybe because you haven't listened."

"I still wouldn't pass line certification."

"That's because line testing is flawed." How many times did he have to say it before they would believe him? "You're a single-level linesman. You'll never pass certification because current testing starts at one and goes up. But you're a linesman all the same."

"And you know this. How?"

"If you listened to the lines, you'd know it yourself. But you won't. Instead, you listen to people like Peters spouting poison and choose to believe them instead." Ean forced himself to calm, for the lines were getting agitated, and that was sure to bring Gruen back with a demand they all get off her ship. "You won't allow yourself to hear. Your mind is closed. Your ears are closed. And as long as they're closed, you'll never make it as a linesman in this fleet. Because the lines have no use for someone who doesn't listen."

Rossi sniggered.

"And you need to learn some things, too," Ean told him.

"What, listening?"

"You need to learn to trust the lines. You're as paranoid as these people. You can't try to kill me every time we attempt something new because you're scared."

"You can't blame me for being scared. You are out of control."

He should shut up now, or otherwise the whole thing would escalate again. Ean gritted his teeth. "You have to trust the lines."

"I trust the lines. What I don't trust is some crazy, out-of-control *human* line twelve who has no idea what he's doing. You've been lucky so far, Lambert, but one day you'll be wrong. And I don't want to be near you when you are wrong because you have so much power, you'll destroy us all. Including the elevens. My job"—he thumped his chest with the arm the paramedic had splinted for him; Ean felt the twinge of pain that came with it—"is to keep us alive since you obviously don't care if we live or die."

He did care. "There's a war on."

"What did I miss?" Fergus asked.

"You jumped a ship cold into the middle of a fleet of ships."

"What *did* I miss?" Fergus asked the Xanto quartet. Lina Vang shook her head.

"The alien ships don't jump into each other."

"Wait." Fergus held up a hand to both of them. "Just wait. Ean, why did you jump a ship?"

"Redmond was trying to steal it." Jakob and the linesmen were from the Worlds of the Lesser Gods, but the captain had been speaking Redmond.

"As if," Nadia Kentish said. "We haven't heard about it. And we were in line training when all this happened."

Rossi pulled himself to his feet. "On the contrary, sweetheart. No one is disputing that Redmond attempted to steal a line ship. They're still chasing the thieves now. It's on the news vids."

Galactic News had picked up the story—Ean could see them running the vid of Scout Ship Three appearing in the midst of the *Eleven* fleet. Then the *Iolo* disappearing.

"Your ship, incidentally. Which you are ignoring." Based on Rossi's malicious smile, that barb was for Ean, though he'd been talking to the Xantos. "No. What we are arguing about is the high-handed way Lambert deals with problems like this. He's like a loaded weapon with all the safeties off. One day, you'll pick it up, and it will discharge."

Ru Li, Hana, and Hernandez came in then. "Linesmen lockdown," Ru Li said to the Xantos. "And you're the last four not in your cabins."

They went silently.

Out in the corridor, Bhaksir finished her call to Sale with a heartfelt, "I wish Radko were here."

So did Ean.

THE *Eleven* chased the *Iolo* for four hours. Captain Yorath, on the *Iolo*, tried the whole time to get another jump. Ean sent the requests through the lines to the *Eleven* fleet ships, where they stopped.

The ships finally got into clear space. Captain Kari Wang gave one warning. "Attention, the *Iolo*. Surrender, or we will fire. You have three minutes to surrender."

The *Iolo* fired on the *Eleven*, but they'd been watching the feeds from the *Iolo*'s bridge all this time. By now they knew how many people were on board and had feeds of every board. They knew where the weapons were aimed. The *Eleven* avoided the shot, and the next one. Then fired a shot of its own.

That was all it took. One shot. A beam of some kind that Kari Wang admitted she had no idea what it did, but one of her eights wanted her to try it.

If it hadn't been for the captain of the *Iolo*'s insisting everyone wear suits, "Because we don't know what this ship can do," there wouldn't have been any prisoners, for the beam sliced the ship open.

Galactic Media hadn't filmed that final battle, but two hours later it was showing on the vids. The image must have come from the *Eleven* itself.

Ean tried to avoid watching it.

EIGHTEEN

DOMINIQUE RADKO

THE SECOND CRATE of iced Gippian shellfish got them down to Aeolus, the largest Redmond world. They left Leonard happily talking about the fate of the other crate—the one he hadn't delivered to Redmond. Tonight, the crew on Captain Engen's ship would dine on fresh Gippian shellfish.

"With Lancian wine," Han had said. "That's what you normally eat them with. "Golden Lake wine from the Radko"—he stumbled over that, recovered—"Estates is best." He looked at Radko, carefully this time.

"I don't know about Lancian wine," Leonard said. "We'll use anything we've got. Now, if you want to avoid official entry, you should slip out the side door here. Bergin, down the end, takes a flat thousand-credit fee."

"Thank you," Radko said.

Bergin dressed like he made a lot of money out of people entering illegally. It was hard to believe he hadn't attracted the attention of the authorities. Then, he probably had. It was as good a way as any of keeping track of illegal aliens on your world.

"Use these noncitizen chits when you purchase anything." He held out four discs, and waited.

"Thanks." Radko handed over chits worth four thousand credits and received the IDs in return. "We're looking for a clinic. Can you recommend one that won't ask questions?"

He paused. She held out a two-hundred-credit chit.

"The more you pay, the better quality advice you get."

"She's only asking a question," Han said.

Radko added another two hundred.

"Fabro's clinic. Two blocks down. They're discreet. They take chits." Bergin pocketed the chits. "Welcome to the center of the universe." He smiled at Han. "It's a pleasure doing business with you."

Han scowled.

Radko led them out of the building. The wind nearly blew them away. She'd forgotten the wind. She would have liked to walk faster, but they had to move at van Heel's pace. Van Heel was trying to hurry, but it was obvious every step was painful, and pushing against the wind didn't help.

"I'm sorry I—"

"Save it, van Heel. There's no need to apologize for being injured in the line of duty. Not unless you were being stupid." Then Radko smiled at the other woman. "It will be nice to have you whole again, I admit."

"You think it will be nice." Van Heel paused. "I can't wait."

"Is this the first time you've been injured?"

Van Heel nodded.

She was holding up well.

"Have you ever been injured?" Chaudry asked.

"A few times. I had a dislocated shoulder and a hairline fracture in my ankle not that long ago." Radko smiled at the memory. "What they call friendly fire."

Had Ean accidentally injured any others on her team? Bhaksir and the others didn't know when to step aside.

"Someone on your own side? But that's—"

"He was saving our lives at the time." And the Alliance. Not to mention acquiring a fleet of spaceships for them. "You'll like him, Chaudry."

She missed him.

FOUR hundred credits didn't buy much of a medical center. It was clean, but the prefab walls were full of holes and the equipment so old that Radko didn't recognize the model.

"I'd almost rather stay injured," van Heel said.

The medic looked tired, and his scrubs, while clean, had a brown stain down one side. Someone had bled on him, and he hadn't gotten rid of the stain.

"Blaster wound," he said, as if he saw them every day. "You're lucky it hasn't turned septic."

Chaudry bit off a protest, then meekly followed the medic into the room. Radko and Han came with them.

"I don't normally do this with an audience." Yet he didn't kick them out. He swabbed van Heel's injury, then dropped the swab into a scanner and inspected the readings. "At least it's clean. Someone knows something about cleaning wounds."

Radko silently pointed to Chaudry.

The medic nodded and disinfected a patch of van Heel's uninjured skin, then sliced a small piece off. The disinfectant must have had numbing properties, for van Heel didn't complain.

What happened if your whole skin was too badly burned to take a starter sample from?

"Regen takes hours. There's no point staying around to watch it." The medic put the sample into nutrient, then slid the sample and nutrient into a small opening on the side of the regenerator.

Radko got the hint. "We'll leave you here, Chaudry, while we look around. Call us if anything happens." A proper regeneration required three sessions. She'd bet none of this doctor's patients ever stayed for more than one.

RADKO used the noncitizen chit Bergin had given her, and more credit chits, to hire an aircar. The money was running out faster than she'd like, but she didn't want to use her own credit unless she had to.

The aircar had a massive engine and enormous stabilizers. They found the reason for them as soon as they took off, for the buffeting wind was strong.

The first thing Radko did when they were in the air was bring up the satellite views of the street TwoPaths Engineering was on.

The buildings here were buttressed up against the castle wall. Had it been Lancia, Radko would have assumed that Two-Paths was part of the family of the Factor of the Lesser Gods because Lancia would never allow a commercial company—especially not one from another world—so close to the castle. All it would take was some well-placed explosive—they had some with them—and they could blow a hole in the wall and get into the palace.

She didn't need to zoom in to see that the TwoPaths building was well protected, for it had the characteristic wavy outline of a building covered with a security netfield. Which meant she wouldn't get inside without blowing the net. It was a lot of security for a site TwoPaths listed as a warehouse.

Lucky for them, a net generator was big—it worked on similar principles to a Pandora field diffuser—and the generator itself was normally situated outside. Not only that, people who relied on such nets tended to think they were enough security.

They wouldn't have much time once the net was down. TwoPaths would have a private security firm on call.

There was a yard on the east side, with a generator-sized structure close to the wall. There would be a door behind that, for someone had to service the generator.

So, get in, take out the generator, and enter via the back door.

Abutting the yard was another shop. They could blow the wall, but they couldn't hide the fact they had been there. They could misdirect, however, and make people think it was an assault on the palace.

Radko turned her attention to the shop next door. It was a sweet shop that—according to the travel guides—was famed throughout the Worlds of the Lesser Gods. Radko had never heard of it.

She clicked off the screen, and said to Han, "Let's be tourists."

They used the aircar to hop from one major tourist spot to another around the Factor's palace, checking out potential escape routes.

"The wind in this place," Han said, as the aircar rocked. "I'd hate to live here."

Radko was glad of the powerful engine and stabilizers; otherwise, they would have been blown from one side of Aeolus to the other.

"It's huge," Han said. "Almost as large as the palace at Baoshan."

It was. She landed the aircar as close as she could, and they explored further on foot.

TwoPaths Engineering was a blank, featureless building. There were no windows on the lower level and only a few on the levels above. The blue shimmer of the security net was noticeable here on the ground. The street was full of cameras. They'd never get in unannounced. Radko's initial plan, using the sweet shop, looked the most promising.

The line for the sweet shop was out the door.

Radko had plenty of time to check the location of the cameras. There was one on the outside of the shop, and one camera from TwoPaths facing the shop door.

A discreet plaque outside the TwoPaths door stated, THESE PREMISES ARE PROTECTED BY MES SECURITY.

Once inside the sweet shop, she could see a rear door behind the counter which led to a cool room or a kitchen. A conveyor belt of sweets rolled in from out the back, continuously replenishing the supply. The servers were human, part of the archaic charm of the shop. As she waited to be served, Radko looked up, pretending to be bored. There were two cameras, both of them aimed toward the counter.

How much protection did TwoPaths have out the back?

What was she looking for when she got in? The report itself? Or evidence of what Redmond was doing there? Both, if she could get it, and most importantly of all, information on why they expected to have access to a twelve soon.

THEY took a room in a hotel close to the TwoPaths building. It was a tourist hotel, horrendously overpriced because of its proximity to the castle. Radko checked the street views. No one went into or came out of TwoPaths Engineering.

Van Heel came back whole and new-skinned.

Chaudry was pleased with the result. "But you will be careful," he said. "Really, you should have three sessions of regen. This is only the first."

"I can use my arm," van Heel said, flexing it. "And it doesn't hurt anymore. I'm happy."

Chaudry should never have been a soldier. He should have been a doctor. Instead, he'd be a linesman. But a linesman could also be a doctor. If they had linesmen who were engineers, why not linesmen who were doctors?

They ate a room-service dinner. On the *Lancastrian Princess* it would be midmorning. Ean would be training linesmen or looking at alien ships.

Don't think about her old life.

"Here's what we do," Radko said. "Tonight, we break into TwoPaths Engineering by going through the back of the sweet shop." She sketched a rough plan on her comms. "I saw three cameras. They looked like basic Schwetters to me. We need to disable them, set them onto a loop of some kind. Can we do that?"

Van Heel nodded. "It will be easier if we know which security firm they're with."

"MES."

"Good. I can hack them. What else?"

"TwoPaths has a security net. I think the generator is in the yard out back. We'll have to blow a hole in the wall to get to it, but it shouldn't be hard."

"Blowing a hole in the wall," Han said. "Won't someone hear us?"

Radko patted the box of explosive. "You've never used this stuff before. It's quiet."

"I've never done any real soldiering before this trip. Except marching."

"Me either," Chaudry said. "I'm thinking maybe Stores wasn't so bad, after all."

If Chaudry chose to adopt his line heritage, he'd never work in Stores again.

THEY spent the rest of the day making plans.

Radko insisted they all take time out to rest. She sent Han and Chaudry off first, afterward van Heel and herself. When she woke, it was midnight. The wind sounded as if it had eased a little. Van Heel was still asleep, and Han was yawning over his screen.

"Where's Chaudry?"

Han stifled another yawn. "Balcony."

Radko went out to talk to him. "How do you feel?"

He leaned on the railing and looked up at the stars. "I didn't see the stars on Redmond. This is only the second time I have seen stars from another world."

The first time would have been when he was with House of Isador. That was on Centaurus, which was close to Old Earth. Radko had seen the stars on Centaurus. They were a long way away.

"Nothing compares to seeing stars in space. Down here on planet, it's nothing really." Especially when obscured by city lights.

"When I joined the fleet, I thought that's what I'd be seeing. Stars in space. Other worlds. Fighting."

"Yet you ended up in Stores."

"It's funny, isn't it. When I was a boy, all I wanted to be was a doctor. Until—" He broke off, and looked away.

Radko started to softly sing the fleet anthem. "The stars my destination."

He took up the chorus with her. "I rise. I rise."

His voice was clear and light. Radko hadn't needed confirmation, but this was it. He was definitely a level one.

The song died away. Radko let the silence extend.

"Stores isn't so bad," Chaudry said.

Yet he could have been a linesman.

"Tell me, why did you choose to fail line certification?"

Chaudry stiffened. "You don't choose to fail. You certify or you don't."

"You're a one, Chaudry. You couldn't have failed. Not unless you did it deliberately. More to the point, once you failed, why didn't you go back to medical studies?"

She let the silence extend again.

Chaudry turned back to watch the stars. "Do you have a partner out there, back on that ship you came from?"

It was a clumsy attempt to change the subject. It wasn't going to work, but she answered it anyway, to keep him talking. "There's someone I like, but he doesn't know it yet." And he never would, either, for Michelle had first rights. And she missed him more than anything right now. "How about you?"

He shook his head. "There was a girl at fleet academy, but she just thought I could introduce her to linesmen. She didn't know—"

Radko turned her back to the stars. She could guess. "That a failed linesman is nothing to a certified linesman."

"Yes." It was just a whisper.

"You're not a failed linesman, Chaudry. You're a one."

"When I made line training, my parents were *so* proud of me. They cautioned me, of course, for not all linesmen made certification. But they were so proud. But a level-one linesman is nothing. Worse than nothing." He ran his hands through his hair. "I knew what I was long before the ceremony. I could only ever feel line one. I couldn't do that to my parents. It was better they didn't know."

"How do you fail line certification?"

"You pretend you're trying, but you're not doing anything really."

Level ones were rare. How many others had done the same thing? "And you didn't want to be a doctor anymore?"

"I wanted to die."

So he'd become a soldier. What was that old joke they used to tell when she was in training? Join the fleet; see the galaxy; shoot people. Or have them shoot you. Which explained the comment on Chaudry's psych profile that he wasn't fit for war duty.

"But they put me in Stores."

Radko smiled at the plaintive tone. "At least we have decent psych people at headquarters." She turned back to look at the stars, in the direction of the Haladean cluster. It wasn't bright enough to see, but she knew it was there. "Have you seen your family since?"

"I pretended I was away on training last time they came to Baoshan."

"Because you failed them?"

"You probably think it's silly."

"I failed my parents, too." Would she ever see them again? Did she care if she didn't, except as guilt if Yu did something in revenge? Thank the lines Jai the Younger and Hua were close as siblings. Surely their mother, Dowager Empress Jai the Elder, could be relied on to save her youngest daughter if need be. Radko hoped someone like Vega had apprised Jai of the possibility. "My ship is my family."

"And you lost that when you came to us."

She hadn't thought about Sattur Dow and Yu until now. "Probably." Vega wouldn't be able to fix it. She banged her fist on the railing hard enough to hurt.

"I'm sorry," Chaudry said quietly.

One man shouldn't have that much power. "He destroyed my life." He was trying to destroy the New Alliance. He was trying to destroy Abram and Michelle. If he did that, he'd destroy Ean, too, and everyone on the *Lancastrian Princess*.

If he did that, she would destroy him.

Radko took a shaky breath. "Sorry, Chaudry. I've been trying not to think about it."

"Sometimes it helps to talk."

Said the man who'd joined the fleet because he wanted to kill himself. "Do you still want to be a doctor?"

Chaudry stretched. "We should go inside."

She laughed and reached out to stop him. "Don't change the subject, Chaudry. This is important."

"Why?"

"Because a doctor who is also a linesman is a rare find indeed."

"Only a one." It came out bitter.

"Especially a one, since line one shows the health of the whole ship. A doctor who is a level-one linesman would be perfect." And very much in demand. Chaudry would have his pick of ships in the Lancian fleet. But he'd go to the *Eleven* or the *Confluence*. She knew that already.

"Line one shows the state of other lines," Chaudry corrected. "You don't need a doctor to fix lines. You need a linesman."

Radko smiled, grim and satisfied in the dark, and lonely, too, for she missed her ship. She missed her job. She missed her linesman.

"It shows the state of the whole ship, Chaudry. Human and line. Sure, you need a linesman to fix lines, but as for the rest, that's only partially right. That's what the cartel teaches you, and the cartels are wrong."

"Wrong?"

He was a linesman. He couldn't hide the hope in his voice. Linesmen, especially single-level linesmen, always wanted to believe there was something more.

Radko smiled again. "No line is superior to any other. We have learned so much about the lines in the last six months. Think about what you want for the future, Chaudry. At the end of this assignment, I'll ask again. If you want to work with the lines, or in medicine, or both, we'll do everything in our power to make it happen. We need people like you."

She turned and led the way inside.

NINETEEN

DOMINIQUE RADKO

VAN HEEL HACKED into MES's system, put the security cameras onto a loop, and routed the alarm back to Radko.

Once that was done, Radko took fifteen seconds to break into the sweet shop.

They passed through a storeroom with prepared sweets, then the kitchen, and finally a second storeroom containing raw materials. Bags of sugar and nuts, some form of syrup, and other items Radko couldn't identify. Even better, the wall out here was painted, not plastered, so the outline of each pre-fab block was clear.

Radko tamped the explosive down around the blocks. It went off with a soft whumph. They kicked the blocks out.

The net protecting TwoPaths Engineering wasn't alarmed, at least not that Radko could see. She pressed the OFF button.

It whined to a halt. The loudest thing so far.

Radko indicated to Han and Chaudry to stand on one side of the door, van Heel and herself on the other.

They waited.

No one came.

She broke the lock, and they piled inside.

They found themselves in a storeroom, with shelving and cupboards around the walls. The packaging was from a mix of worlds. There were boxes from the Worlds of the Lesser Gods, some from Redmond, and even one from Lancia, with HAEMOGLOBIN TESTER on the side.

Chaudry stopped at a box of tubing in clear plastic bags. "Intravenous sets." He stopped at another box. Meters of some sort. "These are medical supplies."

"We have to find their control center," Radko said. They

could speculate later why an engineering company required medical supplies. Their first job was to neutralize any security in the building before someone called for backup.

One minute.

They passed through three more storerooms, one with huge, glass-door refrigerators full of frozen, prepackaged meals.

"This is starting to get creepy," Han muttered.

"Shh." But Radko agreed. This setup was more like a hospital than an engineering lab.

Two minutes.

She heard a sound outside the room they were in and stopped. She motioned for the others to do the same.

If they stayed here, they were sitting ducks. "Chaudry, find us some cloth to cover our faces." She beckoned to Han. "Cover me. Blaster on stun. I'll drop as the door opens. Spray anything higher than me but keep out of the line of fire."

How many security people would you have on night duty at a lab? Three, maybe four? It depended how important the lab was.

Chaudry arrived back, carrying blankets. "It's all I could find in a hurry."

"They'll be good." Radko looked at van Heel and Chaudry. "Stay out of the line of fire."

She heard muttered information being passed through a comms. Someone knew they were there. If it was security outside—which was a logical assumption—they'd have help on the way. There was no time to waste.

She dropped to the ground, pressed the button to open the door, dragged a fast-acting gas grenade off her belt, armed it, and rolled it out.

Something swished above her head and thudded into the wall at the back even as the door closed again.

At least two people outside the door started coughing and choking.

"Blankets on." Radko wrapped one around her own face. "And don't breathe as you run through the gas." She checked what had come through the door. A tranquilizer dart.

"They're using tranqs, people, so beware." She opened the

door again and fired through the choking smoke. A long sweep around. At least two thuds.

She kept firing as she exited. Another thud.

Van Heel tripped over one of the fallen guards. Chaudry grabbed her and kept running.

One door at the front of the building was open, light streaming out. Logically, it would be the control room. Radko entered at a run, and fired at the sole occupant, who was still rising to pull out his weapon.

"Close the door," she ordered Chaudry.

She found the alarm, turned it off. Only then did she allow herself to take a deep breath.

"What now?" Han asked.

Radko turned to the wall of screens. "We find the labs."

Except there weren't any labs. There were three operating theatres down here on the ground floor, plus some examining rooms. Upstairs were glass-walled rooms around a central office. Ten of them were occupied and nearly all the occupants wore Sandhurst uniforms. Linesmen.

"It's not a lab," Chaudry said. "It's a hospital."

The patients showed signs of distress. One huddled in a corner, crying. Another lay on her bed, strapped down. Her face was badly scratched, and the tips of her fingers were bandaged. Another kicked the glass of the walls. The glass didn't break. It bounced, like Plexiglas.

Linesmen. Line experiments.

And they expected to have access to a twelve soon. Never.

In two of the examining rooms, Radko saw alien artifacts. She stepped closer to the screen to be sure. Artifacts that could only have come from one of the alien line ships.

Someone was supplying Redmond with items from the line ships.

Someone from the New Alliance.

Someone with access to alien artifacts would have access to Ean.

Radko swung around. "Van Heel, find the patient records. Copy them. Everything you can. Han, stay here with van Heel and watch the screens. Chaudry, collect the artifacts from the examining rooms." She tapped the ones she saw, to show him what she meant. "All of them. If you see something you don't recognize, especially anything that talks to you, anything that makes a noise, anything that reminds you of space, grab it as well."

Chaudry blinked at that but nodded.

He'd need something to carry them in. Radko looked around for a box, couldn't find one. "Use your blanket to wrap them in. There'll be an orderly around somewhere, so be alert." It was a hospital. They must have someone watching the patients.

"I'll check the office upstairs." If the report was anywhere, it would be there. "Open comms. All of us. Let's go."

She left Chaudry filling his blanket and ran up the stairs.

Three walls of the office were Plexiglass from waist height and looked out onto the linesmen's rooms. The back wall was stone; the same heavy stone they'd seen earlier when viewing the palace walls. There was a door in the wall. If Radko had her directions right, the lab led directly into the palace.

Radko looked around for a safe. There wasn't one. There were two desks, both with drawers. She tried the drawers.

The first one held sweets from the shop next door, and something that looked like dried fruit. The second was locked.

Han said, low and urgent, "Whatever you did stirred up a nest of people. They're all running for you."

Radko pulled her weapon.

The door to the palace burst open.

She fired, instinctively. One. Two. Three. Before she knew what was coming, using the desk as shelter. The answering fire hit the desk, and heated it, but the desk remained unscathed.

Four.

They hadn't been expecting opposition. They would be now.

"Four coming up the stairs," Han said. "Two in the lift."

Radko flipped some explosive out of her belt, tamped it around the drawer entry.

"Get out of there," Han said.

"Get Chaudry and go. I'll meet you outside." This desk was indestructible for a reason, and Radko was sure she knew what that reason was. It was the safe. If there was a copy of the report in this room, it would be in that safe.

"They're carrying weapons of some type. I can't identify them."

"Did you hear me? Outside. All of you. Chaudry?"

"Going," Chaudry said.

Radko raced behind the other desk to shelter from the blast.

"First group coming in," Han said. Two slightly in front.

Radko could see them. They could see her. But the wall had the distinctive shimmer of Plexiglass. They couldn't shoot through it. They had to enter the room.

The first burst in through the door. The blast from the drawer slowed them enough for Radko to get the first two shots in. One of their weapons skittered across the floor.

A tranquilizer gun.

She gestured threateningly with her blaster at the two orderlies—for they were dressed like orderlies—who paused outside the door. She ran for the drawer.

A comms. Yes. She snatched it up.

Someone, somewhere, was shouting.

"Two more coming behind these."

"Han. Get the hell out of there. Where are van Heel and Chaudry?"

"Gone."

"Good. No heroics. Now go."

More people burst through from the palace door. They had blasters; the orderlies had tranquilizers. Radko took her chance with the orderlies. She raced for the door, firing as she went. She made it outside.

The Plexiglass stopped the blaster fire.

Radko waved her blaster threateningly at the orderlies. "Come near, and I'll fry you."

They backed away.

"Farther," Radko said.

"There are two more coming up the stairs," Han said urgently.

Radko fired toward the stairs, still staring at the orderlies in front of her.

Someone screamed, and there was the thud of someone falling.

The orderlies backed away.

Radko raced for the stairs. "Get the hell out of here, Han," as she grabbed the railings and swung over, holding on till the last minute to slow her fall and minimize the distance.

There was no answer from Han.

Radko raced for the yard. Made it. Only to pull up as soldiers in the uniform of the Lesser Gods flooded through the entry.

How many people did it take to cover a single break-in?

One of the soldiers at the front raised a tranq gun.

Another team of soldiers blocked the hallway behind her.

There was nowhere to run.

She felt the sting of the dart in her arm. Pulled it out. Only to feel the sting of two more, one in her back and one in her leg.

TWENTY

EAN LAMBERT

THE INVITATION FROM Emperor Yu arrived while the *Eleven* was chasing the *Iolo*.

> The Emperor of Lancia expects the presence of Linesman Lambert at supper.

Ean ignored it until after he came out of regen on Confluence Station. The burn on his leg itched where the new skin had taken; he'd come away with strict instructions on what he couldn't do until after his third regeneration session. But the burn wasn't painful anymore, and he could worry about other things, like how to refuse the invitation without aggravating the Emperor.

But first things first, and the lines always came first. He'd promised Scout Ship Three to the Xantos. He'd somehow promised the *Confluence* it could choose its own crew.

"And we are choosing."

Didn't he know it.

He called Abram. "I want to address the council. We need to hurry assigning ships to worlds. Otherwise, the council won't get to choose." He made the line as secure as he could. "The ships are desperate for linesmen. They'll take any who come along, which is how Jakob nearly got Scout Ship Three. It's a weakness we can't afford."

"Line business." Abram considered it. "It might even settle things because people are worried about—" He grimaced and didn't say the word they both knew was "Lancia." "I'll schedule you to address the council."

"Thank you." Ean clicked off.

"Thank you," came a whispered echo underneath his.

He smiled and turned his attention to the other problem. Declining Emperor Yu's invitation politely.

Rigel's lessons had taught him how to accept invitations from royalty, but they'd never taught him how to refuse them. Ean had declined two invitations from Michelle already, but would the same politely worded refusal be enough for the Emperor?

"So, Ean." He became aware Sale had said it twice. Or maybe three times. "What happened on the *Gruen* this afternoon?"

He was glad it was Sale who was asking. "I'll tell you after you tell me if this is a polite enough refusal for Emperor Yu." He held up his comms and the message he had ready:

It is with regret that I must decline, as I am presently attending to line issues.

"Or do I have to refuse by calling one of his assistants?"

Sale snatched his comms. "Let me see." She scanned the earlier message. "You've had this for hours, Ean. We could have had you there by now."

"Michelle doesn't want me to go to functions."

"This is not an invitation. It's a summons. Shit. Grab your formal clothes. Quickly."

"But—"

"No buts, Ean. Hurry. You can change on the shuttle."

Ean called Michelle as he collected his formal uniform. Michelle was unavailable, so he left a semicoherent message with Michelle's assistant, Lin—which he wasn't even sure would be passed on—and made his way back to the shuttle. Lately, he spent more time in shuttles than he did on station.

Sale called up on her comms. "Ean, supper will be over before you get there."

Dancing attendance on Emperor Yu had never been part of Ean's plans. Not before he'd met Michelle, or after. But the man held his friends' lives in his hands. If even Michelle was worried about what Yu could do, the best Ean could do to keep his friends safe was to do as Yu requested—within reason. He hurried back to the shuttle.

Maybe he could use the time to ask Yu to rethink Radko's wedding.

Sale might have been reading his thoughts. "Don't mention Radko," she said, as they took off at speed. "Emperor Yu never, never, changes his mind. You'll endanger yourself, Radko, Vega, and anyone else who was complicit in it. So don't. Now, you still haven't told me what happened today."

Tell the truth, Radko would have said, simple and from the lines. Plus, it got her off the subject of Yu, and what he could and couldn't do there.

"You know Redmond tried to steal Scout Ship Three."

"The whole galaxy knows."

"They had some sort of magnet. They linked the two ships."

"It's old technology," Sale said, surprising him. "Apparently they used it to link generation ships together. To save on fuel."

"I didn't know that."

"Neither did most of us, but Commodore Favager of Nova Tahiti recognized it. Got quite excited about it."

Clemence Favager was an Old Earth nut. Ean could imagine her getting excited about the use of old technology.

"They were taking a risk all the same," Sale said. "We know ships physically bonded together can jump through the void, but an electromagnetic bond. I wouldn't want to be the first to try it. I'd be worried the bond would break in the void."

Jakob didn't seem the sort who left things like that to chance. "They had probably already tested it."

Sale nodded. "How did they get onto the scout ship?"

"Three of the people with Jakob were linesmen. The ship was happy to let them on." It wasn't the place or the time, but, "The ships need people, Sale. They'll start choosing their own soon."

"Tell that to the admirals, Ean. There's no use telling me."

Sale needed to know because she was one of the people the ships were choosing.

Ean continued with what had happened. "The jump was in ten minutes, and the *Eleven* was four hours away. I couldn't stop the jump."

"Not even with line eight?"

"I don't know how to do it, Sale. I didn't know what to ask. I couldn't get it to understand." Maybe he should have insisted.

Sale put up a hand to stop the flow of words. "It's fine. What happened next?"

Ean blew out his breath. He didn't like to admit the next bit. "The trainees aren't used to training yet. And I'm not—" Sale knew he'd been having trouble; otherwise, she wouldn't have said what she'd said about Peters the other day. "I wanted to stop the jump, and I wanted to move the *Iolo* closer to the *Eleven* fleet. Which meant a cold jump, but Rossi—" He took a deep breath, forced his voice even and smooth. "He doesn't like cold jumps any more than the captains do, and he . . . tried to stop me."

"By stealing Bhaksir's blaster and firing at you?"

He nodded. "Only Rossi's a famous ten, so when Bhaksir tried to stop him, the other linesmen came in to protect him."

"I see."

Sale had the same direct way of looking that Abram and Michelle did, as if she could see right through you.

"Gruen and I will talk to the admirals," Sale said. "You're lucky they have other things to think about today."

"Thank you."

Sale turned away from the boards and looked directly at him. "When you're out of your depth, Ean, you have to learn to ask for help."

"I can manage."

"You can't manage. We have a ship on lockdown because you insist on doing everything yourself. We have a linesman who nearly got his leg shot off."

He'd spent an hour in regen. His leg still itched, but it was fine.

"Another one with a broken wrist, one with concussion, and five with various laser burns. Four people were arrested."

What could he say to that?

"Worse, we have to explain to the admirals of the other military forces what happened."

"I'm sorry."

This time it was Sale who sighed. "Don't be, Ean. It's as much my fault as it is yours. I knew you were having problems. I should have done something about it."

"You're not responsible for me."

"Somebody has to look after you while Radko's not here to do it."

Radko's job was to protect Ean from would-be murderers and kidnappers, not from his own inability to control the trainees.

He was glad his comms chimed then, with a message from Abram. He was to address the council meeting the following day. Even gladder Abram had made it soon.

"If you were a soldier and couldn't fire a blaster, Ean, you wouldn't be expected to teach yourself. Your team leader would help out, ensuring you had remedial help."

He couldn't fire a blaster, and it was one thing Radko had never shown him. He'd asked her once if she was going to. She'd said, "Ean, your weapons are the lines."

"Maybe you should teach me how to use a blaster."

"Are you changing the subject, Ean?"

"No." Maybe. He wasn't sure. "What do I do about the line trainees?"

"Let's see who gets involved before we decide." The shuttle sounded for landing. Sale strapped herself in. "Meantime, we have to survive this supper first."

THE ship welcomed them. Ean sang his own song of welcome as he followed Sale down the corridor. He checked the ship while he did so. Captain Helmo was on the bridge. He felt—or heard—Ean's regard, and nodded. Commodore Vega was at shuttle bay five, waiting for a shuttle to dock.

Commodore Bach, the Emperor's head of security and Vega's equivalent, was in the foyer of Yu's apartment, talking into his comms.

"Everything is in hand, Lord Renaud. I assure you. I have set my staff to attend to it personally." He glanced at Ean and Sale. "You will excuse me, Lord Renaud, but I must attend His Imperial Majesty." He swiped off, then swiped the comms open again. The woman at the other end wore a Lancian uniform, with the same braid Ean had on his own shoulders. "Find out who assigned Yves Han to a covert operation. I want their head on my desk, tomorrow morning."

"Do we rescue Han the Younger?"

"What we do is damage control. And hope certain people never hear about it." Bach swiped off, then looked at Sale and Ean.

"Emperor Yu requested the presence of Linesman Lambert at supper, sir," Sale said.

Bach looked at her epaulettes. "And he's delivered by a group leader."

"Yes, sir. It's a good opportunity to debrief in private."

Bach nodded. "I heard about today. What started it?"

"Started it, sir?" Sale looked as mystified as Ean felt. "Captain Jakob attempting to steal the ship."

"The lockdown of linesmen."

He shouldn't have known about that. It was Abram's area, not Bach's. Not even Vega's, although she knew.

"That." Sale waved a dismissive hand. "You know linesmen. They come in thinking they're the galaxy's gift. We're teaching them new methods. It takes time to adapt. They don't like change."

Sale was as talented at dissembling as Abram and Michelle. Ean hid his smile.

"So they always do this?"

"This time was a little extreme. But there were reasons." Sale saluted. "It's in my report if you wish to read it. But, sir, I must deliver the linesman to supper. If you will excuse me."

"Of course." Bach stepped aside to let them enter. He followed them in.

The walls on the Emperor's entertaining room were covered with TransScreen, a product that had come onto the market just before Michelle had purchased Ean's contract. TransScreen had a smooth surface that showed whatever was sent through to its controllers. This particular sheet depicted a 360-degree panorama of somewhere on Lancia, for the sky had a distinctive purple tinge. Ean could hear the feed from line five as a constant stream, and as he watched, a shuttle zoomed high across the sky. A delayed real-time send, he guessed.

How magnificent would it be to switch the view to the cameras on the outside of the *Lancastrian Princess*? You'd really feel you were in space then.

Or maybe that wasn't such a good idea. Ean didn't like to remember there was only a wall between him and the stars.

He wasn't the only guest. Sattur Dow was there, as was the Factor of the Lesser Gods. Plus assorted support staff. Some of Yu's, some of the Factor's, some of Sattur Dow's. Ean recognized Ethan Saylor, the youth who continually called Vega wanting to talk to Radko.

Two members of Helmo's crew were clearing away the remains of food on the long supper table. Ean's stomach rumbled as he saw that. He hadn't eaten yet.

Yu looked him over as if he were inspecting something he was about to purchase. He glanced at the Factor. The Factor quirked an eyebrow. Ean got the impression that neither of them was impressed.

"So, Linesman," Yu said, and Ean got the impression more than ever that he was being studied as a pending acquisition. "Why is Galenos hiding information about the alien line ships from Lancia?"

He was glad he'd seen Vega's tape of Michelle's meeting with her father. Otherwise, he might have replied that the Department of Alien Affairs was keeping information about the line ships from every world until it was safe to do so.

"Hiding information." Ean managed a creditable Rossi-like laugh. "From Lancia, who gets knowledge before everyone else does. Who sends their own staff out to the *Confluence* every day. Other worlds should be so lucky."

"That isn't what I have heard."

It was a pity Yu hadn't been on ship long, for the lines weren't picking up his emotions enough for Ean to interpret them. "I don't know what you have heard," Ean said. "But if it's not that, I would question your sources."

Yu's eyes narrowed.

The Factor intercepted smoothly. "Tell me, Linesman. What is your opinion of the events today?"

Which events did he mean? The lockdown of the linesmen? Or the attempt to steal Scout Ship Three?

"I'm a linesman, not a politician. If you are looking for opinions, why don't you ask—" Abram, he'd been going to say, but Yu obviously had it in for him. "Mi— Her Royal Highness, the Crown Princess, I mean."

"Assuredly, we will," Yu said. "But does it not seem unusual that a man heretofore known as loyal and devoted to his ruler suddenly tries to steal a ship? One might almost believe that Captain Jakob was framed."

He couldn't be serious. But it seemed he was.

"By whom?" Ean asked, when he finally found enough voice to speak.

"Someone who wishes to keep the Worlds of the Lesser Gods out of the New Alliance."

Like Abram, he meant.

"No," Ean said. "The Factor was not set up. Jakob is working with Redmond. He's sent them messages in the past."

"Messages," Bach asked sharply. "To Redmond. How do you know that?"

Bach's high-tech center he'd set up on board the *Lancastrian Princess* would have picked up the transmissions as well. If Ean and Helmo hadn't destroyed his listening devices.

"We've heard some of them."

"Heard some of them?"

"Jakob sent a message before he left to go home." Except he hadn't gone home. "He was speaking Redmond."

Yu, Bach, and the Factor exchanged glances.

"Why wasn't I informed of this?" Yu demanded.

Now Vega would get in trouble because Ean had opened his mouth. "We were following it up. Jakob had replaced the camera in his cabin with old footage of him sleeping. We didn't have any recordings of what he did or said." Their emotions were stronger now; he was finally picking something up through the lines. Consternation, agitation. "Once we knew more, we would have notified Commodore Bach, of course, but Jakob and the *Iolo* tried to steal the ship before our investigation was complete."

Bach asked, "Do you have proof of this?" while the Factor demanded, "Are you spying on us?"

The lines sang a sudden song of welcome. It took Ean a moment to realize it wasn't because of what the Factor had said, but it was Michelle's shuttle, arriving in bay three. One of two shuttles arriving at the same time.

It was a pity Michelle wasn't here, right now. She'd know what to say. Still, he'd talked himself into this. It was up to him to talk himself out of it.

"We are not spying," for that seemed to be their main

concern. Although he didn't know why, given that rulers spent their lives surrounded by people who knew everything they did. "We look for triggers." It was even true. "Redmond language, in this case, which was what alerted us to Jakob."

The three men looked at each other again.

"You have an alert for anyone speaking Redmond," the Factor said.

"Yes. We do." Ean did, anyway.

"On this ship." Yu looked at Bach, rather than at Ean. "Why would they expect that?"

"Concerned they have spies on board," Bach suggested. To Ean, "You should have informed me, as I am responsible for the Emperor's protection."

Ean nodded but didn't answer.

Yu started to pace. "My own daughter is spying on me now." He stopped close to Ean. "Why is that?"

He was way too close, and according to Rigel, one never invaded the ruler's personal space. Ean knew he was supposed to step back, to give him room.

Ean had learned more about intimidation techniques in the last six months than he had in his whole life. He knew how to respond. He didn't move—back or forward. He curled his mouth in what he hoped looked like disdain, and channeled his best Rossi. "You assume she's spying on *you*."

His hands were clammy. He was sweating. This was as bad as the trainees and had escalated as quickly.

Down in shuttle bay three, Michelle waited for the air to recycle before she could disembark.

A woman exited shuttle bay five. One of Vega's staff frisked her for weapons.

"I see no need for this farce," the woman being frisked said.

"I would be negligent if I allowed you in the Emperor's presence without it," Vega said.

"Clear, ma'am," the soldier frisking the visitor told Vega.

"Thank you. This way." Vega led the woman along the corridor. "I trust you had a pleasant trip, Madam Chen."

"Fine, thank you," Chen said, stiffly.

Ean dragged his attention back to the room he was in. It

wouldn't do to miss something right now because he was listening to the ship. Yu was frowning, almost as if he'd forgotten Ean was there.

The Factor said, "If Jakob is working with Redmond, we must decide what to do about him."

For a moment, it looked as if Yu wouldn't answer.

"Galenos will question him. I would like to be involved in that."

There was emotion here, pungent, and sharp. Ean couldn't pick who it was from, maybe both of them. He tested the taste with his tongue. There was a touch of fear there, too, as if Yu really was worried about what Abram would do. About a man he'd promoted to admiral six months ago.

If he weren't so paranoid, he wouldn't need to be scared at all.

Yu turned his back on Ean. "You are correct, Factor. Admiral Galenos will twist the facts to suit himself."

Ean wanted to leave, couldn't do so until he was dismissed.

Sattur Dow stepped up beside Ean. "I believe you know my fiancée, Linesman."

"Of course I do. Everyone on this ship does."

"But you know her especially well, I have heard."

What had he heard?

Dow smiled at him. "As such, I would like to extend an invitation to our wedding."

There was no way Sattur Dow was going to marry Radko.

"Others on this ship know her better," Ean said, trying to be fair. "They're as much her family as her real family is, and have been around longer than I. You should invite her whole team."

He was saved from the awkward silence that statement caused by the arrival of Vega and Madam Chen. Vega withdrew after delivering the new guest. She glanced sharply at Ean on her way out but didn't say anything.

Chen made straight for Sattur Dow. "I need to talk to you."

"Later."

"I need to talk to you now."

Sattur Dow looked irritated. "Please excuse me a moment, Linesman."

Ean was pleased to see him go. "Of course."

Dow tried to halt at the door, but Chen took him out into the foyer. "Privately."

Ean eavesdropped unashamedly through the lines.

"You set me up." Ean could hear Chen's rage, icy on his skin.

"I have no idea what you are talking about," Dow said. "But drag me away like that in the middle of a conversation again, and I will most certainly set you up."

Ethan Saylor moved in to fill the void. "Linesman." He smiled cordially. "We should get to know each other better since we'll be working together."

"Working together?" Most of Ean's attention was on what was happening outside the door.

"Once your bodyguard marries Sattur Dow," Saylor said.

Ean looked at him. He was serious.

"You sent me to Redmond to kill me," Chen said.

Redmond, again. Why so much about Redmond all of a sudden?

"Maybe we could get together for a drink sometime," Saylor said.

"If this is your way of getting something more out of our agreement, it's not going to work," Dow said. "Where are my plans?"

"What about tomorrow night? After you finish work," Saylor said.

"I don't have your precious plans," Chen said. "You know that already."

"Linesman?"

"You set me up, Sattur." Chen took something out of her pocket. A chit. Ean was familiar with them from his youth. Chits were guarantees of money. You purchased them from moneylenders at above-market rates. They allowed you to move money without the purchase being traced.

She threw it at Dow. "Here's your money. Be warned, Sattur. You think you're too powerful to be reached, but everyone has secrets, you more than most." Chen turned and walked away.

Dow watched her go. He picked up the chit, then came back inside.

"Is there anyone inside there, Linesman?"

Ean blinked. "Sorry," he said to Saylor. "I was momentarily distracted."

Sattur Dow rejoined them. "Apologies, Linesman." He inclined his head toward Saylor. "Ethan, would you please find out what Merchant Chen's problem is?"

Saylor smiled although the smile didn't reach his eyes. "Of course, Sattur." He nodded politely to them both, leaving Ean alone with Sattur Dow again.

The noise in the room dropped. Yu, Bach, and the Factor looked at Ean.

He should have been listening to them, not to Dow.

"Linesman Lambert," Bach said. "When did you first realize—" His comms beeped. He glanced at the screen, thumb about to swipe the message to silence it. He paused, then looked up. "Please excuse me. I must take this call."

Michelle had exited from the shuttle and was making her way quickly along the corridors. Coming this way. She walked so briskly, her bodyguards had to half trot to keep up with her.

"What was in Jakob's message?" Yu demanded, as they waited for Bach to return.

"I don't know." He considered telling them to ask Vega, but Vega would be forced to say he was the one who heard it. He repeated the few words he could remember.

Yu's face, and the Factor's, grew grimmer as they listened. "That's only an approximation."

"Translated?" Yu asked.

"I don't know," Ean said, but Yu was looking at the Factor.

Coming from neighboring worlds, he would know enough Redmond to get by.

The Factor shook his head.

An uncomfortable silence fell.

Ean didn't break it. Instead, he listened to Bach take his call outside the door.

The woman on the comms was the same woman Bach had been talking to earlier. "This had better be important," Bach said.

"I found who assigned Han's son to Redmond."

Redmond again. Why was everyone at Redmond all of a sudden? Including Radko.

"And?" Bach asked.

"Commodore Jiang Vega."

"Vega," Bach said, as Michelle slowed to enter the foyer where he was talking.

Michelle looked at him.

Bach bowed. "Your Royal Highness."

"Commodore Bach."

Bach bowed and waited for her to enter before he turned back to his comms. "Send a code five," he told the woman. He flicked off and frowned down at the screen, then followed Michelle in.

Michelle inclined her head. "Father. Factor. Merchant Dow. Good evening." She nodded at Ean.

"Daughter. So glad you could make my supper. I heard you were staying on Haladea III tonight."

"My meeting finished early," Michelle said. "And I had some security issues I needed to discuss with Commodore Vega."

"We have been hearing about security issues." Yu ignored what was an obvious warning glance from Bach. "You spy on your guests."

"Surely not." Michelle didn't look at Ean, but he knew she knew who had precipitated the accusation.

Yu's comms vibrated discreetly then. And Bach's. And those of an assistant.

Yu ignored his comms. "Yes, apparently you are—"

The assistant raised a discreet hand.

Yu took out his own comms. He glanced at the message, raised a brow in Bach's direction. Bach nodded.

Was that Bach's code five? What was Vega involved in? And if it was Redmond, was Radko involved?

Yu swiped his comms off with force. He looked at Michelle. "We are not finished with this conversation, Daughter, but I have other issues to attend for the moment."

"Of course. My ship is at your disposal, Father."

"The Factor of the Lesser Gods wishes to be present at the interrogation of Captain Jakob. Arrange this, Daughter." He turned to Bach. "We should start now for Haladea III," and glanced at Michelle again. "In case Galenos steps up the timing of his interrogations."

He swept out, the Factor close behind him. Bach followed

them both, calling Helmo for clearance for the Emperor's shuttle.

Sattur Dow, left behind, bowed to Michelle.

"Excuse my rudeness, Sattur," Michelle said. "But I must organize the Factor's request to sit in on the interrogation. Ean," and she indicated he was to leave in front of her.

Ean half bowed to Sattur Dow on the way out. "Good night, Merchant."

TWENTY-ONE

EAN LAMBERT

EAN TRIED TO pull the screens on the shuttle through to the screen in Vega's office. He couldn't.

"It won't be wired for comms," Vega said. "The only time you'll ever get a signal out of there is if someone opens a channel on their comms. You could kill someone in one of those secure shuttles and no one would know. Not unless they recorded it."

He tried for Bach's comms but didn't know it well enough to identify which, out of the thousands around, it was.

Vega made them tea. It was only the four of them. Michelle, Ean, Sale, and Vega. "You're here to save Lambert from his supper?" she asked Michelle.

Michelle nodded.

"At least something makes sense. And you, Lambert. Why the sudden spying on Bach?"

"Because he wants your head," Ean said. "On his desk. By morning."

Vega paused making the tea. "Literally? Or figuratively?"

"He doesn't actually want your head, I think, but he was unhappy with something you did. He called a code five."

"A what?"

"A code five, and not long after that, Yu got a message." Ean was sure that Yu's message had been precipitated by Bach.

"We don't do codes by numbers," Vega said. "Ours are names, like Situation Josiah."

From the way Michelle nodded, Josiah was a real code. Maybe the numbers were a personal code between Bach and his boss.

"Vega, who is Yves Han, and is he or she with Radko?"

Vega spilled the tea she was bringing across to Michelle. She didn't say anything until she'd mopped up and made another glass.

"I want a linesman of my own," she told Michelle. "If we all had personal linesmen, we wouldn't have any need for war, for nothing would be secret."

Michelle's smile showed her dimples. The best smile. "Level twelve. They're hard to come by."

"I still want one. One that *I* control, rather than one that controls me. So, Lambert, where did you hear about Han?"

"Bach was talking about him earlier, to someone called Lord Renaud. He was on the comms to him when we went in to supper."

Not that they'd had any supper.

"He told Renaud he'd deal with it, then he called up this other woman, told her to find out who had assigned Yves Han to a covert operation, and said he wanted their head on his desk by the morning. She called back later—before Michelle arrived—and said she'd found who assigned Han to Redmond. You had. After that, Bach called his code five. I think they went down to the planet so they could talk about you."

"Is that Renaud Han's son?" Michelle asked.

Vega nodded. "Yves Han. He worked for me for two years when I was at Baoshan Barracks. He's very good. He's wasted where he is."

Of course Vega would send good people with Radko.

"I sent three people with Radko. All failed linesmen. She is, after all, uniquely positioned to understand the abilities and difficulties of working with such people."

If it was meant to be an insult, Ean ignored it.

"Two of them had failed certification. Yves Han didn't. He certified with House of Sandhurst. Level seven, and the lines know, we need sevens. He came home not long afterward to attend a function." She looked at Michelle. "He is Lord Renaud's son, after all."

Michelle nodded.

"He stopped off at a hotel before the event. The day some crazy woman blew herself up there. Killed fifty people. Yves Han spent six months in hospital having his body rebuilt.

When he came out he couldn't communicate with the lines anymore. The doctors say there was no brain damage, and that his loss of lines is psychosomatic, rather than physical, in origin. They posit that he was doing something line-related at the time of the explosion, and that it is so intertwined with the memory of the explosion that he shuts down whenever he tries to use the lines."

"And you thought Ean might be able to fix it."

"Lambert's method of interacting with the lines is different," Vega said. "I thought it might be strange enough to bypass any mental blocks."

She might be right.

"Han's father said he was in trouble," Ean said. "He wanted Bach to rescue him."

Damage control, Bach had said. What were they doing on Redmond anyway?

"Let's find out what the trouble is," Vega said. "And let's hope Bach isn't talking to Lord Renaud at the same time."

THE time lag between Lancia and the Haladean sector was nineteen minutes.

While they waited, Sale went down to the mess and came back with plates of supper. "If it's okay with you, ma'am," she said apologetically, and Ean wasn't sure who she was saying it to. "But neither of us have eaten yet."

"I haven't eaten in ages either," Michelle said. "I wouldn't mind something myself."

"Remember the sandwiches when we met," Ean said, and he and Michelle shared a smile.

"I'll never forget."

Michelle's comms buzzed. Her father. Ean thought about tracing the comms.

"Daughter," Yu said. "Call a council meeting immediately. Your betrothed wishes to request a favor of them."

Michelle looked taken aback. "It is midnight. By the time I got them together, it would be time for tomorrow's regular council meeting."

"Are you—"

"Of course not, Father. But I refuse to make a fool of myself organizing a meeting when one will already happen within hours. Nor should you. It was you yourself who taught me to save the fights for the important things. What is this matter which is of such great import?"

"And if Admiral Galenos asked you to organize a council meeting, what would you say? Wait?"

Michelle took a deep breath.

Yu had no right to do this to anyone.

Vega put a hand on Ean's arm. Out of sight of Michelle's comms. He hadn't realized he'd opened his mouth to speak.

"I would tell him the same thing." Michelle took a deep breath. "I will ask that the Factor be allowed to address the council after the regular session. What does he wish to speak to them about?"

"Why, the capture of the *Iolo* and the betrayal of Captain Jakob, of course."

"Very well," Michelle said.

After Michelle clicked off, she stared at her comms. "I don't know how many more favors the council will grant us. We are fast running out of friends."

"Maybe the Factor should have requested it himself," Vega said. "I hear he's fast making them."

Ean thought of Admiral Trask, and his carefully worded warnings. Of how many of the admirals who'd spoken to Ean wanted the Worlds of the Lesser Gods on the New Alliance's side. They could all see advantages having allies close to Redmond. They just didn't like the way it was being done.

Renaud Han called then.

Lord Renaud had been on the vids often when Ean was a boy. This harried, anguished man looked nothing like the elegant lord Ean remembered from his childhood.

"Lord Renaud," Vega said. "I am from the Palace Guard. About your call earlier. Your son. What exactly is the problem?"

They waited for the call to travel to Lancia and back.

Vega didn't give her name, but nineteen minutes later, when the call came back, Lord Renaud looked into the screen as if trying to see her properly. "Captain Vega." His face cleared with relief. "We've met before. You were my son's commanding officer on Baoshan."

"I was," Vega agreed.

"Only it's Commodore now, of course. Congratulations on your promotion."

"Thank you," Vega said.

Neither of her answers would get back to Lancia for another nineteen minutes.

"Lord Renaud," Vega said. "I need to know what trouble your son is in and what we can do to fix it."

Ean dozed while he waited for the reply.

"It's difficult to explain over the comms," Renaud said. Ean heard the hot spike of Vega's impatience. "You see, Yves thinks he was on a job, and I'm concerned my comms are not secure enough."

"Is it bugged?" Vega asked Ean.

"I can only tell about this end."

"Damn. I need answers, bugged or not. Can you make it secure, Ean?"

Ean had no control on ships outside the sector. "No"

"We'll send him into the barracks to get it coded." Vega looked back at the screen. "Lord Renaud. I need to know exactly what happened. I want you to go into the barracks. I'll have someone ready for you. I want you to tell the whole story. They'll record it, encode it, and send it to me. Tell everything, even things you don't think necessary. Do you understand?"

"We could jump the Lancastrian Princess back to Lancian space and pick him up," Ean suggested, while they waited for the reply. "Then he could tell us face-to-face."

"A cold jump. I don't want to be the one to send Helmo to an early grave."

The comms was open; they weren't hiding any of the conversation from Renaud Han.

Nineteen minutes later, the reply came back from Renaud. "I'd be happy to explain it in person. Relieved, actually, and I could talk to Commodore Bach while I'm there."

Vega's annoyance flooded line one. "Lord Renaud, it will take two weeks to get a jump. If you're lucky."

But Renaud was still talking from nineteen minutes ago. "I can be there tomorrow."

This time Vega did turn the comms off. "I don't know what

world he lives in, but it's not reality." She switched back on.
"Lord Renaud. If you are unable to get a ship, please go back
to our original plan. I will have someone from the barracks
contact you."

She clicked off. "Some people don't seem to realize there's
a war on."

TWENTY-TWO

EAN LAMBERT

MICHELLE CALLED IN multiple favors to get the Factor an audience after the day's council meeting. Ean listened to the talk through Orsaya's comms on his way to his own meeting.

"At this rate, she won't have any favors left to call in." Orsaya's voice was as sour as Vega's as she and Ean walked down to the council room with the Yaolin captain, Auburn. "She's definitely using up the goodwill of Aratoga and Balian on this."

Captain Auburn nodded.

Ean wished Yu would hurry up and go home.

Line training had been canceled that day, pending the investigation by the admirals. That wouldn't happen until after the council meeting. One thing less to worry about, at least. For the moment, anyway.

Abram had organized a precouncil meeting for him. A private session where no visitors were allowed, and the recorded discussion was not made available to the general public. Line business was for council ears only.

Ean stepped up to the podium and wiped his suddenly damp hands down the side of his uniform. He had spoken to each council member multiple times, individually and in groups, but today, he was nervous.

"Members of the council, thank you for agreeing to hear me." He looked around at the 140 council members. Michelle and Abram both smiled encouragingly. Ean took a deep breath. "Yesterday, Redmond tried to steal a fleet line ship."

He had their attention. He heard the sound of a glass being placed down after one of the councilors took a drink of water. If he'd been on a ship, he would have heard the gulp that went with it and tasted the water.

He wanted to be on ship. He wanted to know what they were thinking.

He had no idea.

"They very nearly succeeded."

That caused a reaction: a murmur of noise that swelled, then died away.

"They didn't steal the ships." One could always rely on Admiral Carrell, of Eridanus, to speak first.

"No, they didn't," Ean agreed. "But it was close." He spoke before Carrell could speak again. "Do you want to know why it was so close, Admiral Carrell?"

"Well, of course I do. We all do."

This time the murmur was an assent.

"Because Redmond brought linesmen," Ean said. He raised his arm and pointed. He didn't have to calculate a direction. He knew where the ships were. "Those ships out there are so desperate for linesmen, they'll take anything they can get. Even enemy linesmen."

"We have supplied you with linesmen," Carrell said. "Once they are trained, they will be put on those ships."

"I understand that. But the ships are sentient. They don't understand the concept of time. They don't understand why they have to wait. They want their linesmen now. And if we don't start allocating them to various ships, the *Confluence* and its fleet will start to choose its own crew. From anywhere. Even the enemy. Give me a list of which world gets which ship, and I'll introduce them to their linesmen."

"They're line ships," Carrell said. "We choose their crew. When we're ready."

If Ean could convince Carrell, he could convince the rest of the council. "Alien ships are different from any ships we have known before, Admiral. We might have chosen crew for the human line ships, but the alien ships have minds of their own."

The aliens would have been smart enough to have crew ready as soon as a ship was available.

"So you're telling us we have no control over who goes on which ship? Is this a plot by Lancia to grab the *Confluence* itself?"

He was not going to tell anyone about Sale. Not right now.

"I am telling you to sort out which ship each world will get. Sort it out now, and I will endeavor to introduce the ships to their linesmen. Otherwise, I cannot guarantee you will get the ship you negotiate for."

"This is a plot. A plan by Lancia to—"

The noise from the chamber swelled.

"Admiral Carrell." Ean was grateful for his voice training, which allowed him to raise his voice enough to be heard here on world, even without the lines. "Admiral Carrell. Do you know how we stopped Redmond stealing Scout Ship Three?"

He waited until the noise had subsided.

"I promised it a crew of its own. I introduced the ship to its crew." Ean searched the hall for Councilor Shimson. He bowed to him. "Councilor Shimson, Admiral Trask," who was seated next to him. "I promised Scout Ship Three to Xanto."

The council members started talking over each other.

"Why does Xanto get a ship first?"

"How can a ship choose its own crew?"

"You have to stop this happening. Surely you control the ships."

"Intelligent ships. It's a farce, to force us into deciding before we're ready."

"Which ships are choosing? We need more time."

"Mightn't be a bad idea to move faster. We get our own ship, with entrenched linesmen. Lancia couldn't drag it back after that."

The noise of over one hundred people speaking at once battered at him. Ean held his hands up to stop their talking. For a wonder, they quieted.

"These are alien ships. They are sentient." If the members of the council didn't know that by now, they were living in denial. "They don't think as we do. For us to have control, tell me who gets which ship, and I will introduce the linesmen of that world to their ships. As long as they see progress, I think the ships will wait longer."

"And the *Confluence*," Admiral Carrell demanded.

"Give me two linesmen from every world for it. Pledge those linesmen as part of your gaining your own ship."

Someone whose voice Ean didn't recognize said, "But the *Confluence* hasn't got a captain yet."

He really wasn't going to mention Sale. "I'm sure all of you already have a captain in mind. Put their name forward. Let the council decide. Just give the *Confluence* a crew while you're deciding."

He held up his hand for silence again. And got it. "I don't need to remind you of the fragility of the fleet." This was a closed session, after all. Everyone here knew facts that weren't general knowledge. Like how the fleets jumped together unless they had a linesman in control. He wasn't sure if they all knew it had to be a line seven, but they knew the limitations. "If Scout Ship Three had jumped, the whole fleet would have jumped into enemy territory."

He paused, then added, "I urge you to act now to be sure the ships are under your control." Abram and Michelle would have been proud of his double meaning there. "Before it's too late."

He left the council chambers as more animated chatter broke out. This wasn't his decision to make. The council needed time to argue.

Emperor Yu and the Factor of the Lesser Gods were in the outer chamber, along with the media and support staff who were locked out when a closed council was in session.

Yu paced. The man was always pacing. The Factor was speaking with two well-dressed officials. His body language was eloquent. The horror, the shame, the sense of betrayal. It wasn't hard to surmise they were talking about the attempted theft of Scout Ship Three.

If Michelle did marry the Factor, they'd be able to converse in body gestures alone. Michelle and Abram could hold silent conversations, too. Only they hadn't needed grandiloquent gestures. They'd held whole conversations with a raised eyebrow or a twist of lips.

Yu stopped pacing when he saw Ean. Ean was glad of Bhaksir and her team, who fell in around him and marched him out, looking straight ahead. They exited the gallery before the media descended.

"We should stay and see what the Factor says," Ean said.

"No." Bhaksir took him straight to the roof. "We've orders to get you back on ship as quickly as we can."

To be honest, he was glad. Here on world, he was blind and

deaf. He didn't know what was going on. How easily one got used to having access to the lines.

"Can we watch the council meeting?"

Bhaksir nodded, and Ean listened to the regular business until it was time to call the Factor.

The Factor stood before the councilors, tall and imposing. "Council of the New Alliance. I come to you with this plea. The Worlds of the Lesser Gods are vulnerable. Our former ally, Redmond, has deserted us. We stood alone. Then, out of the goodness of your hearts, the New Alliance is considering us as potential allies. You have adopted us and made us feel welcome. And how do we repay you?"

He paused, long enough to let the message sink in but not long enough for Admiral Carrell to interject.

"With treachery. A traitor from my own party. A man I trusted. A man working with my enemy, our enemy, to steal what is yours."

He was a mesmerizing speaker. By the time he got to the end, Ean wanted to applaud.

Some members of the council did.

"What will happen to those traitors? To this man I trusted with my own life? Will they receive the punishment that is due? No. They will languish in a prison for the rest of their life. I ask you, councilors. Isn't that too kind?"

Another pause.

"Will they even give us the information we require? On the Worlds of the Lesser Gods, we deal with betrayers as they deserve. We take them, we break them. We get our answers. And then we destroy them.

"I, the Factor of the Lesser Gods, ask this of you. Let *us* take these people and find out what they know. Let *us* treat them with the contempt they deserve. Allow me to salve a small amount of the harm that was done to my worlds, to the reputation of my betrothed's world. Grant me this means of making amends.

"I will escort them personally. I will ensure the correct questions are asked. I will share this knowledge with you. With *all* of you."

It was a measured dig at the Department of Alien Affairs.

He got applause, and Ean heard Carrell's "Well said."

Afterward, when the noise had died down, Abram asked

the first question. "So you are proposing to take these thieves back to your world and torture them?"

That question raised a chorus of complaints. "Come, Galenos," Admiral Carrell said. "You can't tell me Lancia never tortured anyone."

"I'm not even trying," Abram said. "But I question whether it is necessary. We have efficient questioning techniques of our own. Humanitarian ones. Can we trust that the Worlds of the Lesser Gods will pass the information they receive back to us? If we allow them to take these people and question them, how do we know what results we will get back? How do we know they will be questioned?"

It was the closest anyone had come yet to accusing the Worlds of the Lesser Gods outright of being involved.

Ean couldn't see what Michelle thought of that.

"If you are so concerned about their not doing the right thing," Carrell said, "why don't you send someone with them to oversee that it is done properly."

"Hear, hear," another councilor said. And a second, then a third.

"I propose we vote on the Factor's request that he be allowed to take the criminals back to the Worlds of the Lesser Gods," Admiral Carrell said. "With the proviso that we are allowed to send two observers. One from Lancia, another chosen by the council by vote."

The vote went seventy-one to sixty-nine, the Factor's way. Michelle voted for the Factor's proposal; Abram voted against. It was the first time Ean could recall that Michelle and Abram hadn't voted the same way.

Emperor Yu, from the visitor's gallery, volunteered Commodore Bach as the Lancastrian to accompany the prisoners.

"After all," he told Michelle when they were back on the *Lancastrian Princess*, "we need someone we can trust to oversee the operation."

Ean eavesdropped unashamedly.

"You honor us all." Michelle looked cool and composed, but through the lines Ean could hear how utterly weary she was, could taste the bitterness and the exhaustion. She looked over to Commodore Bach. "I would appreciate it if you would go. I have the utmost trust in you."

Bach bowed low. "Thank you. Be sure that everything I do, I do only for Lancia."

EAN was on Confluence Station when the shuttleload of prisoners boarded the ship Lancia had provided for the trip back to the Worlds of the Lesser Gods. He waited with Sale and Orsaya while it jumped.

How had the Factor gotten a jump so quickly?

"One hopes Commodore Bach's team is enough to cope with whatever the Worlds of the Lesser Gods puts forward," Orsaya said.

Ean wasn't sure he trusted Bach yet.

Renaud Han hadn't called from Baoshan Barracks, either, so he didn't know what was happening with Radko.

He had other things to worry about right now, for Abram, Katida, and MacClennan arrived at Confluence Station. All four admirals from the Department of Alien Affairs. Here to talk about the "incident" at line training yesterday.

Ean, Rossi, and Sale joined them.

Orsaya's staff got them sandwiches and tea. Sometimes, Ean thought the only thing working soldiers ate was sandwiches.

No one talked about what had happened that morning at the council meeting. Instead they talked about the Factor's initial visit to the *Confluence*. And about the visitors' line knowledge in general.

"The Factor was fishing," Orsaya said. "He's heard stories about Lambert."

"Maybe we shouldn't keep it a secret anymore," Abram said. "Enough people know or suspect by now. We also have Sattur Dow asking questions about things he shouldn't know. Someone is feeding him information."

"I thought you ran a tight ship, Galenos," Orsaya said. "I can't imagine your staff giving out information like that."

Abram blew out his breath but didn't say anything.

"Everyone on the *Lancastrian Princess* is reliable," Sale said, her voice cold.

Orsaya smiled. "Well-spoken, Group Leader. We all know that. But Galenos is as aware as we are that someone is passing information to people like Dow. There is a high probability that someone is Lancastrian."

It wasn't anyone on the *Lancastrian Princess*.

"So we come now to yesterday's problem," Katida said. Ean didn't know if it was a deliberate attempt to change the subject.

"I take full responsibility," Sale said. "I was aware of the tension. I should have acted earlier."

No way would Ean let Sale take the blame for something he'd done. "It wasn't Sale. She offered to help, but I wanted to sort it out myself."

"What actually happened?" Katida asked. Her lines were muted, as if she was deliberately trying to hide them. Ean didn't pry. He opened his mouth to answer, but Sale spoke first.

"Lambert had—has—a reputation among other linesman. Many of the multilevel linesmen in this group were aware of that reputation."

"I didn't control—"

"Let Group Leader Sale complete her explanation," Orsaya said.

Ean closed his mouth.

"The problem was compounded by the fact that Linesman Rossi, a known level-ten linesman, attended the training but did not run it."

More nods.

"One linesman in particular, Arnold Peters, has been spreading resentment. In the classes themselves, and outside of them. He is, by all accounts, convincing, and was at House of Rigel while Ean was there. He's telling them horror stories.

"We knew there was a problem. It was manageable until yesterday, when Captain Jakob and Redmond tried to steal the scout." Sale glanced over at Ean and Rossi. "Lambert took corrective action by moving the ship closer to the *Eleven* fleet."

He was Lambert now. No one in Sale's team ever called him Lambert.

"The bastard jumped the ship cold," Rossi said. "He has no consideration for the welfare of anyone else on the ships."

He wasn't going to let Redmond—or the Worlds of the Lesser Gods—steal a ship.

"Linesman Rossi reacted by trying to prevent Lambert from

moving the ship," Sale said. "He grabbed a weapon and attempted to shoot him. Lambert's bodyguards protected him and disarmed Rossi. Except the trainees saw a top-level linesman attacked for no obvious reason. They came in to defend him."

Sale looked at each admiral in turn. "The problem was quickly resolved with the assistance of all crew on board the *Gruen*. However, Captain Gruen demanded a lockdown, as people were still angry. And her ship was damaged."

Katida's lines leaked amusement. "And we couldn't have that, of course."

"No, ma'am," Sale said, then back to all four admirals. "That's all, sirs."

They turned their attention to Ean. Four intense gazes were unnerving.

"Do you have anything to add to the facts?" Katida asked.

He heard the slight emphasis on "facts," both through her voice and through the lines.

"No, ma'am." It felt strange calling Katida ma'am. "Except the fault is all mine. I was in charge." Sale shouldn't blame herself. He'd been running the training. "But I disagree with the implication that I have no concern for other people and their welfare. The jump was perfectly safe. If I only cared for the ships, I would have allowed the ship to be taken. It wanted crew. All the alien ships do." He pressed his lips together before he said anything further.

Katida turned back to Sale. "Do we have a plan for dealing with future problems?"

"We were hoping that as the linesmen learned more about the lines, they would come around."

"If we get rid of Peters?"

"I'm not sure that will solve the problem," Sale said. "Although we have discussed that."

They'd mentioned it. Was that the full amount of their discussion, or had they talked about it elsewhere?

"Peters makes a lot of noise," Sale said. "But they're linesmen. The singles should be realizing the benefits by now and shutting him down, even if the multilevels aren't. But the singles are almost worse than the multilevels. He shouldn't have that much influence. Not on his own."

"So there may be a second troublemaker," Katida said. "Any

idea who?" Her lines didn't sound surprised. None of the others looked surprised either. It was almost as if they expected it.

"No, ma'am. We haven't ascertained that yet."

"The question," Admiral MacClennan said, "is whether the trouble is deliberate, or whether they're just linesmen aggrieved about the training?"

Ean hoped they weren't trying to find excuses to absolve him. "How could it be deliberate?"

"Ean," Katida said, "you truly do need to spend some time in my military. Build up some paranoia."

"Put Burns in," Orsaya suggested. "He's a single. Many people still believe he's Rossi's assistant. There might be some sympathy there."

"What if they think he's a spy?" Fergus worked with Ean. If the trainees turned on him, he'd have no chance.

"I'll put him in a protective suit," Abram said. Ean had a suit of his own back on the *Lancastrian Princess*. He'd never worn it, other than to try it on. "Although we won't be close enough if anything goes wrong. Ean?"

"The lines will look after him." They considered Fergus part of the *Eleven* fleet, and the *Gruen* was an *Eleven* ship.

"You'd better make sure he's safe, bastard."

"I will, but why don't you do something about it as well?"

Rossi crossed his arms over his chest and didn't answer.

Orsaya said, "We'll all be watching to see what we can find. Burns will be the most protected man in the whole of the New Alliance."

Did the trainees realize they'd now be watched by four fleets?

Abram called Fergus up immediately. "Burns, we're placing you on the *Gruen*. Group Leader Sale and Linesman Lambert will explain what you need to do." Then he called Gruen. "We're sending Linesman Burns to the *Gruen* temporarily. Please look after him."

She nodded. "I've sent through a list of damages."

"We'll have it attended to," Abram promised, and clicked off.

What did Gruen do after a battle, when her ship was badly damaged? Hound the admiralty until it was fixed?

After that, they walked down to the shuttle bay together.

"Abram." Ean dropped back.

Abram matched his pace to Ean's. This close there were more lines around his eyes than there had been, and he looked tired.

"Did the council say anything? About getting crew for the fleet ships."

Abram smiled. "You certainly stirred them up. Made them a lot happier, actually. They're scared of Lancia and worried they'll lose their ships to us. Your message this morning gave them a way to be sure they don't, without actually admitting Lancia is a problem. You'll have your ships allocated soon."

"Good. Because the ships are already choosing their own linesmen. The *Confluence* is vetting each linesman who comes on board." And not only the linesmen. Should he tell Abram about Sale?

"Although"—and the corners of Abram's mouth quirked—"your announcement that you've already given one ship away was unexpected." He breathed out, a soft sigh Ean heard through the lines rather than actually heard. "I wish that yours were the only type of problems we had to deal with."

Did that mean he minded what Ean had done? Or that he didn't? Whether he did or didn't, the ships would choose. "Put sentient ships around sentience for too long, and you won't have any choice who goes where."

"So, is it humans who are giving the lines sentience, then? Or is it that the lines, so long being used to a different sentience, are adapting to humans?"

Ean didn't know, but wondering about it had brought back some of Abram's energy and spirit. Maybe it was time to raise the other matter.

"Did you know the captain of a ship doesn't have to be the captain?"

Abram raised an eyebrow.

"Patten isn't the one Confluence Station thinks is in charge. That's a guy called Ryley."

"Malcolm Ryley? Patten's second-in-command?"

"Yes."

"He's probably a better choice," Abram said. "So you say if a ship has a bad captain, it chooses its own."

How bad had Patten been? Ean shrugged. "It chooses its own if it doesn't have a captain." Maybe Ryley had been around longer. Maybe the station liked Ryley better. "It finds someone who looks after it and is there all the time."

Abram didn't get the hint.

"The *ships* are starting to do that."

Abram said, "That may be no bad thing."

There was nothing Ean could say to that.

FERGUS greeted them with, "Have you ever worn one of these things?" Externally, he didn't look any different. Not even bulkier. "They're dreadful."

"They keep you alive," Sale said.

"But still, against a bunch of linesmen?"

"Linesmen who are in the military. Who've been trained to shoot accurately and shoot fast."

"Are they likely to be a problem?"

"Why don't you ask Rossi, over there, who'll be wearing that splint on his wrist for the next three days? Or Ean, whose leg is fresh from rehab."

Technically, the damage to Ean had been done by Rossi, and the damage to Rossi by Bhaksir and her team.

"Why are we expecting problems?" Fergus asked. "Surely, the business of yesterday cleared the air."

"One can only hope," Sale said. "Unfortunately, it seems to have had the opposite effect, and everyone is resentful because that lockdown will be on their record. We want you to find out if someone is deliberately stirring up trouble."

"Peters?"

"Probably not Peters. He's more likely to be a vocal result of whoever is stirring them up."

Fergus nodded. "Anything else?"

"Be prepared. Don't be complacent."

Fergus nodded again.

They walked down to the shuttle bay with him—their second walk for the night—while Sale gave Fergus last-minute instructions. A frowning Rossi accompanied them, the first show of line solidarity in what felt like a long time.

"We'll look after him."

"Thank you."

"The lines will protect you," Ean said.

"That's good to know. Thank you."

What harm could befall Fergus on the *Gruen* anyway? It was a fleet ship; it should be safe.

"See you tomorrow at training." Ean hoped his foreboding was more to do with his concern about facing the trainees again than it was about what might happen to Fergus in the meantime.

SALE, Craik, and her team accompanied Ean to line training the following day. They had a full complement of senior linesmen, with Rossi, Hernandez, and Fergus all present.

"I want to talk to them," Ean told Sale. "Rather than you tell them off, I mean."

Later, facing the trainees in the cargo hold, he wasn't as confident. Gruen had provided her own guards, and they stood ready—with weapons—for any assault.

Fergus smiled encouragement. He, at least, was still whole and safe.

"What happened yesterday was a disgrace to us all, as people, and to the lines you are learning to work with. Some of you have issues with me being your trainer." He paused and looked them over. Peters opened his mouth to say something. "Don't say it, Peters, or I'll be forced to use you as an example."

Peters closed his mouth with a snap. Ean breathed out; that was one battle he hadn't wanted to fight.

"I'm sure you've all had trainers before that you didn't like. Ones you didn't think capable of training you. They weren't necessarily the highest rank in their field, either. Did you pick a fight with your trainers and continuously undermine them? I doubt it. You gritted your teeth and hoped to get through the course."

They were all silent. How much of that was because they were listening to him, and how much of it was because of Gruen's armed guards around the room? Sale's team, too, although they didn't look as menacing as Gruen's people even if they were more dangerous.

"Yesterday was your last chance. You work with the program or you are out."

He took a deep breath. "As some of you mentioned, you're not getting access to the alien ships, even though you think you deserve it." He could tell them now that they didn't deserve it, but they wouldn't believe him. "You have to earn that access. Once you earn it, we'll take you on a tour."

Sale straightened but didn't say anything.

"And who decides when we've earned it?" Peters couldn't stay quiet for long. "You? We know who you'll pick."

"Not me." He looked out over the crowd to the linesmen at the back. Hernandez, scowling at the group. Rossi, arms crossed, frowning. Fergus, stiff in his armored suit. "Since you all know how good he is, Linesman Rossi will deem whether you've earned a trip to the alien ships."

"Don't include me in your crazy schemes."

"We're linesmen, Rossi. We work together."

He watched the speculative looks the trainees shared. Some of them were definitely out to prove themselves. Even Peters looked interested.

"So what earns us a pass?" Kentish demanded.

"You talk to the lines; you hear them when they talk back to you. Rossi will tell you if you're doing it right or not."

"Thank you very much."

Ean smiled. "Let's start training, shall we."

Jordan Rossi wasn't a patient man, or a tolerant one. He listened to each linesman sing, pointed left or right, then moved on to the next. The four Xantos went right, and Ean already knew they could hear the lines, so that meant those on the left needed more training.

Peters was sent left.

Ean went over to him. "Can you feel the lines? Like you do normally, I mean."

"Is this a trick question?"

Ean hid his sigh. *"No,"* direct to Peters, and then to the lines, *"Please tell him no."*

A strong chorus of noes filled the room, mixed in with some of Ean's exasperation. Even the elevens joined in.

Peters looked taken aback.

"Do you mind?" Rossi said.

"Did you understand what I said?" Ean asked Peters.

"No."

Ean didn't push it. He moved on to the next linesman.

Halfway through training, Vega left a message. Renaud Han was in Haladean space. She'd sent him to Confluence Station. She would meet Ean there.

THEY met in the small meeting room off the main control room.

"You got here quickly," Vega said

"I will do whatever needs to be done for my son." It was both a promise and a challenge. "He's not involved. He's an honest boy and works hard. He doesn't know about any of this."

"And what did it take to get a ship here so fast?"

It wasn't the first question Ean would have asked, but Renaud laughed. "I've been smuggling goods for fourteen years now. Getting a ship was the least of my problems."

Vega didn't even blink although Ean did. "You don't strike me as a man likely to become involved in smuggling, Lord Renaud. What could you possibly gain?"

"Isn't that what this is about?" Renaud asked.

Was Radko was chasing smugglers on Redmond? No. Vega wouldn't have sent her there for that. Not unless someone was smuggling war secrets.

"I'm not ashamed of what I did."

"Tell the damn story, Renaud, or I'll feed you a truth drug. We've got more important things than having you procrastinating."

Lord Renaud nodded and blew into his cupped palms. Maybe to give himself courage.

"You need to understand why I did it."

"Tell us, then."

"My son was a monster." Bald and flat, and absolutely honest, according to the lines.

"This son you are trying so desperately to rescue?"

"Of course not. Let me tell it from the beginning."

Vega nodded.

"Yves was . . . you don't need to know . . . but we started sending him away for treatment when we discovered what he was like."

He relaxed as he spoke. Ean thought he might be relieved to tell it.

"We got a look-alike for some of the public functions because, of course, we had to keep up appearances. It wouldn't do to show the Emperor we had a weakness."

Emperor Yu again, controlling everyone's lives. One man shouldn't have that much power.

"Jaxon was a lovely boy. And although Amina never said it to my face, I know we both wished he was our son, and not Yves."

Renaud blew into his hands again. He was trembling now. "Yves got worse, especially once he started line training. There were incidents. Here, and on Roscracia."

House of Sandhurst was on Roscracia, and Vega had said Han trained at Sandhurst.

"One girl." Renaud's voice didn't change, but the wave of horror—bitter and nose-clearingly sharp—overwhelmed the lines.

"The girl?" Vega prompted Renaud.

"Her mother decided to kill Yves. He came back to Lancia for a function. She blew up the hotel. Killed him, killed herself, and fifty other people."

That would be the explosion where Yves Han had lost his line ability.

"They told us that Yves was dead. Then they said they'd made a mistake, and he was in the hospital." Renaud breathed into his palms again. "We think the initial prognosis—that Yves was dead—came from the DNA they got from the bomb scene. Then someone at the hospital recognized Yves as our son. We didn't know Yves had asked Jaxon to stand in for him. Not for weeks. Not until they started the skin grafts and found we were incompatible."

Vega nodded.

"So we went to his parents. They wanted money. For what we'd done to their son." Renaud looked earnestly at them both. "Understand, no one expected Yves—Jaxon—to recover fully. We all thought he'd . . . so we paid them off, provided they came in every week for skin grafts."

Renaud breathed in deeply again. The opposite of Abram, who always blew out. "They're still getting their money.

"Things went well for a while. Yves—Jaxon—recovered, although he didn't remember much at first. Everyone thought he was Yves, treated him like Yves. His parents stayed away, provided they got their money."

A lot of families Ean knew would give up their sons for a regular allowance.

"Did he ever remember?" Vega asked.

"In the end, but, of course, we wouldn't listen. We always changed the subject." Another deep breath. "Tiana Chen found out. I don't know if you know her. She sticks around the fringes of court, finding everyone's secrets and blackmailing them."

"She blackmailed you?"

"Yes. Yves guessed we were being blackmailed. So he joined the fleet." A laugh that was half sob. "I think he felt guilty. He thought it would solve things. Only the entry tests—"

"Would have picked up that he was an imposter," Vega said.

"Yes." Renaud rubbed his hands together again. "I found someone. On Redmond. They agreed to switch the DNA records in exchange for my sending them things from Lancia. Medical supplies, mostly, because the taxes between the two worlds quadruple the cost. There were some things you couldn't send to Redmond, even back then."

Ean shivered. The adopted son would have thought he was fixing things. But he hadn't. He'd made it much, much worse.

"How did you get the items to Redmond?"

"I have a friend." Renaud stopped.

"He won't get into trouble. We're interested in your son, right now."

"He's a good friend. He hasn't done anything wrong."

"I've already said no repercussions for him."

"He exports live shellfish. He gave me access to the ships he uses. He's their best customer. They'll do anything for him."

"So let me get this straight," Vega said. "The boy's parents are blackmailing you. Tiana Chen is blackmailing you. And Redmond is blackmailing you and asking you to smuggle medical supplies and other goods."

"Yves is worth every credit. And I'll still happily pay it."

The truth of that was a high crystal note through the lines.

"So what changed," Vega asked. "You wouldn't be this stressed about something that's been going on for years."

Renaud rubbed his eyes. "A month after the formation of the New Alliance I got a visit from someone. I didn't know him, but he was Lancastrian. Military, I think, but I couldn't be sure. He said, 'We know you are sending items to Redmond. We want you to send things for us, as well.'"

"And if you didn't?"

"They would take Yves and torture him. Suddenly, instead of passing medical supplies, I'm passing fleet plans and . . . alien gadgets and I don't know what else."

"Alien gadgets?" Ean asked.

"I recognized one of them. From the media. A little thing about so big." Renaud cupped his hands.

Ean wanted to ask him to describe it further. He didn't.

"I knew it was wrong. Of course I did. We're at war. I couldn't keep it up, not even for Yves. So I went to Commodore Bach."

"What did he do?" Vega's tone was mild.

"He told me to keep sending the items but to tell him about each shipment. That if I stopped, Redmond would likely make good on their promise to harm Yves. Or at the very least kidnap him and use that to force us to continue sending goods."

Renaud blinked hard and breathed in three times fast in succession, nearly choking himself. He blinked again. "No one saw me go to Bach, but not long after that Yves leaves the barracks without calling me first. He knows we worry if he goes away. He always calls to let us know."

"How often does he go away?"

"Hardly ever. He's a military policeman. He's stationed at Baoshan Barracks."

Who had assigned Yves Jaxon Han to Baoshan? Ean suspected Renaud wouldn't be above dropping a word in the ear of someone in power to get his "son" a job somewhere safe, where the worst thing he was likely to come across were soldiers drunk after a night out. Where the Han family could keep an eye on him.

"When Yves finally calls, he's on Redmond, and he wants Gunter to send shellfish so he can escape. How does he even know we always put the smuggled goods in with the shellfish? Not unless someone is forcing him to call."

And people said the families in the slums were strange.

"Well, it's a mess," Vega said in the silence that followed. "It's also a damned remarkable coincidence. Gunter Wong is one of the few Lancastrians who can still get ships off Lancia on a regular basis. His product has a short shelf life, and he has buyers in Gate Union and Redmond who keep the lines open for him. We follow the shellfish orders."

Abram probably used it, too. The Lancastrian ambassador on Haladea III ordered Gippian shellfish for functions.

"I sent Han on this mission, Lord Renaud," Vega said.

Renaud sagged. Physically and emotionally. Through the lines it was a long, slow, gray relief. Someone should test Renaud Han for line ability.

"So it is a job? He's safe?"

Vega didn't answer that. She turned to Ean. "The team went down with a cargo of shellfish. One of them might have recognized it as a potential escape route."

Radko would even if no one else had.

"Did they get off Redmond?" Ean asked. The most important question.

"I'm not sure yet. But the ship manifest doesn't show any problems."

"Don't you know?" Based on what Renaud had told them, he would have asked, and if Gunter Wong was such a friend, he'd have told him.

"Yves hasn't contacted me," Renaud said. "If he's on a job, I can't compromise him by calling him up."

Surely it was too late to think of that now. "Where did the ship go after it left Redmond?"

Renaud paused, and the lines reluctantly deflated. They really should test his line ability.

"Aeolus."

Ean had never heard of Aeolus two weeks ago. Still, the Worlds of the Lesser Gods was friendly to Lancia. Wasn't it? So why wasn't Radko back by now?

He glanced at Vega. She was scowling at him. She might have given Radko and her team more than one task. Who said they weren't off doing their job?

"I'll see how far Bach got investigating what happened." Vega called Sale. "Group Leader. Arrange secure accommodation for Lord Renaud on Confluence Station." Then she said to Renaud, "I'll keep you informed."

"Thank you."

Ean said, after Renaud had left, "You know Bach wasn't doing anything. Except damage control."

"Damage control. It's an odd phrase, don't you think." Vega frowned. "I wonder if Bach had an operation of his own on Redmond, and our people got in the way."

"Don't you talk to each other?"

"Of course we do, but there are always secret ops." She glared at him, as if he were to blame, but Ean was used to the Vega glare by now. That was her normal expression. "I'll find out."

She started for the door, paused. "I almost forgot. We still don't know about this top secret project Linesman Glenn was working on, but we did find out that House of Sandhurst recently signed a big contract with TwoPaths Engineering to supply more linesmen for them."

TWENTY-THREE

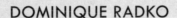

DOMINIQUE RADKO

RADKO CAME AROUND to the sound of two people arguing. They were speaking Standard, but one had the distinct uptrill of a native Redmond speaker, and the other had flatter tones she didn't recognize.

"I've told you before, Commander Martel. No more than two tranquilizers per person. It's dangerous," the Redmond speaker said.

"I'm not putting my crew in danger because your crazy linesmen won't board a shuttle, Dr. Quinn. Argo's got scratch marks down his face that will need regen."

"Two tranquilizers would have been enough."

Radko couldn't move her arms or her legs. She'd taken at least three tranquilizers herself. Would it wear off? She tried to open her eyes. Couldn't do that either.

"We had to get them out fast," Martel said.

"We didn't need to go at all. You caught everyone."

Was her team all right? Were they immobilized like her?

"The lab was compromised. You know the rules. Especially this close to culmination. And remember, this is two weeks after someone stole your report."

"It wasn't my report they stole." But Quinn's tone became more reasonable. "Even so, taking them onto a space station. You know they hate that."

The slight vibration and the murmur of the air supply had been so familiar Radko hadn't realized they were in space. By the sounds, she was on a shuttle.

"They hate everything and everyone." Martel brushed past Radko. She tried to open her eyes again. Still couldn't.

"Any luck?" The voice was directed close to her.

"Nothing." A third voice, as flat as Martel's. Something

dropped onto a surface nearby. "Two comms. Neither of which I can read; they look new. A knife in her boot. An arsenal around her waist, sourced from all over the galaxy. A lot of credit in chits."

The sleeve brushed her again. "This comms looks remarkably familiar."

Radko wanted to be Ean, who didn't need his eyes or ears to see through the lines.

"Redmond military property. It strikes me, Dr. Quinn, that your people are very loose with classified information."

Yet Martel didn't have a Redmond accent. Was he part of TwoPaths Engineering? Or part of a third group they didn't know about?

"You're supposed to be protecting us."

"We're supposed to, Quinn? Wasn't your government doing that? And they're doing a good job, too, as we can all see." From the sudden extra loudness in his voice, Radko knew he'd turned back to look her. "Do you think this one's the leader?"

"I'd guess," said the man who, presumably, had emptied her pockets. "She's got one of Bergin's fake entry chits, but I can't ID her until we crack her comms."

"She'll be Lancastrian." Martel sounded confident. Radko wished she could see him. "Look at her face."

There were benefits to looking like a relation to the Crown Princess of Lancia but disadvantages as well. The disadvantages outweighed the advantages.

"Why would they be so stupid. We've agreed—"

"You heard Bach's call the other day. That guy's father. Only they said he was on Redmond."

Bach wasn't a common name on Lancia. The only Bach that Radko knew was Sergey Bach, Emperor Yu's head of security.

Renaud Han had called someone to get Han out of Redmond. What if he'd called Bach? Why would Bach call these people?

"What else did we find?" the officer asked.

"Comms on the other two."

So two of them had been caught. Which two?

She couldn't do anything for the moment, so she lay and listened. This drug immobilized the muscles but didn't immobilize the mind.

TWENTY-FOUR

EAN LAMBERT

RADKO COULD TAKE care of herself. Ean knew that, and he knew that hitching a ride on a ship guaranteed to deliver a cargo was a smart thing to do. A very Radko thing to do. She was fine.

He wished she'd call, though, and let them that know she was. Except according to Vega, if she called, it meant something was wrong.

The clock in his room showed 03:17 when he finally admitted he wasn't going to get to sleep and made for the fresher. Maybe he'd sleep after a shower.

He listened to the lines and let the water flow wash over him. Ships on both fleets were calm. Except the *Lancastrian Princess*, which was edgy.

Captain Helmo was awake, sitting back in the captain's chair on the bridge, fingers pressed together, doing his captain's equivalent of listening to the lines.

Helmo and Ean had discussed it. Helmo didn't hear anything.

"It's all gut feel, Ean."

"But you must hear something," Ean had protested.

"Instinct, Ean. You know when something is not right, or something needs to be done. It may not even be to do with the lines. Maybe it's experience. Someone doesn't react the way I expect them to, or a ship noise is slightly off."

Ean thought it was more like the cartel-trained linesmen, who learned to push at the lines, rather than tune them. "I think you're getting messages, but you can't interpret them. You think of them as your gut feel, but they're not. You're hearing them."

"Define hearing, Ean," Helmo had said. "No one denies the

lines use sound. I can see that when I go onto one of the alien ships. It's not sound waves that allow you to 'hear' me on the bridge from your room."

"I listen through the lines."

"It's not acoustics that make you sound like a full choir when you sing. A single human larynx cannot physically make the sounds you make. There's something else. You—we—interpret it as sound, but it's more."

However they interpreted it, Ean knew that right now Helmo was sitting in the captain's chair because that was where the "instinct" was strongest. He looked for the origin of the trouble that Helmo was worried about. Yu's quarters. No surprise there.

Yu and Michelle were drinking tea. At least Michelle was. Yu paced energetically around the room. He looked fresh, as if he could keep up the pace forever. Michelle was her usual inscrutable self, but Ean knew how many hours she'd spent awake over the last few nights, and he could feel exhaustion underneath the nagging worry.

"Your arrival has stirred up old worries about Lancia," Michelle said. "Did you think you could come here—with the Factor of the Lesser Gods in tow—and expect nothing to change? Especially not when you brought Sattur Dow with you. The way he's sniffing around the alien ships leads everyone to believe that the first thing you will do when Lancia has enough power is to gift him a ship."

"Of course things have changed. They needed to change. Lancia was being ignored, pushed aside by the other worlds."

"Two weeks ago, Lancia required seven extra worlds voting with them to gain a majority in parliament. Today, they need seventeen. Some change is not good, Father, and this one is bad."

"Everything is working to plan, Daughter."

Something like ice whispered through the lines and raised the hair on Ean's arms. Even the fresher seemed cold, suddenly. The cold had a faint, fizzy, citrus tang to it. It was coming from Michelle.

Her voice showed none of it as she said, "If you have plans, Father, isn't it time you told them to me? Perhaps I can help."

Yu paused. He looked at her, head cocked to one side. "Perhaps it is time. But then what, Daughter? Will you take those plans to Galenos?"

"Should it matter if I did? Galenos is loyal to Lancia."

"Is he? He blocks my every turn. He refuses to let my friends come to the capital of the New Alliance." Yu stopped in front of Michelle. "He advises against my future son-in-law seeing his betrothed's ships."

"We restrict access to those ships inside the New Alliance," Michelle said. "Why should we allow people who are not part of the New Alliance to see them before our own allies do?"

"Our allies? Is not the Worlds of the Lesser Gods a potential ally, too?"

"They have to earn the New Alliance's trust. Having a high-profile member of their party attempt to steal ships for Redmond doesn't help."

Yu waved that away as if it were nothing. "Everyone has traitors in their midst, Daughter. Even I. And you can never tell who is trustworthy and who is not. Six months ago, I had not anticipated that Galenos—a man I trusted to look after my own daughter—would betray me with his own ambition."

A wave of emotion so strong it manifested itself as a stab in the gut. Ean doubled over.

"I don't see why you believe Admiral Galenos is betraying you. He has devoted his life to Lancia."

The emotion was so strong, Ean couldn't tell what it was. He staggered out of the fresher, and went back to sit on the side of the bed.

"Can you be sure he's working for *my* Lancia?" Yu asked.

The waves grew stronger, a sudden tsunami of noise and bitterness—and purple worry. "I cannot believe you would say that about an honorable man like Galenos. Let us stop this farce, Father, and call this entire stupid conversation out for what it is."

"Which is?"

Michelle glanced at him. Ean couldn't read her expression, and he'd bet Yu couldn't, either. "You are trying to discredit Galenos. I can only assume it is because you want to put your own puppet in the council here, and, unfortunately for you, there are only two ways to get onto the council. Wait six years for this term to run out and replace us then, or kill one of us now."

Lancia had been the only world to protest at the six-year term, and the inability to exit—short of dying—once you were elected.

Michelle couldn't be serious. But her lines said she was. No wonder she wouldn't let Abram anywhere near the *Lancastrian Princess* while Yu was there.

"This time, Father, I refuse to stand by and watch you kill an innocent man. A good man, who only has the interests of Lancia at heart."

Yu came to sit opposite Michelle. His overriding emotion was satisfaction. Was he pleased his daughter had seen through his plan? Proud of her for realizing the truth?

"You will have to kill me before you get to Abram."

"Abram now, is it?"

Michelle tilted her chin. "Yes, it is."

Ean sang a song of encouragement through the lines. *"We're here. We support you."*

Captain Helmo heard him. Would Michelle? Probably not. He pushed the full strength of his support through the lines, to the *Lancastrian Princess*, who echoed it and amplified it.

Michelle sat up straighter. Did he imagine her smile? He didn't imagine the glance that she flicked toward the camera facing her.

"I am sorry to hear that." And Yu did look regretful. "You will get over it. And you will have a new life. A political alliance by marriage to cement, allies to manage."

"I have allies to manage here if I can. Your coming here has irretrievably damaged Lancia's standing. If you have any political sense at all, you'll go home and leave us to do damage control." Then she added, bitterly, "If it isn't too late."

"Damage control." Yu rolled the words around his mouth. "I see." Another long pause. "Well, Daughter. I am not going home. Today, I go to Confluence Station as a guest of the Admiral Carrell of Eridanus."

"Carrell?"

"A surprise inspection." Yu smiled. "Being arranged at this very moment. Some members of the council are concerned that the Department of Alien Affairs is not looking out for *all* members of the New Alliance."

A small frown creased Michelle's forehead, but she didn't say anything.

Yu's smile widened. "Before that, I go onto the *Gruen*." He reached across and patted her hand. "I might meet your linesman there. He's so very hard to catch. If I hadn't seen him at supper the other night, I might wonder if he even exists."

Michelle looked away. "I doubt you will see him there. Lambert is taking the trainee linesmen out to the *Confluence* today." Her gaze shifted, and the glance that flicked toward the camera was longer this time.

Message received and understood. *"We will,"* Ean sang although he was fairly sure Michelle didn't hear him. He opened the comms to Helmo, who was sitting forward in his seat now. "If you get a chance, please tell Michelle I got her message. Make it discreet."

Helmo nodded. "Anything else?"

"No."

Ean pulled on his uniform and went out to the main control room. Hana and one of Rossi's people were on duty.

"We're taking the trainees to the *Confluence* today," he told Hana.

The trainees hadn't yet all passed the Rossi test. Peters, for one, was still denying he heard the lines though it was obvious he did. The three trainees from Lancia all said they did, but they hadn't passed the Rossi test, either.

If Michelle had told Yu they would be on the *Confluence*, then that's where they'd be.

The *Confluence* would be happy. More prospective crew. Ean would have to remind it that they weren't all for the *Confluence*.

Hana woke Bhaksir, who woke Sale. Orsaya's guard woke Orsaya's aide, Captain Auburn.

Ean looked at the time. It was 04:02. "There wasn't any need to wake people. We could have sorted this ourselves."

But you couldn't simply tell everyone to meet at a different ship. There were security clearances to organize, shuttles to schedule, and a whole lot of other bureaucracy to cover. How had Yu managed to arrange a visit without anyone's knowing?

If they didn't start now, they wouldn't be ready in time, not unless it was deemed an emergency. Not to mention, if they started organizing it after Yu set out for Confluence Station, it would be obvious what they were doing.

"If you keep this up, Ean," Sale said, "I'm doing the night shifts from now on. What's your problem this time?"

"It's not a problem. We're taking the trainees to the *Confluence* today."

"Since when?"

"Since about ten minutes ago, when Michelle said we were. Yu's coming out to Confluence Station, and the *Gruen*. She said we wouldn't be there because we're training on the *Confluence* today."

"I'll call Admiral Orsaya," Auburn said.

"And the ones Rossi hasn't passed?" Sale asked.

Rossi wouldn't pass up a chance to visit an eleven ship. Not when there was a choice. He'd talk his way into coming along. Somehow. Ean smiled. "Keep them on the *Gruen*. Rossi can train them."

"I thought all the linesmen—"

"Yu didn't mention Rossi." Let Rossi work to find a reason to come along.

Orsaya came out then, as grumpy as Ean felt without much sleep. "Emperor Yu is coming here, you say. We haven't given him permission. I wish the man would take himself and his unwelcome guests and go home. Although I fear—" Orsaya looked away from the Lancastrians and closed her lips on anything else she might have said.

What did she fear that she wouldn't say? The same thing Michelle feared? That Yu was here to kill Abram to get his own seat on the council?

SALE spent the next hour reassigning paramedics and guards from the *Gruen* to the *Confluence* and getting security passes allocated for them.

"At least we've Lancastrian paramedics today. I can't imagine how awkward explaining this would be if they were from some other world."

Bach would have known and told Emperor Yu that the

change had been a late one, but he was off supervising Jakob's interrogation.

Jordan Rossi, allowed to sleep through till breakfast, came out looking refreshed and impeccable.

"I haven't seen this much activity since the last time Lambert did something crazy. What's he done this time?"

Ean got himself tea and nut paste with winter fruits. The one meal Ru Li and Hana couldn't spoil because the nut paste was ordered in from Haladea, and the winter fruits came from the freezer. "I'm taking the trainees who have passed your test onto the *Confluence* for training today."

"Rather sudden, isn't it? Not to mention a total about-face from what you said—was it only yesterday—about not taking anyone onto the alien ships."

"Circumstances change."

"We're taking Ean onto the *Confluence* to avoid Emperor Yu," Sale said. "You're on the *Gruen*, Rossi. With the ones you haven't passed yet."

"Surely you'd be smarter getting all the linesmen off ship."

"We won't undermine Ean like that."

"I see." And Rossi probably did see.

"We'd prefer everyone went," Orsaya said.

Rossi sat back. *"I know what you're doing, bastard."*

"Then do something about it."

Rossi sipped scalding hot tea while he pondered. Ean forced himself to sit and wait. Eventually, Rossi smiled. "Take them over. I want to address them when they arrive on the *Confluence*."

"I don't think I'm going to like this," Sale said.

"You don't have to, sweetheart. Lambert's got a problem. I can fix it."

THEY had an hour before they left for Confluence Station.

Michelle couldn't keep Abram away from Yu forever. One day they'd meet. And Yu would kill Abram.

But if Abram was on ship, line eight could protect him. If Ean could work out how to make line eight come in when he needed it.

Ean found an empty room. *"Let's try the protection again,"* he sang to the line.

He stopped when he saw Rossi standing in the doorway.

"What are you doing?"

"Working with line eight."

"You're pushing at the line," Rossi said. "Like those lines-men you despise so much. The ones who were taught by the cartels."

"I don't despise them."

"Whatever you say. The fact remains; you're forcing the line. On my home." Rossi crossed his arms and waited.

"I wasn't forcing the line."

"You are pushing it to do something you want it to do. Isn't that your definition of force?"

Rossi had a point. Trying to make the line do something in a way it didn't understand could be seen as force. Ean sang a quick apology to line eight.

"Thank you. Now what were you trying to do?"

Ean would have to apologize to the *Confluence* lines tomorrow as well. Right now, he was marveling at the fact that Rossi had come to him to tell him he was doing something wrong. Rossi would never admit to helping someone even if he was. "I was trying to get line eight's protective field to work."

"And all that garbage you tell us about listening to the lines, and *asking* them to do things, rather than forcing them, is just that? Garbage?"

"Of course not." But he had been, hadn't he.

How did you say thank you to a man who wouldn't appreciate your noticing what he was doing? You just said it. "Thank you, Rossi."

"I'm not doing it for you. I'm doing it because you're muck-ing up lines that I fix. I don't need a megalomaniac running around all power and no consideration for what he's doing. You're a level twelve. That doesn't always make you right." Rossi turned and walked away.

Ean watched where he went. Through the corridors, all the way down to the viewport. Ean didn't go to the viewport often. He'd forgotten it was there. He remembered the linesmen, people he'd heard about but never before seen, being dragged out of that same area by Orsaya's soldiers, back when she'd first tried to get the *Confluence* out of the void.

He watched Rossi pick up a half-finished glass of wine. He must have come from the viewport when he'd heard Ean forcing line eight.

Rossi took a mouthful of wine, closed his eyes, and leaned against the Plexiglass as he savored it. Ean tasted the wine along with him. Mellow, like a good Lancian wine should be.

For breakfast?

"Stay out of my mind, bastard."

Ean left him there, losing himself in the music of the lines.

TWENTY-FIVE

DOMINIQUE RADKO

RADKO WAS STILL paralyzed when the shuttle finally landed. She hoped it was the tranquilizer. It was a scarily long time to be helpless. The sounds and the smells reminded her of Confluence Station. They were on a space station. Or a very large ship.

"Take the prisoners down to the cells," Martel ordered. "Get them out of my sight until they're fit to be questioned."

Radko lost track of the time. Here, in the lockup, it was quiet. Ean would have been handy right now. He could have used the lines to see where the others were, see what was going on.

She didn't know how much later it was that her toes and the tips of her fingers started to tingle with pins and needles. Not long after that she found she could flutter her eyelids although it was another hour before she could open her eyes.

She had plenty of time after that to stare at the ceiling. It was made of the same tiles as those at Confluence Station. If she had her knife, she'd be able to prise the tiles off and make her way through the ceiling to escape. Once she could move, that was. Her eyes tracked to the camera set in the ceiling. Of course, they'd know as soon as she tried.

Still, she had inspected Confluence Station thoroughly prior to Ean's taking up residence. A station was a station. If she could get herself and her people into the access corridors, she knew places they could hide.

About the time she could move her arms, Martel arrived back. He wore the navy and pale blue uniform of a Worlds of the Lesser Gods officer, and the pips of commander.

"Ready to talk yet?"

She wasn't sure she could even if she wanted to.

"Amazing stuff, that tranquilizer. I didn't realize how good until now. All three of you are still immobilized."

Still only three. Thank the lines one of them was still free.

"It's a pity because there's nothing I can do to make you answer while you're in this state although I could have fun trying."

Radko damped down the surge of unease.

"Unfortunately, the first captain will be back soon, and he'll want answers, so we don't have the time." He beckoned to someone outside the door. "Get Dr. Quinn here. He must have something to counter the effects of the tranquilizer. After all, they use it often enough."

Five minutes later, Dr. Quinn arrived with two assistants.

"I need her talking in twenty minutes. Pump in a fast-acting truth serum as well."

"I'm not your personal interrogation chemist."

"If you want to keep testing drugs on your linesmen, you'll do the occasional side job."

Martel left.

"Occasional." Dr. Quinn hooked Radko up to an intravenous feed. "This is the second one today."

"The other man did break onto the station," one of the assistants said. "We were lucky they caught him."

Chaudry or Han, it if was a "he." Did that mean they were all captured?

"We were unlucky he had enzymes in his stomach to counteract the truth serum," Quinn said. "First Captain Jakob will bite our heads off for that. And Martel won't take two failures in one day well."

He snapped a solution into the end of the IV. "Monitor that," he ordered one of the assistants. "Don't let it get above 0.3. You," to the other one. "Be ready to give her 700 mls of Dromalan as soon as it stabilizes. And whatever you do, don't give her the truth serum before she stabilizes. If you do, *you're* answering to the commander."

Both assistants shuddered.

Dromalan truth serum took two to three hours to take effect. Once they administered it, Radko had a maximum of two hours before she'd start to talk. She had to escape by then or avoid taking the drug in the first place.

Worse, if a linesman had Dromalan truth serum in their system when they traveled through the void, it destroyed their line ability. Early experiments with the serum had been to improve line ability. It was only later they'd found it useful as a truth drug. If van Heel or Chaudry had been given the serum, the whole team would be stuck in this sector for a week.

Quinn hurried out.

One of the assistants checked the feed. "Get this wrong, and we'll both be dead. Commander Martel is in a mood. So is First Captain Jakob, I hear."

"Because he's coming back empty-handed?"

They both sniggered.

"I heard he got arrested."

The other assistant glanced at the camera, then nudged the one who'd spoken.

Neither of them stood as straight as regular soldiers. Pure medical staff, then. Radko's reflexes would be slow. Could she overcome two untrained people? And if she did, how long would she have to get away? They were on a station, with cameras in every corridor.

Radko waited.

"Stabilized," the first assistant said, finally. "Are you ready?" He looked over to the other assistant. The second assistant checked the syringe of green liquid and nodded. Radko couldn't wait any longer. She rolled off the bed and knocked the first assistant off his feet.

"Hey. You shouldn't be moving yet." The second assistant came running around the bed. Radko rolled under it, came out the other side, and pushed the bed into him. It was a weak push, not enough to push him off his feet even. The assistant was back before Radko could stand. She scissored her legs— just enough to pull him off his stride.

"This is personal now." He fell onto Radko to hold her into place and jabbed his syringe downward. Radko pushed his arm aside. It wasn't much, but the syringe missed her and scraped the assistant's arm, just enough to draw blood.

He cursed, flung the syringe away, and raced over to the basin, scrubbing at the scratch.

If Radko had been closer, she'd have snatched the syringe up. Instead, she rolled away, into the first assistant's legs. He'd regained his feet and was reaching toward the intercom. This time, Radko controlled the roll and brought the assistant crashing down.

She got up and ran. Not that it was much of a run, more of a drunken roll. She focused on keeping on her feet.

She made for the nearest emergency alarm station, clearly marked on the wall, broke the glass, and pressed the hull-breach button. The station's airtight partitions slammed into place over the whoop of the alarm.

Now it was just her and the people in her section.

She ran back to the room she'd exited. Both assistants were gone, as was the syringe. She looked around.

The door had a pop-lock mechanism. Sometimes the luck ran your way.

She reached inside and pulled wires. That one. And that one. In exercises, she could do this in fifteen seconds. She had that now, no more. She pushed the wires together, and counted as the feedback from the electronics built. Ten seconds. Twelve. Fourteen. There was a tiny fizz, and the overload on the wires blacked out the wiring for the doors in this section of the station. Doors around her slid open. Except the breach partitions, of course. They didn't open when you lost power. They had to be opened manually. Once the crew determined where the breach was or wasn't.

She grabbed oxygen and a mask from one of the emergency stations. They'd gas the area soon because they had to be watching what had happened.

Where was everyone?

She ducked into a nearby room. An oxygen cylinder hurtled toward her. She threw herself sideways.

"What the hell?" Van Heel had a second cylinder primed to use. She dropped it with a clatter. "What's happening?"

"Escaping," Radko said. "What's happened with you?"

"Same. I only just got out of that prison they put me in, when the doors all flew open. I should have waited."

"Have they given you any drugs?"

"Not yet."

That was something.

"They were about to interrogate me when they caught

someone else. I thought it was you. There was a lot of excitement about that."

The man Quinn's two assistants had spoken about? The one who'd broken onto the station? Chaudry or Han.

"Grab oxygen and a mask," Radko said. "They'll gas this section eventually." The oxygen tanks also made a primitive weapon, which was better than nothing.

Radko glanced out the door. "Han and Chaudry will be around here somewhere. We need to find them. And we need to arm ourselves with something better than oxygen cylinders." There wouldn't be any weapons in the jail cells. If they hadn't been in space, there wouldn't have been any oxygen, either.

Chaudry was two doors down. Still groggy from the tranquilizer but moving, if slowly.

"Han?"

"Haven't found him yet," Radko said.

They found the two assistants Radko had bested earlier hiding in a cell close to the breach partition. One had his comms out. Radko kicked it out of his hands, and stomped on it. Anything they said would be feeding out to the rest of the station. Chaudry loomed over them, his face scrunched into a mean-looking scowl, threatening to brain them with his oxygen cylinder.

Van Heel finished checking the other rooms. "Han's not here."

Radko looked at the two assistants. It would have been smart to knock them out, but she didn't. "Give me your comms," she said to the other assistant.

He handed it over, keeping one eye on Chaudry.

She made sure it was off, then put it in her pocket. "Stay here. If you come after us, we'll kill you."

She led the way back to her own room. She'd had time to look at the ceiling on this one. "Chaudry, I'm going to stand on your shoulders."

He stood rock solid and silent.

Behind them, she could hear the crew hauling the breach doors open. She pushed the ceiling tile up and swung herself into the roof space. She found the nearest support. "Over here.

Van Heel first." Because Chaudry would be too heavy for just one of them to lift.

Chaudry boosted her up.

"Now you, Chaudry. Push the bed over, stand on it, and we'll haul you the rest of the way."

"You can't lift—"

"Lift your hands, Chaudry, or we'll be caught."

It might have been the shouts of the crew as they pushed the breach doors open that spurred him. It was certainly the shouts that gave Radko an adrenaline boost as she and van Heel hauled him up.

She thought her arms would drop off.

"Go, go," Radko said to van Heel, as Chaudry scrabbled for a foothold along the beam. "That way. There'll be a walkway at the end. Wait for us there. Chaudry?"

Chaudry was nimble, for all that he was bulky. He slipped, but recovered, and crawled along the beam as fast as he could go.

The burn of a blaster singed Radko's boot as she followed him.

Ahead, she heard the unmistakable sound of someone's opening an access hatch. Van Heel, in front, hesitated. Radko pushed past her. "Watch our backs," she ordered, and ran for the hatch.

She was in time to kick the head of the first person entering. He fell backward, and she slammed the hatch shut. It was a pity she couldn't have grabbed his blaster. A weapon would be handy right now.

She motioned van Heel and Chaudry forward. The hatch started to move under her feet. She stepped off quietly and waited. The hatch lifted enough to let the nozzle of a blaster through. A beam on stun, sprayed indiscriminately. Chaudry opened his mouth and Radko motioned him to silence. The user gained more courage and ventured farther into the access space. Radko jumped on the hatch cover, catching the blaster between the edges as she did so. There was a yelp, and the blaster dropped. Radko snatched it up.

Armed, and it felt good.

There was silence from outside.

They wouldn't get far without getting caught. For the

moment, though, they were better off in the access passages than in the main corridors of the station. This way, anyone coming after them had to travel single file. She could pick them off one by one.

Unfortunately, the enemy could pick her team off the same way.

First, they had to get themselves somewhere safe.

The soldiers started shooting at the ceiling. This time the blasters were on burn. Chaudry grunted and jumped back. Van Heel grabbed him before he could fall through the weakened ceiling. They moved back.

Behind them, the first soldier came into sight. Radko stunned them.

"Stop." His voice was familiar. Commander Martel. "You're on a station. Do you *want* to breach the hull?"

The body Radko had downed blocked the way back. Radko leaned close to Chaudry and van Heel, so she could speak softly. "Use the pipes"—and she pointed above—"to help you get across the damaged part. Van Heel first, then Chaudry. Make for the nearest junction. Don't wait for me. I'll catch up."

She fired again over the top of the fallen pursuer. Someone swore and ducked. She hadn't hit him.

The ceiling under Chaudry's feet creaked. Chaudry stopped.

"Get across there," Radko hissed. "Use the pipes."

He started moving again. The overhead pipes creaked.

Radko sweated with him.

He stopped at the other side, with van Heel.

A small piece of paneling dropped away. Someone fired.

"Fire again, and you won't live to regret it." Martel again. "We'll get them at the next entry."

Radko waved the others on. It would have been handy to have Ean right now. He could watch through the lines, know where everyone was and what they were doing.

They moved on reluctantly.

Below her, more people entered the room.

Radko waited until she was sure no one below would fire before she grabbed for the pipes and swung along carefully, keeping her legs raised from the treacherous floor.

She hesitated as she recognized a voice below.

Sergey Bach. Head of Palace Security on Lancia. Commodore Vega's equivalent for Emperor Yu.

"I don't know what the hell you're doing." Bach was practically spitting. "And it's obvious you don't know, either. I feel as if I've walked into a farce. You can't run a station, let alone plan to win a war. Who are these people?"

"Lancastrians," Commander Martel said. "Maybe you could tell us how they got here."

"Lan—"

Another voice cut in. "Why don't *you* tell *us* how that happened, Commodore Bach."

"Lancastrians. Prove it to me."

"We will as soon as we recapture them."

Bach laughed. "How convenient. You balls-up a simple effort to steal a ship—even though we went out of our way to make it easy for you—and you try to draw attention away by blaming us for problems you're having."

"If you made it so easy for us"—this was the man whose voice Radko didn't recognize—"how did the farce of my arrest come about?"

"I got you access to the alien ships. *You* got caught."

Radko smiled grimly. They didn't realize yet, but with Ean around, they'd never steal an alien ship.

The pipe above her gave way without warning. She crashed through the damaged ceiling, onto the floor in front of the speakers.

Three blasters swung toward her.

She recognized the speaker. First Captain Jakob. The Lesser Gods' equivalent of a commodore. The head of the Factor's personal security and Bach's equivalent. She'd looked him up after learning about Michelle's proposed marriage, still doing her job, finding out about potential threats to Michelle and Ean. Old habits.

"Blaster down, nice and quiet."

She put her blaster down and used the hand she was lying on to ease out the comms she'd taken from the assistant. She'd never get out of this alive, not if Bach had this to hide. The most important thing was to let Lancia know he was a traitor.

She managed to push it behind her, and one-handedly thumbed the comms on, praying that it didn't beep. She pressed in the emergency code she knew by heart.

"What's that?"

She realized she'd been whispering to line five, much like Ean might sing. *"Please, don't make a noise."* But the lines didn't hear her, of course.

Bach kicked her blaster away. "My Lady Dominique." His voice was as sour as Vega's could be.

"Lancastrian?" Jakob asked.

"Unfortunately, yes."

Jakob raised his weapon.

Bach knocked his hand away. "Don't kill her. She is cousin to His Imperial Majesty, Emperor Yu. And important to our plans."

He should have let Jakob kill her. Why keep her alive when she might escape and report what he had done?

It was too late, anyway. The comms behind her was capturing all this. Vega would piece it together, and she and Admiral Galenos would chase this traitor down and destroy him.

"Cousin?" Jakob asked.

"You are a traitor to Lancia, Commodore Bach." Radko made her voice clear enough to carry to the comms behind her.

"Doesn't the cousin work for Galenos?"

"She is part of the personal security complement for Her Royal Highness, the Crown Princess Michelle."

Radko kept her voice clear. "You have conspired with Redmond and the Worlds of the Lesser Gods," for they had to be working together. "To attempt to steal an alien line ship. You have betrayed Lancia, and the New Alliance."

"Oh, for—" Jakob spun the control on his blaster. "If someone won't do it, I will."

"You, and Commander Jakob, and—"

Jakob fired.

TWENTY-SIX

EAN LAMBERT

EAN HEARD THE *Confluence*'s *"Welcome home"* as Sale and her team docked.

"This is not their home. That is the Lancastrian Princess.*"*

Abram hadn't understood his message. Helmo would kill him for stealing his crew. So would Vega. Maybe even Sale herself although Sale did give the ship a pat as she came on board. He'd seen Kari Wang do the same thing on occasion, and Captain Gruen, as well. But Sale was a group leader, four promotions away from captain yet.

"We choose."

"You'll get your people soon."

There was no way the New Alliance would give the ship to Sale. Everyone was worried Lancia would take the *Confluence*. That was another reason the ship would never be Sale's.

"Do you know about politics?"

Blue misunderstanding.

"Power factions." Ean didn't have the words to describe it. *"Worlds."*

"Worlds?"

How did you describe a world to a line ship? They must know they were there because they avoided them, but Ean had never seen them depicted on the displays of the ships. *"You know about suns."*

"Suns?"

Of course they knew about suns, and, if his surmise was correct, flicked enemy ships into them. *"Those big balls of energy in space."* He used the tune for Bose engines for energy. *"They have worlds surrounding them."* Line four and line two. *"People live on these worlds."* Line one. *"Our home ships, if you like. Where we come from."*

More blue confusion. He might as well have been speaking gibberish. Which he probably was to the lines. It was like line seven all over again. They could be saying exactly the same thing to each other, but they didn't have the knowledge to link it to something both of them understood.

"Anyway, these factions will send you more people."

"More people is good."

They needed to get Sale away from the ship while those "more people" bonded. And keep her away afterward. Did a ship ever have two "Ships"? Ean didn't think so. But they did bond with new captains if they didn't have one—as was shown with the *Eleven*'s accepting Kari Wang. Best to get Sale off the ship and see what happened.

"Ship is ours."

And he'd have to stop worrying about it while he was on a *Confluence* fleet ship. Let Abram deal with it.

He was glad the shuttle of paramedics arrived then. Forty of them, all wearing Lancian gray. A new batch again, for Ean didn't recognize any of these people. Didn't whoever was in charge of assigning paramedics understand they were taking the linesmen onto the strongest ship in the two fleets? They should have sent experienced people.

None of these paramedics had been on the *Confluence* before. They were a long way past the original group supplied by the *Lancastrian Princess*, Balian's Captain Seafra, and Yaolin's Admiral Orsaya.

There were four shuttle decks on the *Confluence*, each of them immense, each of them easily able to hold the full group of trainees, as well as forty paramedics, Craik's team, and Bhaksir's team.

The deck they used for training was set up for human linesmen, with oxygen tanks spread throughout the vast space. The other three—all of them a long trek through the ship—were closed off. They didn't have breathable air yet. You always had to wear a suit on the *Confluence*, for you never knew when you might step into alien atmosphere.

Before Michelle had bought his contract, Ean had never worn a space suit. Now, he sometimes felt as if he lived in one.

The first trainee shuttle arrived, disgorging forty trainees onto the shuttle deck. Then the next. And the next.

Peters was in the first batch, along with the four Xantos.

Nadia Kentish looked around. "It's as big as a barracks parade ground."

"You'd get used to it," Lina Vang said, but she sounded doubtful.

Scout Ship Three sounded smug. *"Not like me. I'm sneaky and fast, and not too big."*

None of the Xantos answered, but they all looked around, as if wondering who had spoken.

Ean turned to what he had some semblance of control over. "Do you want to talk to them?" he asked Sale.

"Of course."

As Radko would say, "Was the sky on Lancia purple?" Sale always addressed the trainees.

"Who goes first? You or Rossi?"

"Rossi. So I can do damage control if I have to."

Damage control. Ean shivered. Michelle had used those words earlier today, talking to Yu.

ROSSI had an orator's voice, and he knew how to use it. "Linesmen."

He got instant silence.

"The best way to learn the lines is to experience them first-hand. You need to be where the lines are. There are some"—and he glanced at Ean—"who believe you should practice it as some nebulous art in a far-off spaceship, but nothing matches firsthand experience. I, Jordan Rossi, level-ten linesman, know that. That is why you are here. After today, all of you should understand what is different about these lines and how you have to respond to them."

The linesmen broke into spontaneous applause.

Fergus came up beside Ean. "I'm not sure it was wise to let him up there to put you down like that. Jordan may have dropped his plans to become Grand Master, but he's still ambitious. And political."

No matter how much he denied it, Rossi would never willingly go far from the eleven lines, and as Grand Master, he'd have to travel the galaxy. In a way, Rossi had earned the

occasional bagging right. He was stuck here, subordinate to
Ean, and he knew he could never leave.

"If it makes Rossi feel he is in control, I don't care what he
says, as long as he does what needs to be done." At least Fergus was still alive and whole. "How have you been?"

"This suit." Fergus grimaced. "As for the rest."

"On this ship," Rossi's voice thundered, "you will experience the true strength of the lines."

"I've been doing some listening, Ean. I'm sorry to say, but
I think there's a problem with the linesmen Lancia sent in. If
I didn't know better, I'd say they were deliberately stirring up
trouble."

Lancia. Ean wasn't surprised. "It's probably part of Yu's
plan to destabilize Abram." If they had to kick the Lancastrian
linesmen out to save Abram, he'd do it.

Almost as if it were a signal, Ean became aware that
Emperor Yu and Admiral Carrell had stepped onto Confluence Station. Sattur Dow followed.

"Abram? But why?"

"It's a long story." Ean had forgotten Fergus didn't know
the details. But he was a good source of information, and he
knew how to keep his mouth shut. "Fergus, what does Lancia
do to traitors?"

He shouldn't have asked it, not when he'd just said what
he'd said that about Abram.

"Traitors? What have you done to upset Lancia?"

At least he didn't realize the question was about Abram.
"Nothing." Yet, but if Yu challenged Abram as a traitor, he'd
do something about it. "The Factor implied the New Alliance
wouldn't punish the traitors, not as he believed they should be
punished, so we let him take Jakob and the crew of the *Iolo*
home."

Fergus looked at him. "You can't be serious."

Unfortunately, he was. "I was wondering how Lancia punishes someone for treason." He hoped his voice stayed neutral.

Fergus considered it. Jordan Rossi had once said he had a
storage-box mind. Full of facts and figures, all filed neatly
away. It wasn't a function of line seven, so it was something
that Fergus, himself, was good at, outside of line ability.

"I think Emperor Yu has them shot. They have a trial, but if the Emperor truly believes someone is a traitor, the trial is a sham."

That's what Ean was afraid of.

"Lancia has a bad reputation for its treatment of people who betray them. Don't forget Rebekah Grimes."

Abram had executed Rebekah. But she had killed his people.

"Lancia's way is quick, but I wouldn't want to get on the wrong side of Emperor Yu. You tend not to see those people again."

That's what Michelle was worried about. And Ean was now, too.

On Confluence Station, Admiral Orsaya greeted Yu and Carrell respectfully but without warmth. "Admiral, Your Imperial Majesty. You got here fast. It's less than an hour since your clearance came through."

"Times like these," Carrell said, and looked as if he thought Orsaya would agree with him, "the less advance notice the better."

"Where is the Lancastrian linesman?" Yu demanded. "I want to talk to him."

"Linesman Lambert is conducting line training today," Orsaya said.

"We have come from the *Gruen*," Yu said. "There were no trainees."

Maybe it was a good thing they'd woken Sale and Orsaya earlier. Otherwise, the trainees would have still been leaving when Yu arrived.

Ean dragged himself back to what was happening on the *Confluence*. "Thanks, Fergus. I'll let Sale know about the Lancastrian linesmen."

Rossi had finished his oration. Ean had no idea of the rest of what he'd said, but the trainees were happily agreeable.

Sale stepped up to address the trainees. "One day I might kill you personally," she said to Rossi, as they passed.

"She doesn't mean it," Ean sang hastily as the ship lines stirred, especially line eight. *"It's a human way of saying they're annoyed with other people."* He waited till the lines subsided. "Don't say things like that, Sale."

Rossi laughed aloud. "Lines a little out of control, Linesman?"

Sale looked daggers at Rossi. When she turned to Ean, her gaze wasn't much less ferocious. "Can I speak now?"

He nodded.

She raised her voice. "As you can see, it's a big ship." Unbidden—or at least unbidden by Ean—the ship amplified her words, so everyone heard clearly. "You get a guided tour as part of your training, but it is line training. That is what you're here for. That's what you're expected to do." She looked directly at Peters. "Any complaints, and you go straight back to the shuttle."

She looked away, over the crowd, before he could argue. "Access is restricted. Don't wander. We know where you are at any time. If you wander, you get sent back to the shuttle. Understood?"

She held their gaze until most of them nodded.

"Good. We are on a line ship. An Eleven-class. You all know line eleven can be strong. You know the symptoms. You know what to do. We have paramedics here." She indicated the paramedics around the room. "Help your teammates. If you see someone in trouble, do what you can and call the nearest paramedic."

Line eleven had been quiet so far. Or as quiet as it could be. Some of the trainees still had difficulty breathing. The paramedics were already among them.

"Ean."

Ean stepped up. "You know the routine. We will now greet the lines on this ship."

He started with line one. The standard introductory training song. The crew of the *Eleven* called it the Hello Song, and it was as good a name as any.

Here, on the *Confluence*, the lines were strong. Even Peters's eyes widened as line one answered.

Maybe it was as simple as that. They should have brought them onto the *Confluence* first, and all that antagonism would have gone.

Line two.

Sale came over to Ean while he waited for them to sing. "Thanks for the amplification, Ean. It was a good idea."

"That wasn't my idea. It was the ship's." Yes, and ship was feeling pretty satisfied with the praise. "Have you ever sat in the captain's chair, Sale?"

"I wouldn't dream of doing so."

"But you've spent a lot of time on the bridge."

"What's that supposed to mean?"

"Nothing."

Ean sang line three and waited for the trainees to sing it, too, and for the reply.

"Ean, you don't ask questions without a purpose."

Ean ignored that.

Line four. The trainees were more animated, and so was the ship. Not only that, the ships of the whole fleet were listening in. The council had better come up with that list of ships and worlds, for if the ships started choosing people, Ean didn't know what he was going to do.

"I think." What did he think? "I think that you don't always have to be a linesman for the lines to hear you."

"That stands to reason," Sale said. "The *Confluence* knows we're here. It opens doors for us."

"It does?"

"How do you think we get around the ship?"

He hadn't thought about it at all. Initially, he'd asked the ship to open the doors. He'd assumed Sale's team had added human triggers. They'd brought technicians in to add human screens. Engineer Tai had supervised that.

"I'm sure it thinks we're deaf, dumb, and blind, but it recognizes us, weird creatures that we are."

Deaf, dumb, and blind, maybe, but it had recognized that Sale wanted to be heard and amplified her voice. It would do other things for her, if she asked. The way it had shown her the medical center. He'd bet they'd talked about it here on the *Confluence* after they'd discovered the medical center on the *Eleven*.

She could ask . . . what? He looked around for inspiration, and his gaze fell on the electric cart that both Sale and the ship hated so much.

"You should ask the *Confluence* to show you how to get to the bridge fast, Sale. Tell it that you need to get places quickly. Ask for another way."

"And how is it going to understand me, let alone tell me what I want to know?"

"The *Confluence* can sense what you want. Like before, when it amplified your voice."

"The lines can certainly sense humans better than most humans can sense the lines," Sale said. "That's obvious. But we need linesmen to really talk."

"She wants transport," Ean whispered to the lines. *"She doesn't want to use—"* How did one describe a cart? He tried to remember back to what he had felt through the lines.

He should suggest to Abram that Sale be included with the captains when they talked about the lines. But that would give the *Confluence* ideas. Did he care? He liked Sale. She would be good for the ship.

But right now, he had training, and the lines were waiting. He turned his attention back to his job.

Line five.

On board Confluence Station, Orsaya was saying, "I don't know what time the linesmen will be back."

Line six.

All the way up to line ten. And finally, line eleven.

"Gently," Ean cautioned. *"Human lines. Weak."* And line eleven was gentle but it was strong and close, and still took all the multilevel linesmen down.

Nadia Kentish dropped to her knees beside Lina Vang, who'd gone down hard. She signaled to a paramedic. "Over here."

On board Confluence Station, Yu was already preparing to depart. What was the point of going all that way out to a ship and leaving almost immediately? Orsaya stopped to answer her comms. Carrell slowed to wait for her. Dow and Yu kept walking toward the shuttle.

With the strength of the lines on the *Confluence*, Ean could hear and see them as clearly as if he'd been standing beside them, could taste how glad Orsaya was to see them gone.

Dow said quietly to Yu, "She bought it."

Orsaya couldn't hear it, but Ean could, through the lines.

"Of course she did. I knew exactly how my daughter would react, Sattur. She has protected this linesman all along, may even have some personal feelings for him. Of course she would send him to what she perceives as safety."

Yu had deliberately pushed Michelle into sending Ean to the *Confluence*. He'd wanted the linesmen there. Why?

What had they done?

"Sale," Ean said. "We have a problem. I think it's a trap."

"Over here," Kentish called. Ean heard the force of it through the lines. She was a nine, and strong with it.

"Trap?"

The paramedic making his way across to Kentish veered toward Ean. He wrapped an arm around Ean's neck and jerked him back. Ean felt the hard muzzle of a blaster against the side of his neck.

That sort of trap.

Another paramedic pointed a weapon at Sale.

They weren't supposed to be armed. After the riot on the *Gruen*, none of the trainees were allowed to carry weapons.

Other paramedics had weapons out. Half of them made for Ean and Sale. The others circled the fallen and not-fallen linesmen.

Bhaksir pressed her own blaster against the back of the man holding Ean. "Move away from him."

Ean hadn't seen her take her weapon out. Or move. He'd bet the paramedic hadn't either.

"Drop it," the paramedic said to Bhaksir. "Or I kill him." He looked around at the rest of Bhaksir's team, who had their weapons out, too. "All of you."

"Oxygen," Kentish demanded.

"Keep still, and none of you will get hurt."

Kentish stood up.

A paramedic raised his weapon.

Fergus jumped in front of Kentish, deflecting half the blast. They both went down. Scout Ship Three wailed.

The lines came on, urgent, insistent. All ships.

"Radko," and they opened, without request, to show Commodore Vega at her desk, listening to a message. It was sound only. There was no visual.

"Put your weapons down," Sale said to Bhaksir. "We'll let the *lines* sort this out."

Ean, she meant, but Ean was listening with Vega to Radko, trying to see at the same time if Fergus and Kentish were all right.

"You are a traitor to Lancia, Commodore Bach," Radko's words came through the comms. "You have conspired with Redmond and the Worlds of the Lesser Gods to steal an alien line ship. You have betrayed Lancia, and the New Alliance."

Ean heard Jakob's unmistakable voice. "If someone won't do it, I will."

"You, and Captain Jakob, and—"

Then Radko stopped speaking.

"No." Ean's heart thudded in panic. He pushed the paramedic away, ignoring the blaster held to his neck. "Radko."

Ten blasters rose simultaneously.

"Hold," the paramedic yelled to his own team. "Don't kill the linesman." Sweat dripped off his face. "You crazy moron. If I say don't move, you don't move."

Ean hardly heard him. Dead man's message, Vega had called it. The message you sent when you knew you weren't coming home. Was Radko already dead?

He tried to concentrate on what was happening on the *Confluence* but couldn't stop listening with Vega.

If they killed Radko, he would blast them all out of space.

The *Confluence* lines surged. *"Battle,"* and the linesmen who'd started to recover went down again.

The lines on the other ships took up the refrain. *"Battle. Battle."*

Peters, who had recovered enough to understand what was happening, clambered to his knees. "We'll die rather than surrender this ship."

"No surrender. We fight."

"We fight." That was Peters, too, who claimed he didn't hear the lines.

"That woman is Emperor Yu's cousin." This voice had clipped Lancian vowels. Commodore Bach. "He won't take kindly to your killing her."

"If Yu wants to negate our agreement by sending his own team, he would do well to consider the message I send him." Jakob's voice changed, as if he was looking elsewhere. "Find out if she's had the truth serum yet, and if she hasn't, for God's sake give it to her. I want to question her before I kill her."

She wasn't dead yet. Ean breathed again. His legs wouldn't hold him any longer, and he sank to the floor.

"He wants us to move the ship, Ean." Sale looked at the paramedic holding the blaster on Ean. "I can't move it," she told him. "The linesman is the only one who can."

On the *Lancastrian Princess*, Vega said, "Find out where that message originated."

"Ean." Sale's voice was amplified by the lines. He forced himself to look at her. How long would they keep Radko alive?

"He wants you to jump." Her message was clear. He'd jumped ships before, switched places with other ships in the fleet. She expected him to do that now. She also expected that the other ships already knew what was happening. After all, that was what he usually did.

Ean sang the lines open to the bridges of the fleet ships. Both fleets, for there was no time to choose specific ships, and Craik and four of her team were on the bridge here on the *Confluence*. They needed to know what had happened.

"What the hell?" the paramedic said. "What's with the singing? Now?"

If Sale had been Radko, she would have said, "He does that sometimes, it's his way of coping with nerves."

But Sale wasn't Radko, and if he didn't save her, she wouldn't be around much longer to say things like that.

Sale shrugged, as if she wasn't sure. "Ean, the jump."

Another single-level linesman, this one in Balian uniform, said, "We refuse to allow this ship to be taken. If you do this for them, Linesman, you are a traitor. A traitor to the New Alliance. A traitor to Lancia."

"They're traitors anyway," another trainee said. For the Lancastrian linesmen—those who were standing—had produced weapons as well.

"Shit," from the ship, and Ean had to look to be sure Sale's mouth hadn't moved. But the linesmen heard it, every single one of them who was capable of it.

"Did you?" Never mind. It wasn't the time or the place.

The Lancian captors—they were all Lancastrians, Ean realized—rounded up the linesmen. Was Lancia trying to steal the ships?

Fergus struggled to his knees. "I think I'm going to be sick." He crawled over to Kentish. "She's alive."

"Who are you?" Sale demanded of the Lancastrians. "Who sent you?"

"I need that jump, Linesman," the paramedic said, holding the weapon on Ean. "Otherwise, I start shooting people. Starting with that one." He indicated Sale.

"No one will cooperate if you shoot Sale." Least of all the ship.

Line eight was getting louder. So much so that the human eights—all of them singles—were showing distinct signs of distress.

On the *Lancastrian Princess* and the *Wendell*, response teams ran for the shuttle bays.

"Give me the coordinates," Ean said.

Helmo clicked through to Vega. "Are you receiving this?"

"Spacer Radko? Loud and clear. I'm sure everyone is."

"Radko? No, I mean the *Confluence*."

"Tell me."

"The coordinates. Please." Everyone on all 135 ships heard that.

Peters strained forward. "He's as much a traitor as the other Lancastrians. See how none of them are fighting it."

"That's because we're outgunned," Hernandez said. "Group Leader Sale isn't stupid." Hernandez was like Sale, expecting him to swap with another ship. If he did that, he left Radko to die.

The paramedic gave Ean the coordinates for the jump.

Ean read them aloud. "They were 2341.123416.23.21. Where's that?"

"None of your business," but Ean hadn't been asking the paramedic.

Answers came, almost simultaneously, from Helmo and Vega on the *Lancastrian Princess*, Wendell on the *Wendell*, and Kari Wang on the *Eleven*. "Redmond sector."

Which was still half a sector away from the Worlds of the Lesser Gods, where Bach and Radko were. At least where he presumed Radko was. Half a sector. Far enough away that Redmond couldn't reach them before they'd had time to rescue Radko and return home.

As for the people on the *Confluence*. They wouldn't be any

worse off near the Worlds of the Lesser Gods than they would be here.

"Lambert," Vega said. "Don't do anything stupid."

Vega wouldn't give him Radko's coordinates.

"Ean," Sale said. "We need to act."

Ean nodded, and directed his song to line ten. *"Can you take us to where Radko's signal was?"* The lines wouldn't remember the signal if they left it too late.

He realized the lines were already acting, and hurriedly sang line seven in. It wouldn't do to take the whole fleet with him. That would be an act of war.

And this wasn't?

He didn't care. Radko didn't deserve to die. Especially not by Jakob's hand. Or by traitorous Lancastrians'.

But they couldn't rescue Radko without people to do it, and they couldn't do that while the Lancastrians—enemy Lancastrians—were holding weapons on them. And line eight was more than ready.

Maybe Rossi was right. Let the ship do it. Don't try to force it.

"Well," the paramedic said.

"We've already jumped," Sale said.

Line eight was waiting. Ready to protect its people and its ship.

"Linesmen, drop," Ean sang, and put all the force he could behind his words. *"Drop. Drop now, to the floor. If someone near you doesn't drop, pull them down, or they'll be hurt."*

He didn't know how he knew it, but he knew the lines would come in waist high. Maybe they always did. After all, they hadn't exactly measured them, had they.

The lines came in strong to support him, line eleven, too, and if the trainees standing hadn't been single-level linesmen, the strength of it would have knocked them all down. It sent Ean to his knees, and it was a struggle to stay that much upright. *"Drop, all of you."*

The lines took up the chant. *"Drop, drop. All of you."*

"What's going on?" the lead paramedic demanded of Sale.

"Lines. When they're strong, they overpower the linesmen." Although she knew as well as Ean did that the single levels shouldn't have gone down at all. "I need to give Lambert oxygen, or he'll be no use to you."

Ean glanced around. His trainees were all down. And the *Confluence* wouldn't hurt Sale or her people. *"Protect us. Protect Ship from the marauders,"* he sang to line eight.

A tsunami of sound rushed past him. A force-wave that crashed into those standing. They were tossed like flotsam in it. Against the wall. Against the ceiling.

Sale was in the wave's path.

"Sale!"

But the wave flowed around her, and around the paramedic holding his weapon on her.

Sale snatched his weapon while he watched the carnage, openmouthed.

She shot him.

Ean sang a counterwave around himself to protect Bhaksir and her team. The two waves canceled each other out, but he didn't need it, for line eight flowed around them as well.

Above his singing, he heard Sale, amplified again by the *Confluence*. "Trainee linesmen. Those of you who are able, collect the intruders' weapons. Subdue any who resist."

Sale took out her comms and called Craik, who'd been on the bridge all this time. "Where did he take us?"

"Redmond sector," Craik said. "We're still determining exactly where."

"Redmond." Sale's voice was accusing. "You took us where he wanted to go."

"Battle," said the *Confluence.*

Ean staggered to his feet. "Sale, we have to rescue Radko."

Sale's comms sounded. Vega. Ean looked at it uneasily. "Maybe you should answer that when we get back."

Sale glared at him, clicked it on.

"Group Leader Sale," came Vega's crisp tones. "You are near a research station orbiting Aeolus, one of the Worlds of the Lesser Gods. Anything you do is likely to be considered an act of war." She paused, then added, "You are on your own. I repeat. You have no support. Return immediately."

They were still linked to the *Eleven* fleet ships. Ean considered turning the link off, but that was childish. Although there was a lot of activity on the media ships. They were listening in. He hastily sang those lines closed.

"Radko's here," Ean said to Sale. "On that station. She sent a message. She's going to die."

Sale looked at Ean, looked at her comms, then looked at the trainees—busy rounding up prisoners. She looked at her comms again. "There's only one way home, ma'am. We need to fix his problem before he'll fix ours."

She clicked off and watched the Xantos attending Kentish. "How is she?"

Alex Joy shook his head. "She's alive, but that's all we can say for her." He looked from Kentish to Vang, and back again.

Sale looked at Losan, who was nearby. "Take Joy down to the medical store." She scowled at the paramedics. "If I thought any of them were real paramedics, I'd get you to rouse one."

If that was possible. Many of them were horribly still.

"But I don't think any of them are. We haven't got much in the way of medical supplies," she told Joy. "See what you can do." She scowled again. "We've a whole hospital here, and we don't know how to use it." Then she turned to Fergus. "What in the lines did you think you were doing?"

"I had a suit on."

"A suit protects vital body organs. It doesn't protect your head. Or your legs. Not to mention, there's a hell of a concussion as the suit dissipates the blaster heat."

Fergus nodded and winced as he did. "Hell-of-a is an accurate way to describe it, I think."

"Don't do it again." Sale turned to Ean. "What's going on?"

"I'll send you home," Ean said. "Give me a shuttle. I need to find Radko. They are going to kill her."

"Don't be stupid, Ean. We're better armed with you on a ship than we are with you in a shuttle. Although you'd better not lose this ship." She flicked her comms on again, to Craik, on the bridge of the *Confluence*. "What do we have?"

"The station is threatening to shoot us."

"Tell them we'll use the green pulse if they do, so they'd better not try."

"Right," and Craik clicked off.

Sale looked at Ean. "Does the *Confluence* have a green field?"

"Yes." And line eight was ready to use it, too.

"Not yet. Not until we have rescued Radko."

Technically, the Worlds of the Lesser Gods were allied with Lancia—and thus the New Alliance. They should appreciate Radko's uncovering Bach as a traitor, as well as Jakob.

The trainees were rounding up the paramedics who could move, removing their weapons, forcing them into a central circle. Ean tried not to jig impatiently. This had to be done, but every second they wasted here was a second wasted not rescuing Radko.

Sale looked at Bhaksir. "Use what trainees you can to get this lot locked up. Put them in one of the empty shuttle bays, and get Ean to sing the door locked. That way if they cause trouble, we'll vent them into space." She scowled at the paramedics. "I can't believe they're Lancastrian."

She picked out three of the trainees, all single-level linesmen and thus standing, all with rankings on their shoulders. "You, help Bhaksir with the organization. Joy, too, when he gets back. Oh, and none of you try any stupid 'They're Lancian' shit. We're on the same side as you, and we're your only way home. You're right in the middle of enemy territory.

"Ean, block any messages from this ship that's not ours. Some of those paramedics will have comms."

That was easy. *"Only send comms from Ship's people,"* he told line five. *"From our fleet people. You know the ones Ship will let you send."*

It was equivalent to Captain Helmo saying, "No unauthorized comms."

Sale turned toward the bridge. "Come on, Ean. We've work to do."

Ean ran to keep up with her.

At last. It would take them forever to get to the bridge. He was glad he didn't have to be on the bridge to know what was going on. Even the ship seemed infected with urgency.

"Hurry, hurry. Faster."

"I can take a shuttle." It would be faster than having to go all the way to the bridge.

"That's not going to happen, Ean. You'll leave us stranded in enemy space with the most valuable ship in the whole of the New Alliance."

"Technically, the Worlds of the Lesser Gods are not enemies."
Sale snorted. "Does anyone seriously believe that?"

No.

"Slow. Faster."

He was going as fast as he could. Surely the ship understood that.

"Keep an eye on the trainees" Sale said. "I don't want them
turning on us. We're in a really bad position right now. The
only thing between us and the trainees' taking over the ship is
you. Keep it that way."

He should have waited till they'd sorted out the attack here
on the *Confluence*. But Radko might be dead by then.

"I don't know how long the station will hold off firing on
us. We don't know what weapons this ship has."

The *Confluence* was the size of a small city.

"We have a green field."

"Which is useless because we'll destroy Radko, along with
who knows how many innocent people. Tell me about Radko."

But first, Ean checked with line eight. *"Where are your
weapons? What do you have?"*

The overlay of sound almost knocked him over. There were
lots of weapons, all around the ship, although he couldn't have
told Sale where a single one was right now. One of them was
the quiet blue hot blood.

"We have weapons. Lots of them." Breathlessly, for Sale
had started to run. It was a long way from the shuttle bays to
the bridge. "Radko sent a message."

He still couldn't run and talk, let alone sing, but he tried
anyway.

"She said. Commodore Bach," because Sale needed to
know that. "Traitor. With Redmond and the Worlds of the Lesser
Gods. And then he shot her."

"Bach shot Radko?"

"Jakob did."

"What's Jakob doing there? Never mind, Ean. Tell the rest
when we're on the bridge."

He was grateful for that because Sale could run as fast as
Radko. "You really should ask the ship how to get to the
bridge fast." Or he could ask it himself, but he didn't have the
breath for anything but running right now.

"We haven't time to experiment right now."

"Faster. Hurry."

He had a stitch in his side, and the lines seemed determined to push him off course. He nearly ran into the wall once, had to force himself away.

"Faster," the lines insisted, battering him with sound. *"Faster."*

Finally, he couldn't fight the sound anymore. He stopped, his lungs burning. All he could do was stand with his hands on his knees and drag in deep breaths.

Sale was a full corridor ahead of him.

The lines didn't normally push him to do things he wasn't capable of. They were more likely to try to fix it for him. What was he missing?

"Faster," and the lines sounded relieved that he'd finally stopped.

"Faster," Ean agreed, and let the noise push him toward the wall.

Nothing. He was going to walk into the wall. Ean closed his eyes and let the music guide him.

Something jerked, and grabbed him, like the force that grabbed the shuttles. Lines four and three were loud, the other lines finally silent. He opened his eyes. It was dark, but he knew he was moving—horizontally, he thought. Scarily fast. He shot upward, then down, then along again. It was worse than a jump; it was a rushing pneumatic tube, and he was in it.

He shot out the other end, onto the bridge in a rolling heap that he couldn't stop, in time to hear Sale say to Craik, "I've lost Ean. I need to go back for him. Can you manage?"

"Too fast." Lines one, three, and four seemed to be conferring. *"Human. Slower?"* As if they weren't sure they could get it any slower.

Ean hit the wall, bounced off, and finally came to a stop. He got to his feet, choking, trying to catch his breath. His suit had sealed automatically. Wherever he'd been, there was no oxygen.

"He's just arrived on the bridge," Craik said. "Get here as fast as you can."

"But he was way behind me."

"He's here now, Sale. Trying not to throw up."

"Shit."

When he could finally speak, Ean said, "Sale. You should—"

But she was here now, stopping with a skid at the entry to the bridge. "Status?"

Craik shook her head. "No change on station." She glanced over at Ean. "Not sure about him."

"I'm fine." It was a wheeze, but he was fine. He checked the readings on his suit. Radko insisted he always check before he took the helmet off. The air was clean. *"Thank you,"* he whispered to the ship.

All he ever had to do was listen. *"If I don't listen next time, tell me 'faster,' and I'll remember."* At least, he'd try to remember.

Sale asked, "Is Radko alive or dead, Ean?"

"I don't know. Jakob said he wanted to talk to her. That was after he shot her, so I think so."

Please let her be alive.

Sale said, "I need to see the control center on that station. Anything line eight is involved in. And I need to see Bach, Jakob, and Radko."

What was the control center on a station? The administrator's office?

"Bach?" Craik said. "Radko?"

"I'll explain in a minute. Ean?"

He sang up the lines. Station "Ship," anywhere with line-eight activity, then had to flick through each of the cameras to get Radko—and Bach and Jakob—because none of them were linesmen, and the station lines weren't as strong as ship lines. Maybe there was something in Wendell's theory that the more you went through the void, the stronger the lines became.

But speaking of lines.

Ean stopped. "There are a lot of linesmen on that station," he told Sale. "They're all strong, and . . . a little strange." Crazy was the word that came to mind, but you wouldn't have a station full of crazy linesmen. Maybe they'd been trained by a secret line guild on the Worlds of the Lesser Gods and were different. "They're very strong."

Many of them were reacting badly to the presence of line eleven.

"Show me."

Ean put them up on the screen on the wall, a matrix of five

images by four, room by room. He brought a new one up every five seconds, replacing the one that had been there the longest.

Radko would be in the prisons. He could see two people locked in cells. One was a middle-aged woman who was inspecting the walls of her cell with care, looking for a way to escape. The other was a bulky younger man who sat in the center of the featureless room, staring ahead.

The rest of the station seemed to be a minibarracks. A warren of living areas, offices and meeting rooms, some training rooms. They had a huge medical center. The first rooms were empty, but the rest had patients. All of them were linesmen. Some of the linesmen were being attended to. They had the strongest lines. And felt the craziest.

Ean tried not to shudder. It was an insane type of crazy, unhinged almost.

Most of them wore the uniform of House of Sandhurst.

There, finally, in a room on the sixth level. A woman strapped to a chair, with two men standing nearby. One of the men wore the uniform Ean recognized from the Factor's entourage. Jakob. The other wore the gray of Lancia. Commodore Bach.

The woman in the chair moved slightly, and Ean could have cried.

Radko.

TWENTY-SEVEN

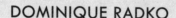

DOMINIQUE RADKO

RADKO WOKE TO cramps, and pins and needles.

Jakob hadn't killed her. He'd stunned her.

She was bound to a chair, arms by her sides, strapped at the shoulders, the waist, the wrists, and around her ankles. The bindings were tight all the way down. She couldn't slip out of them. The ties were behind her, and the seat was fastened to the floor.

She might not be dead yet, but it was difficult to see how she would get out of this.

"Those useless Redmond lackeys," Jakob said. "Their security is full of holes. Look at this." Something spun. She caught the movement out of the corner of her eye, and moved her eyes without moving her head so she could see it better. It looked like a comms. "We didn't even know this was gone until Martel found it among your girl's belongings."

Radko kept her head down. The longer Jakob thought she was unconscious, the better. She could see one pair of polished boots. Worlds of the Lesser Gods boots were a deep navy. These were black. Lancian boots. Commodore Bach was here.

Please let Vega have received her message.

"What is it?" Bach sounded almost disinterested although Radko would bet he wanted to know.

"The report on experiments Quinn is doing on the linesmen. It was stolen two weeks ago. Redmond and TwoPaths Engineering didn't plan on telling us."

Surely they knew it wasn't the original report that had been stolen. Or maybe only Dr. Quinn did, and if no one had said the original report was missing, would they admit to a second one going missing? Probably not.

Radko knew secrets she couldn't afford to give away. Even if Jakob didn't kill her, she couldn't stay alive to blab those secrets out. The question was, how to do the most damage to Jakob and Bach on the way. And somehow steal the comms and get it to Vega.

Jakob must have turned to face her, for his voice got clearer. "We're in a hospital full of doctors, and they can't even administer a drug properly. This time I'll give her the truth serum myself."

"I never thought much of Dromalan truth serum, myself." That was Bach, and the bile rose in Radko's throat just thinking about him.

"It's not my favorite, either," Jakob admitted. "I prefer something faster acting. But there are gallons of this stuff lying around on station. They use it for experimenting on the linesmen."

Bach shuddered, and Radko wanted to do the same. The serum made a linesman more receptive to the lines, but the stronger the linesman, the more damage it did. And you never sent a linesman who'd been doped with it through the void. You destroyed his lines.

"Some of the experiments strike me as barbaric."

"Barbaric or not, they're working. Redmond has done more with linesmen than your world or my world would do in a lifetime, and they've done it in fifteen years."

"We've done some exceptional work of our own, recently," Bach said.

"Not like this. Wait till we get those ships. You'll see what—" Jakob broke off as his comms sounded. Radko saw the shadow of his hand move as he flicked it on. "I told you not to disturb me."

She listened hard, but didn't catch the reply.

"Talk sense, man." Jakob pushed the call onto the wall screen. Radko looked up properly, and saw that was to free his hands so he could fill the syringe with green liquid from the jar on his desk.

The caller was Martel. "The alien ship is here."

"Here?"

"Right in our space." The volume rose as Martel spoke, until he was almost shouting. "Which stupid idiot thought that would be a clever trick? Because it wasn't. It was downright dangerous."

Bach pointed his blaster at Jakob. "This is supposed to be a three-world initiative. The ship was to go to Redmond. Does the Worlds of the Lesser Gods plan on going it alone?"

Jakob waved him away. "It was supposed to go to Redmond. But who cares. We've got the alien fleet. All of them?" he asked Martel.

His comms was going crazy with people trying to call him. He ignored them.

"Isn't one enough?"

Jakob looked at Bach. He ignored the blaster. "They only brought the one ship? You said we take one ship, and it brings the whole fleet. It didn't matter which ship." He lifted the comms to talk into it again. "Which ship is it?"

"Which bloody ship do you think it is? It's massive. And it's close. Oh, and it's threatening to use a destructive green field."

Radko started to hope.

"Contact your man," Jakob said to Bach.

Bach opened his own comms. "Status report, Rigg."

There was no answer.

Bach would only be calling the ship if it was his people who had stolen it. How many Lancastrians were involved in this betrayal?

"Come on," Jakob said. "How hard can it be to steal a ship and send a message?"

An alarm sounded. First in the corridors outside, then over the speaker. Jakob clicked back to Martel. "What's happening?"

Martel glanced sideways. "It's an internal alarm. I'll call you back."

"I hope it's not someone panicking about the ship. We *have* captured it." Jakob clicked off, then added under his breath as he waited for Bach's call to be answered, "We'd better have, anyway. Come on, it can't take this long."

It could if Rigg wasn't in charge of the ship. The lines would be blocking the calls.

Martel called back. He had Dr. Quinn on split screen. Quinn started talking almost before the call was open. "They've attacked our linesman."

"We're not under attack."

"They're all out cold, or screaming, or . . . Do something. Get rid of it. Now."

Radko grinned. The ship out there was one of the eleven ships. Probably the *Eleven* itself. And she knew which linesman would be on it.

Time for a rethink on her action plan.

She spoke softly, under the noise. "Ean. Can you hear me? Flash the lights once if you can."

The lights blinked.

Good. "I need someone to free me."

Bach turned his head to watch her, but he didn't raise his weapon or stop her. Hopefully, he wouldn't realize what she was doing until it was too late.

"I have at least two people on the station with me," Radko said. "Hopefully, three. They'll be in cells. Or two of them will."

"Calm down, Quinn," Jakob said. "You know how the lines on the alien ship affect the linesmen."

Quinn was working himself into his own heart attack. "That's why the ship wasn't supposed to come here. Look at them." He brought up visuals of rooms and corridors. Dozens of linesmen, most of them on the floor, all of them trying to breathe. One of them didn't look to be breathing at all.

If only one ship was here, Ean had used line seven, and they would still be in contact with the other ships in Haladean space. "Vega will identify my team for you," Radko said.

"It felled half the linesmen," Quinn cried.

"See if you can rescue them," Radko continued. "If you can, get them to come here. But tell them I've two armed men here who are as good as any of our own people, and not to underestimate them. If you can't get them here, get them to the shuttles."

TWENTY-EIGHT

EAN LAMBERT

EAN STARTED TO sing open Vega's comms, then realized that the lines were already open to the fleet ships.

"You heard that?" he said to Vega.

"The whole fleet heard it," Vega said. "And you might mention to Sale that instead of ignoring us, she'd do well to leverage off our experience. She has four experienced battle captains here, plus the crew of the *Lancastrian Princess* and Fleet Admiral Orsaya. You have two teams, and a whole station opposing you. Not to mention that based on the rankings on those uniforms, the station is likely to be armed. As soon as they realize they don't have control of the *Confluence*, they'll start firing."

"Heard and understood, ma'am," Sale said.

Ean didn't have time for this. "Vega, do you have—"

"Coming through," Vega said, and it was, finally.

Three images. Ean pushed them up to the screen on the wall.

"The man on the left is Yves Han," Vega said. "The young man in the middle is Arun Chaudry, and the woman is Theodora van Heel."

Ean remembered Chaudry and van Heel. "The prisoners." He sang up the camera views in their cells for Sale and everyone else on the bridge of the *Confluence*, then sang the doors to their cells unlocked.

"Let me talk to them," Sale said.

He turned on the speakers to each cell, sang a comms line open, and connected it between Sale's comms and the speakers. "On your comms."

"Thank you." Sale picked up her comms. "Chaudry, van Heel. Can you hear me? This is Group Leader Sale, on the *Confluence*." She spoke Lancian.

"Yes." Van Heel looked around warily.

"We can see you through the cameras in the room, but we can't hear you. Nod if you can hear us."

They both nodded.

Ean could hear her. Why couldn't Sale? *"Sound on the security feed?"* he asked the station.

"Sound? No sound?"

So however Ean was getting it, he was getting it straight through the lines; from line one, not through the feed he'd redirected for Sale. Who didn't put sound on a security feed?

"Ean. Ean." It was Captain Helmo, as insistent as Abram could be. "Are you listening to me?"

"Listening," Ean said.

"Good. You cannot send those people unarmed into Radko's room. Get them some weapons before they get there. There'll be weapons around. Find some."

Weapons? Right. Line eight would know.

He sang to line eight on the station. *"Show me your weapons?"* Much like he had earlier on the *Confluence*, and again, like the *Confluence*, he got an overwhelming overlay of weapons. "I don't know what's what? Or what's where."

"We have unlocked the doors for you," Sale said to van Heel and Chaudry. "We'll unlock them all the way to Radko. First, we need to arm you." She glanced at Ean. "Are you ready?"

"Working on it," Ean said, cold with sweat. What if he couldn't get them anything? Think. What would Radko suggest?

Get a plan to use with the overlays.

"I need a plan of the station," he sang. To all the lines, for he didn't know which line would be responsible for it.

He got his schematic, and still didn't know which line had given it to him. Maybe all of them.

"And Lambert." Vega's tone was caustic. "Don't sing the station into the fleet. We're in enough trouble as it is without adding theft to our list of crimes."

It wasn't her crime. It was his.

"Understood."

"Understanding isn't necessarily equivalent to not acting, in your case."

Ean tuned her out by singing his request again to line eight.

"Show me your weapons. Only this time, put it on the station plan."

The various weapons were overlaid on the schematic. Captains and seconds conferred, but it was Admiral Orsaya, listening in on Confluence Station, who said, "Level five, that looks like a bank of lockers. It's where we keep the blasters on station here. Might be worth a try."

Ean reoriented himself and the newly escaped prisoners. "I've got it. Locking all the doors except those to the lockers." He'd learned the hard way that the simplest way to prevent anyone from stopping them was to lock the other doors. Everywhere on the ship.

Naturally, that caused a flurry of calls to the engineering section. Or maintenance, rather, for it was a station.

"Right," Sale said to van Heel and Chaudry. "Follow the open doors to the weapons. If anyone stops you, knock them out."

They took off running.

Ean opened the doors for them.

When they had a long stretch of corridor and no doors to open, he sang up the cameras again, and sent them to the captains of the other ships and Confluence Station. A five-by-four matrix, cycling through, one new image every five seconds, with the oldest one dropping off. "See if you can find Han."

He turned back to opening doors for van Heel and Chaudry, and the rest of his attention to what was happening in Radko's room.

He was glad to have something to concentrate on, for the discomfort of the linesmen was starting to get to him. Those who were still left standing, for he was queasily aware that many of them weren't moving.

Why didn't someone give them oxygen?

In Radko's interrogation room, Commodore Bach was saying exactly that. "Give them oxygen, then. Those paramedics were sent with the trainees for a reason."

"What the hell do they need oxygen for? The air on station's fine." Jakob thrust readings in front of Bach.

"Line eleven interferes with the heart-brain mechanism," Radko said. "Their heart tries to pump a different way. If you don't get out there and give them oxygen, some of them are likely to suffocate."

Ean cheered. *"Thank you, Radko. Thank you."*

"And you know this? How?"

"She is one of Galenos's people," Bach said.

"Galenos has a lot of people under him."

"Do you want to save your linesmen?" Radko asked. "Because you should be getting oxygen to them."

"She also works with Linesman Lambert. That's why you need to keep her alive."

"When did you plan on telling me this?" But at least Jakob called Dr. Quinn. Ean followed the call through to the other end, where Quinn was ignoring it.

Jakob called up a soldier. "Get down to Dr. Quinn. I need him to answer his comms."

Ean opened the doors for the soldier as he jogged down to where Quinn was working on one of his linesmen. "Commander Jakob wants to talk to you."

"I'm busy. I've got three linesmen down with heart attacks."

The soldier took out his own comms and called Jakob. "With Dr. Quinn now, sir," and held the comms close to Quinn's ear.

"Dr. Quinn. Your linesman needs oxygen."

"Suddenly you're an expert on what the problem is."

"All of them. They all need oxygen," Ean said.

Radko said, at the same time, "They all need oxygen."

"Why doesn't Dr. Quinn already know this?" Jakob asked.

"I don't know," Radko said. "Any normal doctor would."

Why didn't Quinn know it? It was the first thing Abram and Michelle had tried when Ean had been struck down by line eleven. Thank the lines for Radko, who did.

"I love you, Radko," Ean whispered. "Thank you, thank you, thank you."

He became aware Sale was looking at him. "She's good," he said, and turned back to what was happening on station.

"Send your own soldiers down to do it if Quinn won't," Radko said.

Jakob glanced from her to Bach and back again.

"Works with Lambert," Bach reminded him.

Jakob called up a group leader. "Get oxygen to the linesmen. Every single one of them if necessary."

Ean sang the doors unlocked between them and the linesmen.

Van Heel and Chaudry reached the weapons store.

"Ean," Sale said. Ean was already singing the locks on the cupboards open. "I need to talk to them again."

He sang open the link to the speakers close to the weapons store.

"Take extras for Radko and Han," Sale ordered. "If you can find holsters in a hurry, take them, and take spare blasters. Radko can fire two at once."

And hit separate targets on the bull's-eye with them, multiple times in a row. Ean had been to weapons practice with her.

Now he had to send van Heel and Chaudry back to Radko, avoiding any of the soldiers Jakob had sent to treat the linesmen.

And they still hadn't found Han.

"Sale," Craik said. "You need to see this."

Sale came across to look. "What is it?"

"Not sure yet."

"Ean," Vega said, "the corridor where they're holding Radko. All the way down to the lifts. The security camera is on a loop. Someone has tampered with it. We're not getting the proper image. We can't see it. Someone is hiding out in that corridor. Find out who, and what?"

Ean hurriedly dragged his attention away from what was happening inside Radko's prison room to the corridor outside. "Two men," he said. "Armed."

They were outside Radko's door, one on either side of the doorway, weapons raised. One of the men signaled.

"They're about to attack." Ean readied himself to sing line eight.

The second man nodded.

Ean recognized him from the image Vega had sent through. He changed his tune. *"Unlock the door."*

"We've found Han," he told Vega.

The two men charged into the room together. As they did, Ean saw the first man's face. A man he'd only seen twice but whose features were etched in Ean's memory.

Stellan Vilhjalmsson. Gate Union assassin, and a man who'd already tried to kill Radko once.

"Protect Radko," he sang to station line eight.

"Protect? Radko?"

"In the room. That one." How did you explain to a strange line what you wanted it to do? *"The protection field."*

Human-built lines didn't have alien knowledge behind them. One thing was for sure. The *Havortian* had never used its protective field. The *Lancastrian Princess* and the *Gruen* must have learned it from the *Eleven*.

For a frantic few seconds, Ean considered singing the station into the *Confluence* fleet, no matter what Vega said. Instead, he sang the lights down in a panicked hope that if they couldn't see Radko, they couldn't fire on her.

The emergency lights stayed up, and they weren't run on lines.

"Sale. Radko's in trouble."

"So are we, Ean. A class-two warship's just arrived."

"Two now," Craik said.

TWENTY-NINE

DOMINIQUE RADKO

JAKOB LEFT THE images of the linesmen on-screen. Radko didn't relax until she saw the first soldiers arrive with oxygen. There was something about watching linesmen, and not being able to help, that made her feel helpless.

"I'm not liking the silence from your man, Rigg," Jakob told Bach.

"You know ops. They seldom go to plan," but Bach looked at Radko as if he wanted to ask if she knew what was happening.

Radko would rather spit on him than tell him anything.

Jakob's comms sounded.

"Warship *Hellfire* in position," reported the man who'd called.

Another call followed immediately after. "Warship *Brimstone* in position."

"About time something went to plan. Attack the alien ship."

"What about my people on that ship?" Bach demanded.

"They're not responding. We can only assume they're not in control."

Radko hid her grin. He'd be right about that.

The door opened.

Radko heard the distinctive hum of a blaster on stun. Jakob collapsed.

Stellan Vilhjalmsson. And Han.

Vilhjalmsson had fired.

The lights went out, leaving emergency lighting on the floor as the only source of illumination. The sound of Ean singing came through the speakers. Line eight, Radko guessed, but nothing happened.

Han's weapon was pointing at Bach. He made an "Oh" of

recognized horror, pushed his blaster up and away at the last moment, and fired into the ceiling instead.

Bach's own weapon was out by then.

He fired.

Han went down.

There was no associated smell of burning. Bach, at least, had his blaster on stun.

Bach turned to Vilhjalmsson. Vilhjalmsson had already moved. Bach fired wide, to where the assassin would have been if he'd moved at his usual speed.

"You're slowing down, Vilhjalmsson."

Even Bach knew the assassin.

Vilhjalmsson grunted. "If it saves my life."

Van Heel and Chaudry burst into the room.

"Fire on the right," Radko said, urgently. "Van Heel, take the man on the right out."

Thank goodness the lights were too dim for her to recognize Bach immediately. Otherwise, she'd stop, like Han had.

Van Heel fired. She missed but distracted Bach long enough for Vilhjalmsson to kick the weapon out of Bach's hand.

"Chaudry. Get me out of this chair."

"I can't see," Chaudry said.

"Ean."

The lights came back up.

Van Heel made a sound somewhere between a moan and a gasp. "Sir." She started to hold out her weapon.

"Don't," Radko said sharply. "He's a traitor. Chaudry," for Chaudry didn't seem to recognize him and was stolidly working on the fastenings. "Cover Bach. Don't let him near a weapon. Van Heel, come and free me."

Chaudry covered Bach.

Van Heel came over to work on the clips. She lowered her voice. "Do you know who he is?"

"Of course I do. That makes his being a traitor even worse."

"How do you know he's a traitor?"

Bach seemed to watch Vilhjalmsson, rather than them, although Radko was sure he knew exactly what they were doing and would seize any opportunity.

The restraining bands around her shoulders fell away. She

flexed them as she watched Vilhjalmsson. That last kick seemed to have done some damage, for he was moving carefully, and a light sheen of sweat showed on his face.

"Why were you working with Han?" She had to assume he was, for he had worked against Jakob and Bach.

"Escape, pure and simple. It suited us both." He spoke through clenched teeth. "Han was the only one left when I arrived at the labs on Aeolus. He'd overheard where you were being evacuated to. We joined forces to get onto the station. Unfortunately, I was captured not long after. He found me while he was looking for you."

"Radko." Ean's voice was urgent through the speaker. "You have to hurry."

The bands around her wrists fell away.

"I can't control line eight on the station. It doesn't understand."

"That's fine, Ean. We're good. We're armed," as van Heel handed her a blaster.

"What happened to the woman, Sale, who was telling us what to do?" Chaudry asked. He, too, was watching Vilhjalmsson— with the professional eye of a doctor. "We need to stabilize your back."

"Sale's here," Ean said. "You need to get to a shuttle, Radko. The station commander has weapons ready to fire, and he's sent soldiers down to where you are. If you don't leave soon, there won't be any passages to leave by." A pause. "And we've got a problem our end."

Radko knew what that problem would be. "Two warships?"

"Yes."

Warships weren't something Radko could worry about. "You worry about the warships, Ean. We'll get to the shuttles. Right," she added, as van Heel loosened the bindings around her ankles. She stood up. "Let's go." Radko pointed her weapon at Bach. "Chaudry, can you take Han?"

Chaudry hoisted Han over his shoulders in a fireman's carry. "Ready."

"I've sung the doors open," Ean said. "Hurry."

Radko stopped first, to go through Jakob's pockets. He had three comms. She took them all, and made sure they were zipped securely in her pocket before anything else. Then she indicated with her blaster. "You're coming with us, Bach. You'll be tried for treason against Lancia."

Bach smiled faintly. "We'll see." He moved toward the door. "Which way?"

"Follow the open doors," Radko said.

They turned left outside the door because the passage to the right was blocked by massive breach doors. Ean, bless him, had closed every single door they didn't need. They moved as fast as they could but, hampered as they were by Chaudry's load and Vilhjalmsson's back, they were slow.

Every soldier on ship would be at the shuttle bay by the time they got there.

Radko didn't think about that. Worry about what you could control, trust Ean to do the rest. All the same, she'd be glad when they were on the *Eleven*.

"What weapons does Captain Kari Wang have ready?" she asked Ean.

There was a momentary silence, then a sheepish "Um" from Ean, through the speakers.

She knew how to read Ean. "You're not on the *Eleven*?" But the ship was an Eleven class. There was only one other Eleven-class ship. "You brought the *Confluence*."

THIRTY

EAN LAMBERT

"EAN," SALE SAID. "Turn this ship. Now."

"Turn how? Turn where?" She'd be smarter telling the ship direct.

"Seventy degrees any way. One of those warships is pointing directly at the shuttle bay where we've housed the prisoners. Move Ean, move it now."

The ship was already turning.

"Thank you."

Ean hadn't done anything. He added his own thanks. *Thank you. What Sale wants, you give. Okay?*

"Of course."

"Hit," Craik said. "One of the big cargo bays in section six. Can't tell the damage."

The *Confluence* was already closing the breach doors.

"Weapons," Ean sang to line eight. *"What have you got?"* Because he knew that's what Sale would ask next.

He was swamped with the same overlay that had overwhelmed him before.

"We're sitting ducks here," Sale said. "Ean, I need weapons. And don't give me that green protective field."

Ean seized on the only one he recognized. *"That one."* Quiet, blue, hot blood. "Sale, which ship do you want to aim at first?"

"Shit." A two-second pause. *"Hellfire."*

"Which one's that?"

Another second while Sale oriented herself between human screen and alien displays. "That one."

"That one," Ean whispered. *"Do it now. Do it quick."*

"I need weapons, Ean. I need them yesterday."

"Coming." But they were in the void, and he wasn't sure if Sale heard him. Line eight released the weapon, then they were out again. A blue ball of flame engulfed *Hellfire*. Ean was ready for the metallic smell of hot blood that flooded the ship, but he still staggered. The lines on the *Hellfire* went dead.

"Shit. Was that you, Ean?"

"It was the ship." Sale needed to learn what the ship was doing for her.

He took a moment to see what was happening on the station. Radko was taking forever to get to the shuttle bays.

The commander had stopped trying to call Jakob, stopped trying to get through the locked doors. He turned his attention to the *Confluence*. "Weapons, armed." He didn't have a full crew at the weapons bay, but he had enough to man and load them.

"*Hellfire* is no longer firing," Craik said.

Hellfire was a dead ship. But the *Brimstone* was still firing.

"Nice shooting, Ean," Sale said.

"You should compliment the ship."

Sale looked at him, then said, "Thank you, ship," but she turned back to Ean immediately.

"You should always thank the ship."

"Right, I get the message. Now what do we do about the other ship, and how long is this one out for?"

"We can't use the blue thing again. It takes time to recharge."

"We need a miracle, Ean. We're undermanned, we have no idea what this ship can do yet, and no one to do it for us."

He couldn't give her a miracle. "*Hellfire* won't fire again, it's dead. I don't—"

"Perfect. Thank you. Open the comms to the bridge on the *Brimstone*."

He sang the comms open for her.

"*Brimstone*," Sale said. "This is the *Confluence*. We have destroyed the *Hellfire*. If you don't want the same fate, cease fire now."

Ean had just told her they couldn't do it again yet. He turned his attention to the other problem, because the commander on the station had received a weapons ready from the gunners. He diverted the commander's comms into the speakers in the corridor where Radko was.

"Gunnery one," the commander said. "Fire a salvo in a three, two, five pattern. We're not aiming to destroy the ship yet, only scare it."

Chaudry stopped. "They're firing at us."

"No they're not," Radko said, barely audible under the instructions and calls from line five. "Those are the instructions from this station. They're trying to fire on the *Confluence*. Keep moving, Chaudry."

"If they're firing on our rescue ship," van Heel said, "they'll destroy it before we get there."

"Keep moving. Ean's deflecting the orders. Hurry on, he can't do it forever."

Radko always understood.

"Small single-man craft exiting the *Hellfire*," Craik said.

"They're lifepods," Ean said.

"Correction, lifepods," Craik said at the same time.

Bhaksir called Sale then. "Prisoners are secure."

"What?" Sale said. "That was hours ago."

According to the time on Ean's comms, they had been in the Worlds of the Lesser Gods less than half an hour.

"Can you get Ean to lock them in?"

"He's busy."

Ean used lines eight and three of the *Confluence* to sing the air lock secure. In doing so, he lost control of line three on the station momentarily, and two soldiers made it into the passage.

"Radko," he called. "There are two armed soldiers heading your way."

Radko didn't give any indication she'd heard, and no wonder, for he was piping all the comms into the corridor. If he stopped that, the commander would get his order to the gunners.

Radko rounded the corner and almost ran into the soldiers.

They went down before Ean realized she had fired. She'd always had good reflexes.

AFTER what felt longer than the longest forever in the void, Radko's group reached the shuttle.

"In, in," Radko said. "Don't forget, Bach's under arrest. Don't let him near a weapon. Strap yourself in," she ordered Bach. "All of you."

Ean kept singing the commands into the empty corridor as Radko piloted the shuttle out of the bay.

The commander realized his commands weren't getting

through. "Get down to the gunner's station," he ordered someone. "Tell them to fire."

Ean locked all the doors.

"What the hell? Use the emergency tunnels."

"An unauthorized shuttle has left the station," someone at
another board said.

"Tell them to shoot the shuttle, instead," the commander
said to the person who was unscrewing the emergency hatch.

On the *Confluence* bridge, the only sound was Ean singing.
Ean didn't know what agreement Sale had made with the
Brimstone, but it wasn't firing at them.

He kept singing as the *Confluence* grabbed the shuttle and
brought it in.

Chaudry grabbed the arms of his seat. "We're hit."

"No," Radko said. "That's normal."

"Felt like a hit," van Heel said.

"It wasn't."

Ean stopped singing when the shuttle was safely inside one
of the small air locks on the *Confluence*.

"Comms back, sir," someone on the station said.

"About time," the station commander said. "Fire on that
blasted ship."

"Take us home," Ean sang to the *Confluence*.

They entered the void as the first gunner pressed the fire
button.

"WELCOME home, *Confluence*," Captain Helmo said.

"Radko's got prisoners," Ean told Sale. "Two of them."
Was Vilhjalmsson a prisoner?

"Prisoners. Right. That's where we started. It seems so
long ago now." Sale called Bhaksir. "Stay where you are.
We're coming down. Ean says we have a couple more for you."

"Faster?" Ean asked the ship.

"Faster." Confirmation, affirmative.

Sale had already started running. She thumbed open her
comms as she ran, "Ma'am," to Vega. "We've at least forty
prisoners. The fake paramedics, some Lancastrian linesmen,
and two prisoners Radko brought back from the station."

"Lancastrian?" Vega bit off anything more she might say.

"Sale." Ean and the ship called together. "Wait."

She paused. "What's wrong?"

"We'll use the faster," because he had no idea what it was called. At least she'd stopped. "This way," and let lines three and four guide him to the wall.

Sale kept talking to Vega. "We've around a hundred—"

They were sucked into the tube and jerked sideways. Then up, then down, then sideways again, and finally expelled into the shuttle bay, where Ean bowled over three trainee linesmen.

Ean heard the distinct snap of breaking bone. Two linesmen stayed down. One of them was Arnold Peters.

Lines three and four conferred. *"Still too fast."*

Sale picked herself up. Her voice shook as she continued. "Hundred linesmen who need medical attention. One linesman is badly injured. Blaster burns. Other problems are line-related. Except Burns, who took a blaster in his suit." She looked at the linesmen Ean had knocked over. "At least two with broken bones from friendly fire."

They didn't need the comms, for the lines were still wide open.

Ean heard Jordan Rossi, somewhere in the background, "Lambert strikes again."

Bhaksir beckoned to Alex Joy and Hernandez, and pointed to the two injured trainees. They came over.

"Sorry." Ean tried to help, but they didn't want him to. He limped away.

"We'll send shuttles," Vega said. "We don't have room for them here. Send them on to Confluence Station. Admiral Orsaya?"

"I'll need paramedics and guards."

"Done. Sale, once Lambert returns to a thinking, functioning linesman, get him to move the *Confluence* closer to Confluence Station. And if you're listening, Lambert, there's a difference between *moving* and *jumping*. There's also such a thing as 'too close.'"

"Hear that, ship?" Sale said, as she tucked her comms back into her pocket. "You move. You don't jump. And you don't move too close."

"How close? Where?"

"Closer to Confluence Station," Ean said.

The ship started to move.

"What's it doing now, Ean?"

"Moving closer to Confluence Station."

"Shit." Even though that was what Vega had suggested. "How does it know when to stop?"

"Sale will tell you when to stop," Ean told the *Confluence.*

"Ship will tell." A little smugness there. They could worry about that later.

Ean said to Sale, "I said you'd say when we're close enough."

"Sh—. How am I supposed to tell it that? And what constitutes close enough anyway?"

Helmo said, "We'll let you know with plenty of margin."

Sale took the comms out of her pocket again, looked at it, and put it back. "Make sure it's a big margin because Ean will have to stop the ship. There's no way it's going to do it for me."

"Yes we will."

Ean could have told her she'd insulted her ship, but the bay where Radko's shuttle was had finished recycling, and Radko was exiting. Bhaksir and her team covered them.

Radko spared a quick glance around the massive shuttle deck, then looked him over.

Ean relaxed for the first time since Radko had disappeared into the shuttle bound for Lancia. This was how it was meant to be, with Radko back, by his side.

Although, there was something odd, based on the way she looked at him. Then he realized his helmet was still in place from his trip through the tubes. He grinned at her and kept watching her as he checked his readings before he unclipped it. "Hi." He couldn't stop smiling, looking at her, whole and healthy and alive.

Sale looked the prisoners over. She scowled on seeing Bach. The lines echoed something like betrayal. "You're the reason I joined the Royal Guard in the first place."

"Then Galenos poached you," Bach said. "He always hand-picked the best."

Van Heel watched them. Sale, to Radko, to Bach, and back.

The best thing about the *Lancastrian Princess* crew was they trusted each other. If Radko said arrest Bach, then Sale and Bhaksir arrested him. They didn't argue about it.

"Our crew, too."

Ean ignored that.

Sale turned to the other prisoner. "Captain Vilhjalmsson. Why am I not surprised?"

"I am. Surprised, I mean." Vilhjalmsson had put up his hands as soon as he saw Ean. "Especially since I'm helping Team Leader Radko."

Team leader. She had a team of her own to look after now. Chaudry, van Heel, and Han. She wouldn't be his bodyguard anymore. Ean pushed away that niggling worry. "Helping. Last time you tried to kill her."

"Linesman, I know now the folly of doing that on a ship that you control." He looked around. "Interesting ship, by the way. It's almost worth getting arrested to see this."

Chaudry lowered Han carefully to the floor and looked around. Ean tried to see it as the newcomers would see it. Soldiers from multiple worlds, half of them still on the floor, many of them with oxygen. Kentish, surrounded by people trying to keep her alive.

"What happened?" Chaudry asked. "A war?"

Something like that. Only it was their own people who'd started it.

Two single-level linesmen came up with oxygen.

"He's been stunned," Radko said. "Oxygen won't help."

Chaudry checked Han over. "He'll be fine." He looked at Vilhjalmsson, then over at Kentish. Ean heard the hum of uncertainty through line one, and it wasn't *Confluence* line one.

The lines were certainly listening, though.

In fact, the whole of the *Confluence* fleet was considering Chaudry.

"Yes."

"That one."

The *Confluence* cut over the top of them all, strong and loud and brooking no dissent. *"This one is mine."*

"Yours," agreed the other ships, and all 1,291 lines exuded satisfaction. *"We like him."*

Ean watched Chaudry make his way toward Kentish. "Radko. He's a linesman."

"I know. Level one?"

He nodded.

Radko looked at van Heel. "She's a linesman, too."

"If you're looking at me," van Heel said. "I'm no linesman.

I did training, sure, but I failed certification." She wasn't bitter about it, so for her it was a long time in her past.

"I'll tell you what I think she is. Turn around. I'll tell Sale and Bhaksir."

Ean turned around so he couldn't see her. But after everything that had happened, the lines were wide open. He couldn't block them. "I can see. You're holding up eight fingers."

Radko clasped her fingers together under her chin and smiled. A proper smile, that showed off the dimples that were so like Michelle's. "It's good to be home, Ean."

Ean smiled, too, as he turned around. "It's good to have you home."

"We're glad you're back, too," Bhaksir said. "Couldn't you have left a user manual or something?"

"It's simple, Bhaksir. He's a linesman. He thinks like a line. Remember that, and you'll be fine." Then Radko sighed and looked at Bach. "Can I borrow your comms, Ean? I need to call Admiral Galenos."

He handed it over. He hadn't used it much recently. He was getting used to working direct with the lines. "You can keep it, if you like."

"And if we need to track you?"

"That didn't seem to bother him last time he was without a comms," Vilhjalmsson said.

"You're fishing, Vilhjalmsson. Ean, can you make this secure, please? As secure as it can be."

"With him here? He works for Gate Union." They didn't normally show people what Ean could do.

"Point taken. Let's do this outside. Bhaksir, van Heel, you've got the prisoners."

"I still fail to see why I'm a prisoner. After all, I was trying to rescue you."

Radko stopped at the door. "Last time I rescued you. You repaid me by stealing something from me."

Ean followed her out.

"I missed you, Radko."

"I missed you, too, Ean." He heard the truth of it through the lines.

He smiled at her and kept on smiling as he sang the comms line secure. "How private do you want this call?"

"Very private," and her face turned grimmer than he'd ever seen it before.

"I'd better tune the others out, then." He sang the other ships out of the loop, even the *Lancastrian Princess*, which was her home ship, and she should have been reporting to Vega.

"Do you want me to go back in there?"

Radko shook her head. "Sir," into the comms as Abram answered. "A private word with you, if I may." She stressed the "private."

"Give me a moment."

How much did Abram already know? He must know about the attempt to steal the ship. All the admirals would by now. If they didn't, they'd hear it on the news vids soon enough, for Ean could hear the linesman from Galactic News.

"I'm telling you, Coop. That wasn't an exercise, no matter what they put it out as. You go after the full story."

"The success of your last call has gone to your head, Christian."

"Have I been wrong before? No. Go after the story, Coop."

"Line secure," Abram said, and Ean dragged his attention away from the Galactic News ship.

"Thank you, sir." Radko paused a moment. "I arrested Commodore Bach for treason, sir."

Abram was off ship, so Ean couldn't tell what he was thinking. "Where is he?"

"On the *Confluence* at the moment, sir. I plan to transport him to Confluence Station."

"I'll meet you there."

The first of Orsaya's shuttles arrived as Radko and Ean went back inside.

Sale put Bhaksir in charge of the prisoners and Craik in charge of the trainees. "Load the injured first—prisoners and linesmen. Then the rest of the prisoners, and finally the rest of the linesmen."

They ran out of stretchers before they finished loading the prisoners. Luckily, it wasn't too far to Confluence Station, and the next two shuttles were well supplied.

"That's it," Sale said, as the last trainee was loaded. "Let's go."

They took Bach and Vilhjalmsson on their own shuttle.

As they waited for the air to cycle at Confluence Station, Bach said, "I want His Imperial Majesty present when we talk to Galenos."

"No," Ean said.

"He has the right, Ean," Sale said.

"I don't care. Yu is not getting anywhere near Abram."

"Why not?" Radko asked.

"Because Yu wants to kill Abram. To get his seat on the council."

Bach's mouth turned down in a twisted smile, leaving Ean with the uneasy feeling he was missing something. Off to one side, Vilhjalmsson's eyes widened. It was the only change in his expression.

Maybe one day Ean could keep his face as expressionless. And remember not to blab personal Lancian information to their enemies. Vilhjalmsson didn't need to know about Yu and Abram.

"Fair point," Sale said, and turned back to the other prisoners.

"When Galenos arrives," Bach said. "I will make the same request of him. He will be obliged to grant it."

Sale looked at Radko. Radko took out her comms.

Ean hastily sang it secure for her. This time, they couldn't go outside to hide what he was doing.

"Sir, Commodore Bach requests the presence of His Imperial Majesty when we question him."

Abram blew out his breath. "Transfer Bach to the *Lancastrian Princess* instead."

"Ean says the Emperor is trying to kill you."

"Probably." Abram didn't look surprised.

He'd known about it.

"We can't let you go, sir."

"You have arrested the Emperor's right-hand man, Radko. I can't let you face that alone."

"I'll release him, then."

"Thank you, Radko, but His Majesty will catch up with me eventually. Let's not sacrifice your work. I will meet you on the *Lancastrian Princess*." Abram clicked off.

Ean became aware he'd taken Radko's hand in his own. She gripped tight.

He stayed close to Radko as they exited the shuttle. He wouldn't have changed what he'd done, but it had brought Abram into the very danger Michelle had worked so hard to avoid. Yu would arrest Abram. He had an excuse now because Ean had taken the ship without permission, and Sale's team, who should have demanded he come home immediately—with a weapon to his head if necessary—had stayed to help. Abram, as head of Alien Affairs, was responsible for the alien ships. He was responsible for what happened on them. Was forcing the linesmen onto the *Confluence* part of a plan to discredit Abram?

Ean called Michelle. She'd tried so hard to prevent this meeting. She didn't answer. She was already talking on her comms to Abram.

The call was nearly over. "I'm sorry, Misha. I have to do this."

"I know."

Ean couldn't tell what she was thinking.

"Take care. See you soon."

He shouldn't be listening in, but Michelle was clearly hiding her thoughts. From him? Or from Abram?

EAN and Orsaya watched Captain Auburn march the last of the paramedics down to the cells and tried not to think of the meeting ahead.

He wiped his palms down the side of his trousers. Maybe he should sneak in a blaster. He didn't know how to fire one, but how hard could it be? Point and grip.

"Katida is bringing in her own warship to transport the prisoners to Haladea III," Orsaya said. "Given they were attempting to steal an eleven ship, we deem it's better to get them onto a world as fast as we can."

"Especially since they were trying to steal the whole fleet." It was hard to concentrate on mundanities. "They knew they could take one ship, and all of them would go."

Radko looked shattered, and Ean didn't know what to do about it. Short of begging Yu not to arrest Abram.

They watched four members of Bhaksir's team march a handcuffed Commodore Bach onto the shuttle.

"But then, it's easy to see how they knew so much," Orsaya's voice was harsh.

Ean didn't answer.

Sale was giving last-minute instructions. "Bhaksir, full report to Orsaya about what happened with the trainees."

Bhaksir nodded.

"Craik, you're responsible for the injured. And for getting the trainees back to the *Gruen*."

Not the Lancastrian trainees; they were prisoners.

"Tell Gruen to keep them under lockdown, and if a word of this emerges before the Department of Alien Affairs says it can, whoever leaks it is out of the program."

Craik nodded.

"The three spacers who came with me," Radko said. "Can someone look after them?"

"Hana, Ru Li," Bhaksir said. "You're responsible for looking after Radko's team. Look after them well, or you'll have Radko to answer to later."

"Yes, ma'am."

Sale looked at their last prisoner. "Admiral Orsaya. Prisoner Vilhjalmsson will likely escape if he's imprisoned in a regular cell."

"I don't see why I am a prisoner. I was working with Radko."

"You're in enemy territory," Sale said.

"You and I will talk, I think," Orsaya said. "The images the *Confluence* sent back of the inside of that station—the experiments on the linesmen—looked most interesting."

Ean shuddered. "How do you know they were experimenting?" But then, Orsaya had seen everything Sale and her team had seen, and one thing she knew well was linesman.

"I would think it obvious. Their reactions to line eleven. The references to Dromalan truth serum, which, before it became the favored drug of interrogators everywhere, was used to enhance line ability until they realized its side effects. I wouldn't mind Dr. Quinn's notes."

Ean had to force himself not to move away. "You're not experimenting on any of the linesmen here."

"I wouldn't dream of it, Ean. I know what you can do with the lines. But it would be good to see what they did."

"You should ask Vilhjalmsson about Quinn's work," Radko said. "He stole the report I was sent to collect."

Orsaya's eyes gleamed.

"I sent it on to Markan straight away," Vilhjalmsson said. "I was worried someone might steal it back."

"She would have, too," Ean said.

"Pity." Orsaya motioned to more of her staff to cover Vilhjalmsson. "Be extra careful with this one. He's a trained assassin and works directly for Markan."

The little group of Sale, Bhaksir, and Craik broke apart.

"Talk to you when we get back," Sale said. "If I'm not in jail."

Ean and Radko followed them onto the shuttle. Bach was already seated, restrained at the wrists and ankles. "You won't be in jail."

"You think not. Disobeying a superior officer comes to mind."

"You didn't disobey anyone."

Sale looked at him.

"I should be in jail then. Not you," Ean said.

"On a line ship. That'd be effective."

They both glanced at Bach and fell silent.

"You're not telling me anything I don't know already," Bach said.

"That's for sure," Radko said grimly, but they were all silent for the rest of the trip.

THIRTY-ONE

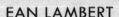

EAN LAMBERT

VEGA AND A team of guards waited for them as they docked on the *Lancastrian Princess*.

"His Imperial Majesty is in his apartments," Vega said. "Admiral Galenos will be here soon. Group Leader Sale, I expect a report on my desk by the time this meeting is over."

"Yes, ma'am." Sale left to record her report.

"Speaking of reports." Radko unzipped a pocket, took out three comms. "One of these is a copy of the report Callista OneLane acquired. Unfortunately, Vilhjalmsson got the original. He's already sent it on to Admiral Markan."

Vega nodded and handed the comms to one of the people with her. "Decode it. I want that report when I come out of this meeting."

The meeting. What could Ean do to prevent Yu's arresting Abram for treason? He checked the *Lancastrian Princess*. *"Is everything all right?"*

"Waiting," came the reply.

Helmo was in the captain's chair, sitting back, letting his instinct tell him what was happening. Michelle was working at one of the screens in her workroom. Yu and Sattur Dow were smiling over a drink in Yu's quarters.

As Ean watched, Abram's shuttle signaled that it had arrived. Helmo stood up. "Give Galenos's shuttle permission to land. Inform Her Royal Highness he is here. Vanje, you're in charge. I want you on the bridge, staff on alert."

He left at a brisk walk.

After Michelle received Vanje's call, she moved over to a cupboard on the wall. Ean could hear through the lines that the lock was coded only to her, Abram, and Helmo. She took out a small, needlelike weapon and slipped it into an inside pocket of her jacket.

Had Michelle just armed herself?

She whispered something that might have been a prayer, her emotion too raw for Ean to read properly—or too raw and personal for him to want to read—and started for the meeting.

The atmosphere in the large meeting room was suffocating. Ean found it hard to breathe. Ship lines were a dirge.

Ean checked the other ships in the *Eleven* fleet. On Confluence Station, armed soldiers in Balian uniform were loading prisoners onto a shuttle. Orsaya's captain, Auburn, and two teams of Yaolin soldiers stood ready to assist if required.

Katida and Orsaya were dining with Jordan Rossi and Stellan Vilhjalmsson.

Both admirals looked grim.

Ean suppressed a shiver.

Radko said, quietly, "Relax, Ean. Do what you do naturally. Things have a way of working out."

They wouldn't work out all the time. You only had to miss once, and Ean didn't even understand what the problem was yet. It should have been simple. A Lancastrian traitor, trying to steal the ships. But it wasn't about that at all. It was about a ruler who was prepared to frame a good, honest man to gain a seat of power.

He breathed in deep. There was no word in Abram or Michelle's vocabulary for failure. Not in Radko's, either. There were just setbacks to be overcome. Abram was right when he'd told Radko that Yu would catch up with him eventually. Keeping Abram away from Yu wasn't the solution. Getting Yu to change his mind was.

Helmo arrived, followed quickly by Michelle, and finally Abram.

Abram smiled at Michelle, nodded to Helmo and Ean's group, then looked at Bach, still cuffed at the wrists. "Commodore Bach."

"I request His Imperial Majesty be present at this meeting," Bach said.

Michelle nodded—once—though the refusal was pouring out of her. A hot yellow denial through line one.

"I shall request His Majesty's presence," Vega said.

Ean watched Vega's brisk march through the ship to the Emperor's quarters.

Yu was still holding court with Sattur Dow. Guards in pairs stood at attention around the room. Two behind Yu, two off to one side, another two near the door. Tiana Chen and Ethan Saylor were among the silent observers. Chen's hands were balled into fists as she glowered at the back of Dow's head. Ean wished her glare were more lethal.

Vega saluted, then stood to attention. "Commodore Bach requests your presence in the large meeting room."

"That was quick." Yu looked pleased as he stood up. He turned to Sattur Dow. "Sattur, would you like to be present at this historic occasion."

"I don't think Yu is expecting this," Ean said. "But he is expecting something."

Bach said, "You should refer to him as Emperor Yu, or His Imperial Majesty."

In Emperor Yu's quarters, Vega said, "It would be inappropriate to invite a civilian to this meeting. This is a matter for the Crown alone."

Yu towered over her. "You presume to tell me what to do?"

Vega inclined her head and turned away. "The large meeting room, Your Majesty."

Ean's back itched until she was around the first turn in the corridor. "He's bringing Sattur Dow."

Abram blew out his breath but didn't say anything.

Ean didn't want Sattur Dow in the same room as Radko. If Dow attempted anything, he wasn't sure what he'd do. He'd think of something.

The Emperor swept in three minutes after Vega arrived. He'd changed his clothing and was now wearing a traditional, wide-sleeved, ceremonial jacket. He was accompanied by Sattur Dow and the full team of guards.

Helmo made a face, and Ean got a strong sense through the lines that this was unexpectedly fast.

Yu smiled when he saw Abram, stopped smiling when he saw Bach under restraint. "What is this?"

Vega spoke before anyone else could. "Please be seated, Your Imperial Majesty. Merchant Dow." She indicated the seats around the table. "Team Leader Radko has returned and is ready to make her report to Admiral Galenos and me. Commodore Bach has requested your presence."

"Radko." The Emperor rolled the word around his tongue. He looked closely at Radko, then at Michelle and Abram, and settled into a seat. "Cousin. So you are back. And just in time." He smiled at Sattur Dow, then waved a hand. "Report."

Radko looked to Abram, then to Vega, who nodded brusquely. "Go ahead, Team Leader."

"My mission was to meet with a trader on Redmond and investigate the sale of a report purportedly about line experiments."

Sattur Dow started. Ean watched him closely.

"Our team managed to contact the seller, but we weren't the only ones after the report. Gate Union sent someone in as well. Stellan Vilhjalmsson."

Abram made a face but didn't interrupt.

"Redmond soldiers attacked the shop just after we arrived." She looked to Vega and Abram. "Unfortunately, Vilhjalmsson got away with the report."

"So you failed," Yu said.

Radko turned back to stare him in the eyes. "Of course we didn't fail, Your Imperial Majesty." Cold and professional.

Ean wanted to cheer.

"We traced the report to a Redmond company, TwoPaths Engineering. Specifically, to a TwoPaths site on the Lesser Gods world of Aeolus. Right against the palace wall, actually."

Did Ean imagine it, or did the Emperor sit up straighter?

"The Lesser Gods?" Vega asked.

"Yes, ma'am. We discovered later that the experiments were a joint venture between TwoPaths Engineering, and the militaries of Redmond and the Worlds of the Lesser Gods." Radko glanced at Bach. "We discovered artifacts that could only have come from the alien line ships; could only have come from one of the New Alliance worlds. From someone who had access to the alien line ships."

"Enough," Yu said. "We don't need the details."

Ean moved to stand close at Radko's back.

"I sent Radko on the mission," Vega said. "*I* need the report. And there is the matter of the consequences. If you prefer not to be here, by all means, there is no obligation to remain. Commodore Bach requested that you be here."

Yu looked at Abram. Ean couldn't see any reason for the look, especially since it was Vega who'd spoken. Or for the look he shared with Bach afterward.

Yu waved irritably. "Proceed."

"We were captured attempting to retrieve the report and the artifacts," Radko said. "The site was a laboratory and a hospital. They appeared to be experimenting on linesmen."

The linesmen Ean had heard on the station. No wonder they had seemed crazy.

"After our capture, the people in charge there believed the lab had been compromised. They withdrew the linesmen from Aeolus and took them to the fallback lab on the space station I was rescued from."

The Emperor stood to pace. Everyone seated rose, as was custom.

It was better to be standing. More voice for the lines when Ean needed it. He was starting to worry that Radko's report was putting her in danger. Would Emperor Yu leave her alive to testify against Bach?

But then Yu would have to imprison them all. Including Michelle. He wouldn't do that. Would he?

"We have heard enough." Yu turned to Bach. "Free this man."

Vega said, "Commodore Bach is under arrest, Your Majesty. For treason against Lancia."

Ean was surprised Yu didn't order her immediate demise.

The Emperor glanced at his guards and at Bach again.

"If it pleases Your Imperial Majesty, I would prefer to have the issue resolved." Bach bowed low.

Yu turned to Radko, who stared him down again. Ean readied himself to sing, for the tension was a sudden crackling energy that tasted like ozone on his tongue.

Line eight was ready. It might not know what it had to do yet, but it was ready. He could hear it, now he was listening properly to the lines. He didn't have to force it to work his way. It was ready to work its own way.

"Continue," Yu said.

Radko glanced at Bach. "I was about to be interrogated when the Factor's bodyguard, Jakob, came in with Commodore Bach." She paused again, then continued, flat and harsh and unlike her usual tone. "Jakob accused Bach of having had him arrested. Bach countered by saying he had given Jakob access to the ships, and that Jakob was the one who had mucked things up. Then Jakob said Bach had promised that if they brought one ship through, the whole fleet would come. But it hadn't."

She tilted her chin and looked directly at Bach. "It was obvious to me that Commodore Bach was working with Captain Jakob to steal the *Confluence* fleet. When the opportunity arose, I arrested him and brought him home to face trial."

"It's a grave accusation," Abram said to Bach.

"It is," Bach agreed. "But I am loyal to Lancia."

Michelle rubbed her arms, as if she was cold. "Loyal. As in attempting to steal a New Alliance fleet and hand it over to our enemies."

Ean remembered, suddenly, the earlier conversation between Yu and Sattur Dow, with Dow saying, "She bought it," and Yu's reply. "I knew exactly how my daughter would react, Sattur. She has been protecting this linesman all along. Of course she would send him to what she perceives as safety."

Maybe Bach was telling the truth.

"This isn't about killing Abram to get onto the council at all, is it," Ean said. Emperor Yu had set the whole thing up. "That was to distract us, and keep Abram away from Michelle, because together they might suspect something. Yu tricked us into going out to the *Confluence* today so *Lancia* could steal the ships. This isn't Bach's plan, it's Yu's."

For a moment, the silence was absolute, except for the whispering of life support.

To Ean, that sound was gradually overcome by a stronger susurrus of betrayal. It came with a strong, sweet scent. Who would believe betrayal could smell so beautiful?

Yu's smile had the same dimples his daughter had.

"Why?" Michelle's voice broke on the words. "You have destroyed Lancia's future."

"Future, Daughter? When we are treated like second-rate citizens here? Everything we want, everything we do, has to go through a committee and be voted on. Where is the power Lancia once had? Given away. By you and Galenos. We have no wish to be part of a government in which we are power-less."

"Whether we want to or not, we have to be." They could have been the only two in the room. "We had two choices. Give in to Gate Union and become a second-rate world, for Gate Union would never let us remain a power. Or join up with the New Alliance and use the one lucky break we had—Ean and the alien fleet—to give us a chance at starting afresh."

"We had a third choice."

"Go it alone?" Michelle said. "We can't even get jumps. Most of Lancia's income is derived from New Alliance worlds. Our people would starve; we'd have nothing. How long will Lancia last as a power when we're stuck in our own solar system?"

"Your imagination has become limited of late, Daughter. Are they the only options you can think of? You are right. Lancia doesn't care about the New Alliance. The New Alliance doesn't care about us, either. We have been left powerless and helpless. Because you will not think past the obvious.

"I do not plan on being part of a government I have no control over," Yu said.

"So you planned to steal a fleet of ships and start out alone."

Yu smiled. "Hardly alone."

A fleet of alien ships didn't make it any less alone.

Michelle opened her mouth to speak. Closed it again.

"Warships will not keep Lancastrians fed," Abram said. "Lancia is an old world and has never been particularly fertile. We import half our food and 90 percent of our technology. We can use the alien ships to bomb worlds and ships as much as we want, but other worlds will stop supplying us with goods long before it is effective. That's assuming we had full crews for the ships and could replenish supplies. Which is also unlikely."

Yu spun around to Abram. "I plan for everything, Galenos. Even supplies. Even your opposition."

Michelle put a hand to her head in sudden understanding. "You teamed up with the Worlds of the Lesser Gods."

"Of course I did."

"And when Gate Union stops the Worlds of the Lesser Gods from jumping?"

"Ah, Daughter. This is where you lack imagination, and I can see the future. A grand future for Lancia. Can Gate Union stop Redmond jumping?" Yu looked at Abram again. "Can they?"

"It would be more difficult," Abram admitted. "Redmond controls the line factories."

"Precisely."

Michelle went white. "You conspired with Redmond, as well as the Worlds of the Lesser Gods?"

"Of course."

"Father, Redmond will use you to get the ships, and once they have them, they will spit you out."

"Daughter, you go too far."

"You have already gone too far. Once people know you— we—were behind this crazy plan to steal the *Confluence*, and its fleet, Lancia will be expelled from the New Alliance. You have destroyed us, no matter what we do now."

"Have I not just told you we do not wish to be part of the New Alliance?"

The emotion creeping through the lines from the humans in the room was a fine brown mist that twisted Ean's gut and made him want to be sick. It didn't show on anyone's face, except Michelle's. She was white, her lips parted as if she wanted to speak but couldn't say the words.

"You don't have the alien ships," Abram said. "I presume that was what you brought to the coalition with Redmond and the Worlds of the Lesser Gods. Will they honor an agreement if you don't have the ships? Of course not, because you are no use to them."

"We do not have the ships, Galenos, because of your inter- ference. Had you not interfered, those ships would be in Red- mond territories right now."

Abram smiled faintly. Ean didn't have to listen to the lines to know what he was thinking. Abram had nothing to do with it.

"You may laugh now, but Lancia has decided. This is the future. Choose to be part of it, or be executed for treason." Yu shook his sleeve, and suddenly there was a blaster in his hand.

Ean was the only one who jumped. The only one who reacted, even. Had the others known Yu had a weapon?

Michelle put her hand to the inside of her jacket.

"Execute me," Abram said. "But first, let's talk about the fundamental flaw in your plan."

Yu raised his blaster.

"Hold." The needle weapon was in Michelle's hand. So fast Ean hadn't seen her pull it out. "Touch Abram, Father, and you are a dead man."

There wasn't any anger in her, only a steely determination very like her father's.

"The fundamental flaw, Galenos," Yu said. "The fact that Lancia doesn't control the line ships?"

"Exactly," Abram said.

"No. My daughter does, through her level-twelve linesman."

After that, things happened so fast it was a blur, but at the same time, it was like forever in the void, and Ean could recall each event clearly.

Yu swung his weapon around to Ean.

Radko grabbed her blaster.

Yu's arm kept swinging. Past Ean. To Michelle. "I can fix that."

His finger tightened.

"No!" Ean and line eight were swamped by a massive blast of denial. Ean wasn't sure he was the one who'd invoked line eight at all, but Yu went down.

Burned almost beyond recognition by Abram's blaster.

Stunned into immobility by Radko's blaster.

Thrown back against the wall by line eight.

Yu's guards fired on Abram and Radko, but line eight sang true. The blaster fire bounced back. Half of them went down under their own fire.

By then, Vega and Helmo had their blasters out.

"Nobody move," Vega said.

Commodore Bach stopped Yu's guards with a gesture. "Weapons down."

Michelle attempted to pick something off her jacket. It might have been burned flesh. Her hand shook so much, she couldn't pick it off.

"That's the second time you've shot someone so close I've got body parts over me." At least, Ean thought that was what she said, for her voice was shaking as much as her hands.

Ean was shaking, too.

Abram knelt in front of Michelle and silently proffered his weapon.

"Don't." It ended up a sob. She put her hands on his shoulders, gripping so tightly her fingers were bloodless. A tear splashed down onto Abram's head, then another, and another.

Abram tried to move Michelle's hands off his shoulders. She wouldn't let go, so he put his arms round her waist instead. She fell into his embrace, and they both ended up kneeling on the floor.

Radko moved over to Vega and held out her own blaster.

Vega didn't take it. "You'd be more useful helping me collect their weapons." She nodded at Yu's guards.

"But, ma'am, I—"

"Stunned an already-dead body from the looks of it. Not to mention, you were doing your job." Vega's voice was steady, but her hands weren't.

Radko silently helped Vega collect the blasters. Ean sang line eight to keep everyone safe, could see the field as a hazy, waist-high wave surrounding them.

One soldier surreptitiously lifted her weapon.

Line eight—and Ean—blasted her over to the other side of the room.

"Anyone else goes for a weapon, and I fire," Vega said.

Abram put his own blaster onto the floor and put his hands to Michelle's waist, lifting her as he stood. He wrapped his arms round her. She buried her face in his chest.

It was probably the first time anyone watching had seen her cry. Ean looked away, at Bach, who was watching him.

"It never was for the seat on the council, was it?"

"No. That was to keep Galenos away from the *Lancastrian Princess*. So he wouldn't work out what was happening."

"Was Yu ever going to kill Abram?"

"No. Galenos has always proven loyal to Lancia. He would have come around. It was your contract we wanted. Her Royal Highness held that."

"Were you part of it?" Vega asked. "This assassination?"

"Yes." Flat and bald.

"But why?" Ean asked. "What's Michelle ever done to you?"

"Nothing. In fact, I admire her. But I support my Emperor. I support Lancia. It was obvious to many people that while she held your contract, we would never have control of the alien ships, for Her Royal Highness was committed to the New Alliance."

Ean had seen his contract. He'd signed it. With Michelle, and Rigel, and Leo Rickenback. "If Michelle dies, my contract goes to Admiral Katida, of Balian."

"If the contract owner dies, the contract goes back to the cartel house," Bach said.

That was a standard contract, not Ean's. Michelle, Rigel, and Rickenback's lawyers had spent days on it. But Ean didn't argue. It didn't matter anyway. If Yu had killed Michelle, he would have ensured that Yu never got a single alien line ship.

"You're a fool." Vega came over and cut the restraints around Bach's hands. "But I imagine you're not the biggest fool, for a commodore doesn't come up with plans like this. I suspect Admiralty House at Baoshan may be a little empty for a while. Galenos will not take kindly to a plan to murder Michelle."

"You can't let him go," Ean said. "What if he decides to kill Abram, for killing Yu?"

"That's Emperor Yu," Bach said.

"He's dead. He's not Emperor anymore." Michelle was, and that was too strange to think of now.

Vega said, "Emperor Yu isn't the first of his family to be assassinated by the incoming Emperor. He killed his own father, and his father killed his father before him. If Bach is loyal to the Crown, he will now be loyal to the Empress."

But Yu hadn't been assassinated by his daughter. Abram

had killed him to save Michelle. It might have been better if Radko had done it. At least she was part of Yu's family.

Ean was glad she hadn't, all the same.

"What about your people?" Vega asked Bach.

"They serve the Crown of Lancia. They will support the new Empress."

Technically, they'd been negligent because their job was to save the Emperor.

Vega looked at Yu's guard. "Does anyone wish to complain, argue, or support anyone other than the Empress Michelle?"

There was only one answer to that, and it wasn't "yes."

"Good." She turned to Sattur Dow. "And you?"

At least he'd stopped smiling. "I support the ruler of Lancia."

Of course he did. But he would find the new ruler harder to influence than he had the old ruler.

Ean realized something else. "Radko doesn't have to marry you now." Something too strong to be relief flooded his mind and the lines.

"I am still prepared to take her," Dow said. "Despite the gross negligence she showed today."

He stepped back as Ean stepped toward him.

"I have a lot to offer a wife."

Radko stepped between them. "I am sure we would both prefer to choose our own partners."

Sattur Dow wouldn't.

Abram said, "I'm sorry, Misha. I failed you by staying away you when you needed me most."

Michelle pulled away, and looked at him. She shook her head.

"I will never do that again." Abram kissed her.

A strong hum of satisfaction exuded from the ship. From Ship.

Ean glanced at Helmo. You couldn't see it from his face. It was as expressionless as Abram's was normally.

"Do you mind?" Radko asked quietly from beside Ean.

He looked at her.

"Michelle. And Abram."

Why would he?

She held his gaze. He held his breath. He was drowning, he was . . . a choir in the void. Ean blinked, and shook his head.

She smiled. "Good."

Ean smiled back. "You know, Radko. I'm really, really, really glad you're back."

THIRTY-TWO

EAN LAMBERT

VEGA AND HELMO sent Bach's guards to the cells. "We're locking you down because we want to control news of this ourselves," Vega said. "Lambert, make sure they can't get a signal out."

"It's a bit late for that," Ean said. "The engineer on the Galactic News ship already knows."

Indeed, he was already on at the producer. "Coop. Coop. Something has happened to Emperor Yu. I don't know what, but it's big news. Big, big news."

"What, bigger than someone's stealing spaceships? And no, Christian, I'm not calling up the Emperor of Lancia. Five minutes ago, you wanted me to report on stolen spaceships. Which weren't stolen at all, incidentally. At least, not according to the Department of Alien Affairs."

"You know Spacer Grieve always misdirects. If he didn't say outright someone hadn't stolen that ship, then someone probably did. But Coop, what about Emperor Yu?"

Ean realized suddenly. "That engineer on the Galactic News. I assumed he was a six because he's an engineer. He's not. He's a one." He was picking up emotions from the lines in much the way Tinatin did, except his pickup was a lot more accurate. Tinatin was probably already giving Kari Wang her own garbled version.

"Well then," Radko said. "It goes to show, you shouldn't assume. Ever. Especially for someone who relies so much on listening."

It was good to have Radko back.

"Lambert," Vega said. "When you've quite finished, can we have lockdown on the soldiers, and on Sattur Dow."

It would be a pleasure. "We should stop comms from everyone in Yu's party."

"Do it."

Ean sang instructions to the ship. No communications in or out for any visitors. Only comms for Michelle and Abram, Vega, and Captain Helmo and his regular crew.

Bach tried his comms. "Impressive. I see why Lambert was so important. And we can train linesmen to do this?"

"Provided you get the right combination of lines," Vega said.

NEITHER Michelle nor Abram was the sort to spend much time whispering romantically to each other.

"Lancia knew as well as you did that the old Alliance was dead," Bach said, when the room had been cleared, and they were settled with tea. Michelle, Abram, Vega, Helmo, Bach, Ean, and Radko. Radko had been going to stand against the wall in her usual guard position. Ean was glad when Michelle motioned for her to sit down with them.

"I need all the support I can get today."

So Radko had left the wall and come to sit beside Ean.

"We could see we were better off in the fledgling New Alliance than we were as a secondary world in Gate Union," Bach told Abram and Michelle. "Until you started to send back reports of what the ships could do. What the linesmen could do—particularly a level twelve—and we realized how much power we had at our fingertips."

He wasn't talking about himself here when he said "we." He meant the Lancastrian admiralty, and the palace. Had he even agreed with what they were doing? They'd never know.

"Emperor Yu sounded out his daughter; the admirals sounded out Galenos. Unfortunately, both of you were determined to work with the New Alliance. So His Imperial Majesty looked elsewhere. Redmond and Gate Union were having problems. After Redmond tried to implicate Gate Union in the destruction of the *Kari Wang*, it was obvious to everyone that their alliance was fracturing. And Sattur Dow knew of a way we could approach Redmond."

Abram raised an eyebrow.

"Renaud Han," Vega said.

"Yes." Bach gave a twisted smile. "He was smuggling for

Redmond in return for silence about his son." Renaud Han, paying silence money for a secret that wasn't a secret at all. "I don't know how you found out about it."

Vega didn't say it was coincidence.

"We knew Tiana Chen was blackmailing him, didn't know Redmond was until Chen started working with Sattur Dow. When Dow wanted something sent to Redmond, she organized it for him through Renaud's smuggling links."

Two people couldn't deserve each other more.

"What were they blackmailing Renaud over?" Abram asked.

"The fact that Han is not his son," Radko said.

Ean looked at her. She hadn't been there when he and Vega had interviewed Lord Renaud.

"He's supposed to be a linesman." Radko smiled at Ean. "He's right-handed."

"His son joined the fleet," Vega told Abram. "Except his DNA didn't match the Han family's. So Lord Renaud paid someone on Redmond to fix the records, opening himself to blackmail from Redmond, too. They got him to smuggle medical supplies."

Abram blew his breath out, didn't say anything.

"Lord Renaud's life is his own to destroy," Bach said. "Our concern was contact with people in Redmond."

"Let me get this straight," Abram said. "You used the contacts Renaud made while smuggling to approach interested parties in Redmond. To offer them the alien ships in return for being part of a new alliance of Redmond, Lancia, and the Worlds of the Lesser Gods. How did the Lesser Gods come into it?"

"They've been working with Redmond for years, building ships based on alien technology. And experimenting on the linesmen even longer. They know more about linesmen than the New Alliance and Gate Union combined."

Ean shuddered, remembering the feel of the lines—the wrongness of the linesmen—on the station orbiting Aeolus.

Red-mint-cinnamon amusement wafted from the lines. "I'd pitch our line knowledge against anyone's," Michelle said.

"Perhaps," Bach said doubtfully. "Regardless, all three powers could see advantages. Redmond had line factories.

The Lesser Gods the linesmen. Lancia brought the ships, and the level-twelve linesman although he was to remain under our control."

Michelle made a sound that might have been a laugh. "Our level-twelve linesman is a thinking, rational human being." Ean was glad Vega didn't comment. "How did you think you would control him?"

Bach's gaze flicked toward Radko. "He has shown loyalty to the woman who is minding him."

"By marrying her off to Sattur Dow," Ean said. "What was that supposed to do?"

"Sattur Dow would expect access to his wife."

"That was never going to happen," Abram said.

Instead, it had triggered the start of events that had ruined Yu's plans. Ean couldn't understand how they'd even expected it to for a moment. Didn't Yu know that Radko couldn't give them access? Although Vega had sent Radko away because they were worried she'd have to.

Vega said, "With Lancia giving away the ships, it would be hard to see us as anything but a lesser contributor to any union of worlds."

"Giving away, Vega? No, I don't think so. We'd still have the linesman."

Michelle's smile was full dimple. "You know, Ean, sometimes I think we should hand you over to our enemies and let them find out the hard way they have no control."

Everyone except Ean and Bach laughed.

"I fail to understand," Bach said.

"You don't have to understand, Bach." Radko's dimples were as deep as Michelle's. "That's what I'm here for. To prevent people like you ever understanding."

The others laughed again.

"Who was involved in this grand plan?" Abram asked.

Bach shrugged.

Michelle and Abram shared a glance. A glance that was a whole conversation in a single look. Like they used to, back when Ean had first joined the *Lancastrian Princess*.

Ean blinked and had to look away. This was how it had been. This was how it would be again.

"Commodore Bach," Michelle said. "As the Empress of

Lancia, I order you to tell me who was involved. Fleet Admiral Galenos, as the head of the Lancian fleet, orders you to tell us who was involved."

Head of the Lancian fleet. Ean wasn't the only one who had to hold in a smile, and the *Lancastrian Princess*'s lines made a choir to match. Lancia couldn't make trouble anymore. Not with Abram in charge. Even Bach looked pleased, and Ean could tell from the lines that he truly was.

Bach half bowed from his seat. "Everyone at Admiralty house was involved. Emperor Yu, of course. Everyone except you and Admiral Galenos." He stopped. "Sorry. Fleet Admiral Galenos."

Michelle nodded.

"His Majesty believed Galenos would come around eventually. He has always had the interests of Lancia at heart." He smiled faintly as he glanced toward Abram. "He might have underestimated Galenos's feelings for you. None of us expected it to come down to Emperor Yu or Crown Princess Michelle."

Everyone on the *Lancastrian Princess* would have chosen the way Abram had.

Helmo must have been thinking the same thing, for he raised his eyebrows. Ean wasn't the only person who shrugged back. As Radko would say, was the sky on Lancia purple?

AFTER that, Vega escorted Bach down to his room and locked him in, while everyone else decamped to Abram and Michelle's workroom.

Helmo went via the bridge. "Give me ten minutes to talk to Vanje. I have the ship on alert."

Radko held Ean back. "Give them five minutes to themselves."

He was glad to have five minutes of his own, just him and Radko. "Thank you for saving my life. Again."

Radko half laughed. "He wasn't trying to kill you, Ean. I should have seen that."

"You would have protected Michelle anyway."

"Yes, I would, but I wouldn't have been fast enough."

Ean thought she would have been.

They started walking slowly.

"Was it bad? The job?"

"It was different. I made some mistakes. There were times I could have used a linesman. Especially a level twelve."

"If you'd taken me with you, I could have helped."

"Wasn't that the whole point? To keep us apart? And without you here, we would have lost the station, *Confluence* fleet, and Michelle. Nor would you have taken the *Eleven* to war."

Maybe so, but next time they'd work something out, so Radko didn't have to go away. But then, there wouldn't be a next time, for the dual enemies of Sattur Dow and Emperor Yu didn't exist anymore.

"Now that you're not engaged," Ean said, "what are you . . ." He stopped.

Radko smiled. He heard it through the lines. "That depends, Ean."

"On what?"

"Lots of things."

What did that mean? He looked at her.

Her smile was affectionate. "Let's see what happens, Ean?"

He wanted to slip his arm through hers. Did he dare? Not quite. Not yet.

They walked in silence for a while.

Even Vega delayed coming back, stopping at her own office to frown down at the decoded report on the desk, then pick it up and start flicking through the screens.

Ean broke the silence, eventually. "We have a problem with the *Confluence*."

"What sort of problem?"

"It's choosing its own crew."

"I thought you wanted crew for it."

"Yes, but it's chosen its own Ship."

"Captain, you mean? Who?"

"Sale."

"Hmm," Radko said. "It's not going to happen, Ean. She'll be good, but no one will ever let her take it. She's nowhere near qualified yet."

"You don't have to be captain to be 'Ship' for the lines. On Confluence Station, Ship is not the station manager, he's a guy called Ryley, who's part of engineering."

"Have you told Abram about this?" Radko asked.

"Sort of. But Abram never followed up on it. And he has been busy with other problems."

"Then he knows, Ean. I wouldn't worry."

"DAMAGE control," Abram said, when they were all back in the workroom. "If Michelle doesn't go back to Lancia soon, one of her younger siblings will take over. But if we don't stay here with the council, we'll lose credibility."

"If we haven't lost it already," Michelle said. "The lines know how much support we lost with my father and the Factor arriving."

"You might get some back now he's dead," Ean said.

He looked at Michelle, who had loved her father despite all he did. He couldn't tell her he was sorry, because he wasn't, so he didn't say anything. He'd talk to Katida and Orsaya himself, and maybe Shimson and Trask. Somehow, he'd convince them things would be better now.

"Whom do we tell first?" Michelle asked. "The council or Lancia?"

"Tell them at the same time," Abram said. "Warn the council we will be making an announcement, then jump the *Lancastrian Princess* to Lancia, so that we get communication between sectors, and make the announcement from the palace at Baoshan. Walk in as you mean to continue, Misha. I'll walk into Admiralty House and do the same."

"Both of you with bodyguards," Vega said. "I will supply them."

"And the council?" Helmo asked.

"We come back for the sessions and spend part of our time here, part there. Until Michelle can sort out a government loyal to her."

"That's a lot of jumps." The terror that Ean associated with Helmo and jumping cold started to seep into the lines.

"We order a lot of shellfish," Vega said.

"They'll pick that up by the third jump," Helmo said. "If not earlier."

Ean had to convince the captains to jump cold. Or they had

to come up with a way to stop Gate Union's blocking New Alliance jumps. Both needed a miracle. Could they convince Vilhjalmsson to get the jumps for them? After all, he needed to get home.

"Do we trust Markan?" he asked. Admiral Markan was in charge of Gate Union military. He was also Vilhjalmsson's boss, and Markan valued Vilhjalmsson, for he had rescued him before.

Michelle choked on her sip of tea.

"No," Vega said.

"Vilhjalmsson was investigating the same thing Radko was. He must know Redmond was about to defect. Maybe you could exchange some of the information Radko brought back in return for jumps. About Redmond. About their experimenting on the lines."

Gate Union had more to lose from Redmond's defection than the New Alliance did. Especially if House of Sandhurst proved to be as deeply involved as they looked to be, for Markan had supported Iwo Hurst's failed bid to become Grand Master. If Hurst proved to be knowingly involved in the experimentation on linesmen—and how could he not be—then Markan stood to lose the support of the line cartels if he didn't do something about it.

Radko shook her head. "Markan already knows. Vilhjalmsson got the original report from OneLane's."

"Ha." Vega brought out the comms she'd been looking at earlier. "The problem is, if he bases his information on this report and tries to replicate it, all he'll do is destroy a few extra linesmen." She tapped the report. "Quinn and his friends think they've found a way to make linesmen out of nonlinesmen. But they haven't."

She couldn't possibly have read the whole report already.

"They find someone with line potential, feed them full of drugs, then test them. All the way up to level ten."

Michelle understood before anyone else did. "Single-level linesmen. It's probably the first time they've ever been tested for every level."

"They've been testing fully for six months now. I'm guessing Lancia suggested that." Vega tapped the comms. "There's a list in here of people who might be suitable for the treatment. Fergus Burns, Mael St Mael. Nadia Kentish."

Failed linesmen.

"They think it's a simple matter of finding the right combination of drugs, and they'll get themselves another twelve."

The lines didn't work like that. "Didn't Bach or Yu tell them?" According to Katida, single lines were a badly kept secret.

"Maybe not," Abram said. "I suspect they kept line-related information close to their chest."

Michelle sighed. "It would have been Lancia's only bargaining tool. Lines and the linesmen."

"However," Abram said, "we may have enough to bargain with Markan. Especially if we do it with the Grand Master of the line cartels present. We can't keep line training and single lines secret forever."

"Vilhjalmsson knows Bach was arrested," Radko said. "If he goes free, he'll take that back to Markan."

Abram tapped eleven-time on the console. "We hand Vilhjalmsson back so he can tell them how Redmond planned to defect from Gate Union. Give Markan information about how line testing is flawed." He frowned. "It's enough to get us jumps to Lancia, but it has to benefit the whole of the New Alliance. Otherwise, we're no better than Yu himself, and they'll still look on us as traitors."

He looked at Michelle. There was a blue snap through the lines. From one of them? Or both?

"Ask for a temporary truce," Michelle said. "Three months. They give us unrestricted line travel. Jumps when we ask for them. We provide all we can about Lancia's plans with Redmond and the Worlds of the Lesser Gods." Her dimple showed. "We'll put Bach in charge of that."

Gate Union needed time to regroup. After all, Redmond owned the line factories. And Markan had elevated House of Sandhurst over the other houses. Their participation in line experiments wouldn't go down well.

"And line twelve?" Vega asked.

"That's not part of the deal. They don't get information about that. Just about the singles."

"We do need to warn some people," Michelle said. "Annette

Jade, for one, as well as Admiral Katida. Balian and Aratoga have both supported us longer than they should have."

They wouldn't be able to hide it from Orsaya, either.

"I'll talk to Vilhjalmsson and Katida," Abram suggested. "While you talk to Governor Jade."

Michelle nodded, and they shared a quick, smiling glance before Abram inclined his head toward Ean. "Linesman, you might ask Admiral Katida to linger over dinner."

THIRTY-THREE

EAN LAMBERT

STELLAN VILHJALMSSON LOOKED as if he should still have been in a hospital.

"Young Chaudry patched me up well enough," he said, in answer to Abram's query. "The medical staff at the station here looked at me as well and pumped me full of drugs. Unfortunately, I need my wits about me, so I can't take too many painkillers. But I will stand, if that's okay?"

Abram nodded, but he didn't sit down either. Nor did Orsaya or Katida. Radko took her normal position over near the wall. Ean perched on the edge of the table.

"Markan must have few people he can trust if he sent you on this mission," Abram said.

"Not really. I went to investigate a stolen report about line experiments. How important could it be? I was bored sitting around headquarters."

It even sounded reasonable, but the lines heard evasion.

"He's not telling the whole truth," Ean said.

Vilhjalmsson looked at him, then at Abram. "Do we have to have the human lie detector in on this meeting?"

Radko dropped her stance to stand straight. Vilhjalmsson flinched. Ean stood up, too.

"Easy," Abram said to them both. He smiled at Vilhjalmsson. "In this room or out there, won't make any difference. He'll still know."

"I confess," Vilhjalmsson said. "I find him rather alarming."

That was the truth.

"So Markan is worried," Abram said.

Vilhjalmsson glanced at Ean as he considered his answer. "You know as well as we do the ramifications of Redmond's choosing to go it alone. They're only ten worlds, but they have all the line technology for the foreseeable future. And if they're actively recruiting worlds—as appears the case with this business of the Worlds of the Lesser Gods—it won't take long for them to become a formidable foe. Especially not if they manage to steal a line ship, which I presume was their plan."

"I think you were worried about more than that," Abram said. "You knew Redmond was building ships based on alien technology."

A tiny spurt of surprise from Vilhjalmsson. Should Ean tell Abram Vilhjalmsson hadn't known that?

There was none of the blue flash of instant decisions as Abram spoke. He must have thought hard about what he would say to the Gate Union man. Calculated dropping of important information that Vilhjalmsson had to take back to Markan was probably part of the plan.

"You also knew they were building weapons based on alien technology. The destruction of the *Kari Wang* proved just how far they were prepared to go."

Vilhjalmsson raised a brow, but that was all the reaction that showed. Underneath, the lines amplified the quickening of his pulse. "Is there a point to this?"

"We want a truce."

Vilhjalmsson tried to laugh, didn't fool anyone.

"A temporary truce," Abram said. "Three months. Time enough for Gate Union to work out what they're going to do. Time enough for them to decide what to do about Redmond. We both know Gate Union is as vulnerable as the New Alliance is if they can't get access to new lines."

Orsaya and Katida were silent. Ean glanced their way. Neither showed any emotion.

"As part of that truce, Gate Union lifts the ban on jumps for three months. Unrestricted jumps for all New Alliance ships. No delays."

Vilhjalmsson laughed. "You offer three months to think about things we're already thinking about. Why would we agree?"

"I can also offer you access to Commodore Bach. He's been working with Redmond for months. He knows who the ringleaders are. He knows the whole plan."

If Vilhjalmsson said he wasn't interested, he'd be lying. Ean didn't need the lines to tell him that. He was more worried about the hum of concern that had come from Katida's line eight. He wanted to tell her to trust Abram but knew it wasn't the time.

"And that's your sweetener?"

Abram nodded. "But I'll add another. We'll tell you why we're looking for failed linesmen."

That wasn't going to be a secret for long, anyway. Plus, they needed to know that. Otherwise, they'd take Quinn's experiments and start destroying more single-level linesmen.

"Offer it to Markan," Abram said. "See what he says. We have all been caught out by Redmond's machinations. We both need time to regroup."

"So you're more desperate for jumps than even we realize, or there's something I don't know."

"Take our offer to Markan, Vilhjalmsson. See what he says."

"I do get out of here, then? I thought I was a prisoner."

Abram smiled. "Organize a jump for me. I'll take you myself, on the *Lancastrian Princess*. Somewhere close to Lancia because I need to take Commodore Bach home. And I need a jump back to Haladea III afterward."

Ean hid his smile. It was clever, and it solved their initial problem. What would Vilhjalmsson say when he found he'd been used to transport Michelle to Lancia to take over as Empress?

"You've a nerve, Galenos. Using me to transport your prisoners for you. Not to mention handing me off in enemy territory."

"Tell me you can't get passage off Lancia if you need it."

"Why should I trust you?"

Vilhjalmsson looked at Ean rather than Abram. Ean stared back and tried to look as trustworthy as he could. And as expressionless as Radko.

Vilhjalmsson considered a while. "I'm tired, I'm sore, and I need to report to Markan. I know there's something I'm missing, but I'll take the opportunity, anyway. I trust I will get there safely."

"You will," Abram said. "I'll leave you to arrange the jumps then. We'll give you a secure line."

Ean nodded. He knew what he had to do.

"*Lancastrian Princess*," Orsaya said, frostily, after her guards had escorted Vilhjalmsson away. "That's quite presumptuous, given all that's happened these last few days. And taking Bach back to Lancia sounds eerily reminiscent of a recent traitor sent back to the Worlds of the Lesser Gods. We know how well that turned out."

Abram blew out his breath again. "Personally, I don't care whether Bach goes or stays. *Michelle* must go to Lancia."

The pause after that felt as long as a ship's passing through the void, and to Ean it seemed he had the same void time to check the other ships.

Governor Jade had arrived on board the *Lancastrian Princess*. Michelle went down to the shuttle bay to meet her personally. "Annette, I appreciate your coming, especially at such short notice."

"My own brand of support," Governor Jade said. "You're under immense pressure at the moment, Michelle. It's the least I can do."

"Thank you. That's what I wanted to talk to you about, actually. Before I announce this to the council. But we'll both need a drink."

Ean watched Governor Jade's face as they walked to Michelle's formal office, the one she seldom used. Jade was bracing herself for bad news.

"Emperor Yu is dead," Abram said. "He, and Lancia's military, were working with Redmond and the Worlds of the Lesser Gods."

Orsaya and Katida stared at him.

"Dead," Katida said. "Are you sure, Galenos?"

"Very sure. I killed him myself."

Another void-long silence.

On the *Lancastrian Princess*, Michelle was telling Governor Jade, "My father is dead. He betrayed the New Alliance, and we had to—" She couldn't continue.

Jade moved in close and hugged her. "Oh, Michelle."

Ean could hear Katida's lines. He expected shock and betrayal. Instead, he heard a wild, singing hope.

"Yu planned to take the alien ships with him," Abram said. "We had given him enough information to know that if one ship jumped, the others would follow when we didn't have a seven singing them apart." He glanced at Ean, and there were smile creases around the corners of his eyes, "Unfortunately for them, they underestimated the impact of line twelve."

"So Lady Lyan is Empress now," Katida said.

"If we can get back to Lancia to consolidate it."

Both admirals finally smiled. The toothy smiles Ean was used to from both of them.

Orsaya's smile was wider. "Vilhjalmsson won't be pleased at being your pawn."

"I think I can offer him enough. If we can negotiate a three-month armistice, we might have a chance at genuine peace between Gate Union and the New Alliance. Our biggest problem right now is the damage Michelle's father did to Lancia's credibility within the New Alliance. Do we have any power left to negotiate these things?"

"The old Lancia doesn't," Katida said. "The new Empress might."

"We'll notify the council," Abram said. "We also need to inform Lancia. It's better to do that there rather than from here."

The buzz of Orsaya's comms made them all jump. One of the guards stationed at Vilhjalmsson's door.

"Captain Vilhjalmsson, Admiral."

Orsaya put it onto speaker.

"I've spoken to Markan," Vilhjalmsson said. "Your jump is in two hours, with a window of one."

Abram grimaced. "Just enough time to get back to the *Lancastrian Princess*. I'll bet that was deliberate."

He clicked off and turned back to Orsaya and Katida. "We'll set up an interim ruling committee for Lancia. Until that's done, we'll spend some time there, but come back here for council meetings and other items as required."

"Markan will know he has you over a barrel," Katida said. "You can't do it without jumps."

"I'll offer him what I can of Yu's plans. I will also, as a gesture of goodwill, tell Vilhjalmsson about the Emperor before he leaves the ship. Speaking of which"—Abram glanced at the now-silent screen—"we'd best get to the *Lancastrian Princess*, given the jump window is so small."

"And while you're away?" Katida asked. "What happens here?"

"The Department of Alien Affairs will run well enough without me."

"And the council?"

Abram smiled faintly and looked across at Ean. "There were only ever three Lancastrians the councilors trusted. Now there's probably only one. Ean, can you make yourself available for any questions or issues the councilors might have? We'll be back for the council meetings."

That meant Ean would stay here, on Confluence Station. If Ean wasn't going on the *Lancastrian Princess*, Abram would expect to have Fergus as the seven to delink the ships.

"Abram, you should know Fergus is—" How did he put it? "Sore. He stepped in front of a blaster. Although he was wearing his suit."

"I'M fine," Fergus told Abram. "A silly mistake on my behalf. Everyone's told me how stupid I was." He shuddered. "And Arun Chaudry explained, in detail, exactly how the heat produces the concussive effect."

"You were lucky," Abram said. "I'm sure it's a lesson well learned. Can you sing?"

Fergus sang to line seven. The sevens answered back.

"You'll do." Abram took time to give quick instructions to Sale—who'd arrived back on a separate shuttle—before he left. "Ean will explain further, but he will report to you for the moment. Help Radko protect him. He'll be spending a lot of time talking with councilors. Orsaya has overall control of the linesmen for the moment."

Katida joined them at the shuttle bay while they waited for Vilhjalmsson.

"I'd love to stay and hear the full story. But I've some fires to fight of my own. I'm looking forward to the announcement." And she rubbed her hands together. "I've lost count of the people who've said to me, 'If only we can be sure Lady Lyan truly was in charge, but we can't.'"

"And now she is." How different would Lancia be with

Michelle in charge? Maybe, for people like Ean, from the slums, there'd be no change at all, but Lancia had a future now. And a place in the New Alliance.

Provided Ean didn't say anything too stupid.

"You'll be fine," Katida said, though he hadn't said anything. "Be yourself, Ean. That's all anyone ever requires of you."

That's all he could be, so that's what people were going to get. "What will happen now, do you think? To the New Alliance."

"We have a future," Katida said. "And if Galenos can pull another rabbit out of his hat, we'll have peace, too."

What exactly was a rabbit, anyway? And why did you pull one out of a hat?

Katida's shuttle arrived at the next bay. She turned to go, hesitated. "You realize some members of the council will take the opportunity while you are away to push for their own captain for the *Confluence*." A strong sense of Admiral Carrell came through the lines. Chocolate, with a bitter aftertaste and a jagged tone.

"It may be no bad thing," Abram said. "Let them feel they have some control. You should push for it yourself, Katida. A sideways promotion this time. Someone political, like your own Captain Terrigal."

A song of affront rolled off Katida, strong enough to make Ean step back. "Are you planning to weaken Balian that much? Terrigal will be admiral when I retire. You know that."

"I do know that," Abram agreed. "And I approve."

"So why condemn him to a ship?"

"Maybe it doesn't have to be that way, Katida. Ean seems to think it doesn't."

Abram had listened. He had understood.

Katida's glance at Ean was sharp. "I thought Ean was all for this bonding."

Ean bit his lip. How did he say it? "The *Confluence* has already chosen its Ship."

"I'll make a deal with you, Katida," Abram said. "I will support your applicant, Terrigal, provided you and Terrigal support my applicant when Terrigal retires. It will work for both of us. Everyone on the council knows Terrigal is ambitious. Your enemies will be happy to have him out of the way."

Vilhjalmsson and his escort of Orsaya's guards turned into the corridor leading to the shuttle bays.

Abram lowered his voice so that the approaching prisoner didn't hear. "And between us, we might be able to hide the fact that we no longer have any say over who controls the ship."

Katida's eyes seemed to see forever. "Sale. It can only be Sale."

Ean breathed deep and didn't say anything.

"Imagine it, Katida. Terrigal will be the only admiral who's ever captained a ship," and Abram raised his voice to normal levels as he turned to greet Vilhjalmsson.

As both admirals turned to their own shuttle bays, the other line eights caught the echo of Katida's eight, and amplified it throughout the fleet. *"Imagine it."*

"ABRAM understood," Ean said to Radko, as they turned to go back to their temporary home on Confluence Station. Or maybe not so temporary for a while.

"Of course he did. He's Abram Galenos."

Sale met them halfway. "Did Galenos say what I thought he said? Emperor Yu?"

"He did," Ean said. "But you shouldn't say it in words, Sale. Not till they make the announcement. There's a level-one linesman on the Galactic News ship, and he picks up everything."

"Now he tells us."

"I'll let Galenos know about him. After this other business." Radko glanced at her comms. "Meantime, I need to talk to Han. Vega says his father is here. They have something to say to each other."

"We put your team in with the linesmen," Sale said. "We weren't sure if we should have put them in with our own or not, but they are linesmen."

Yves Jaxon Han wasn't.

"Thanks."

Radko's three team members came across as soon as Radko arrived.

"I see what you mean about the singing," Han said. "They're all singing."

They weren't, but enough of them were that Ean was pleased. There was one group of five, but most of those practicing were individuals, sounding out their new talents. One of them was Alex Joy, the Xanto. He was singing to line three on Confluence Station.

Ean went over to him. "There's another line trying to talk to you as well." The scout that had claimed the Xantos for its own. "You should listen and reply. It's only polite."

Joy looked at him, listened, then extended his song to include the other line.

The line came back with enthusiasm.

Ean returned to Radko and her team of three.

"How's it going?" Radko asked them.

"Weird," van Heel said. "I think they're all crazy."

"You'll be one of those crazies very soon, van Heel, so you're talking about yourself." She turned to Han. "A private word with you."

Han made a face and followed her out. Ean followed. Han frowned at him.

"I go where Ean goes," Radko said. "Get used to him." She settled in the corridor, left foot up against the wall. "You have to be honest with your father."

"It's kind of hard to—"

Here, Ean could help Radko. "He knows you're not his birth son, if that's what you're worried about. He's being blackmailed by everyone on and off Lancia to keep it a secret. Including Redmond."

"What?" Han turned to Radko. "You told him?"

"Your father told us," Ean said. "Talk to him. Tell him to stop letting himself be blackmailed."

Han walked the rest of the way in silence.

Orsaya's guards stopped them in the corridor where Renaud's apartment was. They recognized Ean and Radko and let them through.

Han turned to watch the guards. "Is he a prisoner?"

"The station's on lockdown," Ean said.

"For what?"

Mutiny, attempt to steal a fleet of spaceships, crimes against the New Alliance.

"Not in your need to know," Radko said. She pressed the comms on the door. "Lord Renaud. It's Dominique Radko. May we come in."

"Dominique." Ean tasted the syllables.

"Don't you ever. Either of you."

"But you introduced yourself as—"

"He's a friend of my parents."

And indeed, he seemed to be, for Renaud, on opening the door, said, "Lady Dominique. It's a pleasure." Then he saw Han. His eyes widened. "Yves."

"Papa."

Father and adopted son hugged each other, laughing and crying.

Ean and Radko backed away.

"It's a crying sort of day." Ean sang the door closed on the Han family, and they made their way back to the control center, and their own people. "How do you feel, Radko? About everything?"

Radko considered it. "Glad to be home," she said, finally, and slipped her hand into his.

Her fingers were warm, comfortable against his. It felt natural. Ean smiled at her. "I'm glad you're home, too."

Want to connect with fellow science fiction and fantasy fans?

For news on all your favorite Ace and Roc authors, sneak peeks into the newest releases, book giveaways, and much more—

"Like" and Follow Ace and Roc Books!

facebook.com/AceRocBooks
twitter.com/AceRocBooks